UNCOMMON ENEMY

JOHN REYNOLDS

Cover design: Based on a painting by Alison Reynolds

Published by
Starblaze Publications
10A Law Street
Torbay
Auckland 0630
NEW ZEALAND

National Library of New Zealand Cataloguing-in-Publication Data

Reynolds, John, 1941-
Uncommon enemy / John Reynolds
1. Title.
NZ823.3—dc 22

ISBN: 978-1877332371

CHAPTER 2

Stuart, with a nod to his parents and younger brother Stephen, and a quick grin to his nine-year-old sister Claire, seated himself at the table for the traditional Johnson family Sunday lunch. Removing his linen serviette from its silver ring he draped it across his knees and began selecting a tasty morsel from the roast his father had finished carving. In response to a question from her father, Claire began to chatter about the Sunday school lesson she'd heard before church that morning.

"Church that morning". Living at home meant that he had to brace himself for the weekly ritual of the morning church service. He smiled to himself. But this morning had been different. As he'd pulled up at the kerb in front of the church and dismounted from his bicycle, he'd seen the young woman. The attraction was immediate – so much so that he had to tell himself to slow down as he parked his bike, removed the cycle clips from around his trouser cuffs and headed straight for the group of young women. Several smiled a welcome as he approached. He was well liked, and suspected that now he had joined the privileged few who were university students, one or two of the church mothers had him in their sights for their daughters.

The young woman was even more stunning in close up. Introduced as Carol Peterson, her flowing black hair, stirred slightly by the wind, encased a face that was nothing short of exquisite. The rest of her was equally attractive. The fabric of the light floral frock flowed effortlessly around a figure that, while slim, filled out appropriately. Expecting the possessor of such beauty to be coolly self-confident, Stuart was agreeably surprised to discover that having been introduced to him –

"Stuart's at Auckland University College," – she answered his questions quite shyly.

She informed him she had come to Auckland's North Shore from Wellington, was boarding with her aunt in Milford and had just secured a secretarial position in the central city.

"You go to the city every day, Carol?" Stuart asked.

"Yes," she replied with a shy smile. "I work in the central city. I go by bus from Milford to the ferry.

With controlled casualness he asked, "What ferry?"

"Oh, usually the one that leaves Devonport at eight o'clock."

As the group moved towards the church door Stuart touched Carol on the arm. "Nice to meet you," he smiled. "Might see you on the ferry sometime."

Momentarily she held his gaze. "Yes, who knows?" she replied before joining the other young women.

CHAPTER 3

Uncharacteristically Stuart was the first one down for breakfast the following morning, wearing his cleanest shirt and tie under his varsity blazer. His mother, always eager to believe the best of her children, took his smart appearance and punctuality as a sign that he was 'making an effort' and greeted him warmly.

"Busy day planned, dear?"

"Yes, Mum, heaps to do."

"That's good. You do enjoy university, don't you, dear?"

"Yes, Mum I do. It's opened my eyes to all sorts of knowledge and ideas that I knew nothing about at all."

"Yes, dear. But you must hold fast to that which is true."

"Oh, I will, Mum. You bet. This marmalade's tasty. Is it new?"

"Not, really. I've been buying it from Mr. Bright's for several months. I'm glad you like it."

Hurriedly finishing his breakfast, Stuart excused himself, hastened upstairs to clean his teeth, check his image in his bedroom mirror and to take some extra time to spread brilliantine oil through his thick black hair. Rapidly descending the stairs he collected his brown paper lunch bag from the kitchen, accepted his mother's requisite peck on the cheek, exited the house and walked swiftly to the bus stop.

He was the first one there.

The bus trip to the ferry terminal at Devonport took an age. Timetabled to link with the 8:00 morning ferry Stuart hoped the bus would be early, thus allowing him time to scan the gathering commuters for a sign of Carol.

However, the trip was at the peak of the rush hour and consequently the bus pulled up at every stop. By the time it arrived at the terminal the bus was filled with passengers and cigarette smoke. Managing to push his way to the front, Stuart was the first off. Entering the terminal he pushed his way through the crowd of men in hats, suits, sports coats and flannel trousers, and a sprinkling of military uniforms. The women, mostly in their late teens or twenties, or past marriageable age, were smartly dressed in knee-length dresses with hats, gloves, and stockings as befitted those who worked in city offices and shops.

Normally Stuart would have joined the other young men in a ritual re-enacted every day. Ignoring the gangplank large numbers of them sought a moment of excitement by lining the edge of the wharf and jumping onto the upper or lower decks of the arriving ferry – their choice depending on the state of the tide. However, giving no thought to the ritual, he began working his way through the crowd assembled near the gangplank area. Anxiously he scanned all the female faces but Carol was nowhere to be seen. As the ferry docked he decided to move to the right hand side of the lowered gangplank and watch the passengers as they poured onto the vessel.

He saw Carol almost immediately. She was talking to a tall man dressed in a dark three-piece suit who looked to be in his early thirties. Stuart pushed through the crowd of people surging up the lowered gangway. As she reached the top he drew level with her shoulder.

"Hullo, Carol!" he exclaimed, rather too loudly. Startled, she turned and in doing so missed her footing on the gangway's edge and fell forward. Stuart and the other man, simultaneously reaching out on either side, caught her before she went sprawling on the deck.

Both men's eyes met above the girl's head.

"What do you think you're doing, mate?" demanded her companion.

"She slipped. Good thing I caught her, mate," responded Stuart, his anger at his own clumsiness more than compensated for by the momentary feel of Carol's body as she staggered upright. He smiled down at her. "Sorry if I startled you, Carol. Hope you're OK. Did you hurt yourself?"

"Hullo, um ..."

"Stuart."

"Yes, Stuart. Of course. Fancy seeing you again so soon."

"Yes. Fancy. I..."

"Sure, you're OK, sweetheart?" interrupted the other man reaching forward and turning Carol's face towards him.

"Yes, Hamish. Quite sure. Let's find a seat."

Including himself in the invitation Stuart walked with the pair to the bow of the ferry and sat down beside her on the long wooden slatted seat that covered the vessel's circumference.

"Oh, Stuart, this is Hamish. Hamish, I met Stuart at church yesterday."

A seagull screeched above them and wheeled away.

"At church. Don't bother with all that stuff myself. Prefer to go yacht racing on Sundays."

Normally Stuart would have agreed, but the 'sweetheart' had irritated him. His uncharacteristic response would have delighted his parents.

"Nothing wrong with Christian teaching. The world would be a lot better place if more people attended church."

Hamish deliberately looked Stuart up and down. His dark suit and conservative tie contrasted with Stuart's university college blazer and grey flannel trousers.

"What brings you to the city?"

Stuart deliberately smiled at Carol before responding.

"Varsity. I'm a student."

"Varsity. Huh. Studying anything useful?"

Carol cut in. "Hamish. That's a little unfair."

7

Her companion laughed harshly. "Come, on, sweetheart, what would you know?"

"So," asked Stuart with a thin smile. "What do you do, Hamish?"

"Business," was the curt reply.

"Hamish came to Auckland to take over the chief accountant's position in his father's construction business," said Carol helpfully.

"Good for you, Hamish," replied Stuart, favouring Hamish with an enormous smile.

The other man gave Stuart a long stare. Then turning to Carol he lowered his voice and pointedly engaged her in conversation.

The clattering of the chains as the gangplank was raised, the whistle from the mate as he unhooked the rope from the capstan and the clanging of the bells to signal the engine room, initiated the familiar throb of the ferry's engines. The steady pulse combined with the strong harbour breeze, the slapping of the water against the bow and the chatter of the other passengers made it hard for Stuart to overhear. Feigning indifference he gazed at the passing panorama of ships, boats, wharves and cranes and the inevitable wheeling seagulls as the ferry made its trip from Devonport towards the terminal at the bottom of Queen Street. His initial elation at finding Carol had subsided with the advent of 'Sweetheart' Hamish. Obviously the older man had plenty of money – what with his flash clothing and the yacht racing on Sunday. Lucky bastard – not only Carol but also the chance to go sailing on Sundays. She'd worn gloves to church and had gloves on now so he had no way of checking the third finger on her left hand for an engagement ring. Mentally he shrugged and turned his thoughts to an attractive fair-haired young woman who'd sat next to him in last Friday's History tutorial.

The noise and movement of the passengers preparing to disembark interrupted his reverie. He was about to follow suit when Carol turned to him and smiled warmly, her large brown eyes staring up into his.

"Stuart, I just realized my new job is near the end of Princes St not far from your university. We might bump into each other again."

Stuart's smile was warm. "Yes, we might." Then, as a tactical afterthought he asked, "Where's your business located, er, Hamish?"

The abrupt response of, "Newmarket," lifted his spirits a little. Newmarket was a fairly long tram ride from the city centre and the university. The opportunities for a lunchtime rendezvous between Hamish and Carol would therefore be limited.

"Nice to meet you, Hamish. And, Carol, as you say, we may bump into each other in the city again. Who knows?" Rounding off his farewell with his most charming smile he turned and joined the line of disembarking passengers heading for the bottom of Queen Street.

CHAPTER 4

The morning lecture on Renaissance History was interesting enough, but as Stuart sat behind the long wooden table scratching notes with his fountain pen, he found it difficult to concentrate. Carol was, in any man's language, absolutely stunning. Furthermore, although apparently linked romantically to Hamish, she must have known that her information about her office location would hardly have pleased the older man. So what was her motive? He shook his head, forcing himself to concentrate. He enjoyed Professor Sterling's lectures. The man had a colourful style, and in contrast to some of the old codgers who consistently read in a monotone from yellowed pages, Sterling often departed from his prepared lecture when he felt that further explanation would aid his students' understanding of the subject.

Stuart watched as the professor paused, gathered his notes into a neat bundle and folded his hands on top of them. His gaze took in the entire small group of third year students.

"Although having no bearing on the subject of your coming exams, I have something of great importance to say to you all. The current world situation does not provide much cause for optimism. Just as the Dark Ages preceded the Renaissance, when the Church attempted to totally control the lives of men, the same thing appears to be happening today in Germany. Any dictatorship is dangerous, but to me, as a scholar, the most disturbing aspect of Adolf Hitler's Nazi government is the mass burning of books by German university students."

His eyes panned the room of silent, attentive students.

"Books by great writers have been publicly incinerated throughout Germany. The Nazi government has not only ordered the public destruction of thousands of works of fiction they have classified as subversive, but also scholarly books that may well be irreplaceable. Such an action is a modern day mirror of the actions of those who controlled Europe during the Dark Ages."

There was no sound as Professor Sterling paused, cleared his throat and leaned forward.

"Be aware, ladies and gentlemen, if this man and his madness is not stopped we may well see the beginning of another Dark Age spread across Europe and beyond. There's not much old chaps like me can do about it, other than to speak and publish papers. But you are the young men and women of a nation founded on democratic principles. I'm afraid my generation has let itself down. The future is now in your hands. Do whatever is necessary otherwise the price we will all be forced to pay will be a terrible one!"

Gathering his notes, Professor Sterling swept from the room leaving behind his stunned and silent students.

It was a pleasant crisp early spring day and during the lunch break with many other university students, Stuart sat in Albert Park munching on his mother's sandwiches and discussing Sterling's words with his close friend Brendan Ritter. Both young men had spent several years in the work force before enrolling at the university – having found the prospect of working their way up from lowly clerical positions in large corporations to be too bleak. (Due to his school success in mathematics Stuart had been urged by his father to take a clerical position in the Bank of New Zealand – "Good safe job, son".) He and Brendan had met in their first year at a History tutorial.

Lying on his back, Brendan gestured upwards towards the eternally motionless statue of the soldier above them.

"He and his mates went off thirty-odd years ago to South Africa to fight the Boers. Didn't do anyone any bloody good. Our chaps thought they were fighting a noble war for Queen and country but wound up fighting farmers like themselves.

War solves nothing. Waste of bloody time. Look at the last show." He accepted the cigarette that Stuart proffered. "Tell you what, mate; if they want me to enlist they're wasting their bloody time!"

Stuart drew deeply on his cigarette.

"Dunno. Prof. Sterling's got a point. This is more than just another war. Hitler and his mates are a direct threat to peace and democracy. Yeah, I know," he went on, seeing Brendan's lip begin to curl, "sounds very noble and all that. But at times we have to defend what's right. If we don't..." He stopped. "What's so damned funny? I'm serious!"

Brendan's look of scorn had metamorphosed into a sly grin, as he directed his gaze over Stuart's shoulder. His eyes flicked back to Stuart, his eyebrows lifted and he nodded. Puzzled, Stuart turned round.

"Hullo, Stuart." Standing on the path was Carol Peterson.

"Carol." Moving swiftly to his feet, he flicked his cigarette away. "What are you doing here?"

"It's a public park." She smiled. "I sometimes walk along to have lunch here. Do you?"

"Yes." He returned her smile. "Yes I do."

"Introduce me, old chap," murmured Brendan, his eyes fixed on Carol.

"Oh, yes, sorry. Carol, this is Brendan. Brendan, Carol."

"*Enchante, m'selle*," said Brendan rising to his feet and reaching for her hand.

"Brendan's done a French paper. It's his subtle way of letting you know."

"Yeah, well, better than reading about long dead people!" He gestured flamboyantly. "History is the past, French is the future!"

"Maybe, mate. But I'd rather be in Auckland studying Maths and History than in Paris waiting for the Germans."

"Wouldn't worry me," he responded, letting go of Carol's hand. "I speak that language even better."

Seeing Carol gazing at both of them uncertainly, Stuart shrugged. "Sorry, we're often like this." His smile was warm. "Do you often come to Albert Park?"

"Yes, like I said."

"Of course." He smiled expansively. "Glad you decided to come today. Have you had lunch?"

"I've brought my own." She indicated a brown paper bag. "How about you?"

"Sadly we've already eaten, *m'selle*," said Brendan with an exaggerated Gallic shrug.

"He has, but I haven't quite finished mine. You'd be welcome to join me." Emphasizing the last word he gave Brendan a long hard stare as he peeled off his blazer and spread it on the grass. "Here, sit down, Carol."

"He studies History, you know. Sir Walter Raleigh is one of his favourite characters," murmured Brendan, taking a final drag on his cigarette and making a show of flicking the butt towards the statue of former New Zealand governor Sir George Grey. He grinned at Stuart and patted the pockets of his blazer.

"Seems I've run out of smokes. Lovely to have met you, Carol. *A bientot*." With a slightly mocking bow he headed down the path towards the university's clock tower.

Settling herself on Stuart's sport coat, Carol tucked her slim stockinged legs demurely under the edge of her skirt and deftly removed her high-heeled shoes.

"How did you find me here?" he asked as he settled himself down beside her.

She smiled. "I didn't actually find you, Stuart..."

"No, of course not. What I meant was..."

"Well, actually, I sort of found you. I came walking along Princes Street and saw all the university students by the park so I decided to walk through. And then I saw you, and your French friend."

"Brendan. He's not French. His father's German and he speaks that language very well. His main subject is Languages

13

so he's reasonably fluent in French. Likes to think it improves his chances with the ladies."

"Does it?"

"You're a lady. What do you think?"

"He seems very charming."

"He obviously thought you were pretty stunning, just like that fellow on the ferry, um…"

"Hamish. Probably."

"Known him long, I suppose."

"Yes, quite a while in fact. We met in Wellington. Our families knew each other for years and he and I grew up together. We started going out while I was in the fifth form. His father wanted to relocate the head office of his construction business chain to Auckland and offered Hamish the position of chief accountant. It was an excellent opportunity for advancement so he took it. Came up here about six months ago."

"So, when did you come to Auckland?"

"Last month."

"To be with him?"

"Not quite. He kept writing to me, telling me how great Auckland was and practically begging me to join him."

Removing her gloves she took a sandwich from her brown lunch bag. Stuart noted the absence of a ring on the third finger of her left hand. Emboldened by his discovery he continued.

"Does he want to marry you?"

"You are a persistent man, aren't you? But, well, yes, as a matter of fact he does."

"And you came to Auckland to be with him. To get married?"

"Mixed motives, actually. It was a chance to, well, get away from home, to another city. My older brother Ian had just joined the army. We'd always been very close so with only me at home it wasn't the same. Mum and Dad don't get on particularly well and I wanted a break. They've always wanted

14

me to marry Hamish so going to Auckland was an ideal excuse to leave."

"And the marriage?"

"Hamish is keen. Mum thinks he's a catch. Plenty of money, successful, job with promising prospects," she shrugged, "and fairly good looking."

Stuart stole a glance at his watch. 12:30. Carol presumably had to be back at work by 1.00 o'clock and he had an essay due by Friday. Time wasn't exactly abundant.

"Didn't mean to be nosey. Just wondering why you didn't marry him in Wellington rather than follow him to Auckland and live apart in the same city."

Momentarily her eyes held his. The coldness of her fleeting glance was chilling before she looked down at the grass.

"Sorry," he said, "I'm being far too inquisitive – treating you like a university research item." Instinctively he took her hand and she made no attempt to withdraw it. "Let's talk about something else. Where's your office?"

"The Northern Club. At the end of the street."

"The Northern Club – that private gentlemen's establishment. Oh, my." He tilted his nose upward with mock exaggeration. "My dear, are you sure you'd be permitted to speak to one such as I?"

Her laughter was spontaneous. Reaching forward she pushed him playfully causing him to fall backwards on the grass. As he was still holding her hand she was pulled forward and fell with her face on his chest. She made no attempt to rise. They lay together for a long moment and then her voice was soft.

"I'm only the office secretary at the Club. Hamish's Dad is a member of an affiliated club and heard they had a position. It's OK. They treat me quite well."

"As long as you exhibit the correct amount of deference," he murmured, his free hand reaching upwards to stroke her long black hair.

"I suppose so. And the Club *is* near the university."

15

"A bonus for both of us."

"Mmmm."

They lay together in the warm sun on the grassy bank barely conscious of the noises of the city drifting upwards towards the Park. A mixture of tenderness, sexual stirrings, and conflicting thoughts about Carol and her relationship with Hamish filled Stuart's head. She'd known him for years, was practically engaged to him. He'd then transferred to Auckland. If she'd wanted to break it off that would have been the time. But instead she came too, and obviously still continued the relationship.

A wolf whistle and giggling interrupted his reverie. They both sat up to see three schoolboys from nearby Seddon Memorial Technical College leering from behind a nearby tree.

"She your girlfriend, mister?"

"Whoo, hoo! You must be in love! Whoo hoo!"

Angry that the boys' puerile behaviour had shattered the moment, Stuart started to get up but Carol reached out and put her hand on his chest.

"It's OK." She rose slowly. "I have to go back to work in a minute."

Her smile calmed him down. "That was lovely. Lunch on the Grass, eh?"

"Yes," she said, "but not quite in the style of Manet."

"Oh." His surprise was genuine. "You know the painting?"

"*Le Dejeuner sur l'Herbe*," she said and then smiled at him. "I loved art at school but Dad said it was an entirely unsuitable career, so I became a secretary."

"And your mum?"

"She agreed. And in any case, she wanted me to marry Hamish. So a secretarial position was a chance to make a few pounds and fill up my hope chest."

"And did you?"

By now they were both standing and Carol was brushing his blazer with her hand.

"Did I what?"

"Fill your hope chest."

"Don't be silly. I left it in Wellington. Told my mother to fill it for me. Give her something to do instead of bickering with Dad."

A clock sounded a single chime.

"Oh dear. Time for me to go."

"I'll walk you along Princes Street." It was a statement not a question.

"Have you got time?"

"Surely. I'll be spending all afternoon in the library – I've got an essay to finish by Friday."

She slipped her arm into his. The tall leafy trees on either side of Princes Street cast benign shadows over them as they strolled past the historic houses on the west side.

Reluctant to discuss any personal issues raised by the lunchtime experience Stuart began to tell her about his university studies. Her questions about university life came in quick succession, and she seemed genuinely interested in his responses. He'd hardly touched the surface when they reached the end of Princes Street and stopped by the Romanesque style Jewish synagogue on the opposite corner.

She glanced across at the ivy-covered walls of the Northern Club. "Must go." She put her nose in the air mimicking his earlier gesture. "They're all frightfully punctual in there."

"Maybe I'll walk this way later in the week." She raised herself on tiptoe and her lips brushed his cheek. "Might see you then. Bye."

He watched her as she began to cross the street. The slight breeze drifting up from Bowen Ave swirled playfully around the hem of her skirt as she reached the other side entered the building.

She didn't look back.

CHAPTER 5

"You lucky bastard! She's a bloody knockout! Where did you find her? Does she have a sister?"

Later that afternoon Brendan had confronted him as he walked past the remnants of the old barracks wall in the centre of the campus – completed eighty years earlier to defend a growing Auckland town against a feared attack from Maori tribes in the south.

"Never you mind. But she is gorgeous, I agree. And sorry, mate, but she only mentioned her brother, Ian." He grinned smugly and shook his head in mock sorrow. "Afraid there's no sister."

"Sod it. So where did you meet her?"

As the two young men walked towards the university library, Brendan's series of rapid-fire questions continued. Stuart soon realized that, apart from a delightfully unexpected sojourn on the grass, and a few details about her family and the apparent boyfriend, his knowledge of Carol was superficial. Yet he was sure of one thing, a determination to discover more.

"Hey, chaps. Heard the news?"

John D'Arcy, a bespectacled student who was in Stuart's Stage Three History class, interrupted the discussion.

"The news? You mean Johnson's new girlfriend?"

"No, you stupid bugger. Adolf Hitler. He's just sent his army and air force into Poland!"

"Good God. Actually attacked the country outright?"

"Absolutely. The British have issued him with an ultimatum to withdraw his army immediately. Otherwise they'll declare war. Look!"

D'Arcy produced a copy of the *Auckland Star*. Brendan read the headline aloud. "Allied Ultimatum to Germany. Ambassadors Take Demand to Berlin."

"Jesus, this means war, for all of us," muttered Stuart. "So much for our glittering academic careers."

"Yep! It'll be off to fight the foe – for you two anyway."

"Whaddya mean?" D'Arcy frowned. "If it's war we'll all have to bloody well go, like last time."

"We won't 'all have to bloody well go', mate. I'm bloody not. Didn't do any bloody good last time and it won't do any bloody good this time. War's a game for mugs. Let the politicians go. It's their fault, anyway!"

"Are you a bloody communist or something?" D'Arcy's face came closer to Brendan's. "We've all got to do our bit to defend ourselves and our country, and the empire, and..."

"Country! Empire! The Germans and the Poles are twelve thousand bloody miles away or hadn't you noticed? Not our war! Let the Europeans get on with it!"

"You're a bloody conchie! You know what they did to those spineless bastards in the last show. Dragged them out to the front line and tied them to stakes. Bloody fine show, too. Cowardly scum!"

"You're not including me in your 'cowards' category are you, mate?" It was now Brendan who moved his face closer to D'Arcy's. "And in any case, it took a lot of guts for those conscientious objectors to stand up against the mindless war machine we've created. So back off and think on!"

"OK, men, you've both made your point," said Stuart, easing himself between the glowering pair. "I don't agree with Brendan but he's right about the courage of the conchies. Anyway, D'Arcy, thanks for the information. Hell of a way to end a day."

"Off you go, D'Arcy!" Brendan grinned with false enthusiasm. "You've got exciting news! There's a war coming! Quick, away and spread the word!" He narrowed his eyes.

"With luck someone will decide to shoot the bloody messenger."

"Listen, you..."

"D'Arcy! Go!" Stuart seized his shoulders and spun him round in the direction of a nearby group of students. "Tell those men! They need to know your news!"

CHAPTER 6

"Join up. Yes, Dad. But I want to finish my degree first."

"Might be over by then, with any luck."

"That's what they said last time. Young men from here scrambled to get to France before the war was over. Thousands of them are still over there – marked by a cross, if they're lucky. It's OK, Dad, I will go but the world can wait a few months."

Stuart and his father rarely spoke at length. However, a looming war, the prospect of enlistment, and the potential effect on Stuart and other family members had brought father and son together later in the evening by the lounge fire. His mother, although distressed by the news, had felt it best to leave the two men to discuss the situation.

"It's inevitable, Dad. Hitler's not going to stop now – Rhineland, Austria, Sudetenland, and now Poland. He's got the bit between his teeth and the Poles won't stop him. Diplomacy and pieces of paper failed once again. We'll have to fight the bastard to stop him."

Normally the swear word 'bastard' would have brought an instant reprimand. But the immensity of the issues did not warrant it. "Ironic," thought Stuart. "As a student Dad still sees me as a grown up schoolboy. Now I'm facing possible military service, I'm regarded as having reached manhood."

"Your mother's pretty distressed, son. Her brother James was killed at Passchendaele and her two cousins, Dan and Brian, never really recovered from their wounds, even though they made it back home. She's a brave woman but the thought of the same thing happening to her eldest son is very hard for her." He paused and stared into the fire for a long moment. "And for me, son. And for me."

It was a rare show of emotion from a man for whom the keeping up of appearances was a central tenet.

"I know, Dad," said Stuart, moved by his father's brief but significant words. "Early days, anyway. We're not at war yet."

"True." Picking up a poker his father thrust it fiercely into the base of the fire. "In the meantime keep up your studies. And be gentle with your mother."

For the next few days Stuart didn't see Carol. He had decided to avoid the eight o'clock ferry as he felt it might cause problems for her. He'd hoped to see her at church on Sunday and was disappointed when one of the young women told him Carol was home with a heavy cold.

Seating himself in the university library, he reached for his History texts. History, next to Maths, had always been his favourite subject from Takapuna Primary where stories of William the Conqueror, Richard the Lionheart and Henry V had stirred his young imagination. His gradual discovery that these men had their flaws did not discourage him as he plunged ever deeper into the complex causes of the historical events that had affected their lives and those of countless numbers of men and women down the centuries. One more essay to go – the role of Kaiser Wilhelm in the events leading up to Germany's invasion of Belgium and France in World War I. Rather too close to home now. Recently he'd read that in World War I New Zealand had sent over 100,000 troops overseas and nearly 20% had been killed on battlefields such as Passchendaele and Gallipoli. And now Europe seemed on the brink of repeating the whole frightful scenario.

As well as being one of his main course lecturers, Professor Sterling was also in charge of Stuart's Monday tutorial group. Tutorials were rare at the university, the system preferring to leave students to study on their own. However, Sterling had instituted a tutorial system for his third year History students that had proved to be very popular. Not only did it allow students to raise questions about material presented in lectures but also required them to present topics to the rest of the group for discussion and disputation. That afternoon was the final tutorial before the exams. The topic was the events leading to the start of World War I. It was Stuart's turn to present his point of view to the other nine students. After much thought he had decided to take the position that the prime responsibility for causing the war was Britain's due to her intransigent behaviour towards the Germans. At 3 o'clock he and the others assembled in the small classroom and, after a few comments about the forthcoming exams, Professor Sterling invited Stuart to make his presentation.

Reading from his prepared notes, and using the blackboard, Stuart outlined the basis of his argument. The resulting discussion became quite heated as each of the students debated the pros and cons. Stuart felt he had managed to deal adequately with the counter arguments and although he enjoyed the challenge, was relieved when Sterling concluded the tutorial with a brief summation and a "good luck for your exams". As Stuart began to collect his papers the professor touched him on the shoulder.

"Young man, I wonder if you would be so kind as to wait behind after the others have gone. I'd like a word."

As the others collected their books and papers, Stuart sat worrying he had overstepped the mark with his arguments. He had deliberately chosen to be provocative as he relished a lively debate, but given the current increasing unpopularity of the Germans he was concerned he was in for a reprimand. As the last student left, Sterling turned to him.

"Now, then, young man – no, stay seated – I was interested by the viewpoint you took in the debate.

"Yes, sir," replied Stuart, uncertainly.

"The point of view you took – do you believe it?"

The question caught him by surprise. 'Believe' and 'beliefs' were words he had heard used every Sunday for years.

In the analytical world of academia they were mercifully absent – until now.

"'Believe', sir?" he responded cautiously. "I don't know if belief comes into it. I think it's a viewpoint for which there is some support…"

"A credible perspective, you mean."

Wishing they'd had been his words Stuart replied, "Yes, sir. There are also strong arguments for other points, er, perspectives but I decided to take that one."

"Any particular reason, Mr. Johnson"

"Well, I knew with the recent news it wouldn't be a particularly popular perspective and therefore I thought it would be a lark, er, challenge, sir, to defend it. Sorry if you thought it was not appropriate."

Sterling chuckled. "Appropriate. Good lord, no, young man. Let's hope we never reach the day when universities start considering the worth of academic disputation on the grounds of 'appropriateness'". In fact, Mr. Johnson, I am bound to say I was impressed by the strength and the logic of the view you expounded. And it certainly provoked a strong reaction."

"Yes, sir, it did, especially in the light of what you said to us about the Nazis after yesterday's lecture."

"I'm glad you said, 'Nazis' and not 'Germans'. The two are not necessarily synonymous." He paused and looked at Stuart. "Now, young man, yesterday I was informed I have received a government research grant to undertake a lengthy study of German foreign policy since the end of the last war. The fact that it could be of some political use resulted in the application being speedily approved. I'm delighted, although I suspect my findings may not be politically acceptable. However, to undertake funded research at this stage in my career is a great opportunity."

"Yes, sir. A great opportunity," echoed Stuart wondering why he was being told.

"Part of the funding allows me to employ a research assistant. I need a free thinker, someone who will not simply follow the political perspectives of the time. Furthermore, I understand from Professor Barnes that you're performing extremely well in Pure Mathematics."

Stuart's eyes widened. "Professor Barnes, sir. Have you been...?"

"Yes," Sterling smiled. "It's not entirely unknown for Arts to converse with Science you know." Seeing Stuart about to speak he held up his hand. "And I'm given further to understand you have more than a passing interest in cryptology."

Stuart started in surprise. "Why, yes, sir."

"Splendid. Could be useful in the future. No, no more questions. The pay's not much but, well, Mr. Johnson, I'd like you to consider it. The position would also enable you to move into postgraduate studies should you wish to continue your studies in the History and Mathematics departments."

"I don't know what to say, sir. I mean, well, this is a great honour, I never imagined..."

"Let's go up to my study," said Sterling, "and go through the paper work. It spells out the research assistant's role, remuneration, conditions of employment and all that sort of detail. You can have some time to think it over, of course, but I would like an answer fairly promptly."

The research assistant's contract was for one year, but the grant was a generous one, and the likelihood of it lasting a further year was almost certain. Furthermore, Stuart would be able to enrol into a postgraduate programme as soon as he had completed his bachelor's degree, and the research he would undertake as Sterling's assistant could be credited towards his studies. The prospect of completing a master's degree in two years' time, with Professor Sterling, and possibly other senior academic staff, mentoring him was impossible to turn down. Although the professor offered him time to think it over, Stuart agreed to sign up immediately.

"We'll commence the research once your finals are over. However, in the interim," said the professor, "I will give you the key to the small History Department library. You may find it useful during the final run up to the exams and it will give you time to familiarize yourself with its contents. It's only for use by staff and postgraduate students so it's a quiet spot, entirely conducive to concentrated research. Its other great advantage is that has an exterior door, which means we can come or go at any time. Downstairs and the second on the right. Here, take good care of the key."

Moments later a dazed Stuart found himself walking across Albert Park down into Queen Street. Opting to walk rather than catch one of the trams that rattled down to the ferry buildings, he made his way towards the bottom of the town contemplating the undreamed of possibilities which had suddenly opened up before him. A postgraduate degree with Professor Sterling as his mentor could lead to a staff position at the university. The prospect was mind numbing. Periodically an academic career had crossed his mind, but aware the opportunities were limited he'd never seriously considered it as a possibility for himself – until now.

His parents had always been disappointed that he'd not been made dux of Takapuna Grammar School. His marks in all subjects had been high through primary school and on entering Grammar he'd particularly relished the various challenges of Mathematics. However, the attractions of the sports arenas and his growing awareness of the young women in his class had resulted in his studies too often taking second place. Although his final Sixth Form marks were high, they weren't high enough and the title of dux had gone to Paul "Swot" Smithers. Acutely disappointed and angry, his father had insisted on a banking career – "keep the boy on the straight and narrow" he'd overheard him informing his mother. Within a week as a bank teller, he knew for him it was the first step into a career wasteland. From his meagre wages he'd managed to save sufficient funds that, with his excellent scholastic record, had enabled him to enrol at university – much to his father's chagrin.

He smiled. "Wait 'till I tell him and Mum this piece of news."

As he crossed Wellesley Street he was brought back to reality with a jolt.

"Late City!" cried the Auckland Star newsboy standing in his usual street corner spot. "Read all about it! Allies declare war on Germany! King George speaks to the Empire!"

The Germans! He'd completely forgotten about them. Now they were poised to smash his hopes and dreams at the incubation stage. He bought a paper and scanned the headlines.

"Bastards!" he said aloud and he began to quicken his pace towards the ferry buildings.

"Pardon?" said a familiar voice alongside him.

He turned round and gasped, "Carol! Apologies for my language, but it's the bloody Germans. They've ruined everything don't you know! Great to see you again. Are you catching the ferry? Where's whatshisname?"

She smiled. "You are in a tizz. 'Whatshisname', as you call him, isn't here. The Northern Club had a bit of a do on so they asked me to work late. And what about you? Swearing your way down the street. Is it because war's been declared?"

"Yes, it is, in a way. Look, I've just had this most amazing position offered to me and now there's going to be a war!"

He'd stopped walking and stood facing her, his fist clenched, staring straight ahead. She touched his arm. "Stuart. What is it? Tell me?"

He glanced up at the large Civic Theatre clock. "Do you have to catch the next ferry? I'd really like to talk to you about it."

She hesitated for a moment and then smiled. "Alright. I've telephoned my auntie to say I'm working late. What is it?"

A tram, its bell clanging, rattled by noisily. The newsboy was doing a roaring trade and around him complete strangers were forming discussion groups – their tongues loosened by the beer consumed at the pubs that had closed an hour earlier at six o'clock. On another occasion Stuart would have joined in but not tonight. It was all too much.

"Too noisy here. Let's walk back to the university."

"OK." She smiled. As before, she tucked her arm into his as they headed back up Wellesley Street towards Albert Park. As they walked, Stuart began recounting the day's events in detail. When he reached the part where Professor Sterling had offered the research position to him, Carol involuntarily stopped and turned round to face him. "But, Stuart, that's a wonderful offer isn't it?"

"Rather. Research assistant positions are very rarely offered to undergraduates. Normally you'd have to have finished your degree, with high marks. But me, I've been offered the position before my finals and," he paused, "I've been given a key to the History library."

"Is that an honour?"

"I suppose it is. I hardly knew it existed. The key's only given to lecturers and selected students."

"Such as you."

On impulse he said, "Like to see it?"

"The key?"

"No, the library," he laughed. "It's got its own outside entrance."

"But what if someone is there?"

"Not likely. This war news will bring everyone out on the street or send them hurrying home. Come on. Have you ever been inside the university?"

"No. But are you sure that…"

"Course I'm sure." He struck an exaggerated pose. "Step aside, you fellows. I am the new research assistant to Professor David Sterling."

He was delighted by the spontaneity of her laughter. He took her hand. "Come on, down here."

28

The exterior door, unmarked, was in a secluded part of the complex. The key fitted easily and with a quick glance round Stuart pushed it open and stepped back. "In you go. I'll find the light."

His mouth was dry as he closed the door. It was partly due to her nearness but also the knowledge that if they were caught, his new position could be seriously jeopardized.

The interior was almost completely dark save for a faint light from an unseen street lamp casting shadows over the room.

"Not sure where the light switch is," he muttered, reaching out towards the wall. Carol had shifted her position and his groping hand, instead of reaching the wall, found the outside of her left breast. Before he could gasp an apology she swung round towards him and placing her hand behind his head, pulled his mouth down on hers. His response was instantaneous. All the hopes and frustrations of the day and the excitement of her in the dark room overwhelmed him as he kissed her long and hard. His tongue found hers and their shudder was mutual. He felt her legs beginning to wilt and, reluctant to let the moment go, supported her with his left arm while his other explored the nape of her neck and her long soft hair. She moaned and her hips moved spontaneously towards his, her left leg sliding upwards over the outside of his right thigh. Through his mounting excitement he wondered if there was a couch in the library or, at the very least, carpet on the floor.

Suddenly, without warning, she jerked her head back and tried to pull away. "No! Sorry, Stuart! No!"

"Carol, what is it? What's wrong?" Although she was standing quite still he could feel her trembling. "Carol, I'm not just, I'm not just out for what I can get."

She reached her hand up towards him and placed two fingers over his trembling mouth. "I know you're not."

The breath of her sigh enveloped him before she gently placed her head on his chest. "Stuart, hold me."

Puzzled, he wrapped both his arms around her in a protective embrace. Yet his arousal had not subsided and her nearness rekindled his desire. Loosening his grip, with his left arm he tried to lift her chin up towards him but, guessing his intention, she kept her head down.

"Carol, you don't have to…"

Her smile was genuine as she raised her head and gazed steadily into his eyes.

"I know, Stuart. Please, just kiss me, slowly and gently."

He did, keeping himself in check even when he felt her begin to respond and push towards him again. The thrill of her presence swept over him in tingling waves but concerned she would shy away again, he limited himself to a long lingering kiss. Not that it was too much of a challenge. She was lovely to touch and to hold. And, in any case, he smiled to himself – it was he doing the kissing and not that other fellow.

The distant chime of a clock brought them both to a realization of reality. Moving slightly apart they stood, trembling slightly. Stuart's long sigh stirred the hairs on top of her head. "You're beautiful, Carol. Just beautiful."

Her response was simply to bury her head in his blazer and murmur, "Do you think we'd better go. If we miss the last ferry…" Her voice tailed off.

Stuart sighed again. "I'm afraid you're right. We'd better be off."

No one was in sight as he carefully opened the door and peered outside. Holding hands, they headed towards the ferry terminus. Neither of them spoke, and Stuart, after the dramatic turns of events during the day, was content to walk with this beautiful girl.

The ferry was half empty and they found a spot at the rear of one of the larger cabins. Usually the taciturn Auckland passengers maintained their own silence during the 20-minute trip to Devonport but tonight most of them were engaged in animated conversations with their neighbours. "Nothing like a war to turn strangers into friends," Stuart mused. Carol had rested her head on his shoulder and appeared to have drifted off to sleep. Feeling protective, Stuart sat listening to the chatter that mingled with the rhythmic thumping coming from the ferry's engine room below decks. All too soon the clanging of the ship's bells and the change in the engine's rhythms signalled the end of the trip.

Carol stirred and opened her eyes. "I fell asleep," she murmured.

"Bit early in the relationship for you to start sleeping with me," he grinned.

Expecting her to respond with a cheeky grin or a playful dig in the ribs, he was nonplussed by the long clay-cold look she gave him.

Behind them came the clattering of chains and a thump as the heavy gangway was lowered onto the ferry's upper deck.

"Come on."

She stood up.

As the tide was at its peak, the ferry was riding high causing the gangway to slope steeply downwards. Pausing at the top Stuart reached out and took Carol's hand firmly as she gingerly made her high-heeled way downward. As he stepped off the bottom onto the terminal's concrete floor she stumbled forward. He caught her in his arms as she fell against him. She leaned her head on his chest for a moment and then looked up and smiled.

"Sorry. Bit tricky in these shoes."

Heedless of the other passengers pushing past them he ran his right hand lightly over her hair.

"You OK?"

She held his gaze and reaching up, touched her fingers to his lips.

"Stuart, I..."

"Carol!" The angry voice cut through the clatter of the passengers' footsteps on the concrete floor. They both turned at the sight of Hamish, his face twisted with fury. Lurching forward he reached for Carol's arm hissing, "Come here, girl!"

Instinctively Stuart put his arm protectively across her shoulder and drew her back.

Hamish lunged again. "I told you to come here!" he snarled.

Stepping in front of Carol, Stuart clamped his hand around Hamish's outstretched arm.

"Not so fast, mate."

Hamish's look of undiluted hatred was followed by a heavy punch to the right side of Stuart's mouth. Its force and its total unexpectedness staggered him. Instinctively he put the back of his hand to his mouth and looking down saw it was smeared with blood.

Furious at the attack Stuart lashed out with a roundhouse right hand that, had it landed, would have certainly floored the other man. In a smooth action Hamish evaded the blow, swaying backwards, his eyes never leaving his opponent. Boxing was a regular feature of the sporting curriculum of many secondary schools and Hamish, by his blow and his stance, had obviously been taught the basics of the craft.

Stuart, who'd been the university's middleweight boxing representative in the previous year's Easter Tournament, sensed Hamish's expertise and adopted a defensive crouch in time to block a second vicious left hook.

"Hey, you chaps, that's enough!"

"Save it for the bloody Germans, mates, not each other!"

The pair had been encircled by a group of male passengers, one of whom, a burly Maori, stepped between them.

"Cut it out! Both of you!" he ordered.

"I haven't finished with you, you bastard!" shouted Hamish trying to push the Maori aside.

Gently but firmly the man pushed Hamish back and, holding him at arm's length snapped, "Watch your language. There's a lady present."

"Perhaps the lady's part of the problem," said another man looking admiringly at Carol who was standing helplessly to one side, her hand covering her mouth.

Angry at the attention he had attracted and unwilling to challenge the well-built Maori and his mates, Hamish swung round to Carol, and seizing her firmly by the arm growled, "Your aunt rang me. You weren't on the 8:30 bus. She was worried sick. I said I'd bring my car down to find you." He glared at Stuart, who stood angrily dabbing his mouth with the back of his hand. "And what do I find? Have you no shame, Carol? Consorting with this varsity bugger!"

"I've already warned you about your language," said the large man, menacingly, "Can't you see the lady's upset?"

"Alright. Alright," responded Hamish hastily. His grip on Carol tightened. "I'm taking the lady home. Her aunt's worried about her."

He tugged at Carol but she freed herself with a quick backward jerk. Reaching into her handbag she pulled out a small white handkerchief and stepped forward to hand it to Stuart.

"Here, Stuart," she said. "I'm awfully sorry about your lip."

With a growl of protest Hamish moved forward to grab her arm but several of the men, whose sympathies were with Carol, blocked his path.

"Thanks," mumbled Stuart. "He took me by surprise; but the blood on your handkerchief? It'll make a frightful mess."

She smiled wanly and, ignoring the increasingly angry Hamish, reached up and touched him on the cheek.

"It's alright, Stuart. The least I can do."

Whirling abruptly she strode straight past Hamish towards the exit.

With a venomous glare at Stuart, Hamish hurried after her calling, "Carol, wait! Wait for me!" as the sound of throaty male chuckles echoed behind him.

"You OK, mate?" asked one of the men turning to Stuart.

"Yeah, thanks." He looked at the reddening handkerchief. "I think the bleeding slowed down a bit. I'll live."

"To fight another day?" The burly Maori grinned.

"Yeah." Looking round the group he smiled awkwardly. "Er, thanks, chaps. Better hurry or I'll miss my bloody bus."

CHAPTER 7

"Morning, Mr Johnson. Good to see you, my boy. Sit down"

Professor Sterling was all affability when Stuart, having knocked on the office door, entered in response to "Come!" The enthusiasm of the often-dour academic at his arrival was solace for Stuart who, over the previous twelve hours, had run the full gamut of emotions. His family had been bad enough, wanting to know how he'd split his lip – the dubious reaction by his father to the lame excuse that he'd tripped and fallen at varsity had irritated him considerably. It was not so much that his father disbelieved his lie but in doing so he had reverted to the all-too-familiar role of suspicious father confronting recalcitrant son. Consequently he'd been in no mood to share the news of Professor Sterling's offer. Added to this the circumstances that had resulted in the injury had marred the memories of his tryst with Carol in the small History library.

His conflicting emotions had boiled over when the following morning at the breakfast table his younger brother Stephen had smirked, "Hey, Stuart, looks like you've been trying to kiss a crocodile."

A very restless night, the view of his swollen lip his bedroom mirror had revealed a few minutes earlier, and Claire's giggle at his brother's witticism had resulted in his reaching over and smacking Stephen hard across the head. Then, ashamed at his action, he had leapt up from the table, grabbed his bag of books and stormed out, slamming the door on the shouts and cries echoing from the dining room.

Arriving at the ferry buildings earlier than usual he had resisted the desire to wait for the eight o'clock boat but had caught the earlier one, with the result that there were few people about when he had arrived at university, where he had made for Professor Sterling's office.

Stuart came straight to the point. "I was wondering, sir, what happens to the research position if I'm called up for military service?"

"Looks like you've recently engaged in unarmed combat, my boy," smiled Sterling.

"Oh, this," said Stuart, touching his swollen lips and smiling ruefully. "Just a minor accident, sir."

"I see. Well, in my opinion it's highly unlikely you'll be called up. Now more than ever the research project has a direct relevance to this new wartime situation. Consequently your position will be considered as being essential war work." Seeing Stuart's frown he asked, "Will that pose any difficulties for you?"

"No, sir, I suppose not. Just that I was expecting to join up and to, well, fight."

"Perfectly understandable. And, when one considers the appalling characteristics of the Nazis, also very commendable. But bear in mind, wars are won by brains more than by brawn. Therefore we'll almost certainly be asked to shift the focus of our research onto German domestic and foreign policy over the past decade in order to assist our government and her allies gain a greater insight into the mind of the enemy.

"That makes sense, sir."

"Of course it does." He smiled. "At times like these young men characteristically respond to their basic instincts by wanting to seize the nearest weapon and dash off to save the world. Of course there's a time for rapid action but there's also a time for a measured, well-researched response. Much more effective in the long run."

Stuart felt considerable relief. The thought of travelling overseas to fight the foe had adventurous appeal, but his studies of World War I had made him all too familiar with the horrors of warfare and the detrimental effect it had had on many of those who survived. Furthermore, undertaking research at home would enable him to be near Carol. He heaved a long sigh. Carol. Ah, yes.

"Having second thoughts?"

Stuart brought himself up with a start. "Oh, no, not at all. It's a wonderful opportunity for me and a chance, as you say, to help the war effort."

"Excellent, Stuart. May I call you 'Stuart'?"

"Yes, of course, sir."

"Splendid. Now what was it you wanted to see me about?"

"Nothing in particular, sir. Only wanted to make sure I hadn't been dreaming."

"You hadn't."

"I am concerned about my exams. The finals are coming up soon and I'm keen to do well. However, as the war has broken out..."

"Look, Stuart, you are to concentrate totally on your studies. I'm happy, as I said, for you to use the History library if you want to but in the meantime, just keep our research project in the back of your mind. When you've finished your finals, take a couple of day's breather then come and see me and we'll begin to plan our strategy."

"OK, sir, if you're sure."

"Absolutely. I've made a start so there will be plenty for you to do when you're ready. Now, I expect you want to get on with some swotting for the dreaded finals, unless there's anything else?"

"No thanks, sir. I'll look forward to seeing you in a couple of weeks, after my finals."

"Excellent." Sterling stood up, stretched out his hand and smiled warmly.

"Good luck, Stuart. I'm sure you'll do very well."

His early morning start meant he had plenty of time in which to begin his final swotting binge. Finding a spot in the library by a window he spread his notes out on the desk, lit a cigarette and began the task of completing the summaries he had been preparing in anticipation of the exam questions. Initially confident of passing with a reasonably high mark, Sterling's offer had increased his level of motivation. Now he not only wanted to pass, but to pass with high marks.

The 11:30 chime of an external clock caused him to pause and stretch. The weather was cool but pleasant and he'd decided to cross Princes Street and sit by the Boer War statue in Albert Park at lunchtime in the hope Carol would turn up. The situation with her was still riddled with contradictions. Her passion and her tenderness showed she had considerable feelings for him. Yet her link with Hamish seemed puzzlingly strong. Perhaps by now Hamish had forced her to confess to their lunchtime meetings or, worse still, the library assignation. Not that he was worried the fellow would take any action – just that he was bound to try to turn it into something sordid.

A few minutes before noon he walked out of the main clock tower building and began to cross Princes Street towards the park. As he paused and waited for a group of cyclists to pass by, he saw Carol walking towards him past the historic houses on the opposite side. She smiled, waved and hurried forward.

"I was hoping..."

"I'd see you," he finished and they both laughed.

"I've got my paper bag. Do you have any lunch, Stuart?"

"Sorry, no. I left in rather a hurry this morning."

She touched his mouth. "Is the swelling's going down?" she asked anxiously.

"Yes. Look, I'm sorry. I've still got your handkerchief." He pulled the crumpled bloodstained piece of cloth from his trouser pocket. "It's awfully messy. Didn't want to give it to my mother."

"Awkward explanations?"

"Yes, and I didn't get the chance to..."

"It's all right, Stuart. Give it here. I'll wash it."

"Thanks. Look, I'm sorry about last night."

"*You're* sorry. Don't be silly. You've got nothing to apologize for. Hamish behaved like a pig. He had no business attacking you like that! And," she paused and her smile had an edge, "I told him so!"

"Well done. What was his reaction?"

"He – he tried to order me not to see you again."

A light breeze brushed the hair from left side of her face.

"Carol, what's that?"

His hand reached out but she drew away, pushing the hair back in place.

"It's nothing."

"Nothing? That mark on the side of your face. It's a bruise."

Involuntarily her hand went up to her face.

"It's nothing, Stuart. I fell against the cupboard when I was getting out of the bath last night."

His eyes narrowed. "You fell."

"Yes, I fell against the cupboard. It's nothing – the swelling's going down."

He tried to hold her gaze but she quickly turned her head away.

"Carol, if I thought for one moment that he ..."

"You'd be wrong. It was a simple accident. That's all." She put her hand on his arm. "Now, as I was saying, I told Hamish we're good friends and I had a right to choose my own friends."

"Good friends?" He smiled, and reaching out his hand, lifted her chin. "Obviously a mistress of the understatement, Miss Peterson."

He was momentarily startled by the look of intense bleakness that filled her eyes before she stepped back and smiled brightly at him.

"Shall we sit here? We can share my lunch. There's not much but we can make the most of it."

"If it's loaves and fishes we could pray for a miracle."

CHAPTER 8

The days that followed were full of excitement and challenge for Stuart. He and Carol started meeting for lunch in Albert Park on a regular basis. Although puzzled by her occasional bleak flashes he had come to the conclusion that in the meantime he was content with the pleasure of her company and to let matters take their course. She had told him Hamish continued to disapprove of their lunchtime meetings but she had refused to stop them. Yet, whenever he tried to further explore her relationship with Hamish, she changed the subject so he finally let it drop. With the memories of the library meeting still fresh in his mind he had twice hinted they should arrange another evening rendezvous, but on each occasion she had changed the subject.

Nevertheless the regular meetings with her buoyed his spirits. He made peace with his family and informed them of his scholarship. Their congratulations were mixed with their obvious relief over his exemption from military service. His father was certainly pleased his son would not have to join the expanding armed forces. Yet the government-funded research position would enable him to hold up his head when telling his neighbours, friends and church members why his son was remaining in New Zealand while others were going overseas on active duty.

Stuart's excellent exam results further lifted his spirits. After hearty congratulations Professor Sterling lost no time in finding him a small office and assigning him a series of research tasks. His weekdays became filled with combing through books, archived newspapers, letters, official government documents and communiqués. As some of the material was in German

Stuart was also able to persuade his mentor to hire Brendan as a part-time translator.

Superficially Stuart's existence was idyllic – a challenging position, a developing relationship with Carol, and relative harmony at home. Yet clouding his horizons were the continuing reminders that there was a war on. Increasingly military uniforms began to appear on the streets. Patriotic speeches from "Where-Britain-goes-we-go" Prime Minister Michael Joseph Savage and other MPs filled the pages of the newspapers, alongside photographs of young Kiwis training and marching in readiness to join the brave boys overseas. Increasingly however, the initial optimism at home was tempered by the realities of the war. The rapid advance of the German army through Western Europe and the fall of France caused widespread concern. Consequently the papers made much of the rescue of the British army at the French port of Dunkirk by the flotilla of vessels that had crossed the English Channel and braved German air attacks to bring the troops back to England.

"It was a great effort, sir," said Stuart as he and Professor Sterling studied the Dunkirk photographs in the New Zealand Herald.

"True," replied the professor. "But don't let it blind you to the fact that Dunkirk was a major defeat. Now virtually all of Europe is under the control of the German army, undoubtedly the best fighting force the world has ever seen."

The deteriorating situation motivated Stuart and Professor Sterling to increase their work rate, seeking to gain any insight, no matter how minor, into the German military and political mind. The fall of France shifted their focus to attempts to research and predict the type of occupation likely to be imposed on the conquered peoples of Holland, Belgium, Luxembourg, France, Norway and Denmark and whether or not this would differ from the brutality of the regime that had been imposed on Poland.

They had also been asked to keep a watching brief on Japan and the USA. Japan's bellicose incursions into China contrasted sharply with the isolationist attitude that appeared to be widespread throughout America. Although President Franklin Roosevelt reflected the considerable sympathy felt for Britain in its battle with the Germany, there seemed little likelihood of his country taking up arms in support of Britain and her allies.

Professor Sterling's privileged position with the government's Ministry of Defence gave Stuart access to censored information showing in grim detail the reality of the war's progress and the increasing success of the German forces on land and sea. The newspapers, magazines and cinema newsreels continued to paint a positive picture of 'our brave boys' but Stuart found it increasingly hard to remain positive when he read the casualty figures of men and material.

It was a cool morning in mid-November when Professor Sterling put his head round Stuart's door and informed him there was a meeting scheduled for 11 o'clock with some military personnel.

"The Prime Minister's Department is considering increasing our funding in order to provide more information for our military intelligence sections," he explained. "A delegation is coming to meet us to discuss the potential of our research. If they see additional possibilities they will recommend an expansion of our operation."

"What are our chances, sir?" asked Stuart.

"Reasonably good I should think," replied the professor. "We'll need to convince them that our research can be applied directly to the nation's war needs. I'd like you to report on your research into the Nazi occupation of Europe, including anything you can find on resistance movements – sabotage, partisan fighters, that sort of thing. The way the conqueror and the conquered behave is always an excellent indication of his ultimate aims and objectives. The conquering of a nation is a lot easier than its occupation. Our visitors might be interested in working with us on ways to undermine the enemy through support for resistance movements."

***

"The military gentlemen have arrived, Professor," announced the departmental secretary.

Professor Sterling and Stuart rose to greet the uniformed members of the delegation. The first to appear was a tall, grey-haired man who strode into the meeting room with outstretched hand.

"Major Richard Thompson, pleased to meet you. Allow me to introduce my team." Turning to the two other uniformed men who had entered the room he continued, "May I present Captain Mark Williamson and Lieutenant Hamish Beavis."

Stuart and Hamish both froze at the same moment, and stood staring at each other in astonishment. "You two gentlemen know each other, Lieutenant?" asked Major Thompson.

Hamish braced his shoulders to display his new uniform with its neat creases and shiny shoulder pips. "Yes, sir, I know Johnson quite well." His top lip twitched upwards. "I'm not surprised he's still a civilian."

Recovering himself, Stuart looked Hamish in the face before shifting his gaze to the man's shoulders.

"I see Mr. Beavis has attained officer status." He beamed. "I hope he has more success in getting his troops to obey him than he has had with a mutual acquaintance of ours."

The snarled response was immediate. "Watch your mouth, Johnson! I'd hate to damage it."

"Beavis!" barked the major.

Hamish froze to attention. "Sir!"

"I don't know what this is about, but may I remind you we are here in a military capacity. You will conduct yourself in a manner befitting a man of officer rank. Do I make myself clear?"

43

"Sir!" responded the still rigid Hamish, staring straight ahead.

Thompson turned to Sterling "I'm sorry about this, professor."

"No need to apologize, Major. Mr. Johnson was also out of order. Now I suggest we all follow the major's advice and remember we are here to serve the cause of our country and should therefore set aside any private feelings." He turned to his assistant. "Agreed, Mr. Johnson?"

"Agreed, sir. Sorry, sir." Stuart, although still recovering from the shock of seeing Hamish in his new capacity, had realized any further aggression on his part could undermine the meeting before it got started.

"Good. That's settled," said Major Thompson. "At ease, Beavis. I suggest, Professor Sterling, we get down to business."

With a scraping of chairs and a rustle of papers, the five men and the secretary seated themselves around the table. Thompson opened the meeting.

"Gentlemen," he began, "it's important for our military to gather an accurate insight into the enemy's thinking, his values and his ultimate goals. Rather stupidly we've made the mistake of not taking the Nazis seriously enough."

"In the hope they'd keep to their own back yard," grunted the professor.

"Exactly," replied Thompson. "However, the fall of France and their occupation of Europe have motivated us to consider ways in which the Nazis could be undermined, other than on the battlefield."

He paused and Sterling nodded. "Over the last few weeks Mr. Johnson has been engaged in extensive research. For the purposes of this meeting I have asked him to prepare a summary of three of his key findings." He held up his fist and raised a finger for each point. "Resistance movements, the attitudes of various sectors of the population towards their new rulers, and collaboration by locals with the Germans." He turned to Stuart and nodded.

"My theme is 'The Nazis as Occupiers'," began Stuart. "The first area I'd like us to look at is resistance movements."

Clearing his throat, he glanced at Hamish. The man's expression was neutral but his gaze was unwavering. As Stuart began speaking he became aware his topic was generating considerable interest. Avoiding Hamish's stare he concentrated on making eye contact with the others in the room. After outlining his methodology and sources of information, he moved on to his conclusions to date.

"What is clear to me is that in Occupied Europe the Nazis are receiving a surprising degree of cooperation among some sections of the population."

The three military men exchanged glances and murmured with surprise. Taking this as his cue Hamish snapped, "That's absurd! The people of Europe hate the Nazis. They'd never collaborate with them."

Stuart, on his home ground and supported by his research, remained calm. The facts he had unearthed were not palatable, but he was confident his sources were reliable. Shifting his gaze towards Hamish he spoke slowly and deliberately.

"My research does not deal with the absurd. I deal in facts and, if asked to develop hypotheses, I do so based on those facts. Therefore they warrant serious consideration."

"'Develop hypotheses'? Huh, typical of these varsity types. Trying to show off by using fancy words to demonstrate they're cleverer than the rest of us." His eyes narrowed. "Listen, Johnson, remember there's a war on and support for Hitler and the Nazis is regarded as traitorous!"

"I think that's enough, Lieutenant," Thompson's tone was sharp but his voice reflected uncertainty. He frowned at Stuart. "Surely you're not saying the Nazis have widespread support in places like Poland, Denmark, Norway, Holland or France?"

"It's difficult to accurately gauge the level. It's unlikely to be wide in Poland, due to the harsh nature of the occupation. And I'm not saying it's widespread, either. But what's clear is that there is support for the Nazis among certain population sections."

"That's ridiculous, sir! They fought to keep the Germans out. And I know they'll continue to fight."

"You 'know', lieutenant? How do you know?" The professor's voice was calm and even.

"Stands to reason, doesn't it?" said Hamish, seeking support from his fellow officer.

"I would hope so," frowned Captain Thompson.

"Hope is one thing, but facts are what we are trying to deal with here, gentlemen," responded the professor. "My young colleague and I have spent many hours sifting through a mass of material, some of it translated from original German sources."

"'German sources'! Are they reading German propaganda at this university, sir? Really, sir, this is too much! We are wasting..."

"Lieutenant Beavis!" his commanding officer's voice resumed its previous authoritarian note. "While I too am surprised at Mr. Johnson's finding, I have no difficulty with these two gentlemen reading German sources. Surely this is the most reliable way of finding out what the enemy is thinking?"

"Yes, sir, but there's more to it than that. Johnson has suspect views. He may even be a Nazi sympathizer. He hasn't joined up; he's remained here at this university while others like me have joined the armed forces. That's pretty suspect in my book!"

"This is too much!" Professor Sterling half rose from his chair and leaned across the table as he addressed himself to Hamish. "You, lieutenant, do not understand the difference between a researcher explaining his research outcomes and a man expressing a personal political opinion. Just because a research outcome is unpalatable, doesn't make the researcher himself suspect. In your case the term 'military intelligence' is an oxymoron!"

"Are you calling me a 'moron'?" snarled Hamish.

The professor slipped back into his chair and sighed. Turning to the major he shrugged. "I rest my case."

Embarrassed at his officer's obtuseness Thompson stood up. "I'm sorry, professor, but under the circumstances it would be best if we left. I would like to hear more of your research but," he looked hard at Hamish, "I will have to reconsider the makeup of my team."

He reached over, briskly shook hands with Stuart and Sterling and left the room.

Hamish, who was the last of the trio to leave, paused alongside Stuart. His words, although soft, were laced with menace.

"Start looking over your shoulder, Johnson."

CHAPTER 9

The news of Hitler's full-scale invasion of Russia caught everyone by surprise and lifted the spirits of the New Zealand population. Parallels were drawn with France's ill-fated military campaign in 1812 in which Napoleon Bonaparte's Grande Armée had been defeated by the terrible Russian winter. The conclusion that Hitler's Wermacht soldiers would eventually meet a similar fate was widespread.

The invasion opened up another area of research for Professor Sterling and his team.

"I'm absolutely staggered at the rapid progress of the German army," he said. "They're well on the way to Moscow." He glanced out of his office window, "However, in a few months there'll be spring blossoms on our trees. That will mean autumn leaves in Russia. The German army won't find the Russian winter an easy environment."

What intrigued Stuart apart from the rapid German advance was the support for its soldiers that came from some sections of the Russian populace. One morning, having barely seated himself at his desk, he received a phone call from Professor Sterling.

"Good morning, Stuart. Could you drop in to my office when you have a moment?"

"Of course, sir," he said. "I'll come now."

As he entered the professor's office he was greeted with, "Here Stuart, take a look at this."

Stuart accepted the photograph that was handed to him. He studied it for a moment and asked, "A German photograph, sir?"

"Yes, from the Russian front in the Ukraine. Rather bears out what you were saying at the meeting with Major Thompson."

With increasing interest Stuart studied the photograph. It showed two blond-haired German soldiers, without helmets or weapons, seated between two pretty girls in traditional Ukrainian dress. All four were spontaneously laughing and applauding.

"Apparently it was taken at some Ukrainian folk festival to which the German soldiers were invited," explained the professor. "Clearly the question of loyalties is as confusing in the Soviet Union as it is in Occupied Europe."

"It certainly warrants further investigation. Have your heard anything more from Major Thompson?"

"Yes, he phoned me an hour ago. Our reports have resulted in their continuing to recognize the value of our work. He's therefore agreed to an increase in our funding."

"Excellent news, sir." Stuart paused. "Did he mention Hamish Beavis?"

"Apparently Beavis has been re-assigned and will not have any further involvement with this office, or, to use the major's words, 'or any of its personnel'".

"That's excellent news, sir, on both counts. Do you think we could offer Brendan some more work?" he continued, knowing his friend was quite happy to support the war effort with his translating skills.

"Excellent idea. His work is fast and accurate and his knowledge of colloquial German is proving invaluable. Would he be interested, do you think?"

"Rather, sir. I'm seeing him after work for a drink so I'll ask him."

During the previous war, legislation had been introduced that required pubs throughout New Zealand to close promptly at six o'clock every night – on Sunday they were not permitted to open at all. The most celebrated result of these drinking laws was the last hour before closing time, known to all as the 'six o'clock swill'. Like all those going for an after-work drink Stuart was aware time was limited. Promptly at five o'clock he left his office and made his way downtown to the De Bretts' pub in High Street.

The noisy smoke-filled public bar, where women were not permitted, contained an increasingly familiar mix of men in civilian clothing and military uniforms. The tiles on the floor carried on halfway up the walls which, apart from the occasional cheaply framed print of a racehorse, boxing or wrestling champion, or rugby team, were bare. The purpose of the establishment was clear – the consumption of copious quantities of beer in the shortest possible time. Standing three deep at the long bar counter, the patrons waited impatiently as the barmen, using long hosepipes, poured beer into the relays of empty glasses and jugs that were constantly thrust forward.

Stuart began to push his way forward through the noisy, packed throng – most of whom were concentrating on downing as much alcohol as possible within the 45 minutes remaining to them. Through the smoke he spotted Brendan in a corner, sitting on a high stool, his head slumped onto one of many tall circular tables screwed to the tiled floor. He was clutching a glass and a half-filled jug of beer was on the table beside him. As Stuart approached with a hearty greeting, his friend barely glanced up.

Puzzled, he asked, "You OK, mate?"

"Not really," slurred Brendan, looking up at Stuart with bloodshot eyes.

"What's the problem?"

Brendan grunted and muttered to himself.

Unable to hear him above the raucous crowd, Stuart leaned closer to his friend's flushed face.

"Sorry, mate, I couldn't hear you. What's the problem?"

Brendan lifted his head and for a long moment looked hard at Stuart. Abruptly he stood up and shouted, "I said I got my bloody call-up papers this morning! But I'm telling you now, loud and clear, I'm not going! They can't make me fight!"

The sudden leap to his feet caused Brendan to collide with a soldier who had been leaning against an adjacent table. As the man whirled round and shouted, "Watch what you're doing you bloody idiot!" he sloshed most of his beer over his nearest neighbour's khaki tunic.

It was Hamish Beavis.

"You!" hissed Hamish on seeing Stuart.

Before Stuart could respond, the man whose tunic had received most of Hamish's beer reached out and grabbed Brendan by the arm. "Hey, you!' he shouted.

Swaying slightly, Brendan turned round and peered at him.

"What did you just yell?" demanded the soldier.

"I'm not going to fight! No bastard can make me!" responded Brendan loudly.

"You been called up?"

"Yeah," said Brendan. "What of it?"

Obviously elated, Hamish grabbed his neighbour and shouted, "It all fits!" He pointed at Brendan and then at Stuart. "This joker is a coward, and his mate Johnson here is a supporter of the Krauts. What a bloody pair. And what a bloody nerve! Drinking in here with real Kiwi men!"

In spite of the high noise level in the pub, the shouting attracted the attention of other men who, sensing a confrontation, began to surge towards the protagonists. Stuart, realizing the crowd was unlikely to show any sympathy towards a man who was refusing to obey his call-up orders, made a vain attempt to calm the situation by addressing Hamish's companion.

"Come on, mate. He's had a few too many. He doesn't know what he's saying or doing. Let's just forget it." He forced a smile and glanced at his watch. "There's only a few minutes drinking time left..."

Cutting across him, Hamish shouted to the growing crowd, "This man's a yellow bastard! And his mate's a yellow bastard! They're both yellow bastards!"

"Yeah, Carol was right. She said your vocabulary was severely limited!" retorted Stuart.

The mention of Carol goaded Hamish into a fury. Swinging his left arm back, he lashed out. This time Stuart anticipated the blow. Hamish had been drinking and his reflexes were slower than normal, providing Stuart time to sway back from the roundhouse punch. Over the past weeks he had gone over and over the ferry building fight in his mind, recreating what he would have done had he known a punch was coming. The images stood him in good stead. Stepping forward with his full body weight he sank his right fist into Hamish's solar plexus. The man collapsed, coughing and vomiting quantities of beer onto the tiled floor.

"He hit an officer, the bastard!" shouted Hamish's companion, surging forward towards Stuart and Brendan.

Several men in military uniform, shouting support, lurched forward to join him but in doing so tripped over the moaning, coughing figure of Hamish. His vomit and the thin layer of beer on the tiled floor caused the men to slide and clutch at one another for support. Each in turn, unable to stay upright, crashed cursing into other men. The result was mayhem.

Fuelled by alcohol and bruised from their falls, men vented their anger on the nearest stranger. Within seconds a full-scale brawl surged across the floor of the public bar. Jugs of beer crashed and shattered on the hard floor adding an additional hazard to the flying fists and boots as with shouts of fury and howls of pain, waves of men surged over the whole area.

Stuart found himself fighting on two fronts – to protect himself and to protect Brendan whose drunkenness made him an easy target. Stuart's sober state did give him an edge over his belligerent attackers who were finding it difficult to swing effective blows in the crush of bodies. At first he managed to

52

ward off most of the punches but inevitably one got through and sent Brendan sprawling. Instinctively Stuart turned to assist and in doing so received a blow to the back of his own head, knocking him down beside his friend.

"Put the boot in!" shouted a voice above them. An excruciating pain shot through him as an army boot thudded into his ribs. Two more equally painful blows followed before another voice shouted, "OK, mates, that's enough!" and Stuart and Brendan were left coughing and moaning on the floor in the corner of the bar while the brawl continued to surge above them. Deciding through his haze of pain that nothing was to be gained by trying to stand, Stuart put his mouth to Brendan's ear and shouted, "Stay here. Don't move. If we get up they'll kill us!"

The blow, the fall and the alcohol resulted in Brendan's drifting into a half-conscious state punctuated by an occasional moan of protest when a foot stood on him or a body sprawled near him. As Stuart lay on the sodden foul-smelling floor, hunched partly in pain and partly as a means of protecting himself from further assault, he heard orders being barked out above the din. The shouting subsided. Summoned by a barman's telephone call the police had arrived in substantial numbers to deal with a familiar problem – a pub closing time brawl.

The police sergeant, aware that at any time his men could be called to another inner city watering hole to deal with the same problem, ordered the barroom to be cleared. Subdued by the sight of a phalanx of blue uniforms, men lurched towards the door and out into the street, assisting their mates who, through injury or drunkenness, were unable to make it on their own. As the last few staggered away the sergeant surveyed the bodies strewn about the floor – some moaning and some lying still.

"Looks like bloody Waterloo," he muttered. "Check to see if any of these layabouts need medical assistance."

The policemen began working their way across the floor checking each man. "Most of them are just drunk, Sarge," said one of the policemen while the rest nodded in agreement. "Bit of blood but nothing serious."

Hearing a load moan, the sergeant indicated the corner where several men including Stuart and Hamish were lying. "Check over there."

Two policemen walked gingerly across the slippery floor towards the group and, as Stuart began to prop himself up, one of them asked, "You OK?"

"Yes, except I got booted in the ribs and it's hard to breathe. He indicated Brendan who had fallen into a deep sleep. "My mate's OK. He only needs time to sleep it off." He began to struggle to his feet and winced as one of the policemen leaned forward and lifted him under the armpit.

"Sore, is it mate?" he asked.

"Yes. Might have cracked something," he muttered as he rose. He smiled wryly at the policeman and gingerly put his hand against his side. "The irony is I didn't even have time for a drink. Came in here looking for my mate and suddenly all hell broke loose."

"That's not true, officer. This man is responsible for the whole bloody mess!"

Turning Stuart confronted the sight of a belligerent Hamish, who had lurched to his feet, and stood swaying slightly and bleeding from a cut above his right eyebrow.

"What do you mean?" asked the sergeant, stepping forward.

"His mate down there," Hamish gestured scornfully, "had his call-up papers this morning. Stood in the corner shouting he wasn't going to join up, that he hated the King, and he hoped the Germans would win. And Johnson here," another scornful gesture, "joined in, egging him on and also shouting seditious comments."

"You bloody liar!" responded Stuart, furious at the man's wild accusations. "You and your army mates started swinging

54

punches and set off the whole thing. And now you're trying to blame somebody else."

"Just hold it, both of you," interposed the sergeant. "Now," he continued, turning to Stuart, "what's this about your mate being called up and refusing to go?"

Stuart chose his words with care. "Apparently he got his call-up papers in the post today. When I came in he had obviously been drinking for a while..."

"Because he's yellow!" interrupted Hamish

"As I said, he'd been drinking for a while," insisted Stuart, trying to keep his temper, "as had most of the men in the pub, including soldier boy here."

His final phrase was ill chosen as the sergeant narrowed his eyes. "Do you have something against the King's officers?"

Sensing the shift in attitude, Hamish cut in. "He certainly does, Sergeant. And what's more he's a supporter of the Germans. I've heard him say so up at that university of his."

"That's a serious accusation, Lieutenant," said the sergeant. He turned to Stuart. "Have you anything to say, young man?"

"Plenty, but you'd arrest me for obscene language in a public place. The lieutenant's accusations are totally without foundation. I support the war effort just as everyone else does. He's pissed off because his girlfriend and I are especially friendly."

"Why, you..."

"Take it easy, Lieutenant,' cautioned the sergeant. "Now then," he continued, addressing Stuart, "I'm not interested in private squabbles about sheilas, but," he continued a little pompously, "anything that undermines national security is my concern. Now, you said you supported the war effort like everyone else?"

Not sure where it was leading, Stuart merely nodded.

"Fine. That's your word against the Lieutenant's. But, what about your mate here?" He nudged Brendan with the toe of his boot and elicited an inaudible mumble.

"He's OK. Unlike me he was fairly drunk. I'll look after him when he comes round."

"I think it's your duty to investigate further, Sergeant." Hamish was determined not to let the opportunity to discredit both men slip by.

"Investigate what?" demanded Stuart. "If he's been called up, so what? No crime's been committed. He doesn't even have to report for several days."

"True enough." The sergeant nodded in agreement. "We'll leave it at that." Turning away he was about to order his men to leave when Brendan chose that moment to wake up. Propping himself unsteadily on one elbow he gesticulated towards the sergeant.

"Don't have to report for several days, eh, mate? Huh. I'll tell you again. I'm not going to bloody well report at all. I'm not going to join their bloody army, navy or air force – or anything else for that matter. They can fight their fucking war without me!"

"See, sergeant! The man's a subversive. Do your duty!"

"Don't be stupid. He's still drunk. Anyone can see that. Let him sleep it off." Stuart was clutching at straws.

The group of constables took exception to Brendan's outburst and began muttering angrily. Unwilling to lose credibility with his men the sergeant turned to two of them.

"Get him on his feet," he ordered.

Mumbling incoherently, Brendan was hauled upright and the sergeant announced he was under arrest.

"But this is ridiculous! What are you charging him with?" protested Stuart.

"Breach of the peace will do for a start," said the sergeant. "There's a war on, mate, and we all have to do our bit. Now move on or you'll be joining your subversive friend."

"Yeah, move on," chimed in Hamish with a leer of triumph. "Just count your lucky stars that..."

"All right, Lieutenant, I'll handle this, thank you." Although regarding the arrest of Brendan as justified, the sergeant was keen to minimize any further complications. "By the state of you I suggest you make your way back to your barracks or your home."

"I wanted to make sure..."

"Now, Lieutenant! Unless, of course, you'd like me to call the MPs?"

At his nod, two of the policemen moved towards Hamish who, having no wish to be involved with the military police, headed towards the door. His shout of "That'll teach you, Johnson!" was lost on Stuart who was more concerned with the fate of his inebriated friend.

"You can see the state of him, sergeant," he pleaded. "The man's in no condition to .."

"Listen, son, he'll spend the night in the cells where he can dry out with the rest of the city's drunks. Then we'll decide in the morning whether or not to charge him. Now, get yourself home and ring the station in the morning." Seeing Stuart hesitate he touched him on the shoulder. "Off you go, now."

"It's OK, mate." Brendan chuckled drunkenly. "These boys in blue are going to take care of me – and they're not the bloody army."

"Take it easy, Brendan. I'll be in touch." Stuart realized his response was inadequate but he had no wish to complicate matters. With a feeble wave to his friend he stepped gingerly out into the street.

Chapter 10

Every time he took a breath his side hurt but he was able to walk, albeit with caution. Instinctively he headed downtown towards the ferry buildings until, passing a department store window, he caught a glimpse of a dishevelled figure clad in a crumpled blazer with a torn sleeve. With a start he realized it was his own reflection. As he paused he felt a chill of the evening wind through his shirt and realized his blazer was quite damp with beer from the bloody floor. He must smell like a brewery. He couldn't go home like this. His parents would be appalled.

Heading back up the street he cut eastwards across Albert Park towards the university. The main building was still open and the few people still around gave him disapproving looks – probably more the result of his aroma than his appearance. Heading towards the History Department he entered the men's toilet and stood in front of the basin where he spent a few moments scrutinizing his sorry appearance in the mirror. His blazer was damp and so were his trousers. "Not a pretty sight," he muttered, stripping off his blazer and wrinkling his nose at the smell. He couldn't do much about the tear but at least he might be able to clean it. He picked up the piece of soap from the basin and rubbed it in a circular motion over the coat. The dampened surface created a light foam and once he'd covered most of the garment, he jammed it into the small wash basin and turned on the tap. The water flowed over the blazer, filled the basin and began cascading over the edge. Hastily turning off the tap he lifted the blazer up. It began to drip, some of it into the basin and the rest onto the floor.

As he stood holding the dripping garment, the door swung open.

"What the devil? Good God, it's you, Stuart! What on earth are you doing?"

Equally startled to see Professor Sterling, Stuart explained about the pub brawl concluding with, "I couldn't go home in this state so the only place I could think of was varsity."

His professor's reaction was to suggest he leave the blazer in the basin where the smell might evaporate and adjourn to his study for a further discussion, adding wryly, "This is hardly the place for us to be seen to be holding an earnest conversation."

Stuart readily agreed, as the September night was turning increasingly cold.

"So, what's to be done?" asked Sterling, once they had seated themselves in the welcome warmth of his study.

"Well, sir, I'm afraid Brendan will be spending the night in the police cells with all the other city drunks."

"Yes. Perhaps he'll swear off the booze after the experience."

"Quite possibly. For a few days at least.

"At any rate, tomorrow morning I'll go to the police station and see what can be done. He's very foolish to carry on like that in a pub full of soldiers. However I should be able to get him released due to his work on our research project."

"Yes that should carry a fair bit of weight."

"Agreed, but he'll have to keep his mouth shut and let me do the talking. Now young man," he looked Stuart up and down, "what about you? You can't go home. Your dishevelled state would hardly endear you to your er, conservative parents."

Stuart smiled wryly. "True."

"Well, there's only one thing for it."

"What's that, sir?"

"You'll have to stay at my place."

"Oh, but I couldn't," Stuart protested.

"You've no alternative Stuart. You can phone from there and explain to your parents we've have been engaged in some research at my home and I've invited you to stay to save myself the trouble of having to run you home late at night. Sound plausible?"

"Well, yes, sir, but are you quite sure?"

"Of course I'm sure. I have a spare room and you're welcome to it. You're lucky I brought my car in today as I normally catch the bus and ferry, to save using my petrol coupons." He smiled. "In any case, young man, travelling with you in that state on public transport would severely damage my reputation in the community. Now, where did I leave my briefcase?"

Within ten minutes Stuart was seated in the professor's 1937 Morris 12 waiting in the queue of cars for the vehicular ferry to transport them across the harbour to Devonport wharf. Growing increasingly tired, and shivering in his shirtsleeves, he was relieved when the car managed to make it onto the ferry's deck as the last one of the fifteen vehicles.

As the ferry began to pull away from the wharf Sterling faced Stuart. "Now, I need to discuss some matters with you."

"Serious matters, sir?"

"Not sure," said the older man. "Now as you know the Allies appear to be able to intercept certain German coded messages."

"Yes," said Stuart.

"We believe that in the last twenty-four hours all German front line commanders have been instructed to stop their advances on all fronts. This has been confirmed by our own troops"

"No further advances, sir? I know our boys gave them a mauling in Crete even though we lost the battle. Maybe the Germans are taking the time to lick their wounds and regroup."

"It's much more widespread than Crete. For example Rommel has just won a major battle at Sollum in the Western Desert. Consequently he's well placed to continue his drive into Egypt with the ultimate aim of capturing Cairo. Similarly,

General Guderian and other German commanders in Russia appear to have halted their advances."

In the increasing wind, the ferry was making slow headway against the whitecaps that thudded in an erratic rhythm against its hull.

"Odd," said Stuart. "From their point of view the German armed forces have been very successful."

"Certainly. They recently captured the major Russian city of Minsk. But, as I said, apparently they've been ordered to go no further, even though their ultimate goal of Moscow now seems achievable."

Stuart gave a short laugh. "You don't think this is a prelude to their suing for peace

Sterling grunted. "I very much doubt it. But whatever the reason, it's unlikely to bring us much comfort, but is something we'll have to keep an eye on in the days ahead."

The clanging of bells, echoes of whistles and rattling of chains announced the vehicular ferry's arrival at Devonport wharf. Forty minutes later the Morris pulled up at the Professor's Castor Bay house overlooking the Hauraki Gulf. During the trip Sterling had suggested they would leave early the next morning, drive to Devonport and catch the first vehicular ferry to the city. He would drop Stuart at the university and then visit the police station to try to secure Brendan's release.

Several weeks earlier Sterling had explained he'd been a widower for the past eight years, but still lived in the three-bedroom home he and his wife had shared for twenty-seven years. The professor had a good housekeeper who took pride in keeping the house up to standard, as the spare room was spotlessly clean. Rinsing out his clothes in the laundry tub, Stuart spread them on a clotheshorse in front of the lounge fire and after relaxing in a warm bath, he slept reasonably well in spite of the pain in his side that he and the professor had decided was a cracked rib.

61

Sterling woke him at 6 o'clock. Two hours later he was in his small office trying to concentrate on some papers.

At 10 o'clock his phone rang.

"Hello, Stuart. I'm phoning from the police station, as I knew you'd be anxious. I had to wait for a while before being able to talk to the duty officer. Curiously enough a couple of soldiers turned up about ten minutes after I arrived, asking about Brendan."

"Soldiers?" responded Stuart, instantly concerned.

"They were both lieutenants. One of them with a plaster above his right eye was that fellow Beavis. The duty officer asked them if they were friends of Brendan. Foolishly, Beavis, who did most of the talking, said they were nothing of the sort and had come to make sure the police officer would be doing his duty and bringing charges against Brendan."

"Why do you say 'foolishly'?"

"Two reasons. Firstly it alerted me to their intentions. Secondly I got the impression the duty officer took exception to being told what to do by the two soldiers. Anyway, I stepped in and introduced myself. I explained that Brendan is engaged in research at the university, which is important to the war effort. I took along a couple of official documents to support my claim which certainly impressed him."

"What about the soldiers?"

"They made a further attempt to discredit Brendan but had to agree he was drunk at the time. Then Beavis started on me."

"What did you say?"

"I didn't have to say anything. The duty officer took exception to their doubting the word and evidence supplied by the 'university gentleman' and advised them to leave the station before they found themselves in serious trouble – officers or no officers. They left muttering inaudible threats. Brendan was then brought to the front desk and I promptly informed him he was about to be released and that he didn't have to say *anything*. Mercifully, as well as being very surprised to see me, he was subdued, hung-over, or both. He signed for his personal effects without a word and now he's waiting for me outside. I'll send him home to rest, to stay out of trouble and come in to work tomorrow." The professor chuckled. "A good morning's work wouldn't you say, young man?"

Stuart chuckled with relief. "That's great news. I'm very grateful, as I'm sure Brendan is."

CHAPTER 11

Stuart had just sat down at the table for the family evening meal when the phone rang.

"I'll get it," said his mother rising and walking out to the hall.

Her, "Hello", was followed by a long silence. The family then heard her voice becoming increasingly agitated. The conversation ended and she walked into the dining room, sat down and stared at her husband.

"What is it, Maude?"

She looked at him and then at her two children. "That was my friend Margaret. She's had the radio on and heard a special announcement. The Germans have dropped some enormous bomb or other on the Orkney Islands."

"Where are the Orkney Islands, Mum?" asked Stephen.

"Just north of Scotland. Your Aunt Marie came from the coastal town of Kirkwall on the largest island."

Stuart frowned. "The Orkney Islands? Why would they want to drop a bomb there? Surely they're not strategically important?"

"The radio said it's some new sort of bomb that has been dropped as some kind of warning. Apparently the destruction on the Islands is really dreadful."

"A new sort of bomb?" asked her husband.

"Apparently the Germans have developed a much more powerful bomb than any that have been dropped in the war so far. Has some special name. Something to do with atoms."

"Stuart, what's the matter?" Seeing her brother put his hand to his mouth Claire reached out and touched him anxiously on the arm.

Stuart looked round at his family. "There've been references to this in some of the documents that Brendan translated for us," he said quietly. "Not sure how, but the allies have been able to intercept some of the Germans' communications regarding new categories of weapons they're developing."

"What sort of weapons?"

"Well, we do know the Germans are developing some sort of rocket with bombs loaded up front that can fly without a pilot. There have also been a couple of documents that indicated they're developing a new type of bomb based on those atomic energy discoveries some years ago by our Ernest Rutherford. The British and possibly the Americans are likely to be researching the same area. However we assumed the Germans were concentrating on developing their armed rockets."

The three of them sat silently for a long moment until his father asked quietly, "If the Germans have developed this atom-type bomb before we have, and it's very very powerful, God help us, they could use it to win the war!" He paused and looked hard at his eldest son. "Is that what you think, Stuart?"

"Let's not panic just yet," he replied. "I'll see if I can phone the professor at home."

Seating himself at the phone table in the hallway Stuart lifted the handset off its hook, placed it to his ear and dialled the number. When the professor answered Stuart leaned forward towards the mouthpiece.

"Good evening, sir. It's me, Stuart."

"Ah yes," came the reply. "I suppose you've heard the news."

"About the bomb? Yes, sir. Is it as bad as it sounds?"

"I'm afraid it probably is, my boy. A huge area has been completely devastated by this one bomb. The Germans decided to drop it on the Orkneys as a warning. Likely to have used an airfield in occupied Norway, courtesy of their puppet governor Vidkun Quisling. They didn't want to destroy a large part of a

British city as they hope to keep it intact for their future occupation. What I've just heard, however, is that they have issued an ultimatum to London demanding an immediate and unconditional surrender; otherwise a similar bomb will be dropped on a British city within forty eight hours."

"Is it the sort of bomb we were discussing the other day, sir?"

"The atomic-based weapon? Yes, it very much looks that way. It has previously unheard of powers of destruction. Who would have thought those bastards would beat us to it?"

Stuart had never heard Professor Sterling swear before. In spite of the gravity of the situation he smiled wryly. Things must be bad for Sterling, however temporarily, to discard his academic objectivity.

There wasn't much more the professor could tell him. Both of them had seen the sketchy information on the Germans development of new weapons but had never imagined the enemy was so far advanced with their atomic research. The conversation finished with an agreement to listen to the six o'clock BBC radio news that evening and to contact each other to share impressions.

Replacing the black handset to its cradle Stuart walked back to the dining room and sat down heavily. He rested his elbows on the table, clenched his fists together and pushed them hard against his mouth, staring straight ahead. His family sat silently watching him. Finally he sighed, shook his head and spoke.

"Professor Sterling says the situation is very grave," he said. He looked at his mother. "As your friend told you, the Germans dropped the bomb on the Orkneys to demonstrate its destructive powers. They've told the British they'll do the same to a city in England unless they surrender within forty-eight hours. He told us to listen to the six o'clock news from London tonight because he's sure Britain will have no alternative but to agree."

They all sat silently and then his mother began to cry. "My aunt often talked about the Orkneys – the kind people, their pretty fishing villages and wonderful historical sites. How could they?"

***

"And so it is with a heavy heart that I announce the British Empire armed forces on land, sea and air will cease all operations against the forces of Nazi Germany."

The family sat in silence by the tall polished radio cabinet as the sonorous voice of British Prime Minister Winston Churchill filled the lounge.

"The government of Nazi Germany has threatened to systematically devastate our historic cities and their civilian inhabitants with their new atomic weapon. Our surveillance aircraft have confirmed that the devastation on the Orkney Islands is on a scale previously unknown to mankind. I have no doubt the Nazis will carry out further terrible action of this kind unless we capitulate.

"More detailed information will be made available to you in the coming days. In the meantime I ask you not to lose faith but to show the spirit that has sustained our island nation and its Empire throughout its long and glorious history."

The crackling of the short wave broadcast ceased and a New Zealand voice announced,

"That was British Prime Minister Mr. Winston Churchill. Here now is the New Zealand Prime Minister Mr. Peter Fraser."

There was a short pause and then Fraser's Scottish burr filled the room.

"People of New Zealand, at an emergency meeting of the coalition cabinet this morning we have agreed that New Zealand has no alternative but to also surrender, particularly as this action is about to be taken by Australia, Canada, South Africa and other parts of the British Empire and Commonwealth.

"Thousands of our servicemen and women are overseas. The British surrender makes them vulnerable to the German forces. Furthermore, as a small island nation that relies for its prosperity on sea trade, we have no chance of sustaining a campaign against a very powerful enemy.

"Be assured your government will do everything in its power to obtain surrender terms that will enable us to maintain the way of life of which we are all so justly proud."

Hearing her stifled sob Stuart leaned forward and put his arm across his mother's shoulder. "Don't cry, Mum," he murmured. "It'll be OK. You'll see."

Momentarily she stopped and looked up at him. The rivulets of tears ran down the lines in a face that had noticeably aged. A series of spasms shook her hunched shoulders.

"No, Stuart, that's the trouble. It won't be OK. Not any more."

Chapter 12

"A letter from Carol, Fred."

Her husband glanced up from *The Dominion*. "You read it Ruth and then I'll have a look through it."

"I've already read it while you were listening to the BBC news.

"How's she getting on? Seeing plenty of Hamish I hope."

Ruth sat down in the opposite chair and leaned closer to the fire.

"She only mentioned him once – sort of in passing. Seems to be enjoying the position at the Northern Club. Also said she'd made some new friends at the local church."

"Female, I hope."

"I'm sure they are, Fred. We both know she went to Auckland to be with Hamish."

"I should think so, too. We're deeply indebted to David Beavis and his son for saving us from the poor house. Furthermore, when Hamish said he'd stand by Carol he was good at his word. Saved my good name from being dragged through the mud. She ought to be damned grateful to him. He's offered to marry her so why doesn't she get on with it?"

Sitting down again he thrust his paper in front of his face to signal an end to the matter.

Used to her husband taking extreme positions on issues great and small, Ruth maintained her position by his chair.

"I'm sure she'll eventually accept Hamish's offer of marriage." She paused. "Doesn't have any choice." There was no response from her husband so she pressed on. "Anyway when Ian comes home I'm sure he'll be a great support for her and for us. A surrender to the Germans is not what we expected Fred, but with Ian back in the family, I'm sure we'll manage in the difficult times ahead. Once Carol has settled down we'll be able to give Ian our full support in making something of himself." She sighed. "I wish we'd heard from him."

Her husband looked over the top of his paper and his expression softened. "I know, Ruth. But there's bound to be a foul up in the mail system with the surrender and all that. Don't worry, the fighting's only just stopped and I'm sure we'll hear something soon."

Soft words from her husband, even under difficult circumstances, were always welcome, and she smiled. "Yes, I'm sure you're right." She stood up. "I'll go and make us both a nice cuppa."

She walked into the kitchen and began to prepare the tea. Putting the teapot and cups on a tray, she carried them through the dining room towards the lounge. At the familiar opening click of the front gate she looked out of the small kitchen window and gasped. Mr. Roberts, the Postmaster, was walking slowly down the winding front path. Everyone knew the Postmaster only came to the front door for one reason – to hand over a telegram from the War Office.

With a splintering crash the teapot, cups, milk jug and sugar bowl cascaded onto the carpet as, trembling, she hurried down the hallway. She managed to call, "Fred!" but she needn't have bothered. Her husband was reaching for the doorknob as Mr. Roberts walked up the front steps onto the veranda.

"Telegram. I am very sorry, Mr. Peterson."

Ruth, who had instinctively stood behind her husband, reached out for him as he crumpled.

CHAPTER 13

"Stuart. Hullo. It's me."

"Are you telephoning me from the Northern Club? You wicked girl! You'll get into..."

"No, Stuart, I'm phoning from railway station. Mum phoned. A toll call from Wellington. It's Ian."

"Ian? He can't be home yet. The fighting's only just stopped."

"No, he's not home. He'll never come home." Her voice faltered. "He's dead. Mum and Dad got a telegram."

An involuntary shiver traversed his upper body.

"Dead? But, the war's over, Carol!"

"I know. But it must have happened a few days before the end, before the, you know..."

She began to cry.

"Before we surrendered. God, Carol, that's appalling! Are you sure?"

"The telegram came today. It said he'd been killed in action in the desert somewhere in North Africa. I'm catching the train in a few minutes. Hamish is coming with me."

"Hamish!"

"Sorry, Stuart, but Mum rang him and he caught a taxi and came straight over. I have to go home. Mum and Dad are traumatized. I don't think they'll ever get over this."

"But, Carol, you can't just leave like this, with Hamish. I have to see you before..."

"Stuart, don't you understand?" He heard her voice catch. "My brother's dead! I have to go home."

There was the sound of a guard's whistle and the muffled shout of a male voice.

"Sorry, Stuart, I have to go. I'll let you know."

The line went dead.

Stuart sat at his desk staring out the window. Her brother was dead and she was travelling to Wellington on the train – with Hamish. The sound of a small crack made him realise he'd snapped in half the pencil he'd been holding. Dropping the broken pieces on the floor he left his office and strode along the corridor to Professor Sterling's where he opened the door without knocking.

The professor looked up in annoyance until he saw the expression on Stuart's face. "Stuart, is there anything wrong?"

Stuart noticed the young woman seated in front of Sterling's desk. "Oh, sorry. Didn't know you had a visitor. Should have knocked."

"It's all right, my boy. Come in. Meet my niece Susan. She's reading English. What's wrong?"

Nodding briefly to Susan he said, "Carol's brother Ian, sir. They've just heard he's been killed. It was only a few days before the bloody war ended." Glancing at Susan he added, "Sorry for swearing."

"Good God. Are you sure?"

"A telegram came. Killed in action. There seems to be no doubt about it. She phoned from the station. Was about to catch the train to Wellington."

"Sit down, Stuart."

Stuart sat down in the chair next to Susan.

"Carol's your girlfriend?" she asked.

"Yes, sort of. Her brother was fighting with the Eighth Army in North Africa. They hadn't heard from him for several weeks but as soon as the surrender was signed they assumed he'd be OK." He sighed heavily. "Bloody war. Bloody Germans." He glanced awkwardly at Susan. "Sorry."

She smiled reassuringly. "That's all right."

"You say she caught the Wellington train a few minutes ago?" asked Sterling.

"Yes, sir."

"Understandable of course. Her parents must be devastated."

"Yes, sir, of course. Unfortunately he went with her."

"Who's 'he'?" asked Susan.

"Hamish Beavis. Her, er, other boyfriend. His parents also live in Wellington. They're family friends."

"Hmm," growled the professor. "No wonder you're angry as well as upset. Nothing much I can suggest except to say these are difficult times and for the foreseeable future at least I doubt if it's going to get much better. But I am sorry, Stuart. This really is dreadful news."

"I know, sir. And I feel so helpless." He clenched his fists in frustration. "There's nothing I can do."

There was an awkward pause and then Susan reached out and touched him on the arm.

"Are you helping Uncle David on the research project?"

Stuart glanced up and stared at her for a moment. "What? Oh, yes, I am."

"I'm sorry if this sounds silly, but I'm off to the 2 o'clock pictures at the Civic to give myself a break. Maybe you'd like to be alone, but maybe, if it's OK with Uncle David, you could have the afternoon off and come to the pictures. There's nothing you can do about the bad news. So?"

A little embarrassed at her forwardness and the probable inappropriateness of the invitation, she shrugged and looked at her uncle. He smiled encouragingly.

"A little unusual but maybe Susan's right," smiled her uncle. "Always been an impulsive young woman. Of course you can have the afternoon off, Stuart. If you want to go to the pictures, well, that's up to you."

Stuart looked at the girl for the first time. Her brown hair was pulled back off a round but pleasant face and her eyes, behind rimmed glasses, were sympathetic. He sighed.

"What's on?"

"A musical, The Wizard of Oz. Do you like musicals?"

73

"Dunno." He shrugged. "They're OK I suppose."

"Look, I'm sorry," she replied with a touch of irritation. "If you'd rather not, I quite understand." She began to stand, smoothing down her dark skirt over her knees.

"Apologies," he said hastily. "I've had a shock, but I do appreciate the thought. I'd like to come. The Civic, you said?"

"Yes," said Sterling, taking his watch from his waistcoat pocket. "You've got 20 minutes. Off you go the pair of you. In any case, I don't quite approve of young ladies going to the pictures unaccompanied."

"Oh, Uncle David, don't be so old fashioned."

"Can't be too careful nowadays, my dear. Now, off you go."

As they crossed Princes Street and cut towards downtown through Albert Park, Stuart felt a jolt as he caught a glimpse of the statues of the Boer War soldier and Sir George Grey.

"You all right?" asked Susan, seeing him check his stride. He shook his head like a boxer after a heavy blow. "Yes, I'm OK. Just a twitch of memory."

"Oh."

Deciding that silence was the best alternative, Susan continued walking beside him. As they approached the Art Gallery he turned to her.

"You're taking English?"

"Yes, second year. I'm loving it. Dad didn't want me to go to university and mum, of course, wanted me to get a job, save some money and fill up..."

"Your hope chest."

She chuckled. "Have you got a sister?"

"Yes, but she's too young for hope chests." With an effort he asked, "Why did your parents finally let you go to university?"

"Uncle David. Told them I'd love it. And he said even if I did get married, I could pass my education on to my children."

"Is that your intention?"

74

She laughed. "Not straight away, of course not. I love the subject and I would like to pass it on as a teacher, not as a mother."

"Hmm."

"Nothing wrong with that, is there?"

"No. A splendid idea. Sorry, I'm not really myself."

"Quite understandable. Never mind, we're here. Have you got enough money for the tickets?" she asked as they joined the queue of patrons seeking escape in the ornate picture palace from the realities of rationing. "I'll buy the ice creams."

"No, it's OK. I'll buy them. Wait while I get the tickets."

"My idea. My treat. Now, you stay in the queue and buy the tickets" She held up her hand as he began to protest. "I'm buying the ice creams."

He held up both palms in a surrender gesture.

"Is vanilla OK?"

"Vanilla. Yes. My favourite."

"Mine too. Anyway, it's the only one they've got."

She smiled warmly and, after a moment's hesitation he smiled back.

CHAPTER 14

"Stuart, is Brendan with you?" asked the professor.

"Yes, sir. We're going through some..."

"Come to my office now, please."

The phone went dead.

"Who was that?" asked Brendan.

"The Prof wants us in his office now."

"Do we have to bring anything?"

"Didn't say so. Just ourselves I suppose. Come on."

After knocking they entered Sterling's office and sat down in front of his desk. He greeted them with a perfunctory nod and then sat with his chin resting on his clasped hands, gazing at the back wall. Stuart and Brendan exchanged glances but continued to sit in silence.

Sterling lowered his hands. "The German government has commanded each of the main British Empire and Commonwealth countries to attend peace talks in Berlin."

"'Peace talks'?" said Brendan. "That's a bloody laugh."

"A euphemism, of course," replied Sterling. "Each country has been instructed to send a delegation, led by their head of state, to meet with German government representatives to discuss peace terms."

Seeing Brendan was about to speak, Sterling held up his hand. "Yes, we're all aware 'peace terms' mean terms of surrender. However, there may be some room for discussion regarding the implementation and administration of the terms."

"One point, if I may, sir?" said Stuart. Sterling nodded and he continued. "You said each delegation was to be led by its head of state. King George VI is our head of state."

"True. I don't think the Germans quite understand that. The assumption is that our new Prime Minister Peter Fraser will head the delegation."

"What sort of delegation?" asked Stuart.

"Good question, and one which leads me to the main point of this meeting," responded Sterling. Picking up a small paperweight from his desk he began twisting it around in both hands.

"The Germans have specified that no military personnel are to be included in the delegation. We have been told we're are to bring Peter Fraser the Prime Minister, his Deputy Walter Nash, Frederick Jones the Minister of Defence and five civil servants from specified ministries. We are also being allowed to include three advisors, providing they have no connection with the military. The government has invited me, due to the work this office has been doing regarding German foreign policy."

"Wow," breathed Stuart. "Go to Berlin. Could be a bit dicey, sir."

"Possibly," replied Sterling. He placed the paperweight back on his desk and faced the two young men.

"I have also been asked to recommend any other personnel who could be useful. If you're agreeable, I would like to forward both your names to Wellington."

"Us, sir?" gasped Stuart.

"Stuart and me, sir?" echoed Brendan. "Why?"

"Sound, logical reasons," replied the professor. "In Stuart's case, he has acquired an in-depth knowledge of German policy and actions regarding the occupation of recently conquered territories. Obviously there is much we don't know, but what knowledge he has could prove invaluable in briefing the other members of the delegation prior to departure. Furthermore, his knowledge will also be useful if there is the opportunity for input from the delegation regarding the coming German occupation of this country."

"And me, sir?" asked Brendan.

"Self evident. You have a considerable fluency in spoken and written German. You've proven your expertise in both translating and interpreting and, like Stuart, you've gained considerable knowledge of current German thinking through the documents to which you've had access."

For a long moment the three men sat looking at each other.

"You're under no obligation, of course," said Sterling. "They are our conquerors and it could be dangerous. I won't put your names forward if you have any doubts."

The younger men exchanged glances and nodded simultaneously.

"No doubts, sir!" Stuart leaned forward in his chair. "I suppose it is a bit intimidating but also a unique opportunity."

"Agreed. I'd be delighted to come." Brendan stood up and thrust his hand towards the professor. "Thank you, sir."

Sterling half rose, shook Brendan's then Stuart's hand and resumed his seat. "Gentlemen, your enthusiasm is commendable and gratifying. This is unknown territory for all of us but, in my view, we may be able to use our knowledge and experience to help our country at this difficult time. Now let's go through the trip in more detail."

The ensuing days flew by. Within a few days the German government approved the list of names submitted by the New Zealand authorities. The three Auckland delegates were informed that in two days they were to take a train to Wellington for a briefing with other members of the delegation. All would then be returning to Auckland for the first stage of a long journey by air to Germany.

Stuart's family was appalled at the prospect. Berlin loomed large in the minds of all New Zealanders as the enemy stronghold, the source of all the woes that had befallen the nation and perhaps above all, the source of all that was repugnant in Nazi ideology.

"You're too young, dear," pleaded his mother.

"Men with more experience should be sent," said his father.

"Berlin," said his brother Stephen, "is on the other side of the world. You might not ever make it home."

His sister Claire simply clung to him, quietly crying.

In spite of his family, and his own disquiet at entering the enemy's lair, he was determined to go. Yes, of course it would be dangerous. Yes, he could be locked up as a hostage or shot as a traitor. He'd read enough reports on Nazi reprisals against those who opposed them in the occupied countries to have some inkling of the possible consequences. However, the Berlin visit was a significant event in his country's history and whatever the risks, he wanted to be part of it. Could his presence make any significant difference, he asked himself. Likely not, but he felt increasingly that surrender should not be synonymous with a complete capitulation. Whatever the realities of the pending occupation he at least would be able to gain some sort of insight into the nation's and his own uncertain future.

And Carol? Since her phone call from the railway station he had heard nothing. He thought of writing or making a toll call to her parents' house in Wellington but then worried this would make trouble for her in an emotionally charged household.

Feeling that he had to do something, he phoned her Aunt Catherine in Milford. Explaining he was a friend of hers from church he asked her to let Carol know he was going to Berlin with the New Zealand delegation and would be returning in about two to three weeks. Carol's aunt was initially somewhat bemused by the phone call, but at the mention of the Berlin delegation she instantly became business-like and said that she would inform Carol when she made her weekly phone call to Wellington.

"Miss Mason, it's important you give the message directly to Carol herself and no one else," requested Stuart, trying to sound both official and pleasant.

"No-one else. Of course, I will, Mr. Johnson," she assured him.

Feeling a little more reassured Stuart thanked her and hung up the phone. He'd just have to live with the uncertainty and concentrate on the major challenge ahead of him.

***

The initial briefing was held at Parliament House. The delegates were introduced to each other and to Prime Minister Peter Fraser, who had taken over in March 1940 after the death of the revered Michael Joseph Savage. Although Fraser was an enthusiastic supporter of the New Zealand war effort, Professor Sterling had reminded both young men on the trip south the new Prime Minister had served twelve months in jail during World War I for opposing conscription. "A complex individual," was his final comment.

The delegates assembled in a meeting room within parliament house where they were introduced to Fraser. On his right hand sat his deputy Walter Nash. Like Fraser he was bespectacled but unlike his leader he had a full head of hair, which, Stuart noted, couldn't seem to make up its mind whether it was parted in the middle or to the right.

Fraser rose and addressed the delegates in a low voice, emphasizing the delegation's responsibility to the nation and his own determination to obtain the best possible terms from the Germans. Occasionally during the speech he referred to written notes. Suffering from poor eyesight he disconcertingly had to lift the papers up close to his face where, with a frown of concentration, he read them through thick-lensed spectacles. Although his voice was flat and calm, Stuart felt that the monotony of the delivery was masking a nervous uncertainty. This was confirmed when at the end of a thirty-minute speech Fraser put down his notes, ran his right hand over his receding hairline, and asked if there were any questions.

The first to speak was Professor Sterling.

"Prime Minister," he began. "You spoke of the restrictions the German occupation force is likely to impose on our population."

"Professor Sterling, isn't it?" interrupted the Prime Minister peering through his spectacles.

"Yes, Prime Minister. What type of restrictions do you envisage?"

"The ones typical of a Fascist regime, of course," responded Fraser with ill-disguised condescension. "Widespread censorship of the press and radio, the use of other forms of communication such as our Film Unit for propaganda purposes, and a general curtailment of freedoms using the predictable excuses about the good of the nation."

Some of the delegates had begun to nod or grunt their agreement when Brendan spoke.

"Um, with respect, Prime Minister, those conditions are now in place here. Your government introduced them last year as wartime emergency regulations."

"Your name?"

Each of the delegates turned to look at Brendan, who was seated at the end of the table.

"Brendan Ritter, sir. I am..."

Fraser interrupted him with a raised palm. He turned slightly in his chair towards his deputy Walter Nash who murmured in his right ear.

"Ritter. Ah, yes." Fraser frowned. "The German speaker from the Auckland University College. You are New Zealand born, aren't you?"

"Yes, sir. Of course, sir," replied Brendan with a touch of indignation.

Fraser's eyes engaged Brendan's in a long cold stare. "My censorship legislation, for your information Mr. Ritter, was enacted by me as the democratically elected prime minister, for the good of the people of New Zealand."

He continued staring at Brendan as if challenging him to offer a contradiction. Wisely, Brendan kept his counsel.

In a voice that gradually rose, the Prime Minister continued. "Your job, young man, is to observe all you can while we are in Germany and to pass this information solely to," he paused, "me." His eyes narrowed. "It is not, I repeat, not your role to question any of my decisions."

Stuart saw Sterling's hand reach under the table and grip Brendan's arm tightly resulting in the young man's muted response of, "Yes sir".

After the final details of transport and accommodation had been clarified, the meeting concluded. At the professor's suggestion the three of them walked together back to their hotel. As they left the grounds of Parliament House and crossed Bowen Street, Sterling turned to Brendan.

"I should have warned you, Brendan. The Prime Minister has two key characteristics."

"Two, sir?"

"Two that were germane to today's meeting. The first is that he does not handle criticism well. He has to be in control and as such requires others to fall into line with his thinking."

"That was certainly obvious today," said Brendon.

"And the second, sir?" asked Stuart.

"As you know, he was born in the Scottish Highlands. His parents were not well off and he had to leave school at twelve and go to work. He immigrated to New Zealand and educated himself by reading extensively and involving himself in local politics. Eventually he gained the highest position in the land. Unfortunately somewhere along the way, he acquired a deep suspicion of academics."

***

The Germans had agreed to allow the New Zealand delegation to begin their Berlin journey by flying across the Tasman on board the Awarua – one of the new Empire Class S

82

30 flying boats that had begun flights between Auckland and Sydney in 1939. The first stage took them nine hours during which time they were served several light meals cooked in the aeroplane's galley. At Sydney they landed smoothly on the waters of the inner harbour and the pilot guided the plane towards the refuelling wharf. The delegates were given an hour to stretch their legs before re-embarking and heading towards Melbourne, Adelaide and Perth.

At Sydney and each of the Australian stops, conversation with the handful of Australian officials who had met the aircraft was at best perfunctory. The Australian delegation had departed for Berlin three days earlier leaving behind a climate of uncertainty. Clearly the rapid capitulation had been as great a shock to the Australians as it had been to their southern neighbours. Although the conversations veered between foreboding and bravado, there was little information on which to base any real predictions as to the nature of either the peace talks or the pending German occupation of Australia and New Zealand.

The western city of Perth was the final Australian stop before the flying boat headed across the Indian Ocean to South Africa. When the plane completed its noisy ascent from nearby Fremantle harbour and levelled off into its flight path the co-pilot came through from the flight deck to announce they were en route to the South African coastal city of Durban. There would be one refuelling stop, at the small island of Mauritius.

"What will await us in Durban, gentlemen?" said Professor Sterling as they settled back into their seats. "Bound to be different."

"Because it's Africa, sir?" said Brendan.

"Yes, but perhaps not in the way you mean. Remember South Africa's white races comprise those of both British and Boer descent. The latter group contains many who were strongly opposed to their country joining us in the war against Germany."

"But their president Jan Smuts is a Boer," said Stuart. "He supported the war."

"True. But there was plenty of opposition to his decision from his fellow Boers. Still early days, but I think we'll find South Africa rather different from Australia."

He was right. After the long trip over the Indian Ocean, in the late afternoon the flying boat glided into a sheltered part of Durban Harbour. As the delegates crowded round the small windows to absorb their first sight of an African city they saw four high-powered motor boats bouncing across the waves towards the aircraft. In a sweeping manoeuvre, each of the boats slithered noisily sideways two abreast in outrider formation providing a nautical escort towards the wharves.

The flying boat was manoeuvred towards a long jetty where several black African men in overalls were waiting to tie it into position. One of the stewards opened the exit door and the Prime Minister stepped out onto the jetty where a uniformed officer thrust a gloved hand forward and in heavily accented English barked, "My name is Colonel Barend Van Zyl. On behalf of the people of the new Suid-Afrika it is my pleasure to welcome you here, Prime Minister Fraser."

The officer then turned and signalled whereupon a band, poised in readiness at the far end of the jetty, struck up a military march.

The remaining delegates exited and grouping around Peter Fraser gazed at the scene that had been prepared for their arrival. Behind the band a battalion of smartly dressed troops were drawn up in precise ranks. As the last of the delegates emerged from the flying boat and reached the far end of the jetty they heard "Parade! Aandag!"

Boots crunched in unison as the battalion snapped to attention.

The officer, facing the assembled delegates, addressed them in a parade ground style.

84

"It is our pleasure to welcome you here to the new Suid-Afrika. Although your stay is a short one we hope you will enjoy our hospitality before continuing your journey to meet our colleagues in Berlin."

He turned towards Peter Fraser. "Prime Minister, we would appreciate it if you would do us the honour of inspecting the guard."

With a flourish he swept his polished sword to a perpendicular position in front of his nose. "Follow me, please, sir," he said and executing a half heel and toe turn, began a slow march towards the assembled soldiers.

Tired from the long journey and confused by the swiftness of the events, Fraser obediently fell into line behind the South African colonel, signalling Walter Nash and Frederick Jones to join him. Immediately four other officers stepped forward and guided the remaining delegates towards a roped off area on the front of the parade ground.

The sound of the military band filled the late afternoon air as the Colonel, followed by Fraser, Nash and Jones moved along the rigid ranks. Stuart, standing with the other delegates, studied the four officers who had taken up positions on either side of the group. The men's uniforms were in traditional British khaki but on closer inspection he noticed the front of the officers' caps were tapered to a German-style high front and trimmed with grey braid. On their lower left sleeve each wore a cuff band bearing the silver-threaded inscription 'Suid-Afrika'. Obviously this was a uniform and a nation in the throes of transition.

Completing their inspection, the party walked to the front of the parade ground. As they reached the front of the rigid ranks the band ceased. Instantly Colonel Van Zyl sprang to attention and looked upwards.

"Jesus," gasped Brendan.

All eyes were drawn towards the flagpole. From its base two soldiers were raising a large flag. The gentle breeze unravelled its folds. The burnt orange rays of the setting African sun caught the flag's base colour – a vivid red. As the folds spread they revealed the central emblem – the black crooked cross of the swastika inside a bright, white circle.

"Presenteer geweer!"

In two precise movements the ranks of soldiers snapped their rifles to the front of their faces in the present arms position. Simultaneously each of the officers swung his right hand up and with open palm in line with the front of his newly tapered cap, stood in rigid salute to the Nazi emblem that fluttered and snapped in the warm Indian Ocean breeze.

CHAPTER 15

At breakfast the following day Colonel van Zyl introduced the delegates to their first German officer, Hauptman Kretschmer. Dressed in an immaculate blue/grey Luftwaffe uniform, Kretschmer clicked his heels, and in fluent English came to the point.

"Gentlemen, your flying boat is to be returned to New Zealand. The remainder of your journey will be completed over the African continent in a Junkers JU 52. It is the model favoured by our Fuhrer in his travels. It is a tri-motor plane that has been fitted out by the German government to make your journey as comfortable as possible. I will be flying the plane. It will be departing in one hour at 10:00 o'clock. Your transport will be leaving the hotel in half an hour. Please make yourselves ready."

Another heel click and brief bow and he was gone. Van Zyl snapped his fingers and a group of fez-wearing black men promptly emerged from a nearby doorway. After a brief conversation with one of them he turned to the delegates.

"Please go to your rooms and assemble your belongings. These boys have been assigned to carry your luggage to the hotel foyer."

"Biggest 'boys' I've ever seen," muttered Brendan to Stuart as they walked upstairs to their first floor rooms, followed, at a respectful distance, by the black men.

Hauptman Kretschmer had been correct. The German plane was fitted with comfortable new seats and, like the flying boat, several bunks were available in the rear. Although the food was well prepared, the delegates missed the friendliness of the New Zealand airhostesses. Their Germanic counterparts were punctual, efficient and unsmiling.

Even Brendan, who tried to combine a warm smile with his German fluency, received little more than "ja" or "nein".

"Berlin should be a laugh a minute," was his rueful response to Stuart's teasing chuckle.

The northern journey over the African continent was uneventful. At the late-night refuelling stop in Nairobi, the delegates were politely asked to remain in the plane so were unable to gain any impressions of the changes in Kenya, one of Britain's largest African colonies.

Dawn was breaking as the Junkers approached Berlin. Stuart, who had managed to sleep reasonably well, woke up, stretched, gazed sleepily out the small window and gasped. Racing towards the plane was a swarm of fighter aircraft.

He seized Brendan's arm. "Wake up, man! We're under attack."

Brendan, who was only dozing, woke instantly. He peered out the window.

"They're ME 109's. German fighters. Don't forget we're in a German plane.

Stuart ran his hand through his hair and shook his head. "Sorry. Forgot. I saw the black crosses and the swastikas and thought we'd bought it."

As the pair watched, the fighter formation split in half. Like their nautical counterparts in Durban Harbour, the aircraft took up positions on either side of the Junkers and as the plane and its new escort descended, the delegates, all now wide-awake, caught their first sight of the German capital.

It had been a long, tiring flight, not made any easier by the sense of increasing unease that filled the aircraft. Now, as they came in low over Berlin, the delegates peered silently out of the windows.

The formation made several passes over the capital city. Obviously designed to announce their arrival to Berlin's citizens, it also provided the delegates with an uninterrupted aerial view of a city that had been uppermost in their thoughts over the past months. Although it was early morning, a considerable number of building sites were swarming with workers and vehicles.

"Bomb damage?"

"Could be, Brendan. But I suspect it's more than that," replied Stuart. "Hitler has great plans for a re-vamping of the central city into what he has called 'Germania'. Apparently it's modelled on Paris, Vienna and Rome, but has to surpass them all in style and splendour."

"All in the best possible taste, *naturellement*," muttered Brendan. "I'm sure the art lovers of the world will hardly be able to contain their excitement."

Communications between the various Commonwealth and Empire delegations had been virtually impossible, as a few days after the surrender the German government had imposed a news blackout that had included cessation of the BBC's London radio broadcasts. They had then summoned each delegation separately at short notice to Berlin to minimize any consultation between them. Consequently at various stages of the journey, with minimal information, the New Zealand delegates had speculated on the nature of the reception that awaited them in Berlin. All expressed the fear they could be subject to a variety of humiliations, ranging from being paraded in public as representatives of subjugated peoples, to prison-like accommodation.

As the ME109 escort planes peeled away the Junkers JU52 began its final descent to Tempelhof Airport. A heavy silence filled the aircraft. The Junkers made a smooth landing and as it taxied to a halt, steps were swiftly moved into position outside the door. The delegates on the left hand side watched a portly man in a dark suit making an attempt to ascend the steps. After stumbling twice he climbed the final few and, having paused to take breath, entered the opened door and stood at the front of the main cabin. Beaming broadly, he mopped his brow and then spread his hands wide.

"Good morning Prime Minister and delegates from New Zealand," he intoned enthusiastically in accented yet fluent English. "My name is Baron Hermann von Muller-Rechberg. I am the Fuhrer's special representative. It is my pleasure to welcome you to the magnificent city of Berlin and to ensure your stay with us will be a memorable one."

The unexpectedly ebullient manner of the tubby German resulted in his opening spiel being greeted with a stunned silence. Leaning across his seat, Professor Sterling tapped Brendan on the arm and nodded in the direction of the Baron. In response, Brendan jumped to his feet.

"Herr Baron, *Vielen Dank für Ihren Willkommensgruß.* Thank you very much for your welcome."

The Baron, impressed by Brendan's relaxed fluency, smiled warmly.

"Prime Minister, perhaps a word from you would be appropriate at this point", said Brendan, looking towards Peter Fraser who was seated in the front seat.

Fraser, seeming out of his depth, rose and faced the smiling Baron.

"Thank you for your words of welcome," he began in his slow monotone. The Baron beamed and bowed. Fraser glanced quickly at Brendan who smiled encouragingly. "My colleagues and I look forward to meeting your colleagues and, er, entering into discussions with them regarding future relations between our two countries."

"Thank you Prime Minister," smiled the Baron, clicking his heels and nodding his head. "Now, gentlemen, if you would be so kind as to follow me, it will be my privilege to introduce you to the remainder of my colleagues."

Fraser turned to the rest of the group and nodded. Assembling in the aircraft's aisle they followed von Muller-Rechberg and their Prime Minister towards the sloping steps.

Exiting from the Junkers, the delegates were greeted by teeming clusters of giant swastikas fluttering from every possible point of the airport's buildings. At the base of the steps, a line of dignitaries waited to receive them. Each New Zealander was greeted with warm smiles and hearty handshakes. Although many in the line wore Nazi armbands on their sleeve, the delegates noticed with some relief that only a few were dressed in military uniform and there was no sign of the black-uniformed Gestapo.

As they neared the end of the line Walter Nash murmured to Fraser, "Perhaps things will not be as bad as we feared, Peter."

"Possibly time for a little cautious optimism, Walter. Possibly not. Time will tell."

Moments later the egregiously smiling von Muller-Rechberg appeared at Fraser's elbow. "Now, Prime Minister and delegates," he began, "we have arranged for you to be transported to your hotel in a convoy. This will enable you to receive greetings from the people of Berlin."

"Greetings?" frowned Fraser.

"Yes. Each of the delegations from Great Britain, Canada, and Australia received the same welcome."

Stuart, noting the omission of South Africa, wondered whether their welcome had been different.

"Like them I'm sure you will enjoy the journey into our magnificent city and the warmth of our welcome. This way, please, Prime Minister."

Tentatively the delegation followed Peter Fraser across the tarmac to a long line of cars. At the front were six gleaming black open-topped Mercedes Benz limousines, their chrome and black paint burnished bright and their engines emitting a throaty idle. On the right mudguards of each was a Nazi flag and on the left, a smaller New Zealand one. Fraser and Nash were escorted to the front car and the others guided in pairs towards the remaining vehicles.

As the youngest members of the delegation, Stuart and Brendan were escorted to the sixth limousine. As they approached, the two German officers standing by the driver's door snapped a stiff-armed Hitlerian salute. One of them smartly swung the passenger's door open and brusquely indicated that the two New Zealanders were to sit in the dark leather rear bench seat. The two officers then took the front seats.

Stuart turned his head and looked back at the rest of the long convoy. From what he could make out, most of the vehicles held a variety of civilians and military personnel except for the one right behind them. The four men in the front and back seats were dressed in identical uniforms – a distinctive black.

Keeping his voice low, he muttered to Brendan, "Don't look now, but directly behind you are the Gestapo boys."

"Wondered why I felt something crawling up my spine," his friend replied. "Looks like we're on the move," he added as their vehicle pulled into line and began moving forward behind the other five limousines. As the motorcade eased away from the Tempelhof tarmac, gleaming motorcycles swept smoothly into position on either side of its flanks.

Suddenly all the vehicles halted. Sirens were heard from the rear of the line and, as the sound came closer, a black open-topped Mercedes limousine, larger than the others, glided down the right hand side of the stationary motorcade. Two officers were seated in the front. The man in the back stood bolt upright staring straight ahead, his left hand on a chromium rail and his other, with palm open, pointed skywards. Wrapped around the left arm of his long brown leather coat was a red swastika armband.

"It's him. Adolf Hitler," murmured Brendan.

As the German Fuhrer's vehicle swung into position at the head of the motorcade, all the vehicles resumed their journey.

All along the route into central Berlin, special stands had been erected. Each was packed with German men, women and children who created a seething forest of perpendicular arms with pale palms thrusting Nazi salutes towards the motorcade. From the crowd came a sustained roar that soared to a crescendo as they caught sight of their leader in the front limousine.

Underpinning the frenzied cheering Stuart noticed a constant rhythmical undercurrent.

"That chant? We heard it on the German radio broadcasts. What is it again?"

"The Nazi chant – 'Sieg heil'."

"Which means?"

"Literally, it's something like 'Hail to Victory'." Brendan gave a wry smile and pretended to look over his shoulder at the vehicle following behind. Then, leaning conspiratorially towards Stuart stage whispered, "Actually, it's more like, 'Three cheers for Uncle Adolf'."

The two young men glanced at the German officers seated in front but there was no reaction. Catching Brendan's eye Stuart shook his head. The Prime Minister had cautioned the delegates on the need to maintain their dignity while not provoking their new masters.

"Unfortunately," he had said, "our location at the centre of Nazi power makes our options somewhat limited."

The journey into the city's centre lasted an hour and a half. The slow pace of the motorcade was designed to provide the spectators with ample opportunity to view their Fuhrer, the leading Nazi military and political dignitaries and the representatives of the conquered territories. At times, pockets in the crowd abandoned their chanting and stiff-arm salutes to cheer and call out to the delegates. The noise made it impossible to distinguish any of the words but it was clear that the cheers were mingled with jeers of triumph. As Brendan remarked, "Deutschland Uber Alles is clearly the order of the day."

Eventually the New Zealand delegation arrived at the Hotel Gross Deutschland near the intersection of Saarlandstrasse and Prinz-Albrecht Strasse.

"Looks brand new," said Stuart gazing up at the imposing columned hotel entrance.

"Probably built on a bomb site," replied Brendan, "but best not to ask."

They were given an hour to unpack and were then politely but firmly invited by Baron Muller-Rechberg onto the extensive hotel balcony from where they had a clear view of the intersection and adjacent streets. Here the orchestrated celebrations continued. Three large tables amply supplied with a variety of food, beer and wine had been placed on the balcony. Seated at each table were two men dressed in suits and wearing Nazi armbands. The Baron introduced the six as "peace delegates who will be responsible for looking after you during your stay".

"Please," he purred as the New Zealanders seated themselves, "enjoy our German hospitality while you learn of our German culture. If you have any questions about our cultural presentations, our peace delegates will be delighted to answer them."

For the next three hours the delegates were subjected to non-stop examples of Nazi-style culture. German bands marched noisily past, a choir of fair-haired maidens clad in traditional peasant garb sang German folk songs, a company of SS Leibstandarte soldiers gave a demonstration of precision military drills, and boys of the *Hitler Jugend* provided a series of gymnastic demonstrations.

Initially some of the New Zealanders asked polite questions of their German hosts but the long-winded responses, coupled with the repetitive nature of the entertainments resulted in the whole party lapsing into a uniform pattern of silent endurance.

CHAPTER 16

The following morning the delegates were informed they would be taken to the Reich Chancellery where the official peace talks would begin. At precisely 9 o'clock the motorcade of the six Mercedes-Benz limousines pulled up outside the hotel foyer. The delegates seated themselves in their same positions and the cars glided smoothly away.

The absence of the cheering crowds gave the New Zealanders the opportunity to study their surroundings more closely. As the vehicles swung left into Prinz-Albrecht-Strasse Stuart heard Brendan catch his breath. Mindful of the two Germans in the front, Stuart nudged his friend and gave him a quizzical look. As their car proceeded down the street Brendan pointed his finger towards a rather utilitarian-looking five-storied building on their left.

Glancing at the two officers in the front seat he mouthed, "Number 8 – Gestapo Headquarters."

Hitler's ostentatious Reich Chancellery designed by his personal architect Albert Speer occupied the entire length of Voss Strasse. As the vehicles glided up to the giant square-columned entrance, the two black uniformed, white-gloved SS Leibstandarte guards who maintained a constant vigil at the entrance snapped to attention and gazed impassively ahead as the delegates assembled on the broad white steps.

Moving to the front von Muller-Rechberg led the party up the marble steps through the entrance.

"On our way I would like to take you through the Great Marble Gallery," he began. "I'm sure you'll be interested to know," he continued proudly, "that it is twice as long as the Hall of Mirrors at Versailles."

It was impressive. A highly polished floor reflected the ornate furniture and the imposing marble doorways that led off to various parts of the Reich Chancellery. High walls reaching up to a plain white ceiling were hung with giant tapestries of classic battle scenes, interspersed with huge framed photographs of the Third Reich's military victories. At precise ten metre intervals, pairs of SS Leibstandarte guards stood at attention opposite each other. As the Baron and the Prime Minister, at the front of the group, reached each facing pair the soldiers snapped their weapons into a 'present arms' position and stared stonily ahead. The cumulative effect of the high ceiling, the long hallway, the huge tapestries and photographs, and the close proximity of the robot-like soldiers, while owing nothing to subtlety, was intimidating. By the time they reached the end of the Great Marble Gallery all the delegates had been silenced by the overt display of German military might.

From the Gallery the delegation was ushered into the grand Mosaic Hall, assigned as the venue for the 'peace negotiations'. Around the tall marble walls pairs of giant grey eagles were inset into giant panels. At the opposite end an eagle with a swastika in its claws surmounted two huge mahogany doors. Men in suits met the delegates at the entrance. They directed them across a gleaming marble floor to a long table placed in the centre and covered in a heavy red and gold tablecloth embroidered with swastika patterns. Seating was provided on dark red Empire chairs, each decorated with the German eagle and the ubiquitous swastika. Slightly under-lit and devoid of any natural light, the area created an air of prescient foreboding.

Standing motionless at regular intervals around the Mosaic Hall were twelve SS Leibstandarte guards each holding a Schmeisser machine pistol in his white-gloved hands.

"Please find the place that has been allotted to you and be seated, gentlemen," smiled von Muller-Rechberg.

Spaced around the table were red leather folders with the name of each delegate embossed on the cover. Peter Fraser was at the top on the right hand side, seated next to Walter Nash and Frederick Jones. Stuart and Brendan were seated opposite each other at the far end. When each of the delegates had found their place and sat down, the Baron clicked his heels, gave a brief bow in the Prime Minister's direction, turned and strode out, leaving the sound of his footsteps resonating from the Hall's cold marble walls.

The dying echoes were followed by an eerie silence. No external sounds penetrated the Mosaic Hall. The stillness was made more intimidating by the presence of the motionless armed guards. For a few moments each of the delegates sat staring at the door through which the Baron had exited, and then one by one they began searching each other's faces for reactions or some guidance. As the width of the table made it impossible for Stuart to talk quietly to Brendan he contented himself with a shrug and a raised eyebrow.

After about a minute had elapsed, Fraser cleared his throat and addressed his colleagues. "Gentlemen," he began, looking down the table, "I'm not sure what is supposed to happen but in the meantime I suggest each of you opens your folder and begins to inspect the contents."

Murmuring in agreement, the delegates reached forwards.

"Achtung!"

The order was barked from the far end of the room. Instantly the Leibstandarte guards snapped into a 'present arms' position. Emitting no sound, the huge mahogany doors swung open. Standing motionless in the doorway, his chin tilted upwards, was a slightly portly man with a receding hairline, dressed in an elegantly cut pinstriped suit.

"Gentlemen of the New Zealand delegation!" the voice of Baron von Muller-Rechberg echoed from the marble walls and ceilings. "The Foreign Minister of the Third Reich, Joachim von Ribbentrop."

Stuart stared at the figure walking confidently towards the head of the table. He'd always been intrigued by the man who was reportedly one of Hitler's favourites. Married to the heir to the Henkell champagne fortune, Ribbentrop had acquired the aristocratic *von* in his name when in his early thirties he persuaded an aunt with a titled husband to legally adopt him. Appointed as German ambassador to Britain in 1936 and German Foreign Minister in 1938, many allied diplomats had regarded him as a man of more vanity than ability. Rumour was that his nickname among his German colleagues was 'Ribbensnob".

Two men appeared in von Ribbentrop's wake carrying a podium surmounted by an elaborately carved eagle. They placed the podium at the head of the table and rested a red leather folder on the bird's extended wings.

As the Foreign Minister approached the table, Peter Fraser, followed by the other delegates, stood up. He extended his hand and Von Ribbentrop gave it a perfunctory shake.

"Good morning, Herr Fraser."

Fraser turned to his left preparing to introduce the other delegates but von Ribbentrop indicated with a wave of his arm that they were to be seated. He turned his back on Fraser and walked over to the podium. Another well-dressed man had now appeared and stood a metre away to the Foreign Minister's right.

Speaking in German, von Ribbentrop addressed the assembled New Zealanders.

"Germany has great admiration for New Zealand and its people," he began. "During the recent battles in the Western desert, Field Marshall Erwin Rommel gained a great respect not only for the fighting quality of New Zealand troops but also the excellent treatment given to the German soldiers that were held as your prisoners – temporarily."

Von Ribbentrop paused and smiling benignly at the listening delegates, nodded to the interpreter on his right. On the word "temporarily" the German foreign minister's faint smile grew broader.

"New Zealand is a stable country populated by well-educated people," he said. "It is our intention to develop a special relationship with your people based on the principles of mutual respect and cooperation. After all your country has a socialist government; our country has a National Socialist government."

Stuart noticed Fraser and Nash exchanging uneasy glances.

"Both are based on the principles of giving strength and happiness to our peoples," continued von Ribbentrop through his interpreter. "We will therefore be establishing a New Order in New Zealand that will be of benefit to all your people."

He paused, brushed a speck of dust from the sleeve of his dark suit, beamed at his audience. When the interpreter had finished he then invited the delegates to open their red leather folder at the title page.

Peace Talks

Berlin

11 July 1941

Terms and conditions of the

final settlement of hostilities

between

The People of New Zealand

and

The Third Reich of the People of Germany

There were only two additional pages. The first elaborated on von Ribbentrop's earlier sentiments regarding the mutual respect between the two nations and the principles of cooperation that would be the cornerstone of the New Order. The second page spelt out the 'peace terms'. As the delegates read through each point, it became painfully obvious that room for negotiation was limited. The German government had obviously decided on the type of regime to be established in New Zealand.

For several minutes von Ribbentrop remained silent but watchful as the delegates perused the document. Then, ostentatiously clearing his throat he continued.

"Tomorrow, gentlemen, you will be given full details of the peace treaty. Unfortunately the Third Reich has received unjust criticism for its disciplined occupation of Poland and other countries. Of course, these are lies manufactured by our enemies. The New Order that we will establish in your country will be based on the principles of mutual understanding and respect. Our prosperity will be your prosperity. Our progress will be your progress."

When the interpreter concluded, von Ribbentrop swept his eyes round the delegates and drew a deep breath. For the first time he raised his voice and, speaking in English, he intoned, "Gentlemen of New Zealand, together we will build a new and glorious tomorrow!" He paused and thrust his right arm stiffly into a horizontal position. "*Sieg Heil!*" he shouted. Instantly the Leibstandarte guards stationed round the perimeter of the hall shouldered their weapons and thrusting their right arms forward echoed the Nazi slogan. As the repeated cry resonated from the marble walls and ceiling, the New Zealand delegates sat uncomfortably on their chairs exchanging uncertain glances.

Abruptly von Ribbentrop lowered his outstretched arm. The chanting ceased but the echoes lingered. Holding both sides of the podium he frowned at the seated New Zealanders then smiled thinly.

"Gentlemen," he said in soft, measured English, "it is a common courtesy among diplomats to acknowledge the culture of other nations and join in their celebrations." He paused, his smile vanished and his eyes narrowed. "Gentlemen, please stand and join with us in a salute to our beloved Fuhrer."

Each delegate turned his eyes towards the New Zealand Prime Minister. There was a long pause and then, signalling to his colleagues to remain seated, Peter Fraser stood to face von Ribbentrop. His face was pale and behind his thick-lensed spectacles he was blinking nervously. He coughed, swallowed and began speaking in his soft Scottish tones.

"Mr. Foreign Minister, on behalf of my colleagues, I thank you for your courtesy and hospitality." He paused and glanced at the interpreter but von Ribbentrop gestured impatiently. "I understand, Herr Fraser. Continue, please."

Fraser swallowed again. "We thank you also for the compliment you have paid to the fighting quality of our soldiers and their treatment of your soldiers."

He paused and met the ambassador's unwavering gaze. "Earlier you spoke of implementing a New Order based on the principles of mutual understanding and respect between our two nations."

He paused again and looked down at the tense upturned faces of his colleagues. "While we respect your right to salute your leader, at this present moment such methods are not part of our New Zealand culture. I will therefore ask my colleagues to confine themselves to standing as a mark of respect between our two nations."

He made a short gesture with his upturned palms and the members of the New Zealand delegation rose uncertainly to their feet and stood silently. Colour had drained from every face.

The interpreter leaned towards von Ribbentrop but was waved impatiently away.

"You will not salute the German Fuhrer?"

"We are standing as a mark of respect to you, to the German people and Chancellor Hitler." The delegates close to Fraser could see his hands were trembling and that he was making a considerable effort to maintain his self-control. "That is all we are able to do at present," he concluded looking at von Ribbentrop.

"You will not salute?"

"We are standing as a mark of respect to you, to the German..."

Von Ribbentrop, while still holding Fraser's stare, made an almost imperceptible movement with his right hand. Instantly two of the Leibstandarte guards sprang forward. White-gloved hands gripped both of the Prime Minister's arms. Von Ribbentrop made a second gesture and the guards snapped to attention while maintaining their unwavering grip. A collective murmur of protest rose from the New Zealand delegates. Instantly a tight circle of soldiers, holding their Schmmeisers conspicuously in front of them, surrounded the table.

The ambassador's smile was devoid of mirth. He held Fraser's gaze and his voice was soft and menacing.

"Herr Fraser, I invite you to reconsider your position. The cooperation of you and your fellow New Zealanders is very important to the continued success of the peace talks."

"Do as he says Peter," muttered Frederick Jones.

"We've got no choice, Peter," said Walter Nash.

Fraser made a supreme effort to control his trembling. Then he spoke rapidly. "Mr. Foreign Minister, you referred earlier to the lies about your occupation of Poland. My people know that the Germans carried out mass executions of thousands of unarmed, defenceless Polish citizens within weeks of the surrender."

Von Ribbentrop opened his mouth but Fraser determinedly pressed on.

"These actions defy every accepted practice of human decency. Therefore, sir, until you are able to demonstrate that such actions are no longer practised by your government, I must advise my delegates to confine themselves to merely standing."

Fraser's Scottish accent and speed of speech was beyond von Ribbentrop's linguistic ability. Beckoning the interpreter forward with a jerk of his head, he listened intently to the rapid, whispered translation. At the conclusion his head snapped upwards. His cheeks had visibly flamed.

"Herr Fraser, I assure you that within the next 24 hours you will have cause to regret your words."

He signalled to the German officer standing behind the ring of troops. The man barked a curt order. In an obviously rehearsed movement, the two soldiers kicked both of Fraser's legs from under him. As the Prime Minister began to fall backwards one of the soldiers drove the butt of a machine pistol into his stomach and with a groan of pain he lurched forward. A blow to the back of his exposed neck instantly silenced him and with a scattering of chairs, his two captors dragged the limp Prime Minister through the huge mahogany doors. Their slamming echoed round the marble chamber.

Several of the New Zealand delegates collapsed into their seats. Others remained uncertainly standing, staring into the emotionless faces of the soldiers who circled them with drawn weapons. The German officer snapped another order and the delegates who were still standing were thrust back into their seats.

No sound interrupted the heavy silence that followed. Then von Ribbentrop heaved a long sigh and, in English, spoke again.

"Gentlemen, I am bitterly disappointed in the behaviour of your former Prime Minister." The emphasis on 'former' was not lost on the listening New Zealanders. "We will resume negotiations tomorrow. Unfortunately, in the light of today's events, it will be necessary to make some adjustments to the peace treaty documents."

He paused and sighed. "You will now be escorted back to your hotel where I invite you to think carefully about the day's events and to resolve that tomorrow, your cooperation with us will be..." He turned to the interpreter and held a brief whispered conversation.

"Full and unequivocal," said the interpreter.

"Full and unequivocal," echoed von Ribbentrop.

After fixing the silent delegation with a long stare he turned and strode briskly from the room.

"You will all please leave now," said the interpreter.

The soldiers grasped the back of each delegate's chair and exerted a backwards pressure causing each occupant to lurch hastily to his feet. The chairs were then swiftly pulled back and the delegates escorted to the exit.

On returning to their hotel the delegates were instructed to assemble on the balcony. The German 'peace delegates' were seated at each table and in addition, three soldiers were stationed at each of the balcony's four corners. Jugs of water, some bottles of beer, and plates of German sausage and sauerkraut had replaced the previous day's generous repast. Awaiting the New Zealanders was Baron Muller-Rechberg. His smooth smile had been replaced by a frown of deep concern. As soon as everyone was seated he addressed the group.

"Gentlemen, I am having difficulty in finding the words to express my disappointment at this morning's proceedings. My colleagues and I have done all we can to welcome you to our great country. In return we expected a much greater level of cooperation from you and your leader."

"What has happened to our Prime Minister?" demanded Walter Nash.

"Be assured, Mr. Nash, your former Prime Minister is being taken care of."

"Jailed and tortured you mean?" snapped Nash.

"Easy, Walter," murmured Frederick Jones.

"Be assured, Mr. Nash that although we regard Mr. Fraser's attitude as unacceptable, he will still be treated fairly by us."

He paused and stared coldly at the group. "We Germans are not barbarians, nor the Huns of your propaganda material. And, gentlemen, I invite you to remember the war is over, you surrendered and therefore we are the victors." He looked pointedly at the armed soldiers. "It is therefore obviously in your interests and the interests of your country to cooperate fully with us."

Brendan stood up. "Herr Baron", he began, "Wir haben Ihre Aussage zur Kenntnis genommen, wollen uns aber versichern, das Herr Fraser sobald wie möglich freikommt."

He repeated the words in English. "We have listened to your statement but we seek reassurance that Mr. Fraser will be released as soon as possible."

"Young man," replied the Baron in English. "You have my assurance Mr. Fraser will be returned to New Zealand. I cannot say when but I can give you my word as a German gentleman."

Brendan opened his mouth to reply but the Baron held up his hand. "The matter is now closed. Please be seated as we have some more German cultural activities that will increase your knowledge and understanding of the peoples of the Third Reich."

Brendan glanced uncertainly at Professor Sterling. With a quick jerk of his head he signalled the younger man to sit down.

"Well, done, mate," murmured Stuart. "But keep your head down for a while."

Barely had he finished speaking when a loud rumbling was heard from the far end of the street. Looming into view came two huge Tiger tanks followed by ranks of goose-stepping soldiers. No music was playing and no orders could be heard. Nevertheless, rank upon rank, the soldiers staring straight ahead goose-stepped down the street in a persistent hypnotic rhythm.

The delegates watched in silent awe as the endless ranks strutted past.

Finally, Frederick Jones, addressing no one in particular muttered, "It's incredible. There must be thousands of them."

"Not necessarily, Mr. Jones," said Stuart. "It may just be the same bunch of jokers marching round and round the bloody block."

The burst of laughter was spontaneous and served to relieve the tension that had permeated the group since the assault on Peter Fraser. Stuart had deliberately spoken in an exaggerated Kiwi accent causing the Baron, confused by the speech and the laughter, to whirl round and glower at him. Meeting the stare Stuart raised his half-filled beer glass in the Baron's direction and smiled.

"I was saying to my friends, Herr Baron, if our soldiers had marched as well as yours we may not have lost so many battles."

The other delegates smiled and laughed. Muller-Rechberg stared uncertainly at the group for a moment and then smiled and nodded before turning to watch the parade.

"Very smooth, mate," murmured Brendan. "But take note of your own warning."

By late in the afternoon the last of the troops tramped past. Taking their cue from Walter Nash, the delegates stretched and slid back their chairs preparing to leave.

Noting the stirrings, the Baron rose. "Please, gentlemen, do take a moment to, as you say in English, stretch your legs. You can see the light is fading. This provides us with the opportunity to arrange a special spectacle that is an integral part of German culture. After a short break you will be invited," he smiled slightly, "to witness a Nazi torchlight parade."

Ten minutes later, when the New Zealand delegates had reluctantly returned to their places, the lamppost speakers crackled into life with a military anthem. Simultaneously, rows of young Germans appeared, wearing an assortment of brown uniforms, under a forest of swastika flags. All were singing in unison with the anthem.

The crackling from the speakers and the singing from the marchers had the advantage of muffling the brief conversations

106

that Stuart and Brendan managed to conduct whilst staring straight ahead.

As the front ranks began to pass, Brendan muttered, "The bloody *Horst Wessel* Song."

"What's that?"

"No, 'who's that?' to be precise. Horst Wessel was a young Nazi shot in a quarrel over his girlfriend."

"His girlfriend? So who shot him?"

"His girlfriend was a whore. They were living together in a Berlin slum. The gunman was a communist. Wessel had written his Nazi anthem a few months before he died and so the Nazi Party decided to transform him into a martyr."

"Charming little story. The man's an example to us all."

By this time the nearest 'peace delegate' was regarding the two young men with some suspicion. Raising his beer glass Brendan smiled winningly at the man. "Die Fahn Hoch!" he called.

For a moment the German glared suspiciously at him. Then, reaching for his own glass he raised it and nodded.

"Die Fahn Hoch," he said.

Brendan, nodding vigorously in reply, downed the remainder of his beer in one gulp, saluted the German with his empty glass and again favoured him with a broad grin. The man studied him for a long moment, gave a thin smile and turned back to watch the procession.

"What did you say?" asked Stuart.

"Simply the title of Horst Wessel's song – Raise High the Flag."

"How does the rest of it go?"

"Can't figure it all out but it's basically something like, 'Raise high the flag, Hitler's banners shall wave unchecked'."

"Obviously penned by a literary genius."

The song was sung and played repeatedly as the flag-bearing ranks streamed past. As the sun began to sink below Berlin's buildings, a flickering of light began to appear from the far end of Prinz-Albrecht Strasse. The music changed to another German march and the first of a series of flaming torchbearers loomed into view.

The illuminated parade, accompanied by an unending stream of German marching music, lasted for several more hours by which time some of the delegates, in spite of the noise, were beginning to slump and doze in their chairs. As the last of the marchers passed the balcony, the Baron stood and addressed the tired delegates.

"We hope you have enjoyed this evening of our Nazi culture, gentlemen" He smiled. "A foretaste of things to come."

Receiving no response he continued. "You are now free to retire for the night. However, before you do, I have to inform you that new arrangements have been made. Each of you will be sharing a room with a peace delegate to ensure, how shall I say, a continuity of communication." He smiled and clicked his heels. "I wish you all a gute Nacht – a good night."

The following morning they faced the realities of the revised 'peace treaty'. The office of Governor-General was to be abolished, effective immediately, and replaced by a Governor appointed from Berlin. Parliament would be dissolved and regional representatives appointed under the control of the Governor and regional Councils. All political parties were abolished – only the Nazi Party would be permitted. Citizens would be permitted to stand for Regional Councils but all appointees would require final approval of the Governor. All government departments and all civil service positions would remain in place, pending a series of reviews by the new Governor's Council and a scrutinizing of all personnel for their 'political suitability'.

The delegates were informed they would be departing for New Zealand later that afternoon. In response to a question from Professor Sterling they were further informed that on return to New Zealand they were to continue in their current positions until the new regime was established. This process was to be determined in Berlin and communicated to the people of New Zealand 'at an appropriate time'. They were assured Peter Fraser was being well cared for. They were instructed make no mention of the 'incident' as the proper authorities would be communicating this to the people of New Zealand – also at an appropriate time.

The return journey was arduous. The Junkers took a route overland through Singapore with no overnight stopovers. At the various refuelling stops the delegates were only permitted to walk up and down the tarmac, and always under the watchful eyes of armed guards.

Finally, relieved, exhausted and apprehensive, the planeload of delegates touched down at Whenuapai airbase, west of Auckland city.

Summing up the thoughts of his two companions, as he emerged from the plane onto a rain-drenched tarmac, Stuart looked up at the dark grey sky.

"So, what now?"

CHAPTER 17

"Here they come," said Brendan. "The vanguard of the victory parade for our brave boys."

"Plenty of people," answered Stuart. "Wonder if there'll be much cheering?"

A month earlier, with the other delegates, the two young men had returned from Berlin. Following their instructions they had resumed their university positions – supplemented by well-paid casual work on the Auckland waterfront. Although the wartime research projects had ceased, the grant money still came through from Wellington so at Professor Sterling's suggestion they continued to collect their weekly allowance in a small brown envelope from the cashier's office in the Registry building.

"I'm sure the funding will end as soon as the Occupation forces take over Wellington's bureaucracy," the professor had surmised, "but in the meantime, consider it a study grant."

The previous day two troop ships loaded with New Zealand soldiers had docked at Auckland. Determined to create a positive impression, the German New Order government had announced a Victory Parade would be held up Queen Street. Through a contact, Brendan had managed to secure a vantage point on the first floor of Milne and Choyce's large department store on Queen Street from where they could watch the parade.

The band appeared first, thumping out Colonel Bogey. Then came the ranks of khaki uniforms with the distinctive lemon squeezer hats and shouldered 303 rifles.

"Bet there's nothing up the spout," said Brendan as the front rank reached the point opposite the window.

The 'Victory Parade' was widely regarded as a misnomer. Certainly, as the New Order-controlled press and the radio stations incessantly reminded them, peace had been declared, and thousands of young men had been saved from death or severe wounds. Furthermore the men who were cheered when they had left in 1939 and 1940 were now returning home to enjoy the peace and prosperity they had helped to secure. Privately, however, very few of the population agreed that the parade celebrated a victory. This was not a parade of brave boys who'd come from cities, towns and farming settlements to fight for freedom.

"Poor buggers are not sure what they're supposed to do," said Stuart. "Look at their faces."

Some of the soldiers stared straight ahead, biting their lips as they marched. A number wore sheepish grins while others, who appeared to be resigned to the new situation, waved to the crowds and occasionally called out greetings.

"See," said Stuart. "Their attitudes reflect those of the whole population – humiliation, sadness and relief."

"Could be worse, you know," said Brendan.

"What could?"

"The occupation. So far the government seems to be doing its best to win our support rather than trying to beat us into submission. Not at all like Poland."

"Maybe, but early days yet. It'll take a lot to convince me that rule by the so-called New Order will be a positive experience."

"You're right, of course." Brendan shrugged. "I was just trying to look on the bright side."

Stuart patted him on the shoulder. "I know, mate, but I'm afraid no matter how you dress it up, the New Order will be the death knell of this nation's freedom."

"Cunning bastards, all the same. Look how they handled the news about Fraser."

Less than a week after the return of the delegates the newspapers had all carried a front-page story on Prime Minister Peter Fraser. It related how he had become ill during the trip

111

and as a result had been receiving the best possible care in a Berlin hospital. Although out of danger he had been advised by his German doctors to give up his prime ministerial role in order to speed his recovery. As a goodwill gesture the New Order government had flown his wife Janet to Berlin to be with him during his recuperation. She had left the previous day.

"Yeah, smart move sending his wife over," said Stuart. "Watch for the carefully arranged bedside photos of the re-united couple surrounded by cards, flowers and caring German medical staff."

"Yes, but will he co-operate?"

"What choice has he got? Beaten up, sick, alone, intimidated. Surrounded by men who've recently conquered a considerable area of the world. And now both he and his wife are under threat. He hasn't much choice."

Following Fraser's resignation, the authorities had moved swiftly to establish their New Order government. Parliament had been suspended, and all government bureaucracies were put under the command of the new Berlin-appointed Governor Claus von Stauffenberg. From the residence of the previous Governor General, Lord Galway, von Stauffenburg announced that elections would be held at a date as yet unspecified. In the meantime, the instigators of The New Order set out to win the hearts and minds of post-war New Zealand.

Wartime rationing was abolished, and a series of government-funded developments in roading, railways and hydroelectric power were launched, with the promise of ample, well-paid employment for returned servicemen. The on-going war on the Russian Eastern Sector (officially called an 'engagement') ensured an increasing demand for wool and meat, thus resulting in a boom period for the farming sector.

Although hostilities had ceased with Britain and her allies, Russia's dictator Joseph Stalin had refused to surrender. Hitler's more belligerent military advisors had urged him to use the new atomic bomb in Russia, but the majority of the Wermacht top brass had been stunned by the power of the new weapon and its ability to lay waste large tracts of land. They reasoned it would be counter-productive to occupy devastated cities and agricultural areas ruined by nuclear explosion. Furthermore, Hitler, motivated more by ideology than military considerations, was not prepared to relinquish the opportunity of conquering and subjugating the 'genetically inferior' Russians town by town and city by city, and he relished the prospect of reviewing victory parades in the cities of Moscow and Stalingrad. Consequently conventional warfare that required considerable manpower, principally with the onset of a bitter Russian winter, continued to be the preferred option.

Three weeks later at the cinema, Stuart and Brendan viewed the first of the New Order newsreels screened before the main feature. The traditional standing for the playing of "God Save the King" accompanied by a screen image of George VI had been deleted from the commencement of the screening, which began with a montage showing bridal couples and young parents smiling awkwardly at each other to the accompaniment of happy music and a smooth voice-over.

"Your New Order government," the commentator explained, "wants to encourage the re-establishment of New Zealand family life. Therefore each newly married couple will receive a generous New Directions grant of fifty pounds

"Fifty quid," muttered Stuart as a buzz went round the cinema. "Maybe I'll qualify as a parson and claim a percentage."

His friend snorted in derision as the commentary continued.

"Your New Order government will also provide a New Birth grant of ten pounds on the birth of each baby. The parents will then receive a weekly New Life child allowance of one pound ten shillings per week for each child until it reaches the age of fifteen."

"There you go, mate. You'd be better off training as a children's Plunket Nurse," laughed Brendan.

113

When the film was over they discussed the new allowances as they walked to the bus stop.

"Smart move by our new masters," said Brendan. "Most of us were raised in the Great Depression and are weary of war." He grinned. "And you can guarantee the returned soldiers will be sick of celibacy."

"Yeah. You watch. Over the next few months Kiwi men and women will be eagerly filling the churches, and marriage beds and then maternity hospitals."

"Which will give them little time to worry about political issues. Smart move indeed."

***

Uncertain of their country's position and their own long-term prospects, Stuart and Brendan had begun holding regular meetings with Professor Sterling to discuss their Berlin experience and the unfolding events at home. The following morning they told him about the newsreel and the implementation of the family allowance payments.

"Yes, it's also in this morning's papers. Ironic, really. At the beginning of the war Peter Fraser set up the National Film Unit to produce weekly items to bolster morale. The Nazis are aware of the power of film and have taken over the whole operation and are using it to promote their form of socialism."

"The government grants will be popular, sir."

"Most definitely. Trouble is they'll divert attention away from the antics of the new Ministry of Culture and Information. It's now implementing a process whereby all newspapers must submit their copy to Ministry officials prior to publication to ensure the content is correct politically. If there are problems, the editor and the reporters are invited to attend re-education seminars."

"At least no one's been shot," said Brendan.

Sterling looked serious. "Not yet, but remember when the Nazis first came to power they built concentration camps to

114

punish and re-educate dissident groups within Germany itself. In my view the new authorities are keen to gain full control of the media as soon as possible and mix it with measures such as the child allowance to keep the population compliant. Have you noticed the *New Zealand Listener*?"

"The free magazine for radio license holders?" said Stuart.

"Yes. Because it's free it reaches the majority of households. Provides an ideal opportunity for the authorities to link the radio and print media together, each one preaching the joys of peace and prosperity under the New Order. Conformity and obedience are the sub-themes of peace and prosperity. For some people it's sufficient, I fear. Rising prosperity is, as the media constantly reminds the returned soldiers, more than their parents ever had."

"Have you remembered the new Governor, Claus von Stauffenberg, is coming to town today?"

The professor frowned. "It's been a great source of debate among my senior colleagues, Stuart. Most of us have decided to stay away. But you two go. I'd like you to report on what happens."

Stuart exchanged glances with Brendan before replying.

"Do you think there'll be trouble?"

"Unlikely. But it's the first time the new Governor will be meeting Auckland mayor Sir Earnest Davis."

"Who's Jewish."

"Yes. As you know I'm not a great supporter of a man who made his money from booze and is reputed to be a womanizer, but at the same time I'd hate to see his race used as an excuse to humiliate him. Today he's the one who'll be symbolically handing over the keys of the city to the German Governor. No-one's sure what to expect."

"We do know von Stauffenberg's not a fanatical Nazi," said Stuart.

"True. He's from a distinguished aristocratic family, and a well-educated intellectual. Furthermore, if you recall, he gained a position in the German high command when he was only thirty three."

"So far he hasn't spouted any anti-Jewish propaganda."

"No, but if he or his Berlin masters want to signal the establishment of an anti-Semitic regime in New Zealand, today could be the time to start."

The following morning Stuart and Brendan walked down to Queen Street and found a position near the front of the growing crowd between the Civic Theatre and the Auckland Town Hall where a special stand had been erected for the occasion. There was a marked contrast between this parade and the earlier Victory Parade. The streets were now hung with Nazi bunting, interspersed with the traditional New Zealand flag. On the previous day German soldiers had erected heavy wooden barriers along the route. Today the soldiers were lined in front of the barriers on both sides of Queen Street.

Punctually at two o'clock the sounds of a military band playing a German march echoed up Queen Street.

"Your mate Horst Vatshisname?" asked Stuart.

"Not this time. Just some tuneless German oom pah pah, with a strong military beat."

A military band, followed an immaculately uniformed goose-stepping battalion of SS Leibstandarte guards, led the parade up the length of Queen Street towards the Auckland Town Hall. The robotic precision of their marching was impressive and many in the crowd viewed them with apprehension. Others, unsure what to do, clapped politely.

As the first ranks began to cross the Wellesley Street intersection, shouts of "Bloody robots! Bugger off!" suddenly came from centre of the crowd.

Two men in dark suits who had been standing in front of Stuart and Brendan, roughly shouldered them aside and plunged into the crowd seeking the source of the shouts.

"Special police," said Brendan, reaching out a steadying arm. "Keep your eyes peeled. They're not too difficult to spot."

Certainly their dress and arrogant bearing made the special police easily identifiable and consequently catcallers, while continuing their caustic comments, were able to avoid them with relative ease. On several occasions when the black-clad men tried to reach a potential trouble spot, onlookers subtly but deliberately impeded their progress. When roughly shoved aside they invariably responded with a look of wide-eyed innocence and a, "Sorry, mate, didn't see you there".

In the centre of the parade was a black Mercedes Benz saloon containing the new Governor and an aide-de-camp. Waiting on the platform sat the councillors and Mayor Earnest Davis. Davis's pinched, unprepossessing features were decidedly gaunt. The film of sweat on his bald head owed more to the tension of the situation than the rays of the afternoon sun, or the heaviness of his civic robes. His effort at adopting a confident, self-assured pose was continually compromised as his eyes flicked nervously between the approaching entourage and the gathering crowd. As the black saloon glided to the base of the stand the mayor rose – further undermining the image of civic dignity by involuntarily mopping the sweat from his visage with his richly embroidered left sleeve.

All eyes were on Governor von Stauffenberg, his aide and two high-ranking German officers as they mounted the steps and joined the mayor on the dais.

"Davis looks a nervous wreck," murmured Brendan.

"Wouldn't you?" answered Stuart.

After the Germans had seated themselves the mayor stepped to the rostrum. He shuffled his notes, looked nervously over the expectant crowd, gripped both sides of the rostrum and, clearing his throat, began his speech. It was carefully worded and brief. He welcomed the new Governor and the delegation to Auckland and expressed the hope this council and the German authorities would be able to cooperate in the future for the benefit of the people of Auckland and the people of New

Zealand. The polite applause that followed his speech was mingled with catcalls that caused a further futile flurry among members of the special police.

As Claus von Stauffenberg stood to make his reply a hush fell over the crowd.

"This is it," said Stuart, watching the tall, youthful, dark-haired figure move towards the rostrum.

"At least he's not in military uniform," said Brendan.

From underneath heavy black eyebrows von Stauffenberg's gaze took in the crowd. In careful English he began by thanking the mayor and his councillors for their warm welcome. He continued by painting a picture of a prosperous future for the nation that would benefit all its citizens. Although he went on to point out that these benefits would be available only to those who joined the partnership offered by the New Order, his speech contained no hint of anti-Semitic rhetoric. At its conclusion Mayor Davis stepped forward and handed von Stauffenberg a large key. Both men then stood together facing the crowd as the band played God Defend New Zealand followed by Deutschland, Deutschland Uber Alles.

"All very civilized, I'm sure," was Stuart's comment. They had returned to university and were walking down the corridor towards his office.

"True," replied Brendan. "Apart from the special police in the crowd, the Gestapo has kept its profile low. Maybe that's the way the Germans are going to rule New Zealand."

"And maybe not," replied his friend, unlocking his office door and pushing it open.

A letter was lying on the floor at his feet. He picked it up and immediately recognized the handwriting.

It was Carol's.

CHAPTER 18

"Ach, watch vat you are doing!" The German accent, like the trench coat, Homburg hat and black tie, had become an increasingly familiar feature of the city crowds since the end of the war. Touted by the press and radio as 'plain-clothes officers recruited to assist the New Zealand police', the special police were regarded with increasing suspicion by the population, well aware of the Nazis' penchant for using security police to suppress dissension.

"Sorry," muttered Stuart. Hardly glancing at the hefty German, he continued to peer down the platform. The station loudspeaker had announced the imminent arrival of the overnight train from Wellington and he wanted to savour every moment of Carol's return.

The hand on his right shoulder was deliberate and heavy.

"Sorry, are you! Your heavy foot, it was sitting on top of mine."

In spite of the man's obvious anger and his own anxiety, a brief smile flitted across Stuart's face at the inappropriateness of the verb. The man's reaction was instant.

"You are thinking this is funny. Ha! Ha! Ha! Is that what you are thinking?"

"No, of course not," answered Stuart. The sound of a train whistle echoed through the station and he instinctively turned towards it. The heavy hand fastened on his shoulder and spun him round. The man then seized the lapels of Stuart's student university blazer and thrust his face forward. His bulbous nose was heavily veined, his breath smelt of beer, and beads of sweat glistened on his forehead.

"To you I am talking, man. Do not your back turn on me when to you I am talking!"

"OK, I'm sorry. I heard the train coming and I am here to meet a friend. I meant no offence." Although becoming angry at the man's behaviour, Stuart was seeking to resolve the situation.

"Then why did you smile when my foot you hurt?"

"I wasn't smiling at you. It was just that, well you used the wrong word. You should have said 'standing' not 'sitting'. But it doesn't matter. I've said I am sorry."

The noise of the train increased as it approached the far end of the platform.

"Sorry. You think you can just say sorry for insulting a German official. Ach! You must realize you are conquered. We are the masters of you stupid Kivis."

"Kiwis", said Stuart instinctively, and instantly regretting it.

"Ach so, you are the clever one with the English. You laugh because I do not speak it as good as you. Do you know…?"

The rest of the man's sentence was drowned in the noise of the engine as it hissed and churned its way past them. Stuart, turning to look as the carriages came into view, pulled against the grip the German was still maintaining on his coat lapels. The effect was immediate.

"So, you make the fun of me and now you try to escape." In a swift and expert movement he spun Stuart round forcing his arm up towards his shoulders. Instinctively Stuart cried out in pain.

"Ach, so it hurts! That is good!"

Thrusting his foot forward the man hooked Stuart's legs from under him, sending him sprawling forward. He crashed into a group of people partially breaking his fall, but he was still winded by the force of his sudden connection with the concrete platform. Instantly he felt his other arm seized and his wrists tugged together. Moments later a pain shot through them and he heard the metallic click of handcuffs.

"Now get up you dirty Kivi!" said the German, hauling him to his feet. Dazed by the fall and shocked by the pain, Stuart staggered upright trying to maintain his balance. He noticed the crowd had drawn back, distancing themselves from him and his tormentor.

"See, you Kivis!" shouted the German, holding his swaying prisoner with one hand. "You will learn, all of you, that conquered you have been! The war you have lost! That we Germans are in charge and you will obey us at all times!"

The platform echoed with the hissing of the engine and the opening and closing of the carriage doors as the passengers disembarked. No sound came from the cluster of expressionless faces staring at Stuart and his captor.

The German grunted. "I see you have nothing to say! Good! You look and you listen and you learn, ja?" He chuckled at his own eloquence. "Now I take this man with me. He will be a lesson learning, ja? And you will all be a lesson learning. Ja, I am thinking so!" He tugged at Stuart's shoulder. "Come, you stupid Kivi. Now I will take you to the Stationmaster's office. I wish to start your lessons soon!"

As Stuart reeled back he saw a movement in the otherwise still and silent crowd. For a moment he was able to focus and gasped as he saw Carol's face staring at him in horror. Their eyes met. Instinctively he shook his head before a rough hand spun him round and sent him staggering towards the station exit.

The Stationmaster's office was located squarely in the middle of the main entrance area. The high ceilings and tall stone pillars had been designed by the original architects to create a powerful, imposing building befitting its location at the hub of Auckland's transport system. As rail was still the principle means of moving goods and personnel from Auckland to other parts of the country the station was the focus of daily transport activities.

The solid, imposing architecture of the railway station had appealed to the German authorities who, conveniently ignoring its British colonial heritage, dubbed it People's Station One. On the basis that thousands of citizens passed through its portals each day, the conquerors had wasted no time in making it a showpiece of the New Order. The stone exterior was treated to a full refurbishment and on a huge flagpole erected at the centre of the structure hung the New Zealand New Order flag. Their obsession with symbols, badges of rank and flags had prompted the new government, on direct orders from Dr Joseph Goebbels' Ministry of Culture and Information in Berlin, to swiftly 'revise' the New Zealand flag by replacing the Union Jack in the top right hand corner with a black *Hakenkreuz* – the Nazi swastika. The rest of the flag, with its blue sea and symbolic Southern Cross, had been left intact. Most of the population, still coming to terms with their new situation, appeared to have mutely accepted the change although incidents of 'desecration' appeared to be on the increase, in spite of the new penalties imposed for 'unpatriotic acts'.

The interior of the railway station had been similarly treated with large New Order New Zealand flags, suspended side by side with their red and black Nazi counterparts. Wisely the authorities had located them high in the roof, thus preventing their being ripped or torn down by 'unpatriotic' persons. Moving gently in the draughts created by the arrival and departure of the trains, they cast shadows on the upper parts of the walls. The effect could have been interpreted as picturesque but for any who cared to look upwards, the undulating shapes created patterns of disquiet.

Still dizzy from his fall and heartsick at seeing Carol, Stuart paid no attention to the gentle fluttering over his head as his captor pushed him towards the Stationmaster's office.

"In here!" ordered the German, pushing the door with his foot. "Stationmaster!" he shouted as they entered the deserted waiting area. "Where are you? For you I have an important visitor!"

A weedy man, hastily buttoning up his regulation jacket and expelling a lungful of smoke, appeared from the office at the side. His ingratiating smile matched his obsequious bearing.

"Good morning Mr. Schroeder. You are well I hope."

Ignoring the servile greeting Schroeder pushed Stuart to a chair in the corner of the room. "Sit!" he ordered and, turning to the official, barked, "This man is my prisoner. He is a subversive. He attacked me! Such behaviour will not be tolerated!"

"No, Mr. Schroeder. Of course not." The official, having completed the final button at his jacket throat, after a cursory glance at Stuart, stood to attention in front of the hefty German.

"I will go for a piss. Then I will phone for a car to take this man away. For that time he will be your prisoner. You will watch him. You will not let him get away. If you do, you will be my prisoner. Then I will have two prisoners, ja?" He chuckled mirthlessly and, with a final glare at Stuart, exited.

The slam of the door echoed through the office. Stuart stared up at the stationmaster who glanced away. Angered at the man's obsequious attitude to the German, he said quietly, "Scared of that bastard, aren't you?"

The man looked shiftily at Stuart and made an awkward attempt to square his shoulders. "Scared? Me? You're joking, mate."

"Maybe, mate," responded Stuart sourly. "All I did was accidentally stand on his foot. Bastard went off his rocker. Threw me on the ground, handcuffed me and shoved me in here."

The stationmaster shrugged but shifted his feet uncomfortably.

"Got a cigarette?"

"Yeah, I suppose so," said the man, glancing uncertainly at the closed door.

"I'd appreciate it," Stuart said. "My head hurts and these bloody handcuffs are cutting into my wrists. Can you do anything with them?"

"Sorry," said the stationmaster, "but I don't have a key. Here." He reached into his pocket and extracted a packet of Capstan. Putting one between his lips he lit it, took it from his mouth and placed it between Stuart's lips. "Have a good draw, mate."

Drawing on the end of the cigarette Stuart felt the soothing effect flow through his body. The man took the cigarette from Stuart's mouth allowing him to expel the smoke with a long sigh. "Again?" Stuart nodded and the process was repeated. Feeling marginally better, he leaned back in his chair and closed his eyes. The phone rang and the stationmaster hurried behind the counter to answer it.

Carol's letter from Wellington had been brief but friendly. She'd explained that in three weeks' time she would be returning alone to Auckland by train and asked him to meet her at the station. She had concluded with 'I have a very important matter to talk to you about'. 'Returning alone' was promising, but the 'very important matter' had left him speculating by the hour. And now, just as he was on the point of finding out, he'd been arrested.

He sighed, opened his eyes and looked around. On the walls were three New Order posters. The first depicted a muscular blond male in lederhosen striding side by side with a Kiwi farm worker. The single word 'Together!' was writ large. The second featured the New Zealand New Order flag with the caption 'Kiwis, at last your own flag!'. Stuart had found them uncomfortable before. Now his circumstances made his lip curl with distaste. The final poster provided him with wry amusement. It showed a young man in a traditional lemon squeezer military hat looking towards a far horizon. Underneath was written, 'Join Up! Discover Adventure! Gain Promotion! Join our fight against the Communist enemy!'

The New Order government's recruiting drive sought to appeal to New Zealand men motivated by adventure and to a lesser extent by the concept of defending the nation against the threat of international Communism. The pay was generous and although cynics pointed out the increasing promotional opportunities were doubtless due to the equally continuing casualty rates, there was a steady supply of volunteers. An increasing portion of recruits came from the ranks of disillusioned ex-servicemen who had found that home and hearth brought with it a plethora of responsibilities for which the occasional unsatisfactory wrestle under the blankets in the dark with the wife was insufficient compensation.

Next to Stuart on a small table was a pile of newspapers on top of which was the latest copy of the Weekly News with its distinctive pink cover page. The photo on the front bore the bold caption, 'The Fuhrer salutes the New Order in London'. The setting was the familiar balcony at Buckingham Palace. Five figures were waving at an unseen crowd. On the right was Sir Oswald Mosley, former cabinet minister and British Union of Fascists leader and now the newly appointed British Prime Minister. Next to him stood his classically beautiful wife, the former Lady Diana Mitford. Adolf Hitler, who had been a guest at their 1936 wedding in the Berlin apartment of Dr Joseph Goebbels, stood next to them. On his left in a medal-bedecked uniform was the former Duke of Windsor, now reinstated as King Edward VIII, and his wife Wallis Simpson. Stuart noted wryly that the American divorcée was not referred to as "Queen Wallis". Apparently the authorities had decided to try and woo the great British public a few stages at a time.

As part of the peace settlement Britain's wartime Prime Minister Winston Churchill had been branded as a warmonger by Mosley and taken into custody. Some had speculated he'd been held in the Tower of London but no one was absolutely sure. Stuart had also read Adolf Hitler was seriously considering re-locating Britain's capital to Oxford. As a vindictive preliminary move he had decreed Churchill's nearby ancestral home, magnificent Blenheim Palace, would be compulsorily acquired and used as Britain's Gestapo Headquarters.

The stationmaster completed his phone call and looked back over the counter.

"It's all right," said Stuart sarcastically, "I'm still here."

"Yeah, OK," replied the stationmaster. "Just doing my job, mate."

"Some job. 'Yes, sir. No, sir, *Jawhol, Herr Hauptman*!'"

"Look, mate, a man's got to eat and feed his family. That's why I took this job as the stationmaster. Not my fault if they've taken over the country. And, anyway," he shrugged, "the job's reasonably well paid and most of the time they leave me alone to get on with it."

"Except in so-called emergency cases like mine. I wasn't looking for any trouble but when I stood on his foot, the bastard who'd obviously been drinking, went bloody berserk!"

"Yeah, sorry. Most of them are reasonably decent, but Schroeder…", the man glanced nervously at the door, "he's got a real chip on his shoulder."

"So what's likely to happen to me?"

The man paused and scratched nervously at the side of his cheek. "Hard to say. Under the new laws…"

"'Patriotic Conduct' laws."

"Yeah, those ones; you could be locked up awaiting trial for an indefinite period."

"So much for the benefits of the 'New Order'. Can't people see that?"

"Some can but what can they do? In any case, if you keep your head down, most of the time you'll be OK as long as – .""

The door swung open and a German officer strode into the room, followed by Schroeder. The stationmaster braced up but the officer, ignoring him, looked straight at Stuart, who felt himself instinctively sit upright.

"Is this the man?"

126

"Jawohl, Herr Oberst. Ich kann...."

"English!" barked the officer. "At all times! Accurate communication with these people is absolutely essential."

"Of course, *Herr Oberst*," answered Schroeder, clicking his heels and jerking his head forward.

Turning to face Stuart the officer barked, "You! What is your name?"

"Stuart Johnson, sir." The 'sir' stuck in his throat but he realized this was not the time for foolish bravado.

"You assaulted this official, yes?"

"No, sir, I did not assault the official. There was a crowd..."

"*Er ist*, er, he is lying, *Herr Oberst*! He assaulted my foot and..."

"Wait!" The German colonel held up his hand. He nodded at Stuart. "Continue."

"There was a crowd at the platform and I had come to meet the Wellington train. I heard the sound of the train's whistle and stepped forward. I accidentally stood on Mr. Schroeder's foot. I apologized, said I was sorry but..."

Unable to gauge from the officer's stare whether or not his story was likely to be believed, he shrugged and tried to adopt the expression of a bewildered victim.

"You said you were sorry? You apologized?"

"Yes, Colonel. I –."

"Ah, you recognize German army ranks?"

"Some, of them, Colonel," answered Stuart hoping that the slight smile on the man's face had gained him a small advantage.

"Good. Please, continue with your story. After you apologized..."

"Yes, after I apologized Mr. Schroeder shouted at me, said I had insulted a German official, grabbed me, threw me down on the platform, handcuffed me and brought me here."

"You are hurt?"

"I have a lump on my head where it hit the platform. But the handcuffs are very tight and causing me pain... sir."

The colonel appeared to be unmoved. "What was your business at the station?"

"Business? Oh, no business as such. I was meeting my girlfriend. She was coming up from Wellington. She had been visiting her parents. They haven't been well."

"They are sick? Our People's hospitals..."

"No, sir, they are not sick in that sense. Her brother Ian, their son, was killed in the western desert a week before the truce. He was their only son." Afraid he had gone too far in referring to the recent war, Stuart shrugged.

The colonel regarded him for a long moment and then shook his head.

"Ach," he sighed. "An unfortunate story. And your girlfriend? Has she been your girlfriend for long?"

"Yes, sir. About five months."

"And you are in love?" The colonel smiled.

"Yes, sir, very much. She's lovely."

"I am sure." He turned to Schroeder. "Release this man."

"Herr Oberst..."

"I said, release this man! Are you hard of hearing, Herr Schroeder, or is it perhaps the effect of too much alcohol? Perhaps I should inquire further into..."

"At once, sir!" Schroeder moved forward and Stuart winced in pain as the blood began to flow back into his hands and fingers.

"I apologize, young man, for your treatment. It is our intention to work together with you and your countrymen." He snapped to attention and favoured Stuart with a stiff bow. "Please, accept my apologies."

"Thank you Colonel," replied Stuart, massaging his wrists.

"Schroeder!" snapped the colonel, indicating Stuart.

"*Jawohl*, er yes." He turned to face Stuart making an unsuccessful attempt to metamorphose his baleful glare into an expression of suitable contriteness. Imitating his superior he bowed and muttered, "Please accept my apologies."

Still angry at his unfair treatment and sensing the man's lack of sincerity, Stuart jerked his head downward in a curt acknowledgement.

Nodding to the stationmaster the colonel turned, and closely followed by his scowling underling, strode out the door.

There was a long silence broken by a deep sigh from the stationmaster.

"You were bloody lucky, mate. But, like I said, some of them are OK, as long as you..."

"Keep your head down," finished Stuart. His expression abruptly changed. "Jesus! Carol!"

As he burst through the stationmaster's office door Stuart noticed the crowd had grown considerably during the previous hour. The high ceiling and the stone masonry of the concourse caused the symphonies of sound to echo and re-echo from all sides. The rapid clack, clack of high heels mingled with the purposeful footsteps of suited businessmen carrying Gladstone bags, the noises of parents coping with suitcases and small children, the queues at the ticket offices and the regular arrival and destination announcements from the loudspeakers scattered throughout the complex. Stuart's eyes swept the crowd seeking for some sign of Carol. In doing so he took care to avoid any eye contact with the occasional man in a trench coat and black tie moving silently on the perimeters, watching from under the brim of a Homburg hat.

A sudden impact caused him to stagger back, gasping for breath. Instantly he was on his guard, but the arms wrapped around him and the face thrust up towards his was wonderfully familiar.

"Stuart! God! I thought I'd never see you again!"

"Carol! Me too." He wrapped his arm around her and held her tight. "How did you know where I was?"

"When I saw what had happened with that German I followed you and saw him take you into the Stationmaster's Office. I didn't know what to do so I sat on the seat over there. I saw the German leave and then return with the important-looking officer. I really thought you were done for."

"So did I. But I managed to persuade the officer the whole thing was an accident. I used you, actually."

She pulled her head back and stared at him with wide eyes. "Me. How?"

"I told him I was waiting for my beautiful girlfriend from Wellington. He ordered his henchman to take the cuffs off me and then, coming to attention, he bowed and offered his sincere apologies."

"Good heavens! Really?"

"Yes, and he made Schroeder, the other fellow, apologize too."

"And did he?"

"Of course. One thing the Krauts are good at is obeying orders. His apology was hardly the epitome of sincerity, though. He's not a man I would like to cross swords with again."

"Yes." She paused and looked serious. "I have to talk to you. You are OK, now, aren't you?"

"Sure. A bump on the head and my wrists are sore but I'll be fine. Now, where's your luggage? I don't want to stay here another minute. I'll catch the ferry with you."

They decided to walk from the railway station to the ferry building. The next boat wasn't due to leave for an hour and the day was pleasant. As they started strolling along Beach Road towards the waterfront Stuart was conscious of her wish to discuss something important and, fearing the worst, attempted to engage her in conversation.

"How are your parents? How are they coping?"

She walked a few steps then stopped next to a small wall and frowned up at him. "Let's sit here, Stuart."

He sat down and placed her suitcase on the ground. She sat for a moment with her gloved hands in her lap and, without looking at him, began speaking.

"Ian's death has been a terrible shock for my parents. When the war stopped they thought he would be safe, which in a way makes it even worse. They'd had two brief letters from him after he embarked in which he sounded cheerful. His last one was a standard army postcard with a drawing of a Kiwi soldier sitting on a pile of sandbags, his helmet tipped back, wiping his brow, his rifle across his bare knees, grinning happily. On the top of the card it read, 'A Merry Christmas'. Along the bottom it read, '2nd New Zealand Expeditionary Force Middle East'".

"How come you know it so well?"

"I used to sit with it in front of me going over and over in my mind where he'd been when he sent it. Inside was a typically brief, hand-written message. Below the printed words 'Wishing you a Merry Christmas and a Happy New Year' he'd written 'Mum, Dad and Carol, from Ian.'"

"Taciturn Kiwi bloke, your brother."

She gave an elongated sigh.

"Yes, he is, er, was. The three of us nearly wore that card out, looking at it and handling it, knowing his hands had also been on it, way out there in the desert." She paused, sighed again and glanced down at her feet. "You've no idea, Stuart, how much I've grown to hate the Germans. They've killed my brother and now they've taken over my country."

"Tell me about it."

"I'm upset at what's happened to our country, but the effect on my parents has been absolutely devastating. All their hopes and dreams were wrapped up in Ian and now," her voice faltered, "and now he's gone."

"I suppose," said Stuart quietly, "you feel inadequate."

She looked up swiftly. "Inadequate? What do you mean?"

"You feel that apart from offering your warmth and sympathy there's nothing tangible you can actually do to compensate for the loss of your brother, their son."

She held his gaze for a moment and then glanced away.

"Stuart they've asked me to promise to do something that would make them both very happy." Her eyes blinked nervously. "Something that would give them some hope for the future."

Stuart felt his stomach turn over.

"They said it would help them to overcome their grief – something they have both wanted for years." She took a breath. "They want me to marry Hamish".

Although his mind was reeling he kept his voice to a monotone. "What did you say?"

"Stuart, my parents owe a great deal to Hamish and his father. Ever since he started taking me out they assumed one day we would be together permanently. For them, Ian, their son was the more important of their two children. He was the one who always got priority and was always praised for everything he achieved. All they wanted for me was that I would make a good marriage – to Hamish."

"What did you say?" he repeated bleakly.

"What could I say? They're both in a dreadful state so I had very little choice."

An army truck full of New Order soldiers rattled past. Stuart stared at it unseeingly. When he spoke his voice was harsh. "So, what did you say?"

"I told them I'd agree to become engaged to Hamish. He had some important government business to do in Wellington so I made him let me come back earlier. Said I couldn't get any more time off work and I had to return. He was so delighted that I'd agreed to the engagement he let me go. He'll be travelling up here on Tuesday night."

Stuart's voice was still harsh. "When's the happy day?"

"Don't know. He's keen to get married as soon as possible but I said," her voice faltered, "I'd like to enjoy the engagement period."

"I'm sure it'll be an unforgettable experience."

She took his hand but he pulled it away.

132

"Try to understand, Stuart. I really had no choice. Mum and Dad would have been devastated if I'd refused."

He sat staring silently ahead.

"Stuart, we can still be friends."

His thoughts swirled. 'Engaged' wasn't 'married' and Hamish was still in Wellington. He breathed deeply and looked at her, the woman he now believed he loved. With a major effort he smiled and touched her gently on the arm. "Of course we can. Now tell me, what do your parents think about the surrender?"

Looking uncertain for a moment she then took her cue. "Oh, Dad wants to try to survive. He thinks the New Order will provide them with a reasonable, safe standard of living as long as we all..."

"Keep our heads down."

"Yes. He keeps saying that. Maybe it helps him make sense of Ian's death. Mum, I'm sure doesn't agree with him although she hasn't said as much. I know she'll never get over the anger, hurt and pain. Deep down she really hates the Germans for killing her son."

"I'm sure that view's shared by thousands in this country. In spite of the best efforts of the New Order, the hatred will continue."

"Yes, but Dad's got a point. We're not being too downtrodden." She saw his frown. "What I mean is we're not being turned into slaves."

"True. But there are various forms of slavery. There's slavery of the body and slavery of the mind. And, as this morning's little incident shows, we're all walking a fine line. While I was sitting in that chair in the Stationmaster's Office I realized not one person tried to interfere or even protest. Schroeder, who'd obviously been hitting the bottle, was insulting not only me but all the other Kiwis. But everybody just stood there."

"You're partly right, Stuart, but only partly. I heard the shouting and couldn't believe it was you. I did hear people around me muttering angrily but, of course, you never know who's listening, especially in a crowded public place."

Suddenly reaching out, she seized his arm in a tight grip.

"You have no idea how I felt when I saw it was you being beaten up. I called your name but the German was yelling so he didn't hear. A man next to me put his hand on my arm and said, 'Careful, love, you'll only make things worse.' So I just stood there, biting my lip to stop myself shouting again."

Stunned by the news of the engagement, Stuart was unsure how to react. "It was a dreadful moment for both of us. But it's over now and I suppose you're keen to get home to Aunt Catherine's." He stood up. "Now, come on, or we'll miss the ferry."

The mellow sound of the *Kestrel*'s whistle echoed round the wharves and the ferry building as it moved out into the stream past the cargo ships at their berths. The cranes were busily transferring their cargoes from wharf to ship, assisted by teams of wharfies. The wharves were full and there were more ships anchored in the stream waiting to disgorge their cargoes and fill their holds with wool, butter and meat. The work was plentiful for the full-time wharfies and the casual labourers (the 'seagulls') like Stuart and his fellow students who earned good casual money loading and unloading the ships. Nevertheless, during the morning and afternoon 'smokos' he had heard dark mutterings from the old hands who had been used to working in a strongly unionized environment. Not only had it provided them with excellent working conditions but also ensured they had a major say in the operation of the country's waterfronts. All the workers knew one of Hitler's first actions on taking power in Germany was to abolish all unions and to make strikes and work stoppages illegal. It was rumoured the same process would be imposed in New Zealand. Some were content that their working conditions were largely unchanged and their wage packets, due to plentiful overtime, were increasing in size. Others were concerned at the implications of being on the losing side, seeing their government replaced and their unions abolished.

The sun was beginning to set as Stuart and Carol sat down outside the main cabin on the long slatted seats. Silently they watched the passing panorama of ships, docks, cranes, small waves and wheeling gulls.

The rattle by his right ear startled him. A teenage boy with a black air force-style cap on his head and a gleaming white diagonal canvas band across the front of his black shirt, stood rattling a collection box. The belt that held up the boy's black shorts was highly polished and bore the motto 'Sure and Steadfast'.

"I'm collecting for the Soldiers Relief Fund, sir. Your support would be appreciated by the authorities." Clearly the boy had learned the patter off by heart.

"Soldiers Relief Fund? That's a new one. What soldiers? What relief?" Stuart was annoyed by the interruption and by the reference to the authorities.

"I think it's something to do with the New Zealand volunteers fighting on the Eastern Front in Russia. I read something on the way up in the papers," said Carol.

"Correct right, madam," answered the boy with a smile. "The brave soldiers fighting the Communists: the enemies of all the people."

"You said 'Relief Fund'". Why do they need relief?"

"They need some nice things to eat and, you know, presents on their birthdays and at Christmas. The brave soldiers are fighting on our behalf." He rattled his collection box again. "Your support would be appreciated by the authorities."

"Jesus, son are you some sort of trained parrot or something?"

Stuart felt Carol's elbow in his ribs as she smiled at the boy. "Your uniform? Isn't it the Boys Brigade? My brother Ian was in the 11th Wellington at our local church."

"Yes, madam," replied the boy politely. "We are being re, um, reconstituted as part of the New Order. The government is granting us extra money. They said they liked our black uniforms so they won't be making any changes and they have given us extra medals to earn. Look," he went on proudly, "I was presented with a new one at last week's church parade." He stepped towards Stuart and bent down to show the medal on the end of a ribbon, pinned to his chest. "It's the Model Citizen Award."

"What did you have to do to earn that?" asked Stuart, forcing himself to sound pleasant.

"I accurately informed my section leader about some seditious talk I heard from one of my teachers at Takapuna Grammar School."

"Good God..." began Carol. This time she was the recipient of a jab in the ribs.

"Very commendable," said Stuart, smiling encouragingly. "What did the teacher do?"

"It was in history class. He told us that Napoleon's Grand Army perished in the snows of Russia, and the same thing could be happening to our volunteers."

"And what did you do?"

"I told our section leader who told the authorities."

"And?"

"The teacher was severely, er, reprimanded. And I received this new badge."

The boy stood closer so Stuart could view the badge more easily in the fading light. It depicted the head of a boy looking earnestly upward. Underneath was written 'Model Citizen'. The head and the motto were encased in a laurel wreath. A chill ran through Stuart. At the base of the wreath was a small swastika.

"Well done, son," he said, digging in his pocket. "Here, thruppence for your fund."

"Thank you, sir." The boy sprang to attention and nodded his head briskly at Stuart who felt increasing discomfort at the guileless boy's news, and the awkward replica of the German colonel's gesture made earlier in the day.

As the boy moved on with his rattle and his patter, Stuart slumped forward resting his elbows on his knees. "Christ, Carol. And there are Kiwis telling each other that if we keep our heads down everything will be OK." He sat up and turned towards her.

"You know, for a while I've been hoping, stupidly, things may get better but you heard that kid in the pseudo-fascist uniform. And he's in the bloody Boys Brigade!"

"Were you ever a member?"

"My parents sent me but I didn't like it. It was Bible Class on the parade ground – heaps of drilling and saluting. I would have preferred the Boy Scouts but it didn't have a sufficiently religious content for my parents. So it was either 'Onward Christian soldiers' or nothing. But I can see the attraction of the black uniforms for our new masters. Very clever tactic. Maintain the semblance of business as usual to lull the masses into compliance and then, through the existing systems, implement the New Order of Model Citizens." He sat bolt upright and his voice rose in an imitation of a citation reader. "On behalf of the Boys Brigade I award you the Most Excellent Order of the Juvenile Automatons!"

"Stuart, please keep your voice down."

"Exactly! 'Keep your voice down' – the new mantra of our new guardians of the New Order. But," and he gesticulated with an outstretched hand as though addressing an assembled multitude, "if we don't keep our voices down and our heads down, we may have to start re-locating."

He paused, lowered his hand. His voice was barely audible above the sound of the waves and the throbbing engines. "Perhaps underground."

Turning unsmilingly towards Carol he took both her hands in his and studied her face. She made no attempt to pull away. His voice was soft. "Carol, beautiful girl, I believe I love you more than I thought it was possible to love anyone. I know you're engaged to Hamish but we both know you don't love him. I understand you're deeply concerned about your parents, but in the end, in the final analysis, it's your life. If you settle for second best, you'll regret it forever."

Reaching up with her right hand Carol put her fingers to his lips. Her eyes were wet. "Stuart. I'm sorry. It's too complex. I have to go ahead with my promise to my parents. I know you don't fully understand, and I don't blame you. Maybe one day you will. But in the meantime I really want us to remain friends and keep talking to each other."

He grunted cynically.

"Look, let's meet on Tuesday for lunch. We can talk some more."

Letting go of her other hand he turned away.

"Please, Stuart."

He glanced back at her and managed a slight smile.

"OK. Tuesday. In the meantime I'll make my motto '*nil bastardo carborundum*'."

"What on earth does that mean?"

As the ferry began docking at the Devonport wharf he stood up. "Never let the bastards grind you into the ground."

Chapter 19

"There's to be a meeting of the departmental heads, tomorrow."

"Oh," responded Stuart, surprised at the abruptness of the statement. He had just dropped into Professor Sterling's office for a chat but dispensing with his usual warm greeting, the professor had looked up from his desk, regarded his young colleague bleakly and then barked out the information. After a long pause Stuart asked tentatively, "Is it an important meeting?"

"Yes. We knew it was coming but it's still a shock when it happens. Here. Read for yourself."

To: All Heads of Department
From: The President, Auckland University College
Subject: Extraordinary Meeting
Date: 28th November 1941

Colleagues

The new Ministry of Education and Culture has instructed us to convene an extraordinary meeting to receive a presentation from their representatives regarding what they term "New Order Regulations governing tertiary curriculum and delivery processes".

I strongly suspect that this meeting will be the beginning of the curtailment of those areas of academic freedom that we have hitherto taken for granted. It is therefore vital that all Heads of Department are present.

The meeting will be held at 10:00am. We have been instructed that no other meeting is to be convened prior to this one. I interpret this as being an attempt to prevent us from planning any initiatives prior to their presentation. After consideration I have decided to comply with the request. However, this should not of course prevent you from consulting with your colleagues over the next 24 hours. Please feel free to contact this office to discuss the matter further with me. However, I advise you against using the internal phone system for anything other than mundane administrative matters.

Please ensure that your attendance at the meeting is punctual.

Breathing a long sigh Stuart handed the letter back. "I told you about the Boys Brigade boy I met on the ferry."

Sterling nodded. "Didn't take them long to move up the system. The Nazis bullied and intimidated their own universities into meek compliance. They regard any organization that encourages freethinking as the enemy. Therefore I'm not optimistic. However, I'd like you to accompany me to the meeting. I've discussed it with the President and he has agreed. You've researched this area extensively, been part of the Berlin delegation, and while there may not be much any of us can do, your perspective could be useful."

"Thank you, sir. I'm flattered."

"Don't be. I'm inviting you for your knowledge and insight, not for false flattery. Now, if you'll excuse me I need to prepare some documents for the meeting. Please arrange with Alice to make an appointment to come and see me tomorrow morning, some time before 10:00."

Bending over his desk, Sterling signalled the conversation was at an end. Stuart, at first a little put out by the older man's uncharacteristic abruptness, realized the news of the meeting was of great concern to him. With an increasing sense of unease he quietly exited to make an appointment with the departmental secretary.

The following morning the heads of department assembled in the main meeting room. The usual hearty greetings and good-natured banter was missing as they seated themselves in a double-L formation. At the top table the President Henry Cooke and Registrar Les Desmond, a recent appointee, sat grim faced, confining themselves to returning the occasional nod of acknowledgement. As requested, all had arrived punctually. Noting that everyone was present Desmond cleared his throat noisily. A hush fell over the room.

"Colleagues, thank you for your attendance." He indicated the three vacant chairs next to the President. "Our, er, visitors have not yet arrived. I suggest we give them a few more moments."

"Always thought fascists made a virtue of punctuality," murmured Joseph Goldman, head of the Philosophy Department, a little louder than he intended.

President Henry Cooke, a humourless, puritanical man who regarded his position as being of the utmost importance to the university, looked up sharply at the comment.

"Could I suggest, colleagues, we avoid confrontational comments such as that? We are the first university college to be visited by representatives from the newly constituted," he glanced at his notes and barely concealed his distaste, "Ministry of Education and Culture. Consequently we will be establishing precedents here that will have a major effect on academic life throughout our country. The process will require reasoned argument and considerable diplomacy. We need to be able to show these people that the continuation of a healthy and vibrant university sector is an asset to this nation and its aspirations."

A low murmur punctuated by some suppressed derisory snorts greeted the final sentence.

"What the President is stressing…" began the Registrar helpfully.

Sharply interrupting the younger man Cooke said, "What I am stressing is that we will do our utmost to retain our integrity and our academic freedom..."

"As critic and conscience of society, Henry?" The speaker was the snowy-haired Professor Don Wilson, head of the English Department, a former All Black and Rhodes Scholar.

Over the past six years the President had been embroiled in a number of controversies involving academic freedom. He shifted uneasily. "I am hopeful..."

His secretary entered the room and murmured in his ear. He stood and turned to greet the three visitors. The first, a tall grey-haired man, was dressed in a neatly tailored lounge suit. The second brought a gasp from the meeting – his uniform was entirely black except for a red Nazi armband on his right sleeve. In his gloved hand he held a high peaked cap, encircled by a metallic braiding underneath a death's head badge and a German eagle. The third man, who carried a grey homburg hat in his hand, was dressed in the civilian garb of the security police. Once they were seated the President nervously turned to his assembled colleagues.

"Er, ah, gentlemen, may I introduce," he glanced at the piece of paper that had been thrust in his hand, "Dr Hans Schulze, Colonel Ludwig Stubbendorf and Mr. Hamish Beavis."

At the sight of Hamish Beavis, Stuart sat rigid with astonishment. Sterling had earlier pointed out that the new German rulers, facing a manpower shortage, would have to maximize their use of the local population to implement the New Order. He had heard that a number of locals were now working in key positions for the new authorities, but Hamish Beavis! He looked at Professor Sterling who was staring open-mouthed at the new trio.

"That's Hamish Beavis, sir!" he whispered.

"I realize that," muttered the professor. "But I'd be far more concerned about his uniformed companion. With men like von Stauffenberg there was some hope. But if the Gestapo begins to gain more power…" his voice tailed off as the trio seated themselves.

The President, his voice betraying his nervousness, interrupted him. "Dr Schulze has asked to address us. He is then prepared to answer any questions you may have." He resumed his seat as the German academic rose and shuffled his notes.

"Gentlemen," he began in softly accented English. "I will be brief and to the point. It is the intention of our new government, your new government, to maintain the role of the university colleges as the primary places of learning."

There was a murmur of assent from some of the staff. Others, filled with foreboding at the presence of the Gestapo officer, remained silent.

"However, there will be some changes. We need to ensure university colleges will implement and maintain programmes which support the government in its efforts to build a new nation founded on the principles of National Socialism. A programme that will be of benefit to all New Zealanders, and not just those few who are privileged to study or work at the nation's universities."

Schulze paused, coughed and shuffled his papers. "As part of this process we will be establishing an Academic Values Authority. This Authority will be under the control of the new Ministry of Education and Culture. It will have the ultimate responsibility for the subject matter taught in all New Zealand universities." He paused and his eyes swept the utterly silent room. "This will include all the reading material that supports the subject matter."

There was a collective gasp from the listening academics.

Looking up, the President made an effort to maintain his self-control. "What will be your role, doctor and the role of your two colleagues?"

The German paused and his eyes again panned the room. "Oberst, that is, Colonel Stubbendorf will be part of the team responsible for the smooth," he paused, seeking the appropriate word and then smiled. "Yes, smooth implementation of the new changes."

"Smooth implementation, doctor? I do not understand."

"Perhaps I can explain, Herr Doctor, with your permission," responded the black-uniformed colonel rising to his feet. "It has been our experience in a number of universities, including those in Germany, that some students have deliberately engaged in unpatriotic acts designed to discredit or even undermine the country's lawful government." His dark eyes swept the room. "It will be my role to support the Academic Values Authority and to ensure all students, and staff," a momentary smiled flickered across his pale features, "cooperate with us for the greater good of the New Order."

Visibly shocked, the President sat quite still. A voice from the back of the room asked, "And what about the third member of your group. What's his role in this glorious New Order?"

The Gestapo colonel's eyes moved to those of the questioner. "What is your name and position?"

"Professor Joseph Goldman, Head of the Philosophy Department," replied the questioner, a little too loudly.

"Professor Joseph Goldman." The colonel paused and then repeated both names with careful emphasis. "Interesting."

He put the tips of his gloved fingers together, nodded to Hamish and then faced the group.

"Mr. Beavis is a financial expert. He will oversee the financial conduct of this university – to ensure it receives the appropriate funds to enable it to continue to operate and," the gloved hands pushed themselves more tightly together, "to ensure those academic staff who support the University Values Authority continue to receive... er..."

He glanced at Hamish.

"Appropriate remuneration, sir," came the prompt response.

"*Genau*, exactly."

Professor Sterling broke the silence that followed. "What qualifications does Mr. Beavis have for this crucial position?"

Stubbendorf glared at Sterling.

"And your name, sir?" he inquired.

"Professor David Sterling, Head of the History Department."

"'David'. Interesting." Another pause and another smile. "Mr. Beavis, who was flown up especially from Wellington this morning, has two qualifications. The first, a thorough knowledge of financial matters. The second?" He turned to Hamish. "You tell them, Herr Beavis."

Hamish scrambled to his feet.

"Of course, Colonel."

He touched the small badge on his lapel.

"Yesterday," he began, "I was enrolled as a foundation member of the New Zealand National Socialist Party. I am looking forward to serving our Party and the nation's interests in my new role." His voice slowed. "I am also looking forward to ensuring the New Order is totally supported by the university." Stuart felt a crawling sensation as Hamish stared directly at him. "And each person in it."

Stuart felt his knee gripped hard. "Sit still and say nothing," murmured Professor Sterling.

Dr Schulze stood up again. "We have with us guidelines for the Academic Values Authority. Herr Cooke, you will arrange for them to be distributed to all departments. You are to discuss them with your staff members who will, in turn, discuss them with all your students."

He clicked his fingers and Hamish placed a small pile of papers in front of Henry Cooke.

"There will also be a series of twice-weekly meetings of your departmental heads with our representatives to discuss the immediate implementation of the guidelines. Be good enough to arrange the first one for this Thursday, at 10 o'clock."

Drawing himself momentarily to attention, Schultz nodded his head, spun on his heels and, followed by his two colleagues, strode towards the door. At the doorway Hamish, the last of the trio, stopped and turned deliberately to face the assembled academics. Raising his right arm he pointed his index finger at Stuart. The sneer that spread across his face was accompanied by a slow, deliberate nodding of his head. As all eyes turned towards Stuart, Hamish gave a short sharp laugh and strode from the room.

CHAPTER 20

"Are you absolutely sure? I know you don't like him but I find it hard to believe."

"So did I at first when he came in with the German academic and the Gestapo Officer. But it was him all right."

They'd met in Albert Park for lunch and were seated under the trees near the band rotunda. The news that her fiancé had joined the Nazis had shaken Carol.

"Doesn't surprise me," continued Stuart. "You'll say I'm prejudiced against him and I am. But unfortunately he won't be the last. The Germans have taken over far more territory than they could ever have imagined, and in a comparatively short space of time. And they're still fighting the Russians on the eastern front. Consequently, to rule effectively, they're going to need the collaboration of a considerable proportion of the population."

"Still unbelievable that Hamish has become a Nazi."

"I saw it with my own eyes."

"Can the university do anything?"

"Apparently the President and some of the departmental heads met the president of the students' union an hour ago. They've arranged a protest rally for early tomorrow afternoon. Although most of them have finished their finals, the word's been put out. A big turnout is expected."

Carol sighed deeply and gazed down at the leaves scattered around the base of the bench.

"You OK?"

"Yes, I'm OK." She glanced up suddenly and for a long moment stared into his eyes.

"Stuart there's something you need to know about me."

"You're not perfect?" He grinned and leaned forward to touch her cheek but she drew back.

"No, I'm serious. I'm still coming to terms with Hamish becoming a Nazi but I need to tell you something about myself first"

"You can trust me, of course."

"There's more to it than that. After what you hear, you may change your mind about me."

He laughed, "Don't be – "

"No, Stuart." She put her fingers gently on his mouth, and seeing the intent look on her face he stopped smiling and squeezed her hand.

"OK. I'm listening."

She pulled her hand away from his and took a deep breath.

"As I told you, I've known Hamish for a long time."

"Yes."

"Both of our parents had been friends for years and so we saw a lot of each other. With the approval of my parents and his father he started taking me out when I was about sixteen. At first it was just fun, just friends, but then he started to get, well, romantic."

She looked away and Stuart grimaced at the thought.

"I didn't mind too much at first. A few kisses and cuddles were quite nice. But then he started becoming more demanding. Kept telling me he loved me and that if I loved him I wouldn't mind going, you know..."

"All the way."

"Yes. He kept on and on, telling me I didn't really care for him, that I was cold, I was unnatural. It went on for weeks."

"Obviously he preferred a subtle approach," murmured Stuart.

"In the end, one Saturday night when his father was out at some Rotary Club function, I finally agreed, just to stop him going on at me." She glanced up at him and then looked back at the ground, scuffling her feet through the leaves that had wafted

148

across the path. "I didn't really want to but he'd been going on for so long, and..."

"It's OK, Carol. Don't upset yourself." He reached for her hand but she pulled away.

"Yes, but you still don't understand. There's more. You see we did *it*. He was satisfied but me, I was left frightened and, um, humiliated, by the whole process." She grimaced and shuddered. "I didn't enjoy it at all."

"Not surprising, under the circumstances. Still it's all over."

"Listen to me, Stuart!" She was becoming distressed but was determined to carry on. She looked him straight in the face. "I got pregnant straight away. From that one time."

"Oh. Bad luck," he murmured, instantly realizing the inadequacy of the response.

"Hamish was furious. He hit me, and called me a stupid cow and then insisted on informing my parents. He told me that although it was my fault he would stand by me."

Shaken by the unexpected news, and not knowing how the story would unfold, Stuart sat staring at her. Neither of them spoke and then, feeling he had to say something, Stuart asked, "What did your parents say?"

"My father was furious. He took Hamish's side and then he asked my mother if she could do anything."

"'Do anything'?"

"Yes, you know, get rid of it."

"Jesus! An abortion? What say someone had reported you to the police?"

"I was too upset to worry about that or to know what to do. Money was no object and my mother knew a woman who was prepared to do it so I was taken to her." She started to shake. "God, Stuart, it was sordid and horrible."

Heedless of the curious stares of passers by, Stuart wrapped his arms around her murmuring, "It's OK. I'm here. It'll be all right."

Her shaking gradually subsided, and she looked up at him with tears in her eyes. "Now, you see what sort of woman I am. Hamish had this terrible hold over me. I had a secret and he had the power to reveal it. Every time I did something to annoy him he would remind me that although he'd stood by me no other man would want me after what had happened. I was too worried about what he said to talk to anyone. Neither my parents nor Hamish's father ever mentioned it again, just carried on as if nothing happened; except that Mum and Dad were both especially nice to Hamish because of the way he'd stood by me."

Feeling Stuart's intake of breath she pressed on. "I felt I was soiled goods. We continued going out together but I did make it quite clear I'd never do *it* again unless we were married. And I've stuck to it, even though it's continued to cause tension between us." She paused, sighed and then tentatively said, "That's the full story. I've never told anyone else."

She stopped talking and buried her head in the lapel of his blazer. Stuart knew she was waiting for his reaction and it would be crucial to her and to their relationship. He took a deep breath and exhaled.

"Whew. Now I understand why you agreed to the engagement. Your brother's death added to the considerable pressure you'd been under for months from your family and Hamish."

"Stuart, there's one more thing."

"More?" He was unable to keep the tension out of his voice.

"Yes." She went quiet for a long moment and buried her face deeper into his lapel so he had to strain to hear her next words. "As the result of the abortion, I won't be able to have any children."

His spontaneous laughter took her by surprise. "Children! Nothing could be further from my mind. It's you I love, Carol. And in any case, if we want children in the future, we'll adopt them. Orphanages are full of kids looking for a good home!"

150

He was conscious that she was perfectly still. "But," he felt her tense, "it does have a happy ending."

"Oh?" she said in a small voice.

"Yes, you found me and I found you. What could be happier than that?"

Reaching down he gently took her by the shoulders and turned her to face him.

"Carol, thank you for telling me. Thank you for trusting me. It makes no difference to me. I loved you before you told me and I love you now. Even more."

CHAPTER 21

He was early for the function and, not wishing to be the first to arrive, parked his car in a side street and switched off the engine. It was raining heavily and the dusk sky was darkening. He lit a cigarette and sat staring unseeingly at the watery patterns streaming across his front windscreen.

The scene was still vivid in his mind. She'd stood by the door with her suitcase at her feet, staring down at him.

"Sorry, Hamish," she'd said, "but I never really wanted you."

His father's grip had tightened on his shoulder stopping him from going to her.

"You'll understand when you get older," she continued. "But I've got a chance to lead my own life and I'm taking it."

A car horn had sounded from the street outside and she jerked round.

"It's that bastard, isn't it?" His father's voice was hoarse.

She shuffled and then smiled without warmth. "Takes one to know one, Dave."

Struggling against his father's grip, Hamish had stretched out his arms towards her. Looking into his eyes, she pressed her hand to her mouth to cover a spontaneous intake of breath. She stood still for a moment and then she shook her head.

"Sorry, Hamish. I've no choice." And she was gone.

Bewildered, he looked up at his father seeking an explanation or a word of comfort, but the man stood staring fixedly at the closed front door.

"Bitch!" he snarled. Then he looked down at his seven-year-old son. "Don't ever forget it, Hamish. Like all women, your mother's a no good bitch!"

That night he went to bed and lay quietly sobbing. Eventually his father came in and stood awkwardly by his bedside – he was never comfortable with tears. The aroma of alcohol was stronger than usual.

"Stop your crying, son" he commanded quietly. "She's not worth it. We're both better off without her."

He touched his son briefly on the top of the head and turned abruptly away.

Throughout the rest of his childhood and into his teenage years his father's sentiments were conveyed to him on a regular basis. Once or twice he'd tried to seek an explanation but his father refused to comment further other than to repeat his derogatory comments about his wife and women in general. In the Fourth Form he first heard the term 'shotgun wedding' and realized it applied to his parents and him.

He'd never heard from his mother again.

He was bright at school, especially in mathematics, and his father's approval at his scholastic success was some compensation for the constant emptiness that stayed with him into his teenage years.

Growing up in the 1930s Depression had not been as harsh an existence for him as it had been for many other children whose fathers were on relief pay at work camps. His father's construction business built up during the prosperous 1920s had expanded into a number of hardware shops. Although the profits from all branches of the business had slowed considerably, there was still sufficient to provide Hamish and his father with a comfortable living.

Other men such as his father's friend Fred Peterson were not quite so fortunate. By 1934 all the savings he had lived on since the stock market collapse had vanished and in desperation he had come to Dave Beavis for help. Beavis was first and foremost a businessman. The Petersons had a freehold house and he agreed to make an interest-only loan to his friend in return for a half share in the property. He also insisted the

Petersons develop a household budget and that regular meetings be held between the two men to monitor the cash flow.

From Hamish's teenage years his father had begun to instruct him in the workings of the business and the boy soon gained the ability to read columns of figures and to understand the factors that contributed towards financial success. Pleased with the boy's progress his father took him to the regular meetings with Fred Peterson and eventually, with the other man's agreement, gave Hamish the full responsibility for handling Peterson's financial affairs. As the New Zealand economy began a slow recovery Hamish, who had left school and was working as a trainee manager in his father's firm, suggested investing some of Peterson's money. When it began to show a steady return the man was deeply grateful.

During his initial visits to the Peterson home Hamish had shown little interest in their daughter Carol. However, when he was invited to her 16th birthday party and saw her dressed in a flowing red frock he was stunned by her beauty. In spite of the increasing success of his financial career he was awkward around women and the few times he'd managed to take them out had left him feeling angry at his inability to communicate easily with them. His clumsy efforts at petting had been equally unsuccessful leaving him frustrated and resentful, especially when the other young men in the firm boasted of their conquests.

His initial approaches to Carol were met with a coy response. She appeared flattered by the attention of an older man and her parents in their turn, still mindful of the financial advice and assistance provided by Hamish and his father, enthusiastically encouraged the relationship. The pair began going out on a regular basis to the movies and the occasional party. The envious looks other men threw in his direction pleased him. Other men desired her but Carol was his…almost.

The longing to possess her physically became an obsession with him and although she tolerated his initial fumblings in her underclothes, she always pushed him away when she felt his urgency. This only served to increase his frustration and he began to accuse her of being cold and frigid.

Finally, on a night when his father had gone out to a business function, he persuaded her to come to his bedroom. There he took her roughly and rapidly. Her cries of pain only served to feed his excitement and at the end he obtained almost as much enjoyment from exerting a final dominance over her as he did from the flood of pleasure that relieved his frustration.

When he pushed himself up from on top of her, the pain and the fear in her eyes only served to rekindle his desire and he took her again, oblivious to her renewed sobs of protest. Finally exhausted and satiated, he sat in a chair and smoked as he watched her hobble to the bathroom.

For the next few weeks she strongly resisted his advances, but one evening when she phoned and asked him to meet her he felt an instant arousal. However, the revelation that she was pregnant infuriated him and he insisted his father and her parents be informed. Hamish had soon realized that in her parent's eyes, Ian was the favourite of the two children. Although they were proud of their attractive daughter they regarded her beauty as an advantage in their goal of having her married and settled as soon as possible so they could concentrate all their resources on assisting Ian to build a career. Hamish correctly counted on them being angry at their daughter for spoiling their carefully laid plans. He felt a smug satisfaction at her distress when it was clear in parental eyes she was cast as the guilty party – the fallen woman who had betrayed their trust.

He felt no remorse at the decision to arrange an abortion. He didn't want Carol and a child – he just wanted Carol. When it was over, he refused to discuss it with her. He began to attempt to resume their relationship, with full parental support. Although she accompanied him without protest to the pictures or on trips to the beach in his near new Morris 8, she became increasingly moody and non-communicative and shied away whenever he tried to touch her. His anger and frustration only fuelled his desire to possess her – permanently.

The offer from the New Order government was a lucrative one. He'd been initially approached by a newly formed New Zealand Nazi Party official as a suitable candidate for Party membership that included an offer of a powerful senior financial position within the new government. His father, after some misgivings, acquiesced to Hamish's wish and agreed to put a new manager into the Newmarket branch of the firm. Hamish's new position delighted him. It not only provided him with a generous salary and expense account, but also meant he would be operating from a defined power base that would give him financial oversight of the nation's university colleges. His first priority would be Auckland University College. He smiled at the prospect.

Carol's agreement to the engagement had not been as enthusiastic as he would have wished and he suspected she was still hankering after Stuart Johnson. He'd discussed Johnson with several new colleagues in the security police and had been assured the new Patriotic Laws gave them sweeping powers to deal with troublemakers, particularly if identified by senior Party officials. Winding down the car window he flicked his cigarette butt into the rain. It was all too easy. He'd seen the shock on Johnson's face at the university meeting that morning. He'd allow a little time for the sweat of fear to intensify and then order the man's arrest.

Once Johnson was disposed of he would be able to take the ultimate step in his goal of possessing Carol – marriage.

His immediate goals were in sight but he would enjoy the anticipation a little longer. Carol wasn't expecting him until the following day and tonight he'd been invited to a Party function to welcome new members. A German member had smilingly informed him the plentiful supplies of food, beer and wine would be supplemented by 'junge Mädchen'. He ran his tongue under his top lip, half-closed his eyes and felt a shudder of anticipation surge through him.

He turned on the key and reached for the starter button.

"Young girls. How young?" he wondered aloud.

CHAPTER 22

The rally of the university student union early the following afternoon started quietly. As the news of the previous day's meeting with the German officials spread throughout the university, students began to assemble in small groups in the quad, seeking further information and debating various courses of action. Opinions were divided about the meeting and its implications and consequently there was confusion as to how the student body should react. The small groups grew into a large, noisy crowd and voices became louder as each student sought to express their opinion above the increasing noise.

On one side of the quad a platform with microphone and a speaker had been set up in anticipation of the rally. At its base the Auckland University College Students Association committee members, their heads close together in a scrum-like formation, were debating their next move. One of them looked up at the increasing throng. Turning back to the group he addressed a tall redheaded youth.

"They don't know what's going on, Ned. Somebody'll have to say something and it has to be you."

Ned Cox shuffled uncomfortably. He had been Student President for a year and had revelled in the prestige that came with the office. Not only had he enjoyed running the meetings but also it had enabled him to mix with the academic staff. Furthermore it had given his love life a new impetus. Often he had fantasized about a glittering academic career once the war was over, but nothing had prepared him for this new turn of events. Yet, someone had to say something and as president it was his responsibility.

"OK. Not exactly sure what I'm going to say, but I'll give it a go."

The crowd grew quiet as he stepped onto the platform and approaching the microphone, nervously blew into it. He gazed at the sea of upturned faces and cleared his throat.

"Gentlemen," he began, and noticing some women students standing in a group on one side, added, "and ladies of course." He laughed nervously but the crowd remained silent. "Um, thank you for coming here today."

"It's not a bloody wedding, Ned!" shouted a voice from the back of the crowd. "Tell us what's going on!"

An affirmative roar galvanized Cox into action. He held up his hand.

"I don't know much more than you do. However I had a brief meeting with senior staff representatives about an hour ago. We have been informed our university college and every other one in the country will be placed under the control of some sort of Nazi committee called the Academic Council. This committee will have the power to decide what courses will be taught and what books will be used to teach these courses."

There was an immediate and angry roar of protest from the student crowd. Cox paused and ran his fingers through his hair. The day was cloudy and cool but he noticed his forehead was heavy with sweat. Again he held up his hand.

"This committee will also, I believe, have the final say regarding the employment of teaching staff. Those who don't support the New Order will lose their jobs and the committee will have the power to appoint their replacements."

"That's a total bloody takeover!" shouted a voice from the centre of the crowd. Echoing shouts of anger spread through the crowd that began to surge towards the platform. A chant of "No takeover!" radiated from the centre in rhythmic waves. Caught up by the vocal momentum, the student president began to echo the chant into the microphone and to beat time with his clenched fist.

At first the cries on the edge of the crowd were thought to be a variation of the chant but when they turned into screams all

159

heads turned and craned to see what was happening. The answer came swiftly and brutally. Several black police vans had suddenly arrived and disgorged their cargo of special police armed with batons. A flying wedge had driven straight into the group of female students smashing them aside and sending them sprawling. With well-practiced speed the wedge, accompanied by a chant of "Move! Move!" surged forward, their batons rising and falling in a grotesque rhythm on the unprotected heads of the tightly packed students. Instinctively the crowd turned to flee but in their panic many slipped and fell causing others to crash on top of them. The wedge flailed at those who were falling and as they fell, stood on their heads and limbs as it advanced towards the platform.

Nick Cox had no chance. From his vantage point he had seen the arrival of the special police and after a warning shout of "Get out of here!" had turned away towards the side of the platform. The shot that hit him in the small of the back echoed around the quad. Some students flung themselves to the ground. Others, heedless of their fellows, redoubled their efforts to escape. Within an astonishingly short space of time the scene had been totally transformed. The special police stood among an array of moaning, sprawling students too terrified to rise or unable to move due to broken limbs.

From the platform came a series of long, spine chilling screams from the student president who lay dying from the bullet lodged in the base of his spinal cord.

CHAPTER 23

Stuart emerged from behind the Old Choral Hall on the Symonds St side of the campus and signalled to Carol to stand still while he peered cautiously round the corner.

"All clear for the moment. Come on."

"You sure?"

"Yeah, It should be OK. I think I copped another cracked rib when that bastard hit me." He tried to take a deep breath and winced. "Getting to be a bit of a habit." He tried to smile reassuringly. "I'll be OK if I don't have to do any running."

"Good thing we were a bit late and wound up on the edge of the crowd."

"Yeah, but we're not out of the woods yet. Come on. We'll head downtown."

"OK, but get rid of your varsity blazer."

Hastily taking it off and removing his wallet and fountain pen, Stuart rolled the garment up and thrust it into a clump of bushes.

"Now take my hand, Stuart, and walk slowly. The authorities may decide to round up participants in the rally. If we're hand in hand, hopefully they'll ignore us."

Moving into Symonds Street they began walking at a leisurely pace. Groups of cyclists and the occasional car went past but there was no sign of any military vehicles.

For a while neither of them spoke. The brutal response to the rally and their dash through the university buildings had left them shaken, bewildered and angry. Finally Carol spoke.

"It's just getting worse and worse. Every day something new and awful happens."

"I know." He squeezed her hand. "And at the moment I don't have any answers. Those bastards back there..."

"Stuart, don't look round but there's some sort of vehicle coming up behind us."

He stopped walking and without looking back spun her round to face him. "It's an army motorcycle. Kiss me! Hard!" he commanded as he slid his right hand behind her head and drew her face towards his.

Wrapping her arms around him she responded instantly. The sound of the vehicle drew nearer and then slowed. Above the noise of the idling motor came a shout and a whistle. Stuart pulled his lips away from Carol's. "Smile," he whispered as he turned in the direction of the sound.

A motorcycle and sidecar had pulled up by the side of the pavement. A soldier wearing a German coalscuttle helmet, with a rifle strapped to his back, was seated astride the bike. In the sidecar, wearing the distinctive high peaked hat and a death's head insignia above the braiding was a uniformed officer.

The soldier was brown skinned.

With a supreme effort Stuart managed what he hoped looked like a sheepish grin.

"Hullo," he said. The soldier grinned but the officer remained stern. "You two anything to do with the university?"

Stuart heard Carol gasp at the New Zealand accent. He squeezed her hand warningly and shrugged.

"Us? University? Hell no." He laughed and glanced fondly at Carol. "Anyway got better things to do with my time. Why? What's the problem?"

"A few nancy boy students kicking up a fuss. Bastards don't know when they're well off. Anyway the specials fixed them. We're helping out, scouting for troublemakers. Where are you two going?"

"My girlfriend and I have been visiting some friends in Grafton. We're walking down to the waterfront to catch the Devonport ferry."

"Known each other for long?"

162

Clinging to Stuart's right arm Carol smiled beguilingly. "Sorry if we're not supposed to be kissing in the street. My fault, officer, it's such a lovely day and I just couldn't help myself."

Both men gazed at her with undisguised admiration. Looking directly at the soldier she murmured, "That's a lovely big motor cycle. I bet it can go fast."

"Yeah, she's a beauty, eh?" He twisted the throttle and the engine roared. "That's enough, corporal," ordered the officer. "Sorry, sir," he replied, as he throttled back, but his grin remained.

Stuart noticed the officer's right hand collar bore the distinctive double S flashings. The upper left hand sleeve of the officer's field grey Waffen SS uniform featured an insignia of an eagle with wings spread, clutching a circular badge in its claws. Inside the circle was a silver fern intertwined with the Nazi cross. Around the lower sleeve was a cuff band embroidered with 'New Order New Zealand'.

With a start Stuart noticed the officer was staring at him. "Just admiring your uniform," he said quickly. "Looks a hell of a lot better than boring khaki."

"Yeah. I like it. We both joined up last week. The new government's offering generous wages and conditions, notably for Kiwis with combat experience."

"Combat experience?"

"Yeah. Me and Corporal Herewini fought with the Eighth Army in the western desert against Rommel's men. Now we're wearing their uniform. Funny, eh?" Although he smiled Stuart sensed the man was gauging his reaction.

"*C'est la guerre,*" he shrugged.

"Sure you're not one of those bloody students?" asked the officer.

"No," replied Stuart. He grinned and shrugged. "I dropped out in the bloody Fourth Form. It's just a French saying of my Dad's. It means, 'that's war'".

"OK," grunted the officer. "Needed to be sure."

Suppressing a sigh of relief Stuart smiled reassuringly at Carol who squeezed his arm tighter.

"Our regiment is looking for good men. The pay's generous, training's exciting and there's an opportunity to go overseas and fight the communists on the Eastern Front."

The soldier murmured something to the officer and he nodded. "Sorry, we'd better get going. We've got a new recruitment station at the Chief Post Office."

He nodded to the soldier who, grinning at Carol, twisted his throttle and called, "Bye, sweetheart!" before engaging the engine and roaring off down the road.

The two of them stood on the kerb and waved. As the machine disappeared down the hill Carol buried her face in Stuart's chest. He wrapped his arms around her and felt her trembling. "It's OK", he said. "They've gone. You were great."

"So were you." Her voice was muffled. "I don't know how we managed after what we've just seen."

"True."

"First Hamish and now those two; and they were in the Eighth Army with Ian." She looked up at him. "Is everyone joining the Germans?"

"I don't think so. But it's more common than most people realize. My research and the translations Brendan did from German war documents showed us that most of the occupied nations formed Waffen SS regiments that fought with the Germans – the Dutch, Norwegians, French, Belgians, even Bosnian Muslims."

"Yet I didn't think our boys would be like that."

"Early days yet. After today's behaviour the New Order government may start to have some difficulty recruiting Kiwis into its ranks."

CHAPTER 24

At Carol's insistence Stuart accompanied her on the bus to Aunt Catherine's in Milford.

"She's a nursing sister. You need expert advice on your ribs with no awkward questions."

"But won't she find it a bit odd, you turning up with a complete stranger with suspected cracked ribs?"

"You won't be a complete stranger. I've talked about my very good university friend Stuart from time to time. And you've spoken to her on the phone, remember." She smiled. "She'll be delighted to meet you.

Aunt Catherine's welcome was indeed warm.

"So you're Stuart. Very pleased to meet you, young man."

Stuart entered the tidy three-bedroom bungalow and was ushered into the lounge.

"I've just lit a fire. Still chilly once the sun goes down," Aunt Catherine explained.

"Stuart had a bit of an accident earlier today, Auntie. He thinks he might have damaged his ribs."

"Indeed," said her aunt adopting a professional tone. "I shall need to examine you, Stuart. In the spare bedroom at the end of the hall there's a dressing gown. If you'd like to remove your shirt and singlet and slip into the dressing gown, I'll conduct the examination here, by the fire."

Two minutes later Stuart returned wearing a large winter dressing gown.

"Good. Now, young man, come and stand over here by the fire and let's have a look at you.

Stepping forward he loosened the gown to expose his chest. Carol reached over and ran the tips of her fingers over it. "Mm. He has got a nice hairy chest, hasn't he, Aunt Catherine?"

"Carol, really!" responded her aunt in mock horror. "Out of the way. This is strictly a medical matter. Go and make each of us a generous cup of cocoa. Now, Stuart, stop grinning at Carol and show me how deeply you can breathe."

Beginning to draw a slow breath Stuart winced in pain.

"Hm," said Aunt Catherine, feeling methodically around his chest and rib area. "You haven't been coughing blood or anything like that, have you?"

"No. I'm OK talking and breathing. It's when I take deep breaths."

"A cracked rib or two is probably all it is. Some medical people swathe the patient in bandages but the more modern approach is to leave the ribs to heal themselves." She frowned with mock severity. "As long as the patient does not indulge in activities of a vigorous or violent nature. Now, Carol, let's have some cocoa."

Sitting by the fire sipping their cocoa, Stuart and Carol described in detail to the horrified Miss Mason, the savage police attack on the students.

"So," concluded Stuart, "we wound up here." He nodded to Aunt Catherine. "Carol was insistent I come and be checked out by an expert."

"You're most welcome, young man. But what an appalling story. Your Hamish joining the Nazis, Carol, and the police attacking unarmed students. Is this the way things are going to be in New Zealand from now on?"

"It looks that way, Miss Mason," said Stuart. "But I for one am not prepared to accept it as being inevitable."

"So what's to be done?"

"I'm not sure. I'll go to varsity early tomorrow morning and see if anything else has happened and then," he looked across at Carol, "we can decide what to do after that. We may find our options are limited. What we don't want to do is rush blindly into some action that will result in our being locked away."

166

Aunt Catherine nodded, then after a thoughtful pause, yawned. "Now, you young people will want some time together, so I'm off to bed. The guest room's all made up, Stuart, and I hope you'll be comfortable."

"I'm sure I will be," he said, "and thank you again for your hospitality."

Earlier Stuart had rung his parents explaining he was staying with a university friend in the city and was now facing the delightful prospect of having Carol all to himself. He glanced at her and smiled. As the door of Aunt Catherine's bedroom closed Carol slid off her chair and on to the rug in front of the fire.

"Come and sit here, Stuart," she said. "We've both had a tough day."

Within moments he was beside her. Snuggling up to him, she slid her hand inside his dressing gown and began to stroke his chest as he kissed her deeply. As their heads drew back she smiled.

"Hmmm, I was right. You have got a lovely hairy chest," she murmured. They kissed again and his excitement mounted.

"God, you're lovely, Carol," he murmured.

She sighed and resting her head back on his chest, gazed at the flickering flames.

"I've got a lot to think about, Stuart. I promised my parents I'd marry Hamish," she shrugged, "and I also promised Hamish. I'm still wearing his engagement ring."

"But, the man's a Nazi. He's not only betrayed his country but he's also lied to you, his fiancée, by not telling you of his intentions – not to mention everything else he's put you through."

"You're right, Stuart, I suppose..."

"No 'suppose' about it! You owe him nothing. You know I love you, and I know you have strong feelings for me, so..."

He felt the tips of her fingers on his lips.

"Promise me something, Stuart."

"Of course."

"Give me a little more time to think it through."

"Time is something we don't have a lot of, Carol. Events are moving very fast."

"I know that. Just give me a couple of days. Please?"

Her face was turned up towards him. Reaching forward he slid his right hand gently under her chin.

"I need a small favour in return," he murmured.

"How small?"

"Very small. Just kiss me again."

Her reply was to lift her face up towards his. Her mouth was soft and yielding and when his tongue found hers they both murmured in pleasure. Gently she pulled away from him and put her head on his chest. He could feel her trembling.

"Carol, surely you and I..."

Her voice was soft but firm. "Stuart, you promised."

Although his long sigh was born of exasperation, he kissed the top of her head.

"OK. I did."

"I think we should both go to bed and, before you get any ideas, mister, you're sleeping in the spare room at the end of the hall. Now, kiss me goodnight."

Lifting her face again, she kissed him.

"Good night, Stuart." She touched his cheek and left the room.

He sat for a few minutes, staring at the dying fire. Then with a quiet smile he rose and made his way down the hallway. The door to Carol's room was closed and he walked quietly past allowing his imagination to dwell on the image of her face framed by her dark hair, resting on the white pillow.

For some time he lay in bed reviewing the events of the day and their implications. A final thought caused him to drift off to sleep with a smile on his face.

"I bet she never kissed Hamish the way she's kissed me."

Chapter 25

The following morning Stuart rose early. He had arranged to meet Professor Sterling later in the morning but was motivated by a need to revisit the familiar university grounds and try and come to terms with the previous day's events. Consequently he caught an early bus that linked him with the 6:30 ferry. In a quick discussion over breakfast Carol had agreed to meet him at lunchtime in Albert Park. She had no idea if Hamish would try to contact her but they decided the wisest course of action would be to go to work as usual.

No mention of the meeting or the brutal police response was contained in the radio news or in the *New Order Herald* the following morning. The authorities had decided to either ignore the event or bide their time before releasing the details with an appropriate interpretation.

Queen St was filling with the usual assortment of citizens making their way to work but due to the relatively early hour few people were about as he entered the university grounds by a path at the edge of the clock tower. Walking towards the back of the Old Choral Hall he glanced round for any sign of movement. Satisfied he was alone he walked over to the bushes where, the day before, he had thrust his blazer. It was still there and, although rather crumpled, appeared none the worse for wear.

Brushing it down he put it on and headed towards the centre of the complex. He stopped short. The length of the old barracks wall was covered in sheets of plywood to which had been attached large notices. He moved closer to the western end of the wall and began to read.

Attention all Staff and Students of the Auckland University College!

Yesterday an unfortunate incident took place at your institution. This incident was the result of the actions of a number of irresponsible student agitators. The authorities in responding swiftly to the incident have detained the President and several senior staff for questioning.

In the interim staff and students are to take note of the following rules that will be strictly enforced.

1. There will be no further meetings of students or staff without the express permission of the Academic Values Authority committee.

2. At any such meetings in the future a member of the Authority or their nominated representative will be present.

3. Effective immediately any staff or students deemed by the Authority to be engaging in any form of unpatriotic behaviour will face instant dismissal and a possible prison term.

In implementing these rules the New Order government reminds staff and students of the following:

The Auckland University College will continue to function as long as it supports the objectives of the New Order.

Those students and staff who adhere to the tenets of the New Order will be generously rewarded through bonus payments and enhanced promotional prospects.

The New Order invites all members of the Auckland University College to work to develop a stable and prosperous society whose benefits can be shared by all citizens.

Signed: Colonel Ludwig Stubbendorf
Security Advisor
Academic Values Authority

Looking down the line Stuart saw that each of the notice boards bore an identical message. He was about to turn away when he noticed something different on several of the notices near the far end of the wall. He moved closer. The top right hand corner of each one bore a large inked stamp. It featured a cartoon of a semi naked man draped across a swastika in a pose analogous to a crucifixion. Underneath was written:

Citizens! The choice is yours! Stop the oppression! Join Fightback!

Stuart gazed at the stamp in wonderment. Obviously there was some sort of resistance movement at work – a movement that must have known when the posters would be put up so they could move in during the night with their stamp. As he stood staring at the image he heard a footfall behind him. He spun round to see a young man whose face he had seen around the university.

"Here!" said the man as he thrust a pamphlet into Stuart's hand. "We will be in contact!"

The pamphlet appeared to have been hurriedly typed and produced on a Gestetner-type machine. When he looked up again the young man had gone. He stood there for a few moments trying to work out the implications of the poster, the young man, and the pamphlet he had hastily thrust into his pocket for later inspection.

Suddenly he remembered what the poster had said about senior staff being taken into custody. Professor Sterling was 'senior staff'. He turned and strode towards the History Department. Letting himself in with his key he dropped his Gladstone bag inside his small office and strode along the corridor to his mentor's door. It was locked. "Still early," he thought and walked back to his office. Picking up the phone he dialled the professor's home number. The phone rang repeatedly and he was about to hang up when a familiar female voice answered hesitantly.

"Yes?"

"Hullo, Susan, it's Stuart. Is the professor at home?"

There was a brief silence before the voice replied, "No, Stuart, he's not here. I was visiting him last night," her voice faltered, "when some men came and took him away."

"Some men?" He felt his stomach tighten.

"Yes, three in dark suits, overcoats and black ties. Two of them were German and the one who did most of the talking was a New Zealander. They said Uncle David was wanted for questioning. They were very polite but very firm. He was told he wouldn't need anything as he would be released as soon as he had answered their questions."

"Where did they take him?"

"I've no idea. Oh, Stuart, I'm so worried. I don't know what to do or who to talk to."

"Nobody does these days," he replied, almost as an aside. "Now look, Susan, the professor's a wily old fellow. I'm sure he'll bamboozle them with his answers and they'll soon let him go."

"Yes, I suppose so. But I'm not sure what to do in the meantime."

"Look, why don't you come into varsity. I'm phoning from my office. Meet me here. In the meantime I'll make a few inquiries and we'll try to sort out some plan of action."

"What say Uncle David turns up here?"

"Leave a note to phone you at my office."

"OK. If you're sure that's what I should do."

"Yes I am. You'll only fret if you stay there by yourself. See you soon."

Replacing the hand piece on the hook Stuart wished he felt as confident as he had tried to sound. For Susan's sake he'd tried to be positive but in reality he had no idea what would happen to Sterling, or his other colleagues for that matter.

Suddenly he remembered the pamphlet. He got up and locked the door before removing the crumpled paper from his pocket. On the front page was the twisted body on the swastika. Underneath was the slogan "Join the Fightback!"

The inside page contained details of all the negative aspects of the New Order and an exhortation for readers not to be taken in by the propaganda that was increasingly filling the newspapers, billboards and airwaves. None of this was new to Stuart but he felt elated somebody was writing ideas that had been developing in his mind over the past few months. He was heartened there was a group who was prepared to resist the edicts of the conquerors and not succumb to blandishments and hollow promises of peace and prosperity. The final page was of particular interest. Headed, "What Now?" it offered a number of alternatives for action. These ranged from slogans that could be painted onto walls, simple acts of sabotage for those working in armaments factories, the writing and printing of anti-government pamphlets, or the joining of armed partisan groups. They all seemed feasible except the last one. There had been no indication that groups were engaged in any form of armed resistance. And even if they were, who were they and how could they be contacted? Or was the poster, in fact, simply a ploy to flush out citizens who were disloyal to the New Order? His mind in turmoil, he sat slumped in his chair going over and over both his personal and the political situations, trying to find some logic and formulate some plan of action. A loud knock on the door startled him. Hastily stuffing the pamphlet into his pocket, he sat upright. The sound of a clock striking 10:30 made him realize he'd been sitting there for some time.

"Who is it?"

"Me, you bloody idiot."

Rising, he unlocked the door. Brendan stood staring quizzically at him.

"Locking the door now, are we?" He entered and sat down. "Planning some subversive activity, perhaps?" When Stuart made no reply he frowned. "You don't look too happy, chum. I came to ask you about those bloody great notices on the old barracks wall. Have you seen them?

Stuart nodded.

"So what's it all about? Do you know?"

Remembering that Brendan had been off with the flu for the previous three days, Stuart began to describe in detail what had occurred in the quad. When he reached the part where Cox was shot Brendan turned pale. He was about to speak but Stuart held up his hand and continued his story by describing the encounter with the Waffen SS pair on the motorcycle and the news of Professor Sterling's arrest. When he'd finished he leaned back in his chair and stared at his friend.

"Christ. Here, have one of these." He proffered a packet of Capstan and scraped a match along the edge of the Beehive matchbox. After his first draw Stuart said, "There's one more thing."

"What?"

"Lock the door again."

Brendan rose, locked the door and returned to his seat. Stuart pulled the pamphlet from his pocket. "While I was looking at the notices early this morning a chap came up to me, spoke a few words, thrust this into my hand and then disappeared. Read it and you'll see why I've locked the door."

Taking the pamphlet Brendan read it through, then ejected a thin stream of smoke and handed it back.

"What do you think?"

"Glad some bastards are doing something. But who are these people?"

"No idea. But what I do know is I can't stand idly by while the authorities arrest and kill varsity staff and students. If we or any of the other university colleges capitulate then all the principles of democracy and free speech will disappear from our country."

"Yeah. Fine words, but the big question is where do we go from here?"

"Not sure, but I get the impression the fellow who contacted me may want to get in touch again. In the meantime, we need to discuss our options."

"Could be a trap of course. But assuming it's kosher, well, we're both fairly good with words, thanks to the efforts of this illustrious institution – your written English is better than mine, and my German is fluent, particularly after all that wartime research. That means we could assist a group such as Fightback with their pamphlets and anti-government propaganda."

"May not be enough. What say they need men to undertake acts of sabotage, shooting Germans, that sort of thing?"

"No reason why we can't do both." He sighed and ran his fingers through his untidy hair. "However I'm not prepared to start trying to shoot Germans without –."

A soft knock on the door interrupted him. Hurriedly Stuart scooped the pamphlet up from the table, thrust it into his pocket and cautiously unlocked the door. He was thrust back as Susan stumbled forward and fell trembling into his arms.

"It's OK, Susan. You're safe here."

She continued trembling and breathing deeply, trying to get a grip on herself. Gradually her shaking subsided and she stepped back. Her face was flushed and she'd been crying. She glanced at Stuart and then caught sight of Brendan.

"Oh, s-sorry. Didn't see you there."

Brendan smiled sympathetically. "That's OK. Had a rough time?"

"Susan, meet Brendan. Susan is Professor Sterling's niece, the one I was telling you about." He looked at her. "Sit down here Susan and we'll make you a cup of tea. You look as if you could use one."

"It's got worse, Stuart," she said as she sat down heavily. "Just after you phoned a car pulled up. There was a loud knock at the door and when I opened it there were two men in long coats, hats and black ties."

"The Security Police?"

She nodded as she made an effort to control herself. "They were holding Uncle David between them. He could barely stand. His tie was missing, his face was puffed up and he was groaning. They walked straight past me into the lounge and dropped him into a chair. They said, 'He wasn't very cooperative. We may have to pay him another visit.' Then they left, slamming the door behind them."

"Jesus," said Brendan. "What did you do then?"

"I rang Dr Rawlings. He came straight away and did a complete inspection. He told us that the upper part of Uncle David's body was covered in bruises, that he had several cracked or broken ribs. He gave him some form of sedative and I left him asleep. I then phoned a couple of neighbourhood women who are around there now. There wasn't anything else I could do and I was worried about using the phone, so I decided to come straight here. Not sure why but," she glanced uncertainly at both young men, "perhaps we should check his office in case there's any documents they could use against him."

"Huh, everything in there could be used against him if they wanted to," said Brendan.

"Yes," replied Stuart, "but it's worth checking in case there's anything really incriminating." He looked at the other two. "Brendan, you stay here and make Susan a cup of tea while I take a look around the professor's study. Most of his material would have been related to the wartime research project."

"Best to get rid of it. And any of your own stuff for that matter."

"Yes. I've got a key. I'll do it now."

Fortunately Sterling was a very methodical man. As a priority Stuart identified all material that had been translated from intercepted wartime German messages on the basis that in the twisted environment in which they all now operated, such activities, even in retrospect, could be categorized as spying. Not wishing to give the impression that all documentation had been removed, he left a number of the professor's speculative reports intact as well as all the pre-war files relating to university activities. He then returned to his office, where Susan and Brendan were talking earnestly. Locking the door he handed the Fightback pamphlet to Susan and, gulping down a cup of tea, he set about removing some of his own files that could be termed incriminating – notably the German translations supplied by Brendan.

Brendan and Susan had been comparing stories of university life and she was looking a little brighter. The pamphlet stimulated further discussion but Stuart, keen to finish his task, let them do most of the talking. By 11.45 he had finished putting all the files into brown paper bags and was on the point of discussing how they could be disposed of when his phone rang. He picked it up.

"Stuart Johnson," he said.

"Hello, Stuart. I met you this morning by the wall and gave you some information."

"Yes, you did."

"You read the information?"

"Yes, I did."

"What did you think of it?"

Stuart paused. "I found it thought provoking."

Both Brendan and Susan lifted their heads up at this point and he nodded to them.

"Would you be interested in learning more?"

"Possibly."

"Good. In half an hour be at the band rotunda in Albert Park. Sit on the seat facing Wellesley St. Someone will drop an item next to you. Pick it up and walk away. Find a place where you won't be observed and read it."

"Will I be...?" The phone went dead.

Stuart sat staring straight ahead.

"What did they say?" asked Brendan.

"I'm to walk over to Albert Park in half an hour, sit down by the band rotunda and wait for someone to drop a package. I then have to take it away and read it."

"Bit cloak and dagger," said Susan.

"Yes." He shrugged. "Sign of the times. But our choices are limited so I'm going to do it. I'm meeting Carol there anyway. Why don't you two join us in our usual spot? We'll discuss it together."

CHAPTER 26

As they crossed the road they saw Carol walking towards them. They gathered in a group on the footpath while Stuart updated her on the morning's events. Appalled by what had happened to Professor Sterling, Carol, having reassured him she hadn't heard from Hamish, questioned his wisdom in going to the rendezvous.

"Yesterday we agreed that something should be done."

"True, but I didn't think it would involve risky circumstances like this – and so soon."

"Neither did I but I can't stand by and do nothing while people are being beaten and killed. And you three can keep an eye on me in case anything goes wrong."

Seeing he was determined, Carol nodded her agreement. The group chose an area near the central fountain that gave them a clear view of the rotunda. The strength of Carol's hug had a desperate feel about it. "Please be careful, Stuart. You mean so much to me," she whispered. He smiled reassuringly, turned and walked towards the rotunda.

Albert Park looked no different from any other day of the week but as Stuart moved cautiously forward he imagined hostile eyes behind every tree. The welcome shade the giant gnarled trees normally provided now took on an ominous appearance as a light breeze caused the shadows to flicker back and forth on the path in front of him. Familiar bird sounds and the occasional noise from the city took on a sharp edge and even his soft footfalls on the grass seemed to contain a gentle menace.

Reaching the green slatted bench by the rotunda he sat down and tried to convey the impression of a relaxed spectator. On the circular seat inside a vagrant was asleep. On an adjacent seat a woman was scattering crumbs for sparrows and pigeons.

The plump pigeons moved in contrast to the rapid darting movements of the sparrows who, although wary of their larger counterparts, still managed to secure a share of the spoils. As he watched the birds Stuart resisted the strong temptation to seek reassurance by looking back at Carol and the others.

A mother and two children walked noisily past followed by a couple holding hands. Suddenly a groan behind him caused him to jump. He spun round and saw that the vagrant had woken up and was shuffling towards the steps, muttering to himself. Annoyed at his own nervousness Stuart wrinkled his nose at the smell of alcohol emanating from the scruffy figure. The man reached the bottom and gazed blearily around. He shuffled forward and sat down heavily next to Stuart. Gripped by increasing nervousness Stuart cursed under his breath and stared fixedly ahead in case the man tried to engage him in conversation.

A few more uneventful minutes elapsed before the man, with a stupid giggle and an incomprehensible muttering, rose and shambled off down the path towards Wellesley St. Stuart sighed with relief.

A nearby clock striking 12:15 caused him to start and look around. Perhaps something had gone wrong. Perhaps he'd better get out before he was arrested. Perhaps...

Looking down, he spotted a small grubby brown parcel on the seat next to him. It hadn't been there before. The drunk. Of course! He scooped it up and thrust it into his inner blazer pocket. Then, trying to contain his excitement, he rose, stretched and walked back up the path towards the group.

He caught Brendan's eye and jerked his head to the right and then turned towards the campus. Crossing the road and walking down a winding path half-hidden by trees, he glanced back to check that the other three had followed him across Princes St.

The contents of the parcel, opened behind Stuart's locked study door, were anticlimactic. They consisted of a short letter and a hand-drawn map.

"Thought there'd be a Luger or at least a dagger or two," Stuart muttered.

"Or a couple of suicide pills," offered Brendan.

The map provided details of a rendezvous point near the village of Albany, well north of the city environs, and a brief set of instructions. Stuart read them aloud to the others.

"If you wish to fight back against the German occupiers and their collaborators, follow these instructions.

1. Make your way to Albany.
2. Follow the map's instructions until you arrive at the rendezvous point.
3. Be prepared to wait patiently, as the area will need to be checked carefully before contact is made.
4. Do not travel as part of a large group.
5. Dress as if for a tramping trip.
6. Bring a small amount of food and clothing with you. Large amounts will arouse suspicion.
7. If questioned, explain that you are going tramping in the hills.
8. On no account bring weapons.
9. Only come if you are prepared to undergo intensive training.
10. Tell no one of your intentions to avoid implicating them.
11. Commit the enclosed map and instructions to memory then destroy them.

We of Fightback look forward to welcoming you as a comrade in arms."

Putting the instructions on his desk Stuart gazed around the group.

"Sounds like something out of a war novel," said Carol after a pause.

"Trouble is," said Susan, "this not a novel. It'll be our war story."

"If we go ahead," said Brendan. "It's not going to be a jolly jaunt in the country. We're going to be leaving here, discarding our careers, turning our backs on our family and friends and throwing in our lot with a group of people we've never met. It will be hard, dangerous and if we're captured we could be tortured or killed."

"You backing out?" Stuart's voice was quiet but he looked his friend straight in the face.

"You know my views on war," replied Brendan. "But this is my home, my country, my fellow citizens. These people have come here and, despite their smooth propaganda, have resorted to terror and intimidation to establish a fascist government. And anyway, Stuart, what choice have we got? That Beavis character is out to get you and if either of us stays here at university we'll suffer the same fate as Prof. Sterling unless we agree to collaborate." His look was hard. "As things stand you and I have no alternative."

Stuart nodded and then turned to the two women. "But it's different for you two. I'm not sure if the partisan group wants women and if you do join you'll run the risk of capture and God knows what from the German troops and their collaborators."

Exchanging glances they nodded and Susan, after a brief smile, spoke in a low voice.

"We've talked about it and decided the situation has given us two choices – collaborate or escape. My relationship with Uncle David, my work here, Carol's vengeful boyfriend who has now joined the Nazis..." Her voice tailed off and she shrugged.

"The whole situation makes it impossible for us," continued Carol. "Both of us have been horrified at the way the Professor and the students have been treated. We can't stand around and do nothing and we'd never collaborate. And in any case the whole system is threatening our lives and our plans. Even at work I'm surrounded by it. The Germans and their cronies have now completely taken over the Northern Club. All Germans of officer rank or senior bureaucrats have been given a 'Privileged Membership' status. The place is full of them. The original members hardly ever come in any more."

"Do they bother you?"

"Not so far. Most of them are excessively polite. But I can feel their eyes, regarding me as part of the spoils of victory." Seeing Brendan was about to speak, she held up her hand. "When this war started, women were called on to do their bit, join the forces and learn to assemble weapons, drive trucks, that sort of thing. The war didn't last long but what it showed was that women are capable of far more than we're given credit for." She took a long jagged breath and spoke again, more softly. "Two days ago the Nazis shot university students. Yesterday they beat up an elderly university professor. Several months ago they killed my brother. We have to fight back and 'we' means women as well as men."

"Women as well as men," echoed Susan.

There was a moment's silence and then Brendan nodding his approval, mimed a handclap.

CHAPTER 27

"I'm going fishing tomorrow," announced Stuart at the family meal table after grace had been said.

"Oh, that's nice dear," answered his mother. "Sit up straight please, Claire."

"Who with?" said Stephen.

"With whom, dear," corrected his mother.

"Oh, a couple of mates from varsity. One of them has a small launch that his dad said we could borrow for the day. Going out off Rangitoto Island to catch snapper."

"What's your friend's name?" asked his father.

About to use Brendan's name Stuart quickly had second thoughts. "Oh, D'Arcy. He was in my History class."

"Fresh fish would be very welcome. Hope you have plenty of luck, son," said his father.

"Yes, so do I," responded Stuart, relieved he was not going to have to answer any more questions. As the family members commenced their meal his eyes flicked around the table at each of them. The reality of his decision was starting to dawn on him. They were his family and although at times it wasn't an especially harmonious home, the possibility he might never see them again caused him to sharply catch his breath.

His mother looked up. "Are you feeling alright, dear?"

"Yes, thanks, Mum. I was just thinking it would be nice to, um..."

"Yes, dear?"

"Well, how about we have a game of Monopoly after dinner?"

His parents exchanged glances.

"Yes, dear," said his mother uncertainly. "That sounds like an excellent idea. Time we did more things together as a family."

"Yes," said Claire excitedly. "Last time I got Mayfair and nearly beat Stephen."

"Yeah, but you didn't win," said her brother. "You wound up in jail and couldn't collect your rents and I won."

"That's enough, Stephen," reprimanded his father. He turned to Stuart. "What's brought this on, all of a sudden?"

"No particular reason," shrugged Stuart. "Just sort of felt like it."

Although a little puzzled, his parents agreed and once the dining room table was cleared and the dishes washed and dried the family sat around the table, spread out the board and selected the pieces.

As soon as the game began Stuart saw the usual family alliances forming. He as the oldest was supposed to set the example and play the game without becoming involved in the petty family tussles that so easily developed in such situations, usually between himself and Stephen. His brother had instantly 'bagsed' the role of banker. Although an allegedly impartial role, Stuart suspected that, as in the past, Stephen would if necessary use the position to replenish his dwindling funds. However, aware it was his last night for who knows how long, he was determined to do his best to maintain a positive atmosphere.

As always he played his game in support of Claire. He laughed with her when she bought a string of properties and commiserated with her when, once again, a spell in jail resulted in her losing them. When Stephen was finally declared the outright winner Stuart was the first to congratulate him, which had the advantage of taking the wind out of the boy's sails and reducing the usual boastful recounting of his success.

The result was the family, particularly his parents, enjoyed the game more than usual. The reduction in sniping between the brothers enabled both parents to gradually relinquish their roles as monitors of acceptable behaviour and simply join with their three children in an enjoyable family activity.

Stuart slept badly that night. The success of the Monopoly game had added to the complexities of the decision that he had come to. Outside of the security of the family he had found a new level of maturity in his relationship with Carol. Yet he was aware of the security that home gave him. Even the parental reprimands provided him with the comfort of familiarity. Several times during the evening he had wanted to share his plans with the rest of the family but each time he realized that the knowledge, however slight, could severely compromise them in the future. Again he reconsidered the wisdom of his decision to join the Fightback group. Once again he concluded his association with the university college and Professor Sterling, and Hamish Beavis's new position of power, left him very little choice. If he stayed he would almost certainly be arrested and his family would suffer by association. Simply disappearing therefore seemed to be the lesser of two evils.

The next morning he rose early in order to pack his canvas rucksack with as much as possible without having to answer too many questions. His father and brother called out their good-byes to him and left. Although he wanted to say something to them, he wasn't sure what, and in any case he didn't want to rouse their suspicions.

As he pulled the rucksack's leather straps through the buckles to tighten the top flap he noticed his hands were trembling. He sat down heavily on the side of his bed and forced himself to breathe deeply. His thoughts were a vortex of contradictions. With Carol he was forsaking his home, his family and his career and embarking on a journey, which although causing his blood to quicken, was riddled with uncertainties. For the umpteenth time he asked himself, "Was this the only option? Was there a better, safer way for him and for Carol? Could he be certain of her support?"

The gentle hand on his shoulder made him spin round.

186

"Have a good day's fishing, you lucky thing," said Clare

"Oh, Clare. Yes. Thanks, I will."

"Stuart," she said, smiling up at him, "will you promise me something?"

"What?" he asked uncertainly, his suspicions aroused.

"Take me with you, next time. I'd love to go fishing."

His laughter of relief was tinged with a sharp sadness. He reached out and hugged her to him.

"Of course. Love to."

"Good. Thanks. I knew you'd say yes." She hugged him back. "I'm really lucky to have a big brother like you."

His eyes stung and he had to make a conscious effort to reply in a normal tone.

"OK. Now behave yourself at school today."

The grin she gave him turned to a frown.

"Stuart, is something the matter?"

He tossed his head and laughed as best he could.

"Yes, I'm desperately unhappy because I have to go fishing instead of going to varsity today."

She studied him for a moment and then laughed.

"Stuart, you really are silly sometimes." And she ran off down the stairs.

He stood listening to the sound of her receding footsteps.

"Maybe you're right, Sunshine," he said.

His mother, as usual, had made lunch for him and, as an unspoken reward for the previous evening, had "included a few other nice little goodies to share with your friends, dear".

Smiling at her, he accepted the well-filled brown paper bag.

"Thanks, Mum. You're a good mum, you know."

"Am I, dear? You've never said so before."

"Well, maybe I should have." He put his arm around her and gripped her shoulder. "I love you, Mum," he said quietly and before she could reply he walked out the front door with a renewed stinging in his eyes.

CHAPTER 28

The trip to Albany took most of the morning. They had agreed to travel as separate pairs but to catch the same bus in order to keep watch for each other. They'd also agreed to write a short note to their families to be posted the same morning – a note that would provide almost no information but would at least prevent their parents from assuming their children had met with an accident and calling the police.

Earlier in the morning they had boarded the yellow North Shore Transport bus near the blacksmith's shop in central Takapuna and headed to Northcote where they had then caught the bus for Albany. It was a warm Saturday morning and the bus, which was half full, was soon winding up the gravel roads towards its destination. The rural scenery, with sheep, cows and small houses, drifted by as the vehicle made its ponderous way northwards, pausing from time to time to pick up or set down its assortment of passengers.

Initially Stuart, along with the other three, had been keyed up at the prospect of joining the resistance group. However the familiarly tranquillity of the countryside had resulted in its becoming somewhat anticlimactic. Nevertheless the occasional military vehicles with the swastika and the silver fern painted on the side were sharp reminders that rural New Zealand life was not the same. A further and unrelenting reminder of the New Order came from large billboards now dotting the roadside at regular intervals. Stuart had seen most of them before but as the bus pulled up at a stop Carol nudged and pointed to a new billboard alongside the bus shelter. It featured a Maori soldier, dressed in New Order military uniform, leaning forward with his bayoneted rifle thrust in front of him. Ghostlike, in the background, a traditional tattooed Maori warrior brandished his long-handled taiaha in an identical pose. The poster caption read, "Fight the Communist enemies of the Maori people! Join up now!"

"That's the second one I've seen targeting Maori men," said Carol. "That young soldier on the motorbike wasn't an isolated example."

"More's the pity," sighed Stuart. "The Maori Battalion mauled Rommel's troops in the Western Desert, and the Germans are smart enough to recognize good soldiers when they see them."

With a lurch the bus moved away from the stop and headed towards a long hill, the heat mixing with the occasional petrol fumes as it ground its way upward. Stuart felt Carol's head fall onto his shoulders and, comforted by her nearness, closed his eyes and drifted into a light sleep.

He awoke with a start to the sound of shouting. The bus had ground to a halt behind an army truck at the top of the hill. The bus driver was standing outside on the grass verge next to several armed New Order soldiers who were lined up beside a man with sergeant's stripes. The shouting that had awoken Stuart was coming from a man standing in the aisle at the front of the bus. In spite of the heat he was dressed in a dark suit, black tie and Homburg hat. Behind him stood an officer and two soldiers.

"Passengers!" The special police official's accented voice was unnecessarily loud. "We have stopped this bus to carry out a search." He paused. No sound came from the passengers. "We apologize for any inconvenience but there has been some unpatriotic activity in this area. Therefore it is necessary for us to take precautions to ensure you can continue your journey in safety. You will please take all your belongings, exit from the bus and stand where the soldiers tell you."

Stuart felt Carol's fingers dig into his arm. "It's OK," he said. "Keep calm. We've got nothing incriminating on us.

We're going to visit friends and then go hiking in the country. Just do as they say."

The pair made their way down the narrow aisle. Stuart was thankful the authorities had not yet had sufficient time to implement a system of identity cards for all New Zealand's citizens. As they passed Brendan and Susan who were standing by their seats, his eyes briefly met those of his friend's but neither man showed any sign of recognition.

Descending the steps the passengers were instructed to stand in a line by the roadside. Stuart noticed the army officer, two soldiers and the special police officer were moving systematically down the aisle of the bus, checking under the seats and on the luggage racks.

"If you have any possessions, ladies and gentlemen, please place them on the ground in front of you," said the sergeant, whose accent was also Germanic. There was a rustle of noise as the passengers complied. "Thank you. Now, from your possessions, take two steps backwards."

"And keep your thumbs down the seams of your trousers," muttered a male voice in the middle of the line.

"No talking!" barked a soldier standing on the left-hand side of the line. His local accent was local.

"OK, mate, take it easy," responded the male voice. "We're just bloody bus passengers. What are you going to do? Shoot us with your big new gun?"

At the murmur of mirth the soldier blushed and shifted uncomfortably.

Turning his head sideways Stuart saw that the comments were coming from a tall, slightly dishevelled dark haired man.

"Your co-operation is…" began the sergeant when the dark haired man interrupted him.

"Hey, Brownie! I didn't recognize you! What are you doing in that uniform?"

The soldier looked sharply in the direction of the speaker.

"It's me, mate," continued the dark haired man. "Last thing I heard was that you'd joined up and gone overseas to fight the Germans. S'truth, Brownie, what the hell are you doing now?"

The soldier cleared his throat. "Er, g'day, Eric. Didn't recognize you. Er, how would you be?"

At this point the army and the special police officers stepped off the bus. The army officer glared at the soldier. "What is going on here, Brown?" His accent was local.

"Christ! Another one. What's the matter with you jokers?" Eric addressed the officer. "You an ex-digger too, mate? If so, have you no bloody shame?"

Catching Brendan's eye Stuart frowned fiercely and shook his head.

By now the other two soldiers had exited from the bus and were standing behind the officer. "Excuse me, sir," said one of them, "we found these." He held up two beer bottles. "One was empty."

"What of it?" snapped the officer.

"I think it belongs to him, sir," answered the soldier, indicating Eric. He grinned uncertainly. "Maybe had one too many."

"Yeah, they're mine," said Eric. "What of it? You bully boys going to confiscate my bottles of beer? Wow, that will really show your Berlin bosses how brave you are!"

"Enough!" barked the special police officer. He turned. "Brown, place this man under arrest. We will take him into custody for further questioning!"

Eric laughed, but with a nervous edge. "Come on, Brownie. Don't be a mug. I'm not doing any bloody harm."

The soldier, who had begun to move towards his friend, hesitated.

"All I had was a couple of beers and –"

"Silence!" shouted the German. He stepped forward and swept the palm of his right hand across Eric's cheek with a loud 'Thwack!' causing him to stagger backwards.

The sound hung in the heavy air for a moment.

"Hey! No need for that!" Brown shouted stepping towards the German. "He's just a bit drunk. He meant no harm!"

"Yeah, Brownie's right, you bastard!" shouted Eric who, recovering from the blow, began to move forward. The German promptly drew a Luger pistol from his inside his jacket. "Get back, you fool!" he shouted but Eric, angry at the unexpected blow, kept advancing.

The shot echoed through the valley.

Eric's chest exploded with the force of the close range bullet sending him sprawled on his back, his left leg twitching.

"You shot him! You shot my mate! You bastard!"

The spray of bullets from Brown's Schmeisser machine pistol sliced into the plain clothed German, pulping his dark suit. As he fell everyone else dived to the ground.

"Get him!" shouted the army officer, jerking his head up and groping for his holstered pistol. Another burst of fire and the officer collapsed, twitched and lay still.

"Brownie!" The voice was one of the other two soldiers sprawled in the dirt. "Don't shoot, mate! Please!"

Clutching his smoking weapon, Brown looking at the sprawl of people and the three bodies. Red rivulets were flowing steadily from underneath the corpses and mingling with the brown earth. From his position on the ground, Stuart could see the soldier was trembling. With open palms held out in front of him, he rose to his feet.

"It's OK, Brownie," he said quietly. He turned to the sprawling soldiers. "Leave your weapons on the ground and stand up slowly." The men looked at each other uncertainly.

His voice was steady as he continued. "Brownie, your mates are going to stand up. Give me your word you won't shoot them."

"I won't shoot them." He lowered his Schmeisser. "I won't shoot my mates."

The soldiers rose to their feet and stood looking at Stuart.

"There'll be hell to pay over this," said the taller one.

"Knowing the Germans, you can be sure of that," replied Stuart. "They hate to lose any of their own outside of a battle zone."

"What do we do?" The other soldier, a smaller man, had removed his helmet and was nervously playing with his red hair.

The sounds of snapping twigs caused Stuart to whirl round, only to catch a final glimpse of the bus passengers and driver disappearing into the nearby area of bush.

"Yeah, Stuart," said Brendan quietly, moving alongside him. "There's still a fair way to go, we've no transport, and…" he swept his hand over the scene, "this mess could bring a Blitzkrieg Boys backup group here at any moment."

Grunting an acknowledgement Stuart then turned to the three soldiers who were clustered uncertainly together.

"Had enough of playing soldiers with the Blitzkrieg Boys?"

"'The 'Blitzkrieg Boys'?"

"Yeah. A sarcastic label for you Kiwi glory seekers who've joined the New Order armed forces."

The men shifted uneasily and the tall man looked sideways at Stuart. "Like I said, there will be hell to pay for this. And we'll be the ones to cop it. But why did you ask that question about us having had enough?"

Carol and Susan joined Brendan. Stuart noticed his friend was carrying the officer's Luger.

"Look, we haven't got much time," he said, "but these men could come with us."

"Come with us, Stuart?" murmured Brendan. "You sure? Hell of a risk."

"Their truck'd be useful."

"Us? Who's us?" interrupted Brown.

"We're heading towards a rendezvous." Stuart glanced at Brendan and the two women who exchanged glances and then nodded. "A rendezvous with a local resistance group."

"Could, er, could we come with you?" said the small soldier tentatively, looking at his mates who eagerly nodded.

"Possibly," answered Brendan. He looked at Stuart and then at the three soldiers. "But you've been fighting for the Krauts. How do we know you can be trusted?"

"Look," replied the soldier, "All of us thought it would be OK to join them. They promised good pay and told us we wouldn't have to harm or kill any of our own people. Then they bloody put us on this search duty and we had to watch some of the Germans arresting locals and beating them up. We hated it but we couldn't do anything. Now we can, eh, chaps?"

His two companions nodded vigorously.

"How far away is the rendezvous point?"

"Apparently near Albany School at the end of the straight."

"OK. I think that's about five miles."

"Look," said Brown. "I'm the driver of that army truck. We're all in deep shit, and like us, you need transport to get away from here bloody fast. The school's not far by truck. If one of the soldiers gets in the front with me and the rest of you get in the back, we'll set off down the road. If we see another army vehicle we'll simply wave. When we get near the school we'll ditch the truck and head across country to the school."

"We've no choice, Stuart," said Carol. "Someone could come past at any moment."

Brendan nodded his assent.

"OK," said Stuart, "but I'm staying in the front as a precaution."

He turned to the red headed soldier. "Give me your helmet and tunic. Carol and Susan, take the soldier's weapons." Seeing one of the men about to protest he barked, "Hand them over. You've no choice."

After an exchange of glances and a mutual shrug, the soldiers handed their Schmeissers to the two girls.

"Now, all of you, in the back. I'll ride up front with Brown."

He glared at the soldiers. "No funny business, you men. We're all in this together but for the moment, we have the weapons."

CHAPTER 29

Once the decision was made the group moved swiftly. The unarmed soldiers, followed by the two women and Brendan, scrambled over the tailboard as Stuart and Brown climbed into the cab. The motor started and the truck roared away. Stuart had ordered the soldiers to drag the bodies behind a hedge – a decidedly unpleasant job as the officer's body had been dismembered by the long burst from Brown's machine pistol – and to pick up any debris. At the redheaded soldier's suggestion ground sheets were taken from the truck and draped over the bodies to prevent swarms of flies attracting unwanted attention. Hopefully inhabitants of any passing vehicle would pay little attention to an empty bus parked by the side of the road.

"Take it easy, Brown," warned Stuart, as the truck lurched around a corner and slid sideways in the loose gravel. "Don't want to draw attention to ourselves."

"Sorry, just want to get away and have time to think. It all happened so quickly, one minute the bus had been pulled up and the next minute I was ..."

The soldier was beginning to babble. Stuart leaned across and gripped his arm. "Going to be OK, mate. Just take it easy and slow down. We'll soon be safe and you'll have plenty of time to debrief."

The truck slowed as Brown eased his foot off the accelerator. "How much further do you reckon?"

"Another five minutes. Then what?

"We'll ditch the truck and go on foot. You chaps will have to get rid of your uniforms otherwise you might get shot at by the resistance group."

"Bloody ironic, isn't it. We'll soon be on the run from the German authorities and we're also possible targets for your resistance people. Talk about the bloody Devil and the deep blue sea."

"Not the best, I agree. Hopefully by the end of the day we'll have worked out something."

"Yeah. Anyway, what's the story on these resistance blokes?"

"We're not sure. We got some information on them. They sounded well organized and so we're hoping to link up with them sometime today."

"Why have you decided to contact them?"

"Long story. Tell you later."

"OK. What's with the two sheilas?"

"They wanted to come. No reason why not. From what I've read Russian women are playing a major role as partisan fighters on the Eastern Front."

"Maybe. Doesn't seem right, somehow – pretty women, both of them. 'Specially the one with the dark hair."

"And spoken for – and don't you and your mates forget it!"

Stuart studied the long stretch of gravel road in front of them. "OK, here's the Albany straight. Check there's no-one watching and pull off the road behind those trees up ahead."

There was no approaching traffic and Brown, glancing in the wing mirror, muttered, "All clear. Here goes."

He hit the brakes and as the truck slowed, swung the wheel to the left. In a cloud of dust and a scattering of gravel the vehicle swung onto a small overgrown track. With a graunching of gears Brown eased through the narrow gap noisily snapping branches and scattering leaves and twigs.

"Over there," commanded Stuart and Brown eased the truck under a tall macrocarpa tree. It bounced to a halt and as a small dust cloud drifted past the vehicle's front, the soldier looked enquiringly at Stuart.

"Looks OK. Hang on and I'll check," said Stuart, swinging open the door and dropping onto the ground. The thick trunk of the tree concealed most of the truck's body while the tree's lower branches draped themselves protectively over the roof.

"Looks good to me," said Stuart. "Everybody out. Make sure you don't leave anything behind."

The group assembled at the right hand side of the truck, out of sight of the road.

"Looks clear," said one of the soldiers gazing out over the rolling paddocks in front of them. "Now what?"

"We keep out of sight and continue to head in the same direction." He removed the German tunic and helmet and tossed them in the back of the truck. He looked at the three soldiers. "You chaps must have had plenty of army training in moving through enemy territory. Lead the way and we'll follow you. When you come in sight of the Albany school house, find a place where you can't be seen but from where you can see the building and signal us."

"Then what?" asked Brown.

"We wait until we're contacted," replied Stuart. Although the soldiers had made no attempt to cause any trouble Stuart was aware the situation had far too many unknowns for him to add to the risk by divulging the next stage.

"Stuart, I think we should go now."

He smiled warmly at Carol. Her face was dusty and sweat-streaked, and she looked pale. He reached out and scratched her head. "We'll be OK, my sweet." He nodded to the soldiers. "OK you chaps. Away you go. We'll follow."

"Hang on a minute, Stuart," Brendan broke in. "These men are in enough trouble. We can't send them off without any weapons. At least give them one of the Schmeissers."

Mindful of the pressure of time, Stuart thought rapidly. It was taking a chance. The Schmeisser was a lethal weapon that could easily wipe out any small group. However, if New Order troops tracked the soldiers down they would have no chance. Once captured, they would almost certainly be tortured and be able to describe their companions and the rendezvous point. One weapon was worth the risk.

"OK. Brownie, you take it." He nodded to Carol who handed a weapon to Brown. "Right. Let's get moving."

The soldier trio moved forward, keeping low as they crossed the narrow track. The other three looked at Stuart who nodded and they began following the soldiers' route. A motorbike was heard approaching and the soldiers dropped into the paddock's long grass. The others immediately followed suit. As the sound of the motorbike faded away the trio rose and, led by Brown, moved forward at a crouching run.

Stuart, who had half-risen to watch them, nodded to his three companions. "Good. They seem to know what they're doing. Right. Let's keep moving."

The clouds had cleared completely leaving an unbroken blue sky above them from which the sun blazed steadily down. The summer cacophony of the cicadas mingled with the bleat of the sheep and the soft lowing of the cows that were spread through the paddocks. The two parties moved steadily but with caution – without being told they realized that if any of the animals were startled it could draw attention to their presence. The occasional sound of a car or motorbike, while causing them each time to pause and drop, was reassuringly normal.

The heat, the heavy weapons, their bags and the inevitable tension made their progress tiring. Where the grass was long and the hedges were high, progress was easier. However when they reached a newly ploughed paddock, there was the double challenge of a rutted surface and the lack of any ground cover. Consequently both groups tried to move as fast as possible across the expanses of dirt.

Ten minutes of moving and crouching brought the soldiers almost to the far end of the ploughed area. Stuart and his group were halfway across when the sounds of several slow moving vehicles echoed through the countryside. Both groups dived between the ruts of brown earth and lay still. The vehicles were coming from the south and could therefore have passed the stationary bus. Each of them listened to the ponderous approach trying to interpret the vehicles' intentions from the speed and the sound of the engines. As the noise drew level with the centre of the paddock instinctively they pushed deeper into the freshly ploughed earth. The droning noises grew louder and then continued on down the road.

"Stay down," muttered Stuart. "Let them pass the soldiers."

The engine notes, maintaining their consistency, receded into the distance.

"They've gone," said Susan. "I wonder what they were?"

No one had an answer.

"We can get up now, Stuart," said Carol.

"Yeah, but be careful."

Cautiously they stood up and looked around. Ahead, the soldiers were also rising to their familiar half crouch. One of them glanced back and waved. Stuart waved back and watched them as they moved forward.

Suddenly Carol laughed. Startled at the unexpected sound he turned round.

"Have you seen yourselves?" she asked, pointing at the others. "Talk about mobile mounds of dirt."

"Yeah, well speak for yourself, grubby," smiled Brendan. "But at least we're well camouflaged."

"True. OK, grubs, let's keep moving, and keep your eyes and ears open."

Stuart began moving forward.

"They've stopped, Stuart," Brendan, touching him on the shoulder, pointed ahead. The trio had halted and one of them was looking back and pointing forward. When Brendan waved an acknowledgment the soldier and his two companions dropped into the long grass.

"They must have spotted the school house." There was relief in Susan's voice.

"Yes. Move up in single file and watch them for any sudden movements."

"Surely, Stuart, they're not likely..."

"In this situation we can't be too sure. Remember up until an hour ago they were wearing Jerry uniforms."

Leading the way and keeping low, Stuart headed forward followed by his companions. Susan was right. The behaviour of the officer in killing Brown's friend, the support the other soldiers had shown for Brown's subsequent action and their acquiescence to Stuart's role of leader indicated that their new loyalties were intact – for the moment.

Nevertheless, as they drew closer, Stuart was relieved to see them all lying facing towards the schoolhouse. Signalling the others he moved into a position on the grass beside Brown who was looking through a pair of German Zeiss binoculars.

"Any sign of movement?"

"Not a sausage, just a schoolhouse and a few sheep nearby. Here. Take a look for yourself."

The schoolhouse jumped into view and he panned the binoculars across the full spectrum.

"OK, listen," he said in a low earnest voice. "I'm going forward to sit on the porch just inside the entrance. Apparently that's the rendezvous point. I'm assuming someone will eventually spot me and make contact. The rest of you stay here and keep watch. I'll take the Luger which will leave all of you reasonably well armed in case anything happens."

Brendan handed him the weapon and wrapping his right hand around the butt, Stuart pushed the safety catch forward with his thumb. Catching sight of Carol's face he murmured, "I'm sure nothing will happen, but we need to be careful."

Not trusting himself to say any more lest his fears reveal themselves he hugged Carol briefly and awkwardly and then moved forward at a crouching run. At the edge of the cleared section around the small schoolhouse he paused and scanned the surrounding area. Nothing was moving. He ran forward, mounted the three steps and entered the small porch. He paused to listen above the sound of his breathing. Apart from the steady hum of the cicadas and the occasional bleat, there was nothing. Following the instructions, after a further visual check he sat down on the top step to wait. His beating heart and sweating palms contrasted sharply with the familiar tranquillity of the rural environment. Although the porch faced away from the sun the humidity hung heavily.

Leaning against the porch wall he gradually relaxed. He wondered how the others were faring, how Carol in particular would cope with whatever lay ahead. She'd shown herself to have a considerable resilience but both of them would be facing greater tests in the future. And his family? How would they cope with his absence – little Claire in particular? Already he missed her bright eyes and her trusting smile. It was all just...

The heavy hand on his right shoulder instantly brought him back to reality. As he tried to rise another hand was placed firmly on his left shoulder and he was held in a sitting position.

"Keep absolutely still, mate."

He looked up into the roughly shaven face of a man in his thirties wearing a canvas hat, a faded tartan shirt, grubby shorts and a pair of well-worn army boots. His companion, similarly dressed, carried a Luger in his right hand.

"What are you doing here?" asked the man.

"I was handed a pamphlet at university. It instructed us to come here. My friends are out there in the paddock nearby."

"We know, mate," said the other man. "We've been watching them for a while."

"OK. Can I call them in? They'll be worried."

"Hang on. Your orders stated, 'no weapons'. You've disobeyed that order and have also brought a larger group."

"Yeah, and three of them are wearing bits of Blitzkrieg Boys' uniforms.

"Yes, that's right. Let me explain."

"Be quick then. We don't have a hell of a lot of time."

As rapidly as he could Stuart explained the sequence of events leading to his arrival at the schoolhouse. The two men listened without interruption and when he had finished they both nodded.

"That tallies, doesn't it?"

"Yeah, it does."

"Tallies'?"

"We picked up one of your bus passengers a couple of hours ago. She'd been running away from the scene, hurt her ankle and was resting by an old cowshed. What she told us agrees with your story."

"Look," said Stuart, "I've explained why we disobeyed your initial orders about weapons, and I can't vouch unreservedly for the loyalty of the soldiers. But," he shrugged, "they bring military experience and inside knowledge, and I presume you can use the weapons." He locked eyes with the two men. "My story tallies, so under the circumstances surely worth a chance?"

Both men looked at each other and the man in the tartan shirt nodded.

"OK, you can call your people in."

Stuart started to rise.

"A word of warning," said the first man.

"What?"

"No funny business. Our people have all of you all completely covered."

Instinctively Stuart scanned the low ridges surrounding the building knowing as he did so he would be unlikely to see any sign of life. He walked round the small school building to face the paddock and waved a beckoning signal. Six figures rose from the long grass and moved forward in the now familiar crouching run.

Chapter 30

The hot sweet tea tasted wonderful and it was difficult to refrain from noisily gulping it down as quickly as possible. Not that the circumstances demanded adherence to drawing room manners. On the walls of the woolshed were hung various implements used for shearing substantial numbers of sheep, and in one corner was a stack of tall wool bales made of strong sacking, stuffed with wool and sewn together with large stitches. The aroma of lanolin ingrained in the floor mingled with the smell of the dried sheep's dung that was layered underneath the slatted raised floorboards.

An hour earlier, the two men had led the entire group away from the school. After half an hour's walk along a narrow dusty road they had rendezvoused with a Bedford flatbed truck that had driven them into a long valley. From there they had emerged to a cluster of farm buildings that included the large reddish-brown woolshed surrounded by an assortment of pens and a half-empty sheep dip trough. Inside the woolshed a group of ten men and two women greeted them cautiously and indicated they were to find a place on the floor. Within ten minutes big chipped enamel mugs of tea were thrust into their grateful hands and a plate piled high with thickly-cut chunky peanut butter sandwiches was passed around.

"Reckon you'll be pretty hungry and thirsty," said the man who Stuart had first encountered on the porch. "Take your time while we brief you on the set up. Then we'll have a few questions for you."

Engrossed in slaking their thirst, the seven nodded.

"OK. For starters, my name's Dan. It's not my real name and here we don't have surnames. If we decide you can stay, you'll have to choose another name for yourself as we don't want to know your real name. Guess the reason's fairly obvious."

He paused and they all nodded again.

"OK. This place is run as a proper farm. Some of us are experienced farmers, while others do jobs as directed. The occasional outsiders who come here, like salesmen and so forth, assume it's an ordinary farm and we want to keep it that way. Consequently we can't have a lot of strange people hanging around doing nothing."

Drawing a tobacco tin from his top pocket, he opened it, extracted a thin cigarette paper and a small clump of tobacco and proceeded to roll into a cylindrical shape.

"Now," his voice changed to a sneering tone, "the New Order."

The short mocking laugh of his companions echoed round the woolshed. Smiling an acknowledgment he looked at the group of seven.

"You may have experienced the dark side of this New Order, the aspects not published in the newspapers or broadcast over the wireless. All of us are dedicated to fighting back against the New Order, but that doesn't simply mean playing heroes and killing people. Yes, that's necessary at times but we also need to continue to remind our fellow Kiwis this country is occupied, and the so-called new prosperity comes at a high price – the price of their freedom, their individuality, and their way of life."

Growls of approval and loud comments such as "Good on you, Dan!" drifted up past the exposed beams and echoed off the iron roof.

Smiling an acknowledgement Dan looked again at the seven. "Notice I didn't say 'Comrades'. There are various shades of political opinion here and that's as it should be. However, we are united in one aim – discrediting and bringing down the New Order." He stared hard at the three soldiers. "And eliminating groups such as the Blitzkrieg Boys."

The trio shifted uncomfortably.

"In the meantime you're welcome as our guests. As new recruits you will be carefully questioned and tested. If you pass you will enter our training programme." He paused and looked outside at the fading sky. "Getting late and because of what happened back up the road, hard to predict what the consequences will be. We may have to move into emergency mode at any time so the first thing we'll do is rehearse the procedure. But," his gaze met the eyes of each of the newcomers, "let me remind you that you are not yet members of our group and what we show you now must not be divulged under any circumstances."

"You're going to show us something secret even though we're not members? What happens if you then decide we're not acceptable?" Brown was obviously expressing the question that had been raised in all their minds, especially the three soldiers.

"Good question. Unfortunately I don't have a pat answer for you," replied Dan. His expression hardened. "But be aware that as far as this group's concerned, there's still a war on."

He let his answer hang in the air and then nodded to the man standing alongside him.

"G'day," said the man, stepping forward. He was leaner than Dan and bore a scar across his left cheek. "My name's Tony and I'm in charge of mechanical operations. Please pay close attention."

Moving over to the wall he reached up to one of the supporting beams that ran from the floor to the ceiling. Grasping a small section he carefully pulled outwards revealing a tiny hinged door that had been built into the beam. He reached inside and twisted his hand to the right. There was a loud click followed by a whirring sound. Slowly a portion of the floor, on which a small wool bale had been placed, lifted up. The whirring stopped. The bale lay resting parallel to the floor revealing a neatly cut square hole.

Tony smiled at the astonished looks on the seven faces.

"No need to applaud my modest achievements, friends. But, allow me to introduce you to your new 5 star accommodation."

Walking over to the hole in the floor he made a flamboyant invitational gesture with his right arm. Scrambling to their feet the seven new arrivals hurried over to the hole and peered down. The first thing they noticed was the deep shaft that had been cut at right angles to the floor. On one side was a ladder that followed the wall of the shaft to the bottom.

"Welcome to the Albany Ritz, honoured guests," smiled Tony with a low bow. He turned to Carol. "Ladies first."

Taken aback, Carol looked at Stuart who smiled and nodded. Cautiously she climbed onto the first rung and descended the shaft.

The others followed and on reaching the bottom of the ladder were astonished at the relative sophistication of the facility. Expecting a dank, narrow mineshaft, they were confronted instead by a series of small cubicles of shoulder height. Although the tunnel base was clay, each cubicle had a slatted floor, a bed with a straw palliasse, and an electric light bulb suspended from the ceiling. Each doorway was neatly framed in timber with its own wooden door.

Tony, who had been the last to descend, stood by the base of the ladder smiling proudly at their gasps of admiration.

"You're the first inhabitants, my friends. We were expecting to increase our numbers and so, with the use of some drilling equipment, and plenty of sweat and muscle, we built the Albany Ritz. The dunny's at the end of the corridor. Dry drop I'm afraid but, under the circumstances..." He smiled. "And you'll have to remember to wash before you descend. We haven't yet arranged full plumbing." He shrugged exaggeratedly. "So difficult to get tradesmen at the moment, don't you know."

"How long did this take, Tony?" Susan asked.

"'Bout six months. Put it together straight after the surrender. A group of us realized an occupation of New Zealand by the Germans would be a hideous prospect and some sort of resistance would have to be started." He gestured with his right arm. "I'm proud to say that this concept is being adopted by others in the network."

"Network?" asked Stuart.

Tony smiled and shook his head. "Now, choose your berths." He grinned at the two women. "In anticipation of a variety of needs we do have several double suites."

Catching Brendan's eye Stuart grinned as his mate's face broke into a knowing grin and his left eye slowly closed.

Chapter 31

Like the others, Stuart had made a valiant attempt to remove the day's dirt using the cold tap, grey sand soap and aluminium trough in the small bathroom off the end of the shearing shed. Although the soap on his skin was painful he was determined to make himself as clean as possible.

Carol had used the bathroom and, coming into the cubicle, had simply smiled, jerked her head upstairs and said, "Your turn."

There was a cutthroat razor hanging by the mirror and to make himself more presentable he soaped his face and, after sharpening the razor on the worn leather strop, carefully shaved off the day's growth. He dunked his head in the small basin and pulled it out gasping at the effect of the cold water. For the umpteenth time he wondered if she would be waiting for him when he went back down the ladder or would he once again be put in the position of having to be the sensitive, patient, understanding male. She'd made him promise to give her some time. Well he had, and in between times they'd made a getaway together, survived a shootout, teamed up with a group of Blitzkrieg Boys, met the Fightback members and been initially accepted into their organization. He caught a glimpse of himself in the small cracked mirror, smiled grimly and nodded at this own reflection. "Yes," he murmured, "she's definitely had enough time."

Then, with a final glance in the mirror he left the bathroom and descended the stairs.

The door to their cubicle was half closed and the light was off. The only other light was the cubicle at the end of the corridor that he presumed was occupied by Brendan and Susan.

He pushed the door open and entered.

"Close the door," she whispered. The latch clicked shut and he turned towards the bed. With a slight rustle she moved sideways and lifted the blankets invitingly. Stuart suppressed a gasp when he saw she was naked.

As he slid in beside her he registered the wonderful warmth of her body. Her mouth on his was equally warm and generous and as she slid underneath him she wrapped her arms tightly round his back causing him to involuntarily wince.

"Easy, darling," he murmured.

She giggled in response. "What was it Aunt Catherine said about not indulging in activities of a vigorous nature?"

"She's a wise lady, but not necessarily infallible," he replied, marvelling at the feeling of Carol's flesh underneath his.

"Yes, but I don't want any further damage done to my man," she whispered. "So, turn over."

Unsure of her intentions, he nevertheless did as he was told and rolled cautiously off her onto his back. Before he even realized what had happened she was above him, straddling his thighs with her head leaning down. Her hair fell across his face and tangled itself in both their mouths. Slowly and rhythmically she began to move across his groin and he moaned inside her mouth. Jerking her head back she thrust her left breast towards his mouth and as he tried to absorb it she moaned and shifted her thighs enabling him to enter her.

They came together.

After their trembling had subsided he twisted his head and kissed her. She had collapsed alongside him, her head resting at right angles to his. He kissed her and tasted blood.

Gently he touched her mouth. "Are you hurt?"

"No. I just had to bite my lip hard to stop myself crying out. I didn't want to disturb anyone else."

"By 'anyone else' I presume you mean Brendan and Susan," he chuckled. "I'm sure they're far too self absorbed to worry about us."

She laughed and then she touched his lips. "Mm. I never imagined in my wildest dreams it could be like that. And you with busted ribs as well."

"Fair's fair. You played an active role," he laughed, stroking her hair. "I love you, Carol."

"I know you do, Stuart. And I know now that I love you."

Draped across each other they fell into a deep sleep.

In the early hours of the morning Stuart woke to the feel of Carol's hands gently stroking his stomach. As they moved lower she murmured, "Why, darling, I thought you were asleep."

This time, secure in the knowledge and trust created by their earlier intimacy, their lovemaking was slower.

The next time they woke it was to the sound of a voice from somewhere above shouting, "Breakfast in 20 minutes! Rise and shine!"

Stuart, who was lying on his back, pulled Carol over so her head lay on his chest. "Is this what you anticipated when we caught the bus yesterday morning?"

"God, no. I thought we'd meet up with some scruffy bunch that would probably be living in tents and spending most of their time keeping one jump ahead of the Blitzkrieg Boys. These people are much better organized than I ever imagined – a fully functioning farm, allocated areas of expertise, and this amazing underground facility."

"Yes, and apparently a counter-insurgency training programme. But don't let's underestimate what we're up against – a very successful war machine. We may have come out on top in yesterday morning's skirmish but that will only make the authorities more angry and ruthless."

"How do you feel about the three soldiers?"

"Not entirely sure, yet. In a way they're both a liability and an asset."

"Meaning?"

"Well, they're deserters who had a direct involvement in an incident in which New Order soldiers were killed. That means soon we'll have the bloody Krauts swarming all over this area."

"Yes, but what makes them an asset?"

"Their inside knowledge. They've been through the system so whatever they can tell us will be useful."

"True." She sighed. "Stuart?"

"Mm?" He started to stroke her hair.

"Are we going to be all right?"

"We're going to look after each other; that's what we're going to do."

"Which brings me to Brendan and Susan. Bit sudden, don't you think?"

Stuart chuckled. "Doesn't waste much time, does our Brendan."

"She's really nice, Stuart. I'd hate her to get hurt."

"I understand. Brendan, in spite of his devil-may-care attitude, is a decent bloke. Susan's been through a lot. We all have." He gently stroked her hair. "Each of us is about to take a leap in the dark and we all need someone to hold hands with."

For a long moment she lay still before replying. "You're right. Under the circumstances, that's the best thing we can do. Promise we'll look after each other."

"You have my promise."

"Mine too."

She began to run her fingernails down the centre of his chest. "Hmm, you delicious man."

"Carol," he murmured, "they said breakfast was in twenty minutes and that was ten minutes ago."

"That gives us another ten minutes to work up an appetite," she replied, her mouth closing on his.

CHAPTER 32

"That's it! Over on his back! Use his weight not your strength! Now, let's try it again! Steve, go!"

Stuart took a moment to respond to the new name he had chosen for himself. Then in obedience to the order he leapt forward with his right arm upraised, carrying the wooden knife. Suddenly he was off balance and the thud with which he hit the ground expelled his breath from his body. Carol hurried forward and knelt by his side.

"Darling, I'm sorry. You OK?"

"No 'darlings' in this business, Jacquie. He's OK and you've done well. Hopefully you'll never have to use the technique but if you do, don't forget to follow up. Immediately!"

"Oh, sorry, Ian." Embarrassed, she scrambled to her feet and gripped the wooden knife in her hand. She crouched over Stuart again but this time held the knife to his throat.

"No need for that," he grinned. "I surrender."

"Right, you two, on your feet. Take a breather before we have another go." Ian smiled at Carol. "I have to confess when Dan told me I'd have to train two women I had my doubts. But you two have changed my mind." His smile faded and he looked at her seriously. "But, in a combat situation, do you think you could go through with it? Actually kill your enemy?"

"Yes, Ian." She wiped the streak of sweat from her brow and met his gaze. "The Germans killed my brother. The vilest man I've ever known has become one of them. I saw with my own eyes what they did to the university students and I know what they did to Professor Sterling. Yes, Ian, I believe I could go through with it."

213

The unarmed combat session had been the first of their training programmes. The former Blitzkrieg Boys, having served in two armies, had reached a high skill standard, thus giving Ian plenty of time to concentrate on Stuart, Carol, Brendan and Susan. Like Carol, each of them was motivated by their recent experiences and had proved to be apt pupils.

"That's it for the morning, chaps," he grinned, "and ladies. We'll knock off for an hour and have lunch. Have plenty to eat and drink as we've got a long afternoon ahead of us. Weapons training is always held well away from the main buildings in order to minimize any repercussions from curious visitors."

Strong tea, chunky sandwiches and apples were set up in the woolshed. The previous day each one of them had been extensively questioned about their background, their motivation for joining the partisan group, and their commitment level. At the end of the evening meal the whole group were informed that Fightback had accepted them on a three-month probation period, resulting in an increased atmosphere of camaraderie.

An hour later the sound of the Bedford truck pulling up outside the woolshed reminded them of the job in hand and in response to Ian's orders they clambered onto the flatbed tray at the back. The trip took about thirty minutes, through a variety of small hills and valleys until they arrived at what appeared to be an abandoned farmhouse. They clambered off the truck and Ian explained that the farmhouse was deliberately maintained in a dilapidated state to allay any suspicion. They were then shown a cleverly concealed entrance to an underground cellar that housed weaponry gleaned from a variety of 'unnamed sources'.

"How did you get these weapons here?" Brendan gazed at the arsenal in the cellar. "Surely any large truck runs the risk of being randomly searched?"

"That's the advantage of Albany," grinned Stuart. "As well as a few roads it also has water transport. All this stuff is brought up here at night on small barges, using Lucas Creek."

"Lucas Creek?" asked Sue.

"Yes. It winds its way through heavy bush, past this part of the farm. Tidal navigation is tricky. But," Dan tapped the side of his nose, "if you know your way it's relatively easy, and well away from prying eyes."

Their first afternoon session was spent in practicing with the British bolt-action 303 rifles. Although firing only one bullet at a time the weapon could be loaded with a small magazine and was extremely accurate. They were also taught to load and fire some newly-acquired hand-held Sten guns. The weapon, designed for close range engagements, was useful to a group like Fightback as it could also be fired using German 9mm ammunition. Aware of the weapon's tendency to jam, Ian had all of them repeatedly practice the procedures for stripping and assembling the Stens until they could literally do so with their eyes closed.

For several hours they practised loading and firing from various positions and simulated situations. By the end of the afternoon their ears were ringing and their hands trembling. Although the two women had found it difficult to cope with the weight of some of the weapons, they had proved adept at being part of a captured German MG 34 machine gun crew, efficiently feeding the belts of ammunition through the breech of each gun. It was difficult, noisy work and after the unarmed combat practice, exhausting. Again, the experience of the former Blitzkrieg Boys proved invaluable. They were familiar with nearly all the weapons and willingly supplied support.

Finally Ian called a halt. "Enough for one day. You've all done very well." He smiled and without any trace of condescension added, "In particular the girls. You've handled three different weapons today. Tomorrow we'll revise what we've done and in the afternoon I'll let you have a go at the Bren gun – stripping, assembling and firing. It's a machine gun but like the rifle it uses 303 ammunition and is very accurate when fired off a tripod." He looked around the group. "Now, like me I bet you're all looking forward to a good meal and a relaxing evening."

The men and women needed no further encouragement to scramble on the back of the truck and relax against the wooden sides as it bounced its way steadily along the dirt road. Suddenly it skidded to a halt. Looking over the sides they saw Tony standing in the centre of the track holding a bicycle and waving them to a halt.

"They sent me to alert you. There's a bit of a flap on."

"What's happened?"

"The authorities have discovered the soldiers' bodies and they're swarming over this district in droves. So far they haven't reached our farm but obviously we're on their maps and they could turn up any time. Dan's orders are for Ian to drive the truck back to the house and, if anyone asks, just say he was taking hay to one of the back paddocks. You others are to come with me. I'll take you in a roundabout way that will enable us to recce the house before we finally approach it. We should be OK but the situation calls for caution."

Reluctantly the seven climbed down. Although each had been eagerly anticipating some food and relaxation, they realized that under the circumstances erring on the side of caution made sense. Tony concealed his bike in a clump of roadside bushes and as the truck moved off he beckoned the others to follow him. Climbing up a sharp incline they reached the edge of an area of native bush growing thickly across the tops of the hills. He paused and beckoned for them to gather round.

"The interior's fairly dry so our footprints won't be too obvious. It's fairly thick so try to avoid breaking off any twigs, branches, or fern fronds – a dead giveaway for anyone following us or trying to work out if this area is in regular use."

They nodded and Tony, with the ease of familiarity, entered the bush and moved along a barely discernible path.

The dim interior of the bush was cool and provided a welcome relief from the heat. Consequently, although Tony's pace was brisk, the walk was not unpleasant. For a while a pair of fantails provided light entertainment as they flitted and darted alongside the group, casting tiny shadows in the small beams of sunlight that penetrated the thick green canopy.

After about fifteen minutes Tony stopped and beckoned them forward.

"OK. We now approach with caution. If there are any problems there'll be a signal from the farmhouse. Even so we look for anything unusual, such as strangers or strange vehicles, prolonged barking by the dogs and suchlike."

"What's the signal from the farmhouse?" asked Brendan.

"If the curtains in the kitchen are opened, it's OK to approach. If they're drawn we are to wait here. Similarly, if the exterior light on the woolshed is turned on we are to wait. However, we're always mindful that if we have unexpected and unannounced visitors it may not provide enough time to draw the curtains or turn on the light – hence the extra precautions. Now, as we're coming near the edge of the clearing overlooking the farm buildings, I'll lead and the rest of you stay close and follow my movements."

The bush in front of Tony began to thin and soon the reddish-tinged late afternoon sky was visible through the leaves and branches. Tony slowed and then dropped down some fallen punga logs on the bush's edge. He motioned the others to do the same and, pulling out a pair of Zeiss binoculars from his pack, scanned the farmhouse and surrounding buildings in the distance.

"Curtains are pulled back," he muttered.

His binoculars panned from left to right and then in reverse order. Satisfied, he turned to the group.

"Everything looks fine. Now, one group at a time, we'll head towards the woolshed where someone will be waiting to greet you, hopefully with food and drink. When the first group arrives and it's OK, give us a wave and the second will follow. Once inside the woolshed, if there's any problem you must follow the procedure we've rehearsed and instantly go down into your quarters. Is that clear?"

They all nodded.

"OK. The two women and Steve are to go first. The others and I will follow once you've arrived safely. Go now."

The three stood up and headed down the gentle slope towards the shearing shed. In spite of Tony's reassurance, the recent news and the open space filled each of them with a sense of vulnerability. Consequently it was with considerable relief that they moved past the last of the sheep pens and up the woolshed steps where Dan, with Lisa and Barbara the other two women in the group, greeted them.

"Welcome home," Dan grinned. "All clear, so I guess you could murder a cup of tea and some food."

"Too right," said Stuart. "Any problems so far?"

"Not that we're aware of," said Lisa. "The so-called Albany incident has been given particular prominence on the radio news – the deaths of the soldiers have been blamed on," she paused, "let me get it right, 'a tiny group of terrorist fanatics who will be dealt with swiftly and mercilessly by the authorities'."

"'So honest, law abiding citizens can feel safe and enjoy the prosperity that comes with the New Order,'" added Barbara. "It's not that we've got good memories, but after a while the news broadcasts have an inevitable predictably."

"Yes," smiled Stuart wryly, "Nazi propaganda is not necessarily synonymous with originality and creativity."

As they sipped their hot mugs of tea, from the window they watched the second group making its way across the paddocks and past the sheep pens without incident. Soon they were all gathered round the wool-sorting table eating plates of food that each had fetched from the farmhouse kitchen. Tea-making facilities were standard in many woolsheds, but a fully equipped kitchen capable of making substantial meals would arouse suspicion.

The meal provided a welcome opportunity to relax. The woolshed was warm and dry and the existence of the 'Albany Ritz' was an additional reassurance.

"Cards, anyone?" called Barbara.

"Yeah, great idea," replied Dan. "However, first things first." He looked at Stuart. "Now, as you know, we make it a priority to get rid of any evidence of extra guests. Therefore, every night as soon as dinner is finished, two people are assigned to take the dirty dishes back to the farmhouse, clean them and put them away. Mugs are OK but dirty dinner dishes are not. You and Jacquie can do it tonight, please."

"Fine," responded Carol. She grinned at Stuart. "Come on 'Steve', a little domestic duty will do you the world of good."

It was a five-minute walk from the woolshed to the farmhouse. "Careful not to stumble," warned Carol "If you break the plates we'll all be eating off newspapers."

"As long as it's not the New Order Herald. That's enough to give all of us indigestion."

The dishes were efficiently washed, dried and cleared away with the help of Jason and Tom, the two Fightback members who lived permanently in the farmhouse. Stuart and Carol enjoyed the opportunity of getting to know the other two even though, because the rules did not allow group members to reveal their personal details, small talk was somewhat stilted.

As the last of the dishes were being put away the lights in the farmhouse suddenly dimmed twice.

"Jesus!" snapped Tom. "A vehicle has crossed the cattle stop."

"Bugger," said Jason. "Suppose it had to happen sometime."

"What do you mean?" asked Carol nervously.

"We try to keep the occupants of the house to the minimum necessary to operate the farm legitimately. Anyone else could lead to awkward explanations. Don't know who our visitors are but you two won't have time to reach the woolshed without being spotted. We do have an emergency bolthole in the next room. Tom will get you up there while I answer the door. Move!"

They heard a vehicle crunching up the gravelled driveway as Stuart and Carol followed Tom through the dining room into a small bedroom. Standing on the bed he reached up and touched the ceiling. A panel opened to reveal a small ladder lying across the gap. "Tony's magic," muttered Tom. He grasped the bottom rung and pulled. The ladder came down at right angles to the ceiling.

"Both of you up! The ceiling's reinforced so it's quite safe. But lie absolutely still and don't make a sound until we give the all clear."

The pair scrambled up the short ladder. As soon as they were clear of the gap Tom pushed it back up and closed the tight-fitting ceiling door. They found themselves on a wooden floor from which the sounds of the house could be heard below. Quietly they moved to a side-by-side position and lay still.

Underneath they heard a loud, sustained banging on the front door followed by the sound of footsteps and the door being opened.

"Good evening." The accent was heavily Germanic.

"Good evening." The voice was Tom's. "Is there something wrong?"

"We would like to come in. We have questions."

It was an order rather than a request, as footsteps were heard entering the house.

"Would you like to sit down?" It was Tom's voice.

"Thank you. I am Franz Schroeder, Special Police."

Stuart caught his breath. Schroeder – the German who'd arrested him at the Auckland railway station. He listened more intently.

More footsteps, a scraping of chairs, and then Schroeder's voice continued. "I introduce my two colleagues, Detective Sergeant James Wallace and Special Agent Hamish Beavis."

Stuart felt Carol stiffen as a cold shiver swept over him. He squeezed her arm tightly and with his mouth close to her ear, whispered, "It's OK. Keep still and listen."

There was a further scraping of chairs and then a moment's silence before Schroeder's voice resumed.

"My other men will stay outside. Now, you know about the attack on the Albany road."

"Yes." It was Tom's voice. "We heard about it on the radio news broadcast."

"That is good. We have questioned all of the er..."

"Passengers, Mr. Schroeder."

"Thank you, Mr. Wallace. Ja, we have questioned passengers, from the bus. But two people – a man and a woman. They have disappeared."

"We are searching this part of the country. Have you seen any strangers?" The voice was Wallace's.

"No. We haven't. If we had, we..."

The harsh voice cut him short. "We are particularly interested in the missing man and woman." It was Hamish Beavis. "Their names are Stuart Johnson and Carol Peterson. Have you seen either of them before?"

There was a slight shuffling and a long pause.

"No. Never seen them."

"Why are you looking for them?"

Carol's grip on Stuart's arm was fierce.

"They are associated with the university where there was an, er, unfortunate occurrence a few days ago. They have both disappeared and we have cause to believe they may have been involved in the incident on the Albany Road."

There was a silence. Tom and Jason had decided to say nothing further.

"Their families do not know where they are. However we have reason to believe they may have been passengers on the bus that was involved in the incident," said Wallace.

"Well, we haven't seen them, have we Tom?"

"No. But we'll be on our guard. Do you think they're armed?"

"Very likely." Hamish's voice sounded frustrated and angry. "They may have teamed up with some New Order deserters..."

"Herr Beavis! Enough! To speak of this thing is forbidden. The information is..."

"Classified," prompted Wallace.

"Ja, classified. You will remember that, Beavis."

Although films of sweat were layering themselves over his body, Stuart enjoyed a fleeting moment of satisfaction at the contriteness in Hamish's reply.

"Er, yes, my apologies, Mr. Schroeder. I appear to have been, er, misinformed. There was, of course, no question of desertions."

"Let me, on this matter, be very clear," Schroeder continued. "The New Order government is for the good of all the people of this country."

Tom's sycophantic reply was designed to please the German. "We agree, Mr. Schroeder. Milk and wool prices have never been better."

"And we greatly appreciate the assistance provided by government agricultural agents," added Jason, echoing the obsequious tone.

"Ach, excellent. Our government values the work of the farming peasants."

Hamish coughed.

"The two subversives, Mr. Schroeder." He was concerned to maintain the focus on Stuart and Carol. "They are considered ruthless and will stop at nothing to achieve their ends. It is crucial they are both captured and brought in for," his voice slowed, "special questioning."

Feeling a shudder pass through Carol's body, Stuart positioned his right hand at the top of her head and massaged it gently with his fingers.

"Of course," said Wallace. "Mr. Beavis, through his personal knowledge and recent association with the university, has been assigned to us to assist in the hunting down of these two subversives.

"I have met one of these people," said Schroeder. "With him I have, how do you say it in English, some unfinished business." He gave a grunt of mild amusement and then continued. "You said you have not seen them. You say you support the New Order government. That is good." His voice took on a harsher tone. "You will remember please, that giving help to enemies of the state is punishable by death. Please tell your neighbours of this. Soldiers and a German officer have been murdered." A chair was scraped back and fell clattering to the ground. "Those who spread terror will be punished!"

Other chairs were pushed back, followed by a shuffling of feet.

"We are visiting other houses to tonight," said Schroeder. "These enemies of the state will be found. Tell your neighbours that no stone, er..."

"Will be left unturned, Mr. Schroeder?" It was the detective's voice.

"Ja. No stone. Tell your neighbours." Another pause and a heel click. "We will take our leave."

Stuart and Carol lay still, their thoughts in turmoil at the implications of what they had heard. They listened intently to the sounds of departure and, after a brief silence the outside door opened and closed. A pair of footsteps returned to the room and stopped.

"Stuart and Carol," said Tom softly, "If you can hear me tap twice."

Startled at hearing their real names used, Stuart momentarily paused and then tapped.

223

"OK. We think they've gone but there's always the possibility they've left men behind to watch the place. I've turned the dogs loose and we'll let them roam for a while. If there are any strangers around the property they'll let us know. I'll then whistle them back and if they arrive in one piece we'll be fairly sure everything'll be OK. Can you hang on a little longer?"

Stuart tapped again.

"Good. It's OK for the two of you to talk if you keep your voices low. If there's any sign of danger we'll instantly let you know."

CHAPTER 33

During the next hour Stuart and Carol, their faces close together, whispered a review of the events in the room below. Their greatest concern was the speed with which the authorities had picked up their trail, and the direct involvement of Hamish Beavis. From his tone Beavis was motivated by anger and revenge which dovetailed neatly into the importance that his superiors attached to apprehending those involved in the Albany killing. They were both also worried about the attitude of their new colleagues, who might regard the presence of two identified 'terrorists' as too much of a liability – in which case their situation looked very bleak. The authorities now had copies of their pictures; their families had been contacted and intimidated and were now almost certainly now under constant surveillance. The familiar and secure links of friends, families and work had disappeared. They'd taken the only option open to them at the time and now faced the unimaginably bleak prospect of becoming pariahs, shunned, feared and hunted – in their own land.

Below they could hear the movements of people coming and going but apart from the occasional innocuous comment, nothing of any importance was discussed within their hearing. Their sense

Eventually several pairs of footsteps entered the bedroom and stopped in the centre. The ceiling trapdoor was opened and the ladder lowered.

It was Dan's voice that said, "You can come down now."

Cautiously Stuart stretched out his legs and, when his feet touched the rungs, began to descend. Halfway down he stopped and stared into the room. The faces staring up at them were expressionless.

"It's OK, Carol," he said and completing his descent, watched as she climbed down into the room.

"How're you feeling?" Dan's voice was flat.

"Bit stiff, bit worried," replied Carol, glancing at Stuart who reached out and took her hand.

"Yeah, I bet," said Dan tonelessly. "There's a meeting over at the woolshed. We've got some things to discuss. Come on."

He indicated they were both to go in front of the others. Apprehensively they walked out of the door into the dark yard and headed towards the woolshed.

Four men remained in the farmhouse in case of emergency. The rest were gathered in the woolshed, some on seats, others on the floor and several were perched on wool bales. The inability of the naked light bulbs to reach all the faces created an ominous atmosphere. This was further reinforced by the subdued responses to Stuart and Carol's greeting.

"Sit here," said Dan, indicating two chairs in the centre of the room.

Facing the group Stuart resisted the temptation to make some wisecrack about kangaroo courts, and tried instead to read the faces that surrounded them.

Dan sat at right angles to them, his elbows resting on the large wool-sorting table.

"I presume you both heard all of the conversation that took place in the dining room."

They nodded.

"I also presume you are aware of the increased seriousness of the situation."

They nodded again.

"We have all been discussing its implications. We knew when we began a resistance movement we would be facing some serious problems. This current situation is certainly more serious than we had imagined."

He paused and looked around. A few heads nodded but nobody spoke.

"Although our rule is not to reveal our real identities to each other in case of future interrogations, in your case the authorities have done it for us. Both of you are now classified as terrorists. We have heard your names mentioned on the radio news an hour ago. Schroeder, Beavis and Wallace had photos of both of you so I daresay they'll be in tomorrow's newspaper."

Stuart's eyes swept the shadowy interior. "Obviously we hadn't expected this. And for them to say we spread terror is ridiculous."

"Yes," said Carol. "We've harmed nobody."

"It's a political label, nothing more, nothing less. One group's 'freedom fighter' is another group's 'terrorist'," responded Tony from the back of the woolshed. "Whether or not you've done anyone any harm is irrelevant. If you're labelled as an 'enemy of the people' then that turns people against you and gives the authorities the excuse to deal with you however they please. Reason or logic has nothing to do with it."

There was a murmur of agreement as Dan continued.

"The fact that you're high on their wanted list means an increased risk for everyone here. Aiding, abetting or harbouring a terrorist is a capital offence. Anyone in this room could be hanged for it."

"Look," Carol began falteringly, "we hate the Nazis as much as anyone in this room. We joined Fightback because it gave us a chance to, well, fight back." She paused but there was no reaction. Her voice steadied. "We have no intention of putting anyone, not one single person, in danger on our account."

Putting his arm across her shoulder, Stuart faced the group.

"We're fully aware we're a danger to all of you. We discussed it together while we were left hiding in the ceiling." He glanced at Carol who nodded. "We've made a joint decision. People could be killed because of our presence here." He rose and looked squarely into the faces of those in the front. "There's no alternative. We'll both leave and take our chances. We may

227

get caught but the rest of you will be safe." He reached down and took Carol's hand as she rose and stood alongside him. "Right, Carol?"

"Yes," she said. Looking straight at Dan she continued. "As Stuart has said, we've made a joint decision." Her grip on his hand tightened. "We'll leave tonight."

The spontaneous burst of applause stunned them both. Brendan stepped out of the shadows and seized Stuart's hand while Susan hurried forward to embrace Carol.

"What the hell's going on?" Stuart was completely bewildered at the sudden change of mood.

"We had a meeting and decided to see what your attitude would be to the change in the situation. We wanted to see if you'd put your friends or yourselves first," explained Dan.

"You've passed the test, mate," said a hugely smiling Brendan. "Now we can work out a plan of campaign." He grinned even wider. "Not that I ever doubted you for a moment of course!"

Tony was on his feet again. "Members of Fightback are committed to supporting each other in all situations. That's one of our central tenets. In any case, you're not the only two who are liabilities." He paused and pointed to the three former Blitzkrieg Boys. "Obviously the authorities don't want it known that three of their soldiers deserted. But that doesn't mean they'll be any less rigorous in their pursuit of the deserters or any more lenient with any who have provided them with aid and comfort. We, my friends, are all compromised. In fact we were the moment each and every one of us decided to oppose the oppressors and their cronies and join Fightback. Now," he turned to Dan, "it's been a long night and extra guards have to be posted so I suggest we all turn in and catch up on some richly deserved sleep."

Dan nodded. "Second the motion. There's still plenty of detail to work through but I think we've all had quite enough for one day. OK everyone, let's grab some shuteye."

Half an hour later Carol, having taken her turn at the washbasin, returned to the cubicle and slipped into bed beside Stuart. Throughout the twists and turns of the extraordinary day she had been continually conscious of his strength and support and was looking forward to what was fast becoming the best part of the day – sharing a bed with him.

He was lying on his back and hardly moved as she slid in beside him and rested her head lightly on his chest. She gently moved her hand backwards and forwards across his chest but he barely stirred. Enticingly she slid her bare leg across his legs towards his groin. His only response was to sigh. She lay still for a moment deciding whether or not to persevere and within a few moments she had joined her lover in a long deep sleep.

CHAPTER 34

"You two can't go, and that's an end to the matter."

"Look, Brendan..."

"No, you look, mate, you're known to the authorities. Your photo and Carol's have been widely circulated. Even if you want to play the brave soldier boy, how about considering her?"

"You could be in danger too."

"Possibly. But there's a big manhunt out there and the focus is on you two."

"Hamish Beavis," said Carol.

"Exactly. He's obviously painted the blackest possible picture of both of you in order to gain maximum support for his personal vendetta. If either of you risk going out in public you'd be playing right into his hands."

A collective murmur of agreement echoed round the woolshed. The day had ended and, with double sentries posted, a full meeting was under way.

"OK, OK," said Dan walking into the centre and holding up his hand. "Your enthusiasm for the cause is commendable, Stuart, but Brendan's right. If you get captured you could compromise all of us."

"I hope you're not suggesting that I would..." began Stuart sharply.

"I'm not suggesting anything," Dan said. "Simply bear in mind we're not dealing with a few grubby thugs. We are dealing with powerful sadistic men who have re-invented the art of extracting information in the most painful and effective way possible."

He continued to a murmured assenting undertone.

"Fortunately none of us has had direct experience of their methods. And I don't wish to put anyone in the position of finding out personally. So, Stuart and Carol are staying here."

Dan turned towards Brendan. "Now," he continued, "please summarize the information that's been received and what we plan to do."

With a quick smile at Susan, Brendan joined Dan in the centre.

"In Nazi Germany a resistance movement emerged about a year after the start of the war among medical students at Munich University. It called itself *Die weiße Rose* – The White Rose. It developed in response to the Nazis' stifling of individual freedom within Germany and the cruelty that had been inflicted on Jews and peoples in occupied places like Poland and Russia."

"Define 'resistance movement'," said Dan.

Brendan nodded. "The information we gleaned during the war was very limited. However, it appears that resistance in this case did not involve acts of violence. However the movement's personnel were reasonably successful in the writing and printing of anti-Nazi leaflets which they distributed through the White Rose network that spread throughout parts of Germany."

"Which presumably didn't impress the Nazi government," said Dan

"Absolutely not. The Nazis used their networks of informers to round up the key White Rose men and women. Their university studies were terminated and all were seconded into the armed forces and sent to occupied countries overseas, including New Zealand. Two days ago two of their women," he glanced at this notes, "a Sophie and a Gretchen, managed to make contact with an Auckland University College cell member."

"Could be a trap," said Susan.

"True. But it could also provide us with a direct link into the occupation forces. The University chaps have had a preliminary interview with the women and looked through some literature that they had. However they want a second opinion before proceeding any further."

"That's where Brendan comes in," said Dan. "His German fluency, the knowledge he gained during the war and his trip to Berlin makes him the ideal person. We've arranged a rendezvous with the two White Rose women tomorrow."

"Where?" asked Lisa.

"Best that only a few of us know. All the arrangements have been made. Brendan is to make contact, find out what he can and then report back to us. We'll then take it from there, if he's successful."

He paused and studied the silent group.

"If Stuart and Carol can't go, then I'll go with you," said Susan suddenly.

"Susan, we've already discussed this," began Brendan.

"I know there'll be danger but a hand-holding couple is less likely to attract attention than a lone male." Seeing he was about to reply she held up her hand. "I've done the basic training, and know a little German."

She stood up, smiled and coyly tilting her head downwards minced towards the centre, running both her palms down the front of her light floral frock. Stopping directly in front of Brendan she looked up at him from lowered lids.

"And in any case, if you're going to meet a couple of golden haired Rhineland frauleins," she said guilelessly, "you'd better have me there to keep an eye on you."

The laughter broke the tension. Bernard smiled at Dan, shrugged his shoulders and spread his arms wide.

"Guess you can't argue with that, mate."

CHAPTER 35

The Friday morning walk around the foreshore between the marine suburbs of Takapuna and Milford was deceptively pleasant. The clear blue of the sky mirrored the shimmering hues of the Waitemata Harbour presided over by conical-shaped Rangitoto Island – a familiar landmark to mariners and Aucklanders.

In keeping with their role of a young couple enjoying a day at the beach, Brendan was clad in light trousers, an open-necked shirt, battered Panama hat and sunglasses. Susan was wearing a pretty summer frock with a broad-brimmed straw hat secured by a light blue scarf tied under her chin. Although, like all New Zealanders, Brendan had spent his boyhood in bare feet, his soles had lost some of their toughness and he now wore scruffy but serviceable sandshoes. Assured they would be 'looked after' neither was armed.

The car had dropped them at Hurstmere Road, the main road that paralleled the coast, and taking the side street leading to the foreshore, they had begun making their way along the rocky path past various small inlets. Absorbed by their own thoughts, they walked in silence paying scant attention to the beauty of their surroundings. The light breeze played with the folds of Susan's frock as, entering the Thorne's Bay inlet, she took Brendan's hand and walked across the small beach's warm sand. Reaching the end they clambered back up onto the narrow rocky path and continued to follow its northward contours.

Susan's scream suddenly cut through the stillness. Clutching Brendan's arm she scrambled back from the edge of the path and pressed herself up against the rock wall.

"Silly girl," he chuckled, as the wave that had splashed the hem of her frock hissed away from the base of the path.

"Sorry," she smiled wanly, still holding onto his arm. "I'm a bit tense, that's all. The giant's chair's just around the next corner isn't it?"

"Yes." His hand closed reassuringly over her palm. "It'll be OK. Nothing's likely to go wrong." He looked up at the tranquil sky. "Especially on such a beautiful day."

Nevertheless, his footsteps instinctively slowed as they approached the next corner.

The oversized stone chair, constructed in the 1920s by a local philanthropist for public use, was built of large rocks cemented together and placed on a broad concrete base. It was wide enough for two average sized people to sit and look out across a stretch of rock-strewn sand towards the sea.

"Nobody around," said Susan.

"Looks OK. Come on."

Hand in hand, trying to look like a couple of casual day-trippers, they walked over to the chair. Seating herself on the base Susan smiled up at Brendan.

"Used to love coming here every summer as a little girl." She paused and gazed out to sea. "I distinctly remember the beginning of one summer when I sat on the chair and found I could touch the ground. My dad grinned and said I'd now grown up. Silly really."

"Silly?"

"Yes. All kids like to feel they're growing up but I remember at the time I felt quite sad – as though something had gone forever."

Leaning up against the side of the chair Brendan gazed at the ocean. Apart from several wheeling seagulls and a self-absorbed couple lying on a pair of towels half-hidden by some rocks there was no one else around.

"If this weather keeps up there'll be masses of people here tomorrow."

Susan didn't reply. He glanced down at her. She was staring towards the northern end of the path.

"Brendan, I think it's them."

He turned. Two young women were approaching from the Milford end. Although dressed in light frocks and carrying small cane picnic baskets, from the pallor of their faces and shoulders it was clear they weren't locals.

"Just sit there," he muttered.

Brendan studied the approaching pair. Although his stance was one of contrived casualness he felt an inner tension seep through his body.

A few metres from the chair the two women halted and stood uncertainly for a moment. They were both wearing new straw hats. One of the women showed short wisps of dark hair protruding from under the rim while the other's blonde hair was shoulder length. From above them a seagull gave a sharp, raucous cry. They looked at Susan and Brendan and then at each other. The blonde woman nodded and turning back towards the pair, the dark girl spoke. The loudness of her voice betrayed her nervousness.

"That is a very large chair, is it not?"

"Yes," replied Brendan. "Would you like to sit down?"

Clearly relieved, the two hurried forward.

"I am Sophie Scholl." The dark haired one thrust out her hand.

They shook hands. She turned back towards her companion.

"And this is my friend Gretchen Brandt." She smiled. "Gretchen can only speak a little English." She shrugged. "My English is not so good but we will both try."

Susan stood up and Brendan introduced her to the two women who took her a little by surprise by vigorously shaking her hand.

"It's OK," smiled Brendan. "Germans shake hands with everyone."

"*Was sagen Sie?*" asked Sophie.

"Ich sage, dass man in Deutschland immer die Händedruck machen muss."

"In Neuseeland etwa nicht?"

"Nicht für Frauen."

"I don't think we should be talking in German, Brendan," Susan frowned at him. "It's not because I can't speak it well, it's just that if we're overheard..."

"You're right. I was just explaining that Kiwi women aren't used to shaking hands." He turned to Sophie. "We must speak English while we are here."

"Naturally. We understand," nodded Sophie

Brendan began to explain that it was his job to question the two women and then, if he was satisfied, he would confirm the initial verification by the university cell.

During the conversation Susan studied the girls carefully. Dark-eyed Sophie's brow was continually creased in concentration, watching Brendan intently as he spoke, and regularly nodding her understanding. By contrast whenever Gretchen's blue eyes met Brendan's a wisp of a smile appeared round her mouth, often accompanied by a gentle touch on his arm.

"Blonde hair, blue eyes, classic Aryan beauty. Ideally suited for a Nazi Party recruiting poster," thought Susan.

Several times during Brendan's explanation he had to repeat what he had said, before pausing to allow Sophie to translate for Gretchen. When he'd finally finished, Sophie, after glancing nervously around, reached into her basket and from underneath a white cloth produced a sheet of paper. Moving closer to Brendan, she thrust it into his hand. Looking down he saw it was a leaflet written in German.

"Die weiße Rose."

Both women nodded vigorously.

"It is our White Rose leaflet," explained Sophie. "We printed many of these in Munich. We gave them to the university students. The Nazis were not pleased."

Brendan studied the leaflet for a few moments.

"God!" he exclaimed.

"What?" said Susan.

He carefully checked to see that no one was within hearing.

"Wenn das deutsche Volk..." His voice tailed off as he continued to read silently. He paused and then translated.

"'If the German people are so corrupted and spiritually crushed that they do not raise a hand, then yes they deserve their downfall'." He looked up at Susan. "No wonder the authorities are concerned. The whole pamphlet is an attack on the Nazis and their system. I'm surprised these two are still alive!"

Gretchen touched his arm. "Excuse me, Brendan, what said you?"

He turned to her. "A moment, please." He addressed Susan. "Look, this is taking more time than I imagined. I'm also mindful that the longer we're here the greater the danger. It'll be faster if I do the rest of the questioning in German. Then I'll translate for you."

"Suppose so. Just make sure you stick to the point and don't get side-tracked."

He frowned. "What do you mean?"

"Never mind. Just get on with it."

Turning to the German women he explained they would continue in German, but should keep their voices low. They both nodded in eager agreement.

Sophie explained that at the outbreak of war they were both enrolled at Munich University as medical students. They had initially joined the White Rose group to show their concern at the increasing restrictions on university students and the treatment of German Jews. However the White Rose activities had attracted the ire of the authorities and they had been arrested. Under normal circumstances they would have been charged and imprisoned and possibly executed. However, the vast area of territory unexpectedly gained by Nazi Germany had created an acute shortage of army medical personnel. Consequently they had been ordered overseas and attached to a medical corps. They had assumed their New Zealand posting was designed to take them as far away from Germany as possible. Although they'd been watched closely when they'd first arrived, their surveillance had slackened off over the past few weeks and now they were even allowed a weekly day off to spend as they wished.

Gretchen smiled. *"Wir gehen gern zum Strand."* She laughed and playfully took his arm. *"Neuseelander sind sehr schön."*

The three laughed, partly as a release from their tenseness.

"What's so damn funny?" asked Susan.

"Gretchen was explaining how they love going to the beach to admire the handsome Kiwi men," Brendan grinned.

"Brendan, I thought you were supposed to be checking their validity."

"OK. Take it easy."

"No, don't 'take it easy'. Get on with it."

"Yes, all right, I –"

Gretchen's scream made them whirl round. A sturdy black Alsatian had come racing round the corner, leapt up at the young German woman and was pawing the front of her frock.

"Midnight! Get down! Bad dog!" A small girl came running forward. Seizing the animal's trailing lead she leaned back and dragged it off the frightened Gretchen.

"Sorry, lady," began the girl as an older woman joined her.

"Yes, we're terribly sorry. I told Margaret to keep a firm hold but Midnight's a strong dog and he just broke away." Pulling a small handkerchief from her dress pocket she reached towards Gretchen. "Frightfully sorry. You've got some dirt on your pretty dress."

Gretchen, frightened by the dog and now confused by an unexpected encounter, backed away uncertainly shaking her head.

"Das macht nicht. Das mach nicht."

The woman seized her daughter's hand. "Come away, Margaret!"

"What did the lady say, Mummy?"

"Quickly!"

"But, what did she – ow, Mummy, you're hurting me."

The four watched in silence as the mother urgently pulled the protesting child and dog along the path and disappeared around the corner.

"She was, er, with fright, was she not?"

"Yes, Sophie. Frightened. But that's no excuse," snapped Susan. She whirled round and thrust her face close to Gretchen's. Her voice was low but the words were measured and angry.

"Do not speak German. Do you understand? No German."

"OK, Susan." Brendan reached out and touched her arm. "Gretchen was frightened by the bloody dog. It's not her fault."

Impatiently Susan shook off his hand. Her voice was low and harsh.

"Then whose fault is it? The authorities are looking for us. We're not supposed to draw attention to ourselves. We're supposed to look like a typical young couple enjoying the summer sun. And here we are frightening the hell out of the local population by jabbering away in bloody German."

Sophie put her hand on Brendan's arm.

"I am sorry for any trouble," she began. "It was the dog. Gretchen was..."

"It's OK," replied Brendan. He glared at Susan. "Nobody's fault. But," he turned to Sophie, "we must be very careful. We are all running a great risk. You must not speak any German when you are with us."

The two German women exchanged a rapid whispered conversation and then both nodded.

"We understand, now," Sophie said. "We are very sorry. We will not speak any German."

"No," echoed Gretchen. "No German."

Brendan smiled reassuringly. "OK, Susan?"

Susan frowned and then nodded her head in agreement. "OK, as long as they stick to the agreement."

"Of course. I've studied their pamphlet and believe they are genuine members of the White Rose, which I also believe is a genuine German resistance group. I think we should now proceed to the next stage."

Susan hesitated. "You're sure?"

"Yes, I am. It matches my background information and the communication from the University cell."

Seeing her frowning he asked, "You're still not convinced?"

"Maybe. But before we proceed, we have to check their baskets – and their persons. We've all been taught about concealed weapons."

"Of course." He turned to the two German women.

"Brendan. Just a minute."

He turned back.

"Tell them you'll check their baskets. I'll do the personal searches."

He grinned and spread his arms wide. "Of course, dear girl. I never assumed otherwise."

Swiftly he explained to Sophie the necessity for the search. The basket revealed nothing more than some pieces of bread, an apple, handkerchiefs and lipstick. Using the shelter provided by the Giant's Chair Susan then ran her hands swiftly over each girl's body.

"All clear," she nodded to Brendan.

"Good. Now you are to follow me along the beach. The rendezvous is at the bottom of Milford Road."

Taking Susan's hand he headed north towards the end of the coastal path. When they reached the beginning of Milford Beach the four of them continued in silence across the sand finding some relief from their tension in the wavelets of the incoming tide that swirled around their feet.

"Brendan?"

He stopped and turned round.

"Yes, Sophie?"

"It's Gretchen. She has a, how you say it in English," she lowered her voice and touched her head, "*Kopfschmerzen.*"

"Headache."

"Ja. Yes." She smiled apologetically. "The hot sun, the dog, the worry."

"I understand. There's a shop at the end of Milford Road near the beach. They should have some aspirins."

Both women nodded their thanks.

"OK?" He glanced at Susan who was frowning.

She shrugged. "Suppose so. I won't relax until we're back home, in Albany."

"Me too." He squeezed her hand. "Won't be long now."

The small dairy located at the end of the road sold ice creams and milk shakes as well as basic necessities such as bread, milk, and a limited selection of groceries. It looked deserted as they approached.

"We can all go in, but let Susan and me do the talking," instructed Brendan. He reached forward, opened the door and stepped back to let the women go ahead.

"Oh, excuse me, madam."

The tall German officer, who had suddenly appeared in the doorway, stepped aside narrowly avoiding a collision with Sophie.

The three women momentarily froze. Susan, recovering herself, smiled at the man.

"Thank you officer. Come on girls. In we go."

The German watched them enter. Obviously attracted by the sight of three casually clad young women, he showed no sign of leaving. Crinkling his blue eyes into a smile he doffed his officer's cap to reveal close cropped blonde hair.

"Hauptman Hans Klemperer at your service ladies." He bowed and snapped his polished boot heels together. "It is beautiful New Zealand weather today, is it not?"

"Er, yes, officer, it is a beautiful day," Susan smiled.

The door slammed as Brendan released it and stepped between the officer and the three women. With a conscious effort he worked his features into an ingratiating smile.

"Good afternoon, officer. I am glad you are enjoying our New Zealand weather." He pointed at the man's neck. "Is that an Iron Cross, sir? Where did you win it?"

The German stared at him suspiciously. "France, von Manstein. 7th Panzers," he snapped. He turned back towards the three women who were gathered at the counter where Susan had just asked for a bottle of aspirin.

"Ahh, aspirin," he said jovially. "For the headache. Too much good Auckland sun!" As the others weakly joined his laughter he continued, "So, which one of you has the headache?" His gaze settled admiringly on Gretchen. "Perhaps it is the lovely lady with the blonde hair." Reaching out he touched her cheek. "Your face is quite pale. Perhaps you are not used to the sun."

Gretchen stood motionless; with her mouth half open staring at the officer. The man frowned. "Is my English so bad? Can you not understand me?"

"Yes, officer, she can, but she has a very bad headache and needs to go home."

Susan's forced smile and nervously spoken response caused the officer to frown suspiciously.

"Your Iron Cross, sir? Tell me –" began Brendan

Klemperer waved a dismissive hand and fixed his eyes on Sophie.

"And you, dark-haired lady. Do you have a headache, too?"

Her eyes wide Sophie shook her head.

"I am sorry, officer," continued Susan, "but we really must be going. My friend is quite ill."

The man paused and his eyes narrowed as they flicked between each group member. The heaviness of the humidity matched the heaviness of the silence – broken only by the buzz of a blowfly.

Klemperer's face broke into a wide smile.

"Of course. Forgive me." Reaching the door in two strides he swung it open and stood back. He bowed slightly. "After you."

"Thank you." Susan walked past him closely followed by Gretchen. As the German girl drew level with him she looked up and smiled nervously. He grinned and nodded.

"Bis bald, Fraulein."

"Danke. Bis bald."

Instantly his hand flew to the holster at his side. Brendan, rugby style, lowered his shoulder and charged, connecting with the man's stomach. "Run!" he roared as the officer staggered backwards and crashed into a shelf full of tinned baked beans.

Coming upright, Brendan scrambled towards the doorway. From the corner of his eye he saw that Klemperer, back on his feet, was tugging his pistol from his holster.

A large Chevrolet sedan was parked on the side of the road. Brendan dived left onto the grass and executed a forward roll that brought him alongside the car's front wheel.

A series of shots momentarily obliterated the sound of the incoming tide. Crouching behind the car's front wheel Brendan glanced back. The German officer was clutching feebly at the doorpost of the dairy. A dark red smear was marking his slow downward slide.

"Get in the car! All of you!"

A young man clad in swimming togs and a short-sleeved shirt was standing by the driver's door. His right hand held a smoking Weber pistol.

"How the hell?"

"Later. Get in. Now!"

The three women dashed over and scrambled into the Chevrolet's back seat. The driver, a young woman dressed in a bathing suit and a lemon beach coat, was holding the car in gear. The man with the revolver held the door open as Brendan slid onto the bench seat next to her. As the man leapt in and slammed the door there was a jerk as the clutch was released, and with a throaty surge the big V8 motor propelled the car down the street.

"Easy, Harriet. Don't want to attract any attention."

"OK," responded the woman, easing off the accelerator and swinging the car through the Milford intersection onto Kitchener Road. "Make sure all of you keep alert."

"Yeah. Keep your eyes peeled, but for God's sake try and look relaxed. We've all just been to the bloody beach."

Resting the Weber on his lap the man covered it with a towel. He glanced at Brendan and then at the three dishevelled women in the back seat. "Name's Jim."

"Christ, Jim," said Brendan. "where the hell did you come from?"

"We were your back-up – sunbathing in front of you by the Giant's Chair. When you left after the dog incident we followed you along Milford Beach. Just as well, too. What happened?"

"The German language and the inability of some people to keep their mouths shut!"

The vehemence in Susan's voice caused Jim to turn and face her.

"Explain."

"Take it easy, Susan," said Brendan. "I'll explain. Sophie, you translate for Gretchen."

"These are the two German women from the White Rose?"

"Supposedly!" Susan's voice cut in. "But the way they're going the only white roses we'll see are the one's that'll be placed on our coffins!"

"Susan, cut it out. We live in dangerous times."

"Obviously!"

"And we'll get nowhere quarrelling among ourselves. Now please be quiet while I try to explain what happened. Then you and anyone else can have your full say."

"Yeah," said Susan, folding her arms and sinking back into the large leather seat. "You bet I will."

"I am sorry for any trouble we have given," said Sophie uncertainly. "But please, I think we need to go back to our place soon. Otherwise our people will become..."

"Suspicious. Yes, I understand. We'll arrange it."

"Excuse me, but there is one other thing I wish to tell you. I'm not sure but I think it may be important." She frowned. "Because of the university."

Brendan, who had twisted round to face Sophie, nodded encouragingly.

"Yes, go on."

"In English," said Susan.

"Yes, of course. I will try," said Sophie. "Two days ago we were sent to a house somewhere near here. We were told to help a man who was sick. He was an older man. He was in bed. He had some cuts on his face. He was, how you say it in English, heavy with the drugs."

"Heavily drugged." Brendan frowned. "Was he a German officer or something?"

"No, he was a New Zealand man. The soldiers said he was from the university."

"Soldiers? Were they guarding him?"

"Guarding him?" she repeated. "You mean keeping him from going away?"

"God!" exclaimed Susan suddenly seizing Sophie's arm. "Do you know his name?"

"Um, they would not tell us but I saw a postcard on the bedroom desk. He is a professor."

Susan leaned forward urgently.

"His name? What was his name?"

245

Sophie turned to Gretchen and spoke rapidly. She frowned and then suddenly smiled.

"Sterling. Herr Professor Sterling."

Chapter 36

"You look very convincing, mein Herr," Stuart smiled grimly.

"Huh." Brendan grunted as he completed checking the brim of his hat and the knot in his black tie. "Main thing is to convince myself." He shifted uncomfortably. "These bloody coats are too heavy for our humid weather."

"Yeah. But they look the part. Now let's go through the routine one more time. Firstly, you do the talking."

"Check. No English at all unless you need to talk to the prisoner."

"You've got your identity papers?"

"Check. You've got yours?"

"Check."

"Pistol?"

He nodded grimly. "And you?"

"Check."

"I've got the authorization letter which I'll hand over after I've told them we've come to collect the prisoner."

"Check." Brendan held the letter of authorization on an Auckland Gestapo Headquarters letterhead. "The Gestapo is still getting established but Sophie said the letterhead will intimidate the guards. All Germans are conditioned to responding instantly to Gestapo requests."

"Let's hope she's right. She must have taken a hell of a risk. It looks authentic enough and this gear," he indicated their attire, "looks very convincing."

"OK. But keep well back in the seat and try to avoid looking out of the window," his friend cautioned. "Don't want to be recognised by any of the locals."

The plan, when originally developed, sounded simple enough. Sophie had sent word through the university cell that she could obtain some Gestapo letterhead paper and type out an appropriate authorization allowing Professor Sterling to be collected from his house and taken away for further interrogation. The day chosen had been one when she and Gretchen were scheduled to be on duty at the professor's home.

Brendan, due to his German fluency, was an obvious choice to imitate a special police officer. Stuart had volunteered to accompany him on the basis that the Germans would not imagine his undertaking anything so audacious. Eventually, after a fierce argument, Dan had agreed.

The special police uniform of dark suit, long coat, trilby hat and black tie had been relatively easy to put together from Fightback's 'Costume Department' – their expanding collection of enemy clothing. The car, although a British Morris, was black. On the front mudguards fluttered twin red and black swastika flags. The driver, a Fightback member, wore the uniform of a German private soldier.

It was 20 April 1942, Adolf Hitler's 53rd birthday.

After an incident-free journey the car pulled up on the street outside the professor's house in Castor Bay.

"Best back up the driveway," said Stuart. "Easier for the prof."

"And for us if we have to make a quick getaway," said Brendan.

He removed his hat and ran his fingers through his fair hair.

"OK?" said Stuart as the driver began reversing the Morris up the driveway beside a high hedge."

"Yeah."

The car came to a halt.

"Come on, let's get on with it." Stuart felt his mouth going dry and the thin film of sweat that began spreading over his body owed little to the heavy coat and the warmth of the day.

Brendan, pulling his shoulders back, strode to the front door where, after a moment's hesitation, he knocked loudly.

From inside a radio was playing at full volume.

"It's a marching song about the German troops in Russia," he said.

The song ended and after a pause, a crackling voice shouted, *"Ein Volk, Ein Reich, Ein Führer!"*

The now familiar chant of *"Sieg Heil!"* began.

"Three cheers for Adolf," muttered Stuart.

"Shhh, someone's coming."

The door opened and a corporal, swaying slightly, stood peering at the two men. He wore no cap, his tunic was unbuttoned and in his hand was a half full glass of colourless liquid. For a moment he peered at the two men then snapped to attention while at the same trying to unsuccessfully conceal his glass behind his back.

Brendan glared at him. *"Trinken sie Schnapps, Feldwebel?"* he demanded.

Guiltily the corporal brought the glass forward.

"Es ist der Geburtstag vom Führer. Wir sind..."

Stuart, noting that the birthday of Adolf Hitler was the excuse for the man's unmilitary bearing, relaxed a little.

Brendan thrust the Gestapo authorization in the soldier's hand.

"Wir kommen wegen Herrn Professor Sterling. Wir wunschen gehen, sofort!"

Taken aback, the soldier began studying the letter. With a grunt of impatience Brendan pushed past him, signalling Stuart to follow.

From the radio in a room off the left hand side of the corridor a stream of shouted German, distorted by the shortwave signal, filled the villa. Stuart guessed it was the German leader exhorting his people to greater achievements.

"Herr Professor Sterling!" demanded Brendan over his shoulder as he began to stride down the villa's corridor.

Hurrying after them the soldier called, "Hauptman Stumme!"

The left hand side door opened. Adolf Hitler's crackling voice surged from the room. A German officer appeared at the doorway.

"*Was ist los*?" he began, then on seeing the two Gestapo men, paused and frowned.

In short sharp sentences Brendan repeated his request and signalled to the soldier to show the officer the letter. The officer read it and frowned. His eyes narrowed uncertainly and he began to question Brendan. Taking advantage of the conversation, Stuart moved further down the villa's hallway to the left hand bedroom. He thrust the door open. On a bed, with his back to the window lay Professor Sterling. His face was pale and he appeared to be asleep. Clad in medical uniforms, Sophie and Gretchen sat either side of him. Closing the door Stuart moved to the bedside.

"We have the letter," he said in a low voice. "Brendan is showing it to the officer. I presume he'll be convinced."

"The papers. They are OK, Stuart?" said Gretchen hesitantly. Her eyes sought his assurance. He nodded and patted her on the arm.

"Your clothes also look very authentic," added Sophie. She smiled nervously. "I am sure the officer will let the Professor Sterling leave."

The door swung open. Stumme, with the corporal behind him, stood in the doorway holding the authorization letter in his hand. He looked hard at the two women. Gretchen putting her hand to her mouth coughed nervously. He continued to stare at her for a moment and then turned an unwavering gaze on Stuart.

Pushing his way into the room, Brendan greeted the two women with a minimum of ceremony. He then bent over the professor, removed his glove and rested his right hand on the man's brow.

"Professor Sterling," he said softly, "we have come to take care of you."

The old man stirred. Anticipating a shock of recognition Brendan moved his head forward to prevent the officer seeing the professor's face. The precaution was justified as the man's eyes instantly opened and he gasped.

Seeking to create a distraction Stuart pointed to the letter and brusquely addressed the officer in what he hoped was a convincing accent.

"Die Papiere. In Ordnung!"

The Hauptman frowned and regarded the group for a long moment. Through the walls, the German Führer's voice increasingly punctuated by the rhythmic chants of the multitude, was reaching a crescendo.

The man paused, then nodded.

"Ja. Alles in Ordnung."

Brendan turned to the professor.

"The two nurses will help you get ready, Professor. Then they will assist you to the car. Please cooperate with them. It is in your best interests." He nodded and Sophie and Gretchen moved forward.

"Sie können Englisch gut sprechen," said the officer to Brendan,

"Yes," replied Brendan. "All Germans in New Zealand should learn English."

"Huh," grunted the man. His smile was cold as he carefully replied, "All New Zealand people should German learn!" Turning on his heel he left the room followed by the corporal. A door opened, the radio surged and the door slammed.

"Back to Schnapps and the Führer," muttered Stuart.

"Do we put his clothes on?" whispered Sophie.

"No. Just his dressing gown and slippers," said Brendan. "We must move now."

251

The professor had been sedated and consequently required assistance. Helping him to his feet the two women then moved either side and draped his arms across their shoulders.

"OK?" said Stuart.

They both nodded.

"Lead the way." He nodded to Brendan. "I'll watch the rear."

Cautiously opening the door, Brendan stepped into the corridor. The sound of a German anthem swelled from the radio in the nearby room. Turning back he jerked his head and the two women, with the professor between them, moved awkwardly forward along the polished wooden floor. The sunlight, streaming through the leadlight window of the villa's front door, created soft coloured patterns on the walls and ceiling, contrasting sharply with the penetrating blare of the military anthem. Reaching the end of the corridor Brendan grasped the large brass doorknob. Turning it, he pulled the heavy wooden front door open.

Sprawled on the grass next to their car's front wheel was their driver. A dark stain was slowing seeping out from under his motionless form. Standing above him and facing the doorway was the corporal. Alongside him stood Hauptmann Stumme and two other soldiers. Their rifles pointed unwaveringly at Brendan.

"Step forward, all of you," shouted one of the soldiers in a local accent. "Obey us and you will not be harmed."

"Get down!" shouted Brendan, dragging the door shut and flinging himself backwards. All five went sprawling on the wooden corridor as shots rang out and the leadlight window disintegrated, showering them with glass shards.

"How the hell did they know?"

Stuart crouched against the sturdy door pillar.

"Give yourselves up! The house is surrounded! You can't escape!" came a shout.

Estimating the position of the voice Stuart thrust his pistol forward at the end of his outstretched arms, sprang upwards, caught a momentary glimpse of the leading soldier and squeezed the trigger. The groan was followed by several more shots that buzzed angrily over his head as he dived back to the floor.

"One down," he said.

Footsteps were heard thudding past the outside of the villa.

"They're heading round to the back door," said Brendan.

"Take up a position half way down the hall and cover the door," ordered Stuart.

He turned towards the girls who were huddled near the prone figure of the professor.

"Stay here. I think there's a window open in the lounge."

Crouching down, Brendan took up a position inside the professor's bedroom door facing the back entrance. Stuart, keeping low, dashed across the corridor to the lounge door and shouldered it open. The alcoholic odour was pungent. A German marching song swelled from the tall polished wooden radio cabinet standing in the corner of the room. Two German soldiers, muttering incoherently, sprawled sideways against the far wall. The wide bay window on the far side was open. Thrusting his head out and checking left and right, Stuart hoisted himself over the windowsill and dropped onto the grass, thankful that the radio masked the sound of his landing.

To his right was a tall, thick macrocarpa hedge. Crouching down he heard two shots come from the rear of the house, echoed by the sound of breaking glass. Resisting the temptation to investigate he moved forwards towards the front edge of the villa and peered round the corner. Stumme had joined the sprawled body of the driver. The other soldier and the Feldwebel were crouching behind the car engaging in an earnest conversation while keeping a watchful eye on the front door. Stuart raised his pistol. Although the distance was well within range, he was aware his hand was trembling slightly.

"Easy," he muttered.

Taking two long slow breaths he slightly repositioned his pistol. His eyes narrowed and he squeezed the trigger. The corporal fell forward without a sound. The soldier whirled and looked Stuart squarely in the face. For the barest of moments he registered the man's brown features before squeezing the trigger again. The soldier clutched at his throat in a vain attempt to stop the blood flow before pitching forward onto the body of his comrade.

"It's me. I'm coming in!" he shouted. In three strides Stuart leapt up the steps and onto the veranda and flung open the door. "Get the professor into the back seat of the car," he ordered. "Quick as you can!"

Keeping low he moved down the corridor and slid into a bedroom doorway on the right, opposite Brendan.

"Got the other two bastards out front," he said loudly above the blaring of the radio.

"I think I got one another one. They tried to burst in but when he was hit the others pulled back."

"How many?"

"Not sure. Maybe another one or two."

"OK. Go and help the women. Then get into the driver's seat and start the motor. As soon as you're ready to leave, sound the horn. I'll join you."

"Won't the sound alert the others?"

"Have to chance it. I'm closer to the car than them and by now they're likely to be a bit windy."

His friend opened his mouth to protest but Stuart pointed to the front door.

"Reinforcements could come at any time. Go!"

Crouching low, Brendan moved towards the open front door. As his footsteps sounded on the broad wooden front steps Stuart fired a shot through the broken wooden panel of the back door. An answering rifle shot sent a bullet whining angrily through the empty hallway.

Keeping up against the wall and with his eye glued to the back door at the far end of the corridor, he slid swiftly after Brendan.

"Ein Volk! Ein Reich! Ein Fuhrer!" blared the radio.

"Baaarp!" blared the car horn.

Stuart dashed down the steps and reached the left hand side of the car. Scrambling in, he slammed the door as Brendan released the clutch and with revving motor sent the car down the driveway between the hedgerows. As they emerged onto the road Stuart noticed a smattering of people watching cautiously from the footpath on the opposite side. By the kerb on their immediate left was an empty khaki-coloured Kübelwagen – the small open topped Volkswagen troop carrier.

"Stop!" Stuart ordered.

"But –" began Brendan.

"Now!"

With a jerk the Morris came to an abrupt halt alongside the German vehicle. Resting his arm on the car windowsill Stuart fired at the front tyre. With a faint hiss the vehicle sank slightly to its right.

"OK. Go!"

As the car lurched away Stuart noticed that the people across the road had disappeared.

CHAPTER 37

"What sort of night did he have?"

"Not very good, I'm afraid. He started sweating badly about 3 o'clock this morning. I bathed his head with cold flannels and, after tossing and turning for a couple more hours he went back to sleep."

"I'll stay here and keep an eye on him. You'd better go now and have some breakfast. They'll need you at the de-brief. They'll want to hear what you have to say."

Pausing in the doorway of the little cubicle Susan looked down at her sleeping uncle. She gave a long sigh and walked towards the ladder that led up to the woolshed. It had been an anxious night but Lisa's competency as a nurse reassured her that he was receiving the best of care, under the circumstances. Several times Brendan had come into the tiny room where she was maintaining her vigil and had been very considerate and reassuring. His role in the rescue of her uncle had given her a new respect for him and she was now sure she was genuinely in love with him and not just seeking some comfort in a difficult situation.

"Aufwachen. Wir mussen aufstehen."

The sounds from the adjoining cubicle reminded her that they now had another two guests, the White Rose women. In the car on the way back to Albany it had been decided it would be out of the question for them to return to their medical unit. Consequently they'd accompanied Brendan and her uncle to the farm where they'd been given a cautious but warm welcome and allocated a shared cubicle.

Slowly Susan climbed up the ladder into the woolshed. She still felt tired and heavy after the tensions of the previous day and the night's vigil. Her relief and pleasure at the success of the rescue attempt had been dampened a little by the group's considerable interest in the arrival of the two German women. However the prompt assistance her uncle received had mollified her. She shrugged. In this situation nothing was predictable.

***

Earlier in the day there had been an increased wariness around the farm due to the arrival of the two German women and the story of the professor's rescue. The tranquillity of the morning had done little to change the heightened caution of all members of the group whose eyes kept constantly scanning the surrounding countryside and listening for any change in the familiar daily sounds.

After the morning tasks that included the milking of the six house cows had been completed, the meeting was convened in the woolshed. As well as the usual precaution of leaving two people in the house, four others, using the pretext of making running repairs to the holding pens around the woolshed, had been posted to keep watch outside.

Dan called for silence. "First of all, let me congratulate Stuart and Brendan on the success of their mission. Well done, both of you."

The genuineness of the applause showed that the audacious rescue of the professor from under the noses of the occupation forces had considerably buoyed everyone's spirits.

"We'd also like to welcome our two German guests, Sophie and Gretchen." He smiled. "I never imagined I'd be offering refuge to a couple of Germans but their presence here this morning reminds us we live in volatile times.

Brendan, who was sitting on a wool bale between Susan and Gretchen, leaned over and translated for the German girl who nodded and smiled warmly at him.

"Although they could have been of more use to us working undercover with the German forces, their knowledge of the system will still be an asset."

"Sure, Dan," called out Tony, "but can they shear sheep?"

The laughter was interrupted by the sudden opening of the door at the end of the shed. John, one of the men who'd been assigned to guarding the farmhouse, came bursting in.

"Sorry to interrupt the merriment, Dan," he began.

"What is it, John?"

"A new radio bulletin. It's just been broadcast on the radio that the authorities have sent a company of troops into the Albany village. They have arrested ten local men and crammed them into the small Albany War Memorial Library. They have announced that the people of Albany have been providing aid and comfort to the terrorists. Therefore if the terrorist pair of Stuart Johnson and Carol Peterson do not surrender or are not handed over, five of the men will be shot by firing squad in the main street tomorrow morning, and, if there is still no surrender, five more the following morning."

All eyes turned to Stuart and Carol.

Carol's voice was barely audible. "We'll have to surrender. We can't let ten innocent men die."

"We can't let those bastards get away with this, you mean! If we do they'll use this same tactic every time, all over the country." Brendan had stood up and, having spoken, his eyes circled the walls as if seeking a dissenter.

Dan's response was measured. "We could always consider a raid on the place," he said. "We've been doing the training and they're probably not expecting any sort of structured military response. A couple of us could take the truck into town, recce the place and report back."

"Or we could do absolutely nothing," said John sotto voce.

"Nothing?" came from several voices.

"Yeah, nothing," said John. "You'll likely think I'm a cold-blooded bastard but look at it this way. Up until now the Krauts and their Kiwi cronies have done a pretty good job of convincing the general population that life under the New

Order's not too bad and is going to get better. After all the hillside's not exactly crawling with dissident partisan bands."

"Your point?" Tony's voice was harsh. John was known for his acid tongue and his penchant for frequently challenging ideas that were put forward by other members of the group.

"My point is this. If we do nothing and the bastards carry out their threat and publicly execute these men, what effect will that have on the population? It will destroy most of the goodwill the New Order has worked hard to develop over the past months. The result? Groups like us will have far greater support from all sectors of the civilian population."

"But what about the men they're going to shoot?" said Susan.

"Yes," said Stuart. "Men who are sons, brothers, fathers and husbands."

"Look, all of you," snapped John glaring round the group. "This is not Robin bloody Hood fighting the Sheriff of Nottingham's buffoons. We're up against one of the most efficient fighting forces ever assembled. We will never beat them on the field of battle." Although his voice began to rise, he picked his words deliberately. "The only way we can win is by discrediting the Krauts among all sections of the population – showing them up for what they are, gathering people to our cause and harassing the enemy in any way we can. Eventually the New Order will become more and more desperate, carry out more and more reprisals, and alienate more and more of the common people. The result? More and more people will flock to our banner."

"And do we have to needlessly sacrifice innocent people on the way?" A rumble of support accompanied Tony's question.

"Innocent?" John spread his arms wide. "From what Stuart and Carol have told us, only a few weeks ago innocent university students were shot down in cold blood. And how many of you can be sure Peter Fraser our Prime Minister hasn't been killed by these bastards." A few heads nodded. "Exactly, my friends. We're not the grammar school military cadets enjoying a break from bloody Maths and English. This is war, and, surprise, surprise, in war sacrifices have to be made and innocent people sometimes get maimed and killed!"

With a final long hard look at the group John sat down with his back to a wool bale, took out a tin of tobacco and began to roll a smoke.

After a long silence Tony stood up. "John's right in many ways. This is war, and we need to be reminded the stakes and the risks are high. Furthermore, like any wartime situation, as familiar patterns break down we'll find ourselves facing all sorts of unpleasant choices that will test our loyalties and possibly cause dissension within our ranks."

His pause was greeted by silence and he continued.

"John's probably right when he says the more people the authorities shoot the greater will be the resistance. He paused again. "However, I'm not prepared to stand idly by and let innocent men die." He pointed to Stuart and Carol. "And I'm also not prepared to let these two give themselves up to the Blitzkrieg Boys." He smiled grimly. "It will only encourage them."

The debate continued for a further hour until it was agreed that unless they had further information on the situation in Albany village any plan of action they might decide on ran a considerable danger of failure.

On the basis that Tom and Jason were known to the authorities as local farmers it was decided they would take the truck into the village on the pretext of buying groceries from the local store. In the meantime, those who had legitimate work to do around the farm would continue as normally as possible. All the newcomers would be confined to the woolshed, ready to disappear underground at any sign of trouble.

The next few hours, although tense, passed uneventfully and following the sound of the returning truck there was general relief when Tom and Jason, apparently unscathed, walked into the house with two boxes of groceries. Within a few minutes everyone except those on guard duty had assembled expectantly in the woolshed for the pair's verbal report.

"The place has quite a few soldiers," began Jason, "and a swag of those tedious little Boys Brigade twerps, who are helping out with guard duty and the like."

"We managed to drive past the library," continued Tom, "but several army trucks were parked in front so we couldn't see much. There seemed to be a reasonable number of troops around it with their mates bivvied in a paddock nearby. We both thought they all looked surprisingly relaxed."

Tony asked the question that was on everyone's lips. "So, what's your recommendation?"

CHAPTER 38

The cacophonous explosion of the grenade shattered the stillness of the dark night. The flash of bright orange smeared a momentary silhouette of tents, trucks and sentries across the vision of the watching attackers. Two more explosions followed. Instantly the petrol tanks of three parked trucks ignited in a spectacular domino response.

Above the agonizing screams of the soldiers, Dan's voice roared, "Now!"

Rising from their positions behind a large hedge, the six raced across the road towards the library. Dan, spotting a gap in the burning trucks, sped towards it. A figure loomed in front of him and he squeezed the trigger of his Sten gun. As the figure fell he noticed the uniform – black shorts and a white canvas band across a black shirt.

"Jesus!" Hearing the others behind him he headed straight down the short library path towards the door. On his second burst of fire it disintegrated.

Following the moves rehearsed repeatedly earlier that afternoon, the other five created a crouching half circle with their backs to the library shooting instantly at any signs of movement.

For Stuart, the explosions had triggered off an emotional response bordering on ecstasy. His eyes were wide and as the adrenalin coursed through his system, he shouted a commentary like a demented sports announcer as he shot at the figures momentarily silhouetted in the flames.

"Here's one coming!" Burst of fire. "Got you, you bastard! There's another over there!" Burst of fire. "Great stuff, Tom!" Burst of fire. "That's one for me!"

Behind him he was barely aware of Dan's voice shouting into the library doorway, "Get up, you men! Make a run for it! Get as far away as you can!" Seconds later Dan raced past him shouting to his group, "Come on! Let's get out of here!"

Stuart followed swiftly. As the group reached the other side of the road they linked up with the second smaller group that had been providing covering fire. Stuart called out a prearranged code word and Carol joined him within a few seconds. Earlier in the day her inclusion had led to a brief and intense debate. Initially there had been some opposition to the idea of having a woman as part of the attack team. In response she had presented a short but eloquent rationale based on the fact that one of Fightback's key tenets was that everybody undertook every role. There had been no dissenting response.

The whole group swiftly broke up into pairs as they headed away from the village and spread themselves as widely as possible across the paddocks. Although the military authorities had assembled a large contingent of soldiers, their response to the raid was less than impressive. The size of their force and the absence of any previous attacks on troops by locals had made them complacent. Consequently the soldiers, preferring to sleep or carouse, had assigned the unpopular role of the night guard to the hapless youths from the Boys Brigade supplemented by only a handful of regulars.

As the pairs spread out , spasmodic shots followed them. In most cases they ricocheted off posts well away from the retreating figures, indicating that the soldiers were firing more in hope than in expectation of hitting anyone. Stuart, still on adrenaline high from the action, turned with a laugh to Carol, who was a few paces behind.

"Come on, slowcoach! We've still got –"

The thump in his left leg sent him sprawling. Surprised, he tried to scramble to his feet but fell heavily again. For a moment he lay there and then said, "I think I copped one in the leg. I can't stand up."

Swiftly Carol knelt by his side. "We can't stay here. They'll be following. Here, lean on me and try to stand."

He threw his left arm across her shoulder and levered himself upwards on his right leg. He stood for a moment shaking and then moaned, "Christ! It's starting to throb!"

"There's a patch of bush over there. Let's try and make it and then I'll take a look. Come on."

Progress was slow across the uneven surface of the paddock. Even though Stuart tried to put as much weight as he could on his right leg, Carol staggered and stumbled as she tried to support him.

"Need a hand?" The voice close by caused them to stop and raise their weapons.

"It's OK," said the voice. "I'm on your side. I was imprisoned in the library. We all got away, thanks to your team. You wounded, mate?"

"Yeah, in the left leg."

"OK. Lean on me. I'm bigger than your mate. He can carry the weapons and lead the way."

In spite of the situation they both laughed.

"Yeah, my mate all right. But he's a she."

"A 'she'? How come?"

"Long story," interrupted Carol. She took Stuart's Bren from his grasp and moved forward. "Come on. This way."

After a few more steps they came to a gap in the edge of the bush that led to a narrow walking track.

"This'll be easier," said Carol.

"Where are you heading?"

"With your help, to a point west of here," she said.

"With your friend's wound, wouldn't it be better if we could find water and then have a look at it?"

"Is there water nearby?" The throbbing in his leg was steadily increasing and the thought of cool water on his wound, or flowing down his dry throat was an enticing one.

"Yeah, a branch of Lucas Creek. Over to the right," answered the man.

They were about to resume their journey when the man paused.

"Look, er, my name's –"

"No!" snapped Carol. "We don't want to know your name. And you don't want to know ours. We're on the same side. That's enough for now. Come on."

After five minutes of painful progress they reached the tributary's banks. Carefully the man lowered Stuart to the ground. Dizzy with pain and loss of blood he collapsed onto his back.

"Stay in that position," said the man. He looked up at Carol. "Now, let's have a look at the wound. Got a knife?"

"A knife?" groaned Stuart.

"Yep. We'll have to cut your trouser leg away to inspect the damage."

Fortunately the clouds that had been covering the moon scudded away creating sufficient light for them to make a cursory inspection of the damage. As the man began to carefully cut into the top half of Stuart's trouser leg they could both see it was heavily stained.

"He's losing blood," said Carol, trying to keep the tension from her voice. She pulled a packet from her supply pack. "I've got a first aid kit but it's fairly inadequate."

"Pour some of that disinfectant on the wound and then see if you can cover it with your dressings." The man removed his shirt and began to tear it into strips. "I'm going to have to try a tourniquet to stop the bleeding. I belong to the local volunteer fire brigade and I've done some first aid. Hope I can remember enough."

The pain was acute and several times Stuart lost consciousness as the other two disinfected and dressed the wound and applied the tourniquet. Through his haze of pain he heard them both agree a bullet appeared to have passed right through his upper leg and therefore the priority was to contain the bleeding and prevent infection.

"There's a more bushy area up ahead. We should try to make for it. I played in there with my mates when we were kids, so I know it quite well," said the man.

"But if he tries to walk the bleeding will get worse," said Carol.

"Then I'll carry him. We don't have time to spare. Help me get him up on my back."

Piggyback style Stuart was carried along the bush track. The occasional echo of shouting and rifle fire motivated them to move more swiftly into the deep sanctuary of the inner bush. When the sounds eventually became more distant and spasmodic, the man stopped, and stood breathing heavily with Stuart clinging to his back. "Now, if my memory serves me, there may be a hut somewhere nearby." He paused, peered around and grunted. "Yep, let's try down here."

Two minutes later Carol's brief torch flash confirmed that they were standing outside a hut about the size of a sizeable garden shed. Originally it had been established in a small clearing but this was now overgrown by the encroaching bush. Scattered near the doorway were little skeletons and the curled up remains of small pelts. "Rabbits and possums," offered the man by way of explanation.

The door wasn't locked and inside was a long wide bench, a couple of old chairs propped up against a chipped table on which were scattered some dusty cups, plates and cutlery, a tiny fire place with kettle, a billy can, and a small pile of wood.

"Here," said the man to Carol. "Help me put your mate on the bench." With a sigh of relief he eased Stuart off his back and onto the bench. "There we go, easy does it. Now, make a pillow with your jersey."

Although the pain had eased Stuart still felt sick and dizzy. He felt a coat go over his shoulders and Carol's face next to his.

"Listen, Stuart, darling," she whispered, "we're safe in a hut. We're both going to take it in turns to keep watch. What I want you to do now is to get some sleep."

"Sorry." He groaned. "I should have been more careful. I should have..."

She kissed him gently. "Shhhh. Don't be silly. As you've said before, 'C'est la guerre'. Now close your eyes and go to sleep."

CHAPTER 39

The sound of low-flying aircraft woke him with a start. For a moment he was disorientated and then he remembered. He tried to call out but his mouth was dry and he could only manage a croak. The door of the hut swung open and Carol was by his side.

"How are you feeling?"

"Not sure yet. What are those planes?"

"If I remember my aircraft identification lessons I would say they're the German reconnaissance Feisler Storchs."

"Very likely. Do you think they're looking for us?"

"I would think they're seeking out anyone who could have taken part in last night's raid. I suppose that means us, but I doubt if we'll be spotted. We're too deep in the bush." She stood up. "Feel like anything to drink? There's plenty of water and even some tea although it may be a bit cold."

"Tea? How did you manage that?"

"We lit a fire last night and boiled the kettle and the billy. We decided to risk it as it was dark and windy which minimized the risk of the smoke being seen or smelt. It meant we were able to clean your wound with hot water and also brew some tea from the ration pack."

"How could you see?"

"Old kerosene lamp in the corner. Not much kero in it but it was enough to do the job."

"I felt some pain earlier on. I think someone was dressing my wound." He smiled weakly. "Must have been my lovely nurse." He looked her up and down. "Know something?"

"What?"

"Here you stand in loosely fitting army fatigues, your face is smudged and your lovely dark hair wrapped up in a khaki bandana. Yet you still look incredibly sexy to me."

She smiled and patted the back of her head in a gesture of mock coyness. "Why, sir, I'm here purely in a nursing capacity." He reached out for her but she knocked his hand aside. "Listen, mister, keep in mind you're not well. When I changed your bandage you moaned quite a bit. Fortunately the wound looks fairly clean and the bleeding's stopped. But we're not out of the proverbial woods by a long way." She glared at him with mock severity. "Nurse's verdict is that with plenty of rest, you'll be well on the road to recovery."

"What about our mate?"

"He's outside, well concealed, keeping watch. Tried to tell me about himself but I stopped him. Explained why and he understood. He was certainly in the right place at the right time last night. I told him so and thanked him profusely on your behalf."

"Well done. Now what was it you said about some tea?"

After consuming two cups of lukewarm tea and eating a block of chocolate that they had brought with them in their small ration packs, Stuart began to feel a little better. Smiling his thanks he closed his eyes and fell asleep again.

The sound of low voices woke him. Carol and the man were sitting at the table. He coughed and tried to sit up.

"Take it easy, mate," said the man.

"You've been asleep for hours," said Carol coming over and putting her palm on his brow. You're still a bit hot but a long sleep is just what you needed."

"Yeah. I feel a bit better, but I'm bloody hungry."

"That's what we're discussing. We feel safe here and there's water nearby, but we've run out of food."

"If we stay here, they won't find us, but we'll starve to death," said the man with a grim smile.

"So we think we've got no choice but to try to find the farmhouse. Geoff thinks he knows which one it is."

"Geoff?" interrupted Stuart.

"Not my real name. But we couldn't keep calling each other 'you'."

"Fair enough. Do you think you can find the farmhouse?"

"More to the point, do you think you're up to walking?"

Levering himself off the bench Stuart put his left leg on the floor and gently transferred some of his weight to the right one.

"So far, so good," he said. "But can I walk?"

"Try this," said Geoff. "I think it will fit."

He handed Stuart a slightly crooked but sturdy T-shaped ti-tree branch, the top piece of which was roughly padded.

"All my own work," he smiled.

Tucking it under his right armpit Stuart took a few steps. He stopped and closed one eye, scowling at the watching pair.

"Aaah, me hearties, I be Long John Silver. Now which of ye thieving swabs has stolen me pet parrot?"

They both laughed. "How far do you think you can go, Long John?"

Stuart tried a few steps up and down the cabin's wooden floor. "OK So far. Can I try outside?"

"Hang on, I'll check if the coast is clear."

Opening the door, Geoff carefully looked out and then walked around the outside of the hut. He put his head back in the doorway. "Looks OK. Come on, I'll help you down and you can go for a test drive."

Gingerly Stuart negotiated the two steps and then began a careful circumnavigation of the hut, watched anxiously by his two companions. After several minutes he stopped and grinned. "Not too bad. If I keep the weight off the injured limb, and rest every so often I think my biggest problem will be a sore armpit. You two have done wonders with your bush carpentry and front line nursing."

"That's great." Carol's encouraging smile failed to mask her anxiety as the distant drone of an aircraft sounded in the distance. "We can't stay here much longer. It would be better for all of us if we tried to make it to the farm. It may take a while but as Geoff knows the area and if we're able to identify a few landmarks, we should be able to make it before it gets dark."

"You're right, my sweet. I'm bloody hungry and I'm sure both of you are as well. We should leave now."

Gathering their possessions and removing any signs of their short stay, they checked the sun's position and headed in a westerly direction along a small overgrown bush path with Carol and Geoff carrying the two Sten guns.

Progress was slow, partly from the need for caution and partly because, in spite of his earlier optimism, Stuart's leg continued to trouble him. Seeing him in pain, Carol kept close by, watching him anxiously. They had been travelling for about thirty minutes when, half way up a slight incline, his crutch slipped on a root and he went sprawling.

"You OK?" Carol crouched down beside him and clutched his arm.

"No, I'm not bloody OK!" He shook his arm free and his voice began to rise. "I've been shot in the leg! I'm trying to walk with a crutch made out of sticks on a small slippery bush path! And I have only the vaguest notion of where the hell I'm supposed to be going! No, I'm not bloody OK!"

"Keep your voice down, mate," said Geoff.

Carol reached out to touch his arm but he again pulled away.

"Leave me. Can we rest for a bit?"

Without waiting for an answer he lowered himself by the side of the track and with a sigh stretched out on his back.

Carol and Geoff exchanged embarrassed glances. Finally Geoff shrugged his shoulders and said, "Look I'll go ahead a little to check our bearings and to, er, see if the coast is clear."

The two of them sat in tense silence. Uncertain what to do Carol kept glancing at her lover's prone form, taking care to look away whenever he appeared about to turn his head towards her. They had had arguments before on minor issues but he'd never shouted at her like this. She had fallen deeply in love with him and had marvelled at how well the two of them had coped with the rapid changes in their situation. In some ways the danger, uncertainty and fear had brought them closer together but on the other hand there were times when she yearned for the stability and comfort of a permanent home and a predictable routine. Above all else was the strain of uncertainty, of being unable to make even the most rudimentary plans for the future.

Yes, there was an element of excitement in her new existence with Fightback – the underground hideout, the skills of combat, the camaraderie and the terrifying success of the raid on the Albany Library. Every day her thoughts turned frequently to her brother Ian and each time her determination to avenge his death was renewed. The Albany raid had been the first opportunity to really hit back at the occupying forces and she longed to tell her parents what she'd accomplished – that their daughter had been part of a raiding party that had killed the soldiers of the army that had killed their son, her brother.

Of one thing she was sure. For the first time she had felt like her own person. She had quickly recognized the difference between the discipline of the partisan group and the strict adherence to social mores that had previously been an integral part of her life. She smiled to herself. It may all end in a hideous mess but at least she had been given the taste of an existence as far removed from conformist middle class society as she could ever have imagined. With dizzying rapidity she'd gone from the Northern Club secretarial staff to a wanted terrorist on the run from the German occupiers and an enraged ex-lover.

A deep sigh interrupted her reverie. Recognising it as a Stuart attention seeker she leant over to him.

"How are you feeling now?"

He looked up at her. "OK. The chance for a rest has done me good."

He reached for her hand and squeezed it. She didn't pull it away but let it remain limp inside his.

"Look, Carol, I'm sorry I blew my top. I was tired, my bloody leg was starting to throb and I began to feel dizzy – from the pain or the hunger, or both. So, I...."

She put her two fingers to his lips. "It's all right. I understand. I was worried about you and instead of just watching out for you I adopted the role of the mother hen."

"Yeah, that's part of it. I was also angry with myself for being a burden. No, don't interrupt; what I mean is you've looked to me for leadership and guidance since we began and now, because of my bloody leg, I feel I've let you down."

"You haven't. They told us in the woolshed we're at war and inevitably this brings casualties. Unfortunately you're one of them." Smiled and touched his cheek. "You told me that we have to look after each other. Well, now it's my turn."

She leaned down and gently kissed him on the lips. His hands slid through her hair and she felt his body respond. He groaned as she pulled back and looked down at him.

"A moan of lust or a groan of pain?" she murmured.

"The former. Even when I'm sorely wounded you excite the hell out of me."

A rustle of branches and a snapping twig instantly alerted them. The figure on the track was Geoff who stood grinning at them.

"I see my discreet withdrawal did the trick."

"If you'd withdrawn a little longer, who knows what might have happened," chuckled Stuart. "Look, mate, sorry about my outburst earlier on."

"That's OK." He smiled. "Difficult times for all of us. Now, I checked ahead and there's a break in the bush line with large paddocks and some buildings in the distance. I couldn't see much detail, but I think you should take a look to see if it's your farm."

Refusing any assistance Stuart regaining his feet. Leaning on his crutch he smiled. "Sounds good to me. How far is it?"

"If we take it easy, about ten minutes."

Stuart grinned at both of them. "So why are we standing round yakking? Let's start moving."

Geoff's estimation was accurate and ten minutes later they neared the edge of the bush line.

"You two wait here" He handed his Sten to Stuart. "Cover me. I'll take a quick dekko then if it's OK you can come forward."

Stuart carefully balanced himself with the Sten. They watched as Geoff moved forward to the edge of the bush, paused and looked carefully out through the tree branches at the paddocks in front. Turning his back, he gave them the thumbs up and stepped out into the open.

The shot and the echo sounded a split second after Geoff's head disintegrated into a bright scarlet pulp spray. For a moment the pair stood rigid.

"Jesus, they're out there!" whispered Stuart.

"Come on!" Carol's voice was desperate. "Give me your Sten. We can't stay here. Come on"

As fast as they could they moved off the track into the interior of the bush. Behind them they could hear the sounds of men's shouts mingling with the revving of engines.

"There's quite a few of them and they're well equipped," said Stuart.

The noise behind them was increasing with every passing moment. Carol, a few steps ahead, paused and pointed.

"Down here!" she said.

Without asking why he followed her awkwardly down a slight slope to an area where the bush was dense. She peered forward, pushing the branches aside.

"Look," she said, indicating a cluster of moss-covered boulders. "There's some sort of small cave in there. We'll never outdistance them. Quick. You go in first and I'll try to cover the entrance."

Hobbling forward Stuart pushed aside a tangle of overhanging fern fronds and branches found himself in the dank interior of what appeared to be a small cave. The darkness and the slippery floor nearly caused him to fall but, having steadied himself, he felt round for a place to sit. Having pulled the branches back into place, Carol groped her way towards him.

"Hope it'll work," she said.

Suddenly a loud explosion followed a flash of light. Carol gripped Stuart's arm and opened her mouth. Another explosion and a torrential downpour answered her unspoken question.

For several minutes they sat listening to the rain thrusting its way through the trees and hammering on the roof of their tiny haven.

Carol opened her mouth but he held up his finger.

"Shhh," he whispered. "We need to listen."

As if on cue, the sounds of men moving along the track began to come closer. They either had little knowledge of bush craft or were very confident as their progress was characterized by heavy, slithering footsteps, snapping branches and loud voices. As they came closer to the track by the cave a loud "Halt!" was heard. All movement stopped. They heard a voice giving brief staccato-style orders in German. After a pause this was followed by orders in English, delivered in a similar style.

"You are too noisy. Move quickly and quietly. Do not snap the branches. Do not speak. Proceed with caution. Search the bush for the enemy. They could be very near."

The group then began moving off again. The tension was instantly increased, as Stuart and Carol, crouching in their dank dark refuge with weapons at the ready, were less able to accurately assess the soldiers' positions. All they could hear were the occasional footfalls and swish of branches. Several times even these sounds ceased and the ensuing silence plucked incessantly at their nerve endings. Both had their eyes fixed rigidly on the entrance to the cave. The silhouettes of the twisted branches, the flickering shadows, flashes of light and the rustle of the foliage caused by the occasional breeze unmercifully taunted and teased their imaginations.

Gradually the sounds faded but at least twenty minutes elapsed before either of them in whispered conversation, agreed they should try to confirm the enemy had moved on. Cautiously Carol began to move the branches aside, pausing every few seconds to listen. Then, putting her head through the gap she peered round. Nothing appeared to be moving. She eased herself outside the cave and crouched by the entrance. A warning cry and a flapping of wings accompanied the hasty departure of a tui, but the brief noise elicited no response.

"Stuart," she said in a low voice, "I think it's safe."

"OK. Let me have a look."

He emerged. Together they stood stock still, straining for any unnatural sounds.

"I think it's all clear."

"Now what?"

"They're obviously combing this area and have key spots under surveillance which is why Geoff copped it. I think our only course of action is to follow the soldiers at a distance. They're unlikely to retrace their footsteps without good reason."

"But where are they heading?"

"Roughly in the direction of the farmhouse, as far as I can tell." The tone of his voice showed the ordeal in the recesses of the cave and the continuing pain in his leg had taken its toll. "If, I mean when, when we find it we'll check it out very carefully and then, when the time is right, make contact."

She shrugged. "We've not much choice. But we'll have to be extra wary."

More cautiously than before, they began to move forward. For a time the bush track remained unchanged but then it divided into two paths, the smaller one of which went off at a tangent. A brief inspection of the damp ground showed the soldiers had continued along the main section.

"How about a change of plans," said Carol. She indicated the smaller track. "This one could take us to the edge of the bush from where we can check our position. If it shows us nothing we can always come back and resume our journey on the original track."

Stuart nodded his agreement. His armpit was becoming chafed and his leg was throbbing painfully. Any chance, however slight, of spotting the farmhouse was worth a change of plan. His hopes lifted a little when they began to see a thinning of the bush and in front of them a glimpse of a broad paddock stretching up a long slope. Mindful of Geoff's fate, near the edge of the clearing they both lay flat and pausing frequently, slithered their way forward.

Stopping behind a tall tree at the edge of the clearing they paused, listening. On Stuart's nod they cautiously stood up. Carol pointed with her chin.

"Look. A road. Recognize it?"

Shaking his head Stuart said, "Too far away. But that big slope looks a little familiar."

The grass in the paddock was long and after a quick discussion they decided to move cautiously through it to the summit of the slope from where they might be able to gain a more accurate view of their position.

Their approach, in a series of low, slow movements, took longer than expected but eventually they reached the top and lay there panting from their efforts. The sun that had followed the downpour had been a welcome relief after the dampness of the bush, but was now causing them both to sweat uncomfortably.

"OK so far," said Stuart. "But we can't lie here forever. Can you get up slowly and see if you recognize any landmarks? Keep your Sten at the ready."

"As always," she replied, beginning to rise. "Just wish we knew –"

From the base of the slope the shouted orders followed by sound of a barking dog froze the words in her mouth.

"Los! Los! Vorwarts! Beeilt euch!"

The excited barking of the dog blended with the cocking of machine pistols and rapid booted footsteps.

Carol flung herself on the earth next to Stuart.

"Schmmeisers!" he muttered. "Bastards. A quick burst! Straight and fast! On my command…"

A helmet appeared over the crest.

Chapter 40

The intense pain caused him to cry out. Confused voices swirled around him during his brief periods of semi-consciousness and he was aware of being jolted up and down and pulled and pushed by many hands. At other times he woke with the sweat pouring from him and was vaguely conscious of soft voices and hands providing him with cool water. Yet, although the bouts of pain at times seemed to recede, every time he moved or was moved by others, piercing spasms traversed every part of his body.

Voices and images dissolved in ever-changing patterns. Carol's hands reaching out to sooth his brow, his mother reprimanding him for his foolhardiness, faces of leering German officers and New Order soldiers with Kiwi accents, smiling benignly at him and calling him "mate". The face of Hamish Beavis appeared in various guises, sneering menacingly or standing with an arm around Carol gloating with triumph. Other times he found himself stumbling and falling over the prone bloodied bodies of Boys Brigade youths, who sat upright and shouted abuse. New Order soldiers whose bodies, cut to pieces by machine-gun fire, suddenly came together and leapt to their feet, causing him to grope for his Sten gun. The images vanished and he was in his office at university, calmly poring over his books when Professor Sterling entered and smiled at him. About to speak, the professor was suddenly seized and pulled back by unseen hands obeying shouted orders. Stuart found himself in the university quad. Bleeding students sprawled on the ground stretching out their arms to him, pleading for assistance. A young woman, her face streaked with blood, rose from the group. She staggered towards him and seizing him by the shoulders began to shout his name.

"Stuart! Stuart!"

Waking with a jolt he found himself staring into the eyes of Carol. She had him by the shoulders and was gently shaking him.

"Stuart, darling." Her voice was calmer. "It's me. It's me! Carol! Everything's OK! You've been really sick, some sort of fever. But we think the worst is over." She held out a glass of water. "Here. Drink this."

His eyes fixed upon hers, expecting them to disappear at any moment and to be replaced with some hideous image of violence and death. Instead she stayed in his vision, smiling gently and talking tenderly to him.

Sipping the water gratefully he then shook his head in bewilderment. "I don't understand. We were both shot, weren't we?"

"No, darling, you were wounded in the shoulder and I twisted my ankle badly. The soldiers surrounded us and I thought we were done for. But remember how you thought that slope looked familiar?"

"Yes."

"It was the one by the old farmhouse where we do our weapons training. Ian and some of the others were checking their weapons when they heard the firing. Just as the soldiers surrounded us they came over the hill, caught them by surprise and wiped out the ones we hadn't killed."

"God! Then what happened?"

"They managed to carry both of us to the truck and drove back to the farmhouse. They got us down here in the Albany Ritz with a few minutes to spare. When the New Order troops arrived on a house-to-house, everything was normal. Barbara and Lisa were in the kitchen preparing the evening meal; Tom and Jason were out milking the house cows. They all admitted they had heard shots in the distance, hoped nobody had been hurt and reiterated their support for the New Order due to the excellent prices the farmers were getting for wool, meat and butter."

"Were the soldiers convinced?"

"Apparently. A couple of them came into the woolshed. We heard them walking about above us and we were worried you'd start moaning or shouting, but Lisa had given you painkiller injections and you stayed sound asleep. Our chaps had managed to load all the soldiers' bodies on the truck and hide their weapons. It also rained heavily for most of that night so all signs of the skirmish were obliterated. Since then planes have flown over occasionally, and a couple of days ago some soldiers came back sniffing around. Consequently we've had to lie low down here but Tony and Jason have continued to go into the village for supplies as usual."

"Why haven't the Krauts gone on the rampage arresting and shooting hostages?"

"From what we can gather, they're in a difficult situation. They need the populace on their side and they need the farmers to keep producing for the Russian war effort. They're worried about having to cope with widespread rebellion, sabotage and civil disobedience. We think there's a major dispute between the Germans' two main factions, one led by Governor von Stauffenberg who wants the long term goal of winning hearts and minds and the other by the Gestapo who want swift and brutal reprisals."

"Who's winning?"

"No idea." Tony had entered the cubicle and was standing in front of the bed. "Hopefully we are, in the end."

He held out his hand.

"You've had a rough time, mate. Great to see you sitting up and talking sense for a change."

"Thanks. Obviously somebody's been taking care of me and I'm really grateful."

"It's OK," said Tony. "You took one in the shoulder but Lisa said there's been no infection. The bone is healing nicely and she thinks you will be as right as rain in about a month. Your leg's also healing nicely."

"She's invaluable."

Tony smiled. "Yeah. Her knowledge about such things has been invaluable. And she's also been ably assisted by the two German girls."

"Are they settling in OK?"

"Yeah. Suppose so." He grinned wryly. "I think some of the group is still coming to terms with providing refuge for a couple of Germans. Their prime responsibility has been keeping an eye on the professor who's still pretty crook, and they've done that well. And they were also keen to help out with looking after you."

"I look forward to thanking them."

"Sure. But the person you should really thank is this little lady here. She has been at your side night and day, soothing you, bathing you and talking to you as you thrashed about like a bloody marlin on the end of a long line!"

"Oh, Tony you exaggerate," said Carol. "We agreed at the beginning we would always be there to support each other."

Smiling at Stuart she reached for his hand.

Tony grinned again at Stuart. "Great to see you on the road to recovery, mate. We'll bring you upstairs later when the sun's gone down and you can catch up on all the news."

Reaching out he shook Stuart's hand warmly and left as Stuart and Carol turned back towards each other.

After the evening meal it was decided a celebration was in order. A small beer ration was brought into the woolshed, enough for two glasses per person, and a wind-up gramophone placed carefully on a table in the corner. Additional personnel were posted on sentry duty while the rest of the group celebrated not only the success of their rescue mission but Stuart's initial recovery.

John had been assigned the task of keeping the gramophone supplied with a steady stream of 78 records that, although in

282

some cases were scratchy and prone to jump the grooves, added considerably to the party atmosphere. As the evening wore on, Stuart and Carol remained relaxed in a corner of the woolshed catching up on the news. They both noticed that in another corner Brendan and Susan were engaged in a tense conversation.

"What do you think's bothering those two?"

"Dunno," shrugged Stuart.

"So why do they both keep looking at the two German women?"

Stuart held up his hand. "Listen."

Instantly on the alert, Carol sat bolt upright.

"It's OK," he laughed. "John's playing my favourite melody; the W.C. Handy classic The St Louis Blues." He got cautiously to his feet, and bowed exaggeratedly to Carol. "May I have the pleasure of this dance, ma'am?"

"Are you sure you can manage?"

"Quite sure."

"Then, sir, I accept your invitation." Taking his outstretched hand she got to her feet and he drew her close.

"What about your leg?"

"It'll be OK if we take it easy."

As they began to dance to the music Stuart smiled down at her. "I owe you my life, Carol."

She smiled back. "The others helped too. And, in any case, we both agreed."

"To do what?"

"To look after each other."

Reaching up she kissed him as they continued to move gently with the music.

CHAPTER 41

"How are you feeling, sir?"

Professor Sterling lifted his head slightly from the pillow as Stuart and Brendan entered his cubicle.

"Not too bad under the circumstances."

Stuart tried not to gasp at the weakness in the professor's voice. His pallor and the thin film of sweat across the top of his head added to the impression of a man who was having difficulty finding the road to recovery.

Pulling two wooden apple boxes from the corner Stuart flipped them on their sides. Both young men sat down.

"If you're not well enough…" began Brendan.

The professor's hand appeared from under the grey army blankets and waved impatiently.

"Don't be ridiculous. Delighted to see you both." He looked at Stuart. "You've been having a pretty rough time, they tell me."

"Yes, sir – my own fault. I was so cocky after the raid on the Albany library I got careless. Nearly cost me my life." He paused. "How about you, sir?"

"Not too good, I'm afraid. When I was taken in for questioning they hit me repeatedly in the stomach. When I fell to the floor, they then resorted to the time-honoured tactic of putting the boot in. Not very imaginative but very painful."

"Bastards," said Brendan. "What were they trying to do? Get some sort of information from you?"

"Strangely enough, I'm not sure if they knew themselves. I think it was more a matter of intimidation than extracting any hard information."

"So, why did they decide to let you go home?"

"When they realized there wasn't much point in beating me any more. I was in a bad way and kept passing out. I do remember at one point regaining consciousness and hearing an argument going on between the Germans and a couple of the New Zealanders. The latter were expressing reservations at my continued ill treatment."

"Huh," grunted Stuart. "Big of them."

"Well, they may have won the day because the following morning I was taken home. Don't remember much. I was fairly heavily drugged."

"To ease the pain?"

"Maybe, Stuart, or to keep me docile. They intended using me as an example to intimidate my academic colleagues." He sighed heavily. "Susan was horrified when she saw me but I urged her to get away before she was next on the list."

"She hated leaving you, sir," said Brendan.

"Yes, I know," nodded the professor. He looked hard at Brendan. "She means a lot to me, young man. I hope you're taking good care of her."

Brendan shifted awkwardly and folded his arms. "Of course, professor."

Sensing the awkwardness, Stuart changed the subject.

"What impression did you get of Sophie and Gretchen, sir?"

"Limited, I'm afraid. They spoke German most of the time. Sophie tried her English out on me when the German doctor wasn't around but even then I think I was heavily doped up." He smiled wanly. "Pretty girls, though. Especially the blonde. What do you think, Brendan?"

"Er, yes sir. You seem to be in good hands with both of them. And they're keen to improve their English. Sophie's improving rapidly but Gretchen needs more assistance. I'm the only fluent German speaker in the place and therefore..."

"It's all right, young man," replied Sterling. "You don't have to justify yourself. Now, if you'll excuse me, gentlemen."

"No, sir, I wasn't…" began Brendan, when Stuart touched him on the arm. The professor had already fallen asleep.

Chapter 42

"'Sheep'. That's the plural of 'sheep'".

"Not one sheep, two sheeps?"

"No. One sheep. Two sheep."

"So. One cow. Two cow?"

"No. For most nouns you add an 's' for the plural. But not for sheep."

"English. It is not, how you say, 'logic'?"

"'Logical'. True. There are many exceptions. But you are doing well, Gretchen. You are a good student."

The German girl, her face framed by her blonde locks, smiled prettily up at him.

"You are a very good teacher, Brendan. You have taught me all about the New Zealand animals and the farm words. I am now trying to talk to the other people in the group."

"Yes, and they are happy to help you. That's why you are making such excellent progress."

It was a warm summer's morning. For the past few days Brendan had scheduled an hour of one-on-one teaching with the German girl while Susan was assigned to looking after her uncle. She was less than happy but had been unable to counter Brendan's argument that Gretchen's English needed to improve in order to avoid any communication difficulties in an emergency, and he was in the best position to teach her.

"After all," he added, "Sophie and Gretchen have taken very good care of your Uncle David."

Seated on a grassy mound by the edge of the sheep pens, Brendan was dressed in a light shirt, shorts and boots and Gretchen in a light summer dress. In spite of a gentle breeze the heat from the morning sun was beginning to increase.

"Brendan, it is becoming too hot. Can you walk with me over to those trees?" She pointed to the sprawling patch of bush on the edge of the paddock. "You can teach me the names of the birds and the trees."

He glanced sharply at her. Her smile was guileless, and after a brief look over his shoulder at the woolshed he stood up. "OK, but only for a little while. They don't like us wandering off."

As they walked across the paddock towards the bush line Brendan began a rapid series of vocabulary testing questions while at the same time aware the real reason was to cover his contradictory feelings. Gretchen, the breeze tugging at her skirt, skipped lightheartedly ahead of him, turning to answer each question before laughing and moving away again.

The cool, dark bush offered a relief from the hot, bright sun. Gretchen entered ahead of Brendan and as he stepped over a spreading fern and onto the narrow track she turned towards him.

"Now, just above you is a tree called –"

The rest of the sentence was stifled as her open mouth made immediate contact with his. For a moment he stood stunned then his hands slid in parallel up behind her back and cradling her head, pushed it more firmly against his. He felt her right leg slide over his thigh and the folds of her light dress brush provocatively against his bare legs. He moaned and slid his hands down her back and under her skirt. He gasped as his hands encountered only bare flesh. Swiftly he lifted her upwards and in an instant response she locked her bare legs around his thighs and thrust her tongue deep into his mouth. Staggering a few steps off the track he sank on his knees into a nearby grassy patch where, with her legs still wrapped around him, he lowered her down.

"*Liebling!*" was her single shuddering cry as he entered her.

***

288

As their breathing subsided Gretchen giggled.

"What's funny?"

"I come all this way. To another part of the world and I find two things."

"Yes?"

"How much I hate the Nazis and how much I love you."

He leant down and kissed her.

"Why do you hate the Nazis so much? Is it only because they have stopped freedom among university students?"

She shook her head.

"You can explain in German, if you wish."

"No, English is your language. I will try to explain and if I get, um..."

"Stuck".

"Ja, stuck. Then you will help me."

"OK." Again he kissed her lightly. "Tell me."

"OK. But you must promise not to tell anyone else."

"Of course."

She gazed at him steadily. "I am Jewish."

"Jewish?" he asked incredulously, running his fingers through the blonde tresses spread on the grass.

"Brendan, not every Jewish person has black hair and a large nose. I have a mother and a father and two sisters. My two sisters are fifteen, and *zwillings*."

"Twins?"

"Ja, twins."

"Are they OK? I mean..."

"My father is a doctor of Engineering. The Nazis are not stupid. They need many many engineers to help the army in Russia. They told him he can keep working and my two sisters can still go to school. And me? I must join the army. I have no, um..."

"Alternative?"

"No alternative. The Nazis tell us what to do and where to go, and if we do not obey their orders we will be sent to a KZ."

"What's that?"

"*Konzentration* camp. Same word in English I think."

"Yes. I have read a little about them. Camps for political prisoners."

"Yes, but also for Jews – just because they are Jews. No other reason. Many Jews go there and never return." Her blue eyes flashed with malevolence. "I hate the Nazis!"

CHAPTER 43

"It's important none of us goes wandering off. We need to know where everyone is at all times."

"Yes, sorry, Dan. I was just trying to improve Gretchen's vocabulary."

Dan held up his hand. "OK. We have to be extra careful now. The authorities will be bloody furious at the success of our raid, the rescue of the professor and the killing of their soldiers. They'll almost certainly be increasing their surveillance of this whole area."

"I understand. It won't happen again."

"What won't?" demanded Susan, emerging from downstairs into the woolshed.

"Oh, hi Susan, just a little misunderstanding. Nothing at all to worry about." Brendan's exaggerated brightness caused her to frown suspiciously.

"What's going on?"

"Nothing, Susan. Nothing at all."

At the sound of Gretchen's voice Susan turned and regarded the brightly smiling German girl with undisguised acrimony.

"Huh! If you say so, then I should be worried." She turned to Dan. "What's the problem?"

Sensing the undercurrent, Dan frowned. "Well, it's just that Brendan and Gretchen went outside for her English lesson..."

"It was a nice day," began Brendan.

"And then they disappeared," continued Dan. "We didn't know where they were and were about to implement an alert when they turned up." He looked at Brendan and Gretchen in turn. "They've acknowledged the importance of the rules and," he shrugged, "assured me that it won't happen again. So, no real harm done."

"Your turn, Gretchen." Susan's voice was ice cold.

"My turn? What do you mean?"

"It's your turn to look after Professor Sterling. You're half an hour late."

"Yes, of course."

With a final look at Brendan, Gretchen hurried down the ladder to Sterling's cubicle.

"And as for you, mister, I'd like a word. If you can spare the time of course."

***

"Jesus, mate, you really pick your moments don't you."

The sun was going down as Stuart, dropping his cigarette on the ground and stubbing it out, glared at the crestfallen Brendan leaning up against the side of the faded red woolshed wall

"I know. It's just that she was all over me and, well, come on, mate, can you really blame me?"

"Susan's worried sick about her uncle. Christ, Brendan, don't you think that under the bloody circumstances..." Stuart, at a loss for words, shrugged helplessly.

Brendan looked uncharacteristically crestfallen. "She guessed, of course. Women have an instinct for this sort of thing. Told me we're no longer sleeping in the same cubicle." He shrugged. "I suppose I could always suggest to Gretchen..."

"No bloody way! Dan wouldn't put up with it. You know how he keeps stressing that we keep our personal problems to a minimum. If you start sleeping with Gretchen it will cause all sorts of problems. What was her motive, anyway?"

"Well, without wishing to sound too egotistical, she fancies me."

"Maybe," said Stuart. "Did she make the running?"

"Yes, you could say that. She's also in a dangerous situation and a long way from home. She's just seeking some solace."

"What about Susan? Her position's not exactly a piece of cake."

"Yeah, you're right I suppose."

"Yes, I am you dumb bastard. So spare a thought for her. Remember that some of the group members are still a bit wary of having two Germans here, so we don't want to create more trouble." He glared at his friend. "Best thing you can do tonight is to stay upstairs and bed down on a comfortable wool bale. Forget about women and concentrate on preparing to play your part if there's any sort of emergency."

CHAPTER 44

Driven by a howling westerly wind the rain descended in biting sheets. It was too wet to venture outside for any form of training, so most of the time was spent in strategy meetings in the woolshed. Mindful of the heightened dangers the meetings included a variety of drills and procedures to accommodate a range of emergency situations. Stuart noted with wry amusement that Brendan, having spent the night on a wool bale, threw himself into the drills with a total commitment.

He and Carol had spent part of the night discussing the triangular situation while, like everyone else in the underground hideout, being constantly disturbed by the racking coughs coming from the professor's cubicle. Brendan had told him about Gretchen being Jewish, and he'd told Carol on the basis that she needed to be kept fully informed, but that she must keep the information to herself. Finally, having decided that both he and Carol would talk to Brendan and Susan as soon as possible, try to offer advice and stress the importance of not letting their personal problems compromise the safety of the camp, they fell asleep in each other's arms.

After the lunch break Stuart and Carol had been assigned to take the dishes back to the farmhouse. Sophie and Gretchen had been rostered with Lisa to prepare the lunch in the farmhouse kitchen so remained there.

"Put them in a pile while I have a squizz outside," said Stuart as they completed gathering up the plates and utensils.

He began to open the door. It was nearly ripped from his hand by the crosswind. Lowering his head he stood on the top step and, narrowing his eyes against the wet stinging sheets of rain, peered into the sodden gloom. Nothing suspicious was distinguishable and the only sounds were the periodic moaning of the wind and the constant rain tattoo on the corrugated iron woolshed roof.

Stepping back inside he walked over to Carol and scooped up a pile of dishes.

"All clear. Just bloody wet. Come on. Let's join the drowned rat-race for the farmhouse."

Hunched up against the elements, they hurried down the steps and began the brief trip across the open ground from the woolshed.

The shout that echoed above the noise of the wind caused them to pause in puzzlement. The second shout of "Halt! Don't move!" froze them in their tracks.

Four helmeted figures in heavy coats and carrying Schmeissers were racing towards them from the building's western side. Half blinded by the rain Stuart strained to make out details of the soldiers as he felt Carol pressing up against him. A further shout caused both of them to turn to see two more armed figures approaching at speed from the opposite direction.

Stuart twisted his head around to where Carol stood pressed up against his shoulder.

"Keep still and we'll try to bluff our way out!" he said loudly above the noise of the elements.

Aware of the hollowness of the advice he was unable to add anything as the leading soldier slid to an abrupt halt in front of him and peered into his face. Using the rain as an excuse Stuart tried to tuck his head into his hunched shoulders.

"You!" demanded the soldier. "What are you doing?"

What he had hoped would be a relaxed chuckle came out as a nervous laugh. "Carrying dirty dishes to the farmhouse kitchen," he answered, thrusting the plates towards the solider.

"Watch it!" barked the soldier, taking a step back.

"They're only dirty dishes. Now, do you mind? We're getting cold and wet standing here."

Another soldier positioned himself between the pair and the farmhouse.

"We don't mind in the least. And if you mind, that's tough," he growled. "Now, let's have a good look at both of you."

Reaching swiftly forward he thrust his hand under Stuart's chin forcing it upwards. The unexpectedness of the action caused Stuart to lurch backwards against Carol. The dishes slid from his wet hands and splintered noisily on the ground.

"Too bad," laughed the soldier. "Saves you washing them."

The second soldier, following his companion's example, stepped in front of Carol.

"Let's have a good look at you, sweetheart," he said. Taking a clump of her hair he pulled downward causing her to gasp with pain and tilt her face upward towards his.

The first soldier thrust the barrel of his Schmeisser under Stuart's chin to force his head higher and peered closely at him.

"I think we've got him," he said loudly to the other soldiers who had now formed a semi-circle around the pair.

"I think we've got both of them!" answered his companion. Twisting his head in a half turn he shouted, "Call him, Wilson!"

A tall soldier turned his head, cupped his hand to his mouth and shouted, "Sir!

Sir! Over here, sir! We've got both of them!"

Stuart, unable to speak or turn his head, strained his ears above the sounds of the wind and rain. The voice that sounded in his ear caused a shiver to run through him that owed nothing to the elements.

"Got you!"

Hamish Beavis's face appeared inches from his nose.

"You poncy little varsity prick. I knew I'd get you in the end."

Through the driving rain Stuart could see Hamish was wearing a long black leather coat with a braided SS officer's cap featuring the death's head in the centre. He realized the only hope of getting out of the situation was to attract the attention of the others in the woolshed. Drawing his head back slightly to relieve the pressure from the soldier's weapon he shouted above the noise of the elements.

"Brave little pervert, aren't you, Beavis. Easy to abuse me when one of your minions has a gun stuck in my face. You wouldn't be so brave if it was one-on-one."

"You'll get your chance, Johnson, don't you worry."

"Like your flash new cap, Beavis. What's the death's head signify? Dead from the neck up?"

Under the circumstances the glancing blow to the side of Stuart's face was not unexpected. Fortunately, hampered by his heavy leather greatcoat and the driving rain, Hamish was unable to land the blow accurately and its effect was minimal.

Thrusting his head towards his antagonist Stuart shouted as loudly as he could.

"You're a filthy little ratbag, aren't you, Beavis! Wonderful example to your soldiers! How to hit people when they can't hit back! Great bloody Nazi hero!"

His adversary's face contorted and Stuart prepared himself for a second blow. Instead the man hissed, "You snivelling bastard! I'll hurt you where it hurts the most!"

Beavis's face disappeared and Stuart heard him take two squelching steps.

"Carol. Sweetheart." His laugh was loud but devoid of mirth. "Your fiancé has arrived to rescue you. And to take care of you."

Taking her cue from Stuart, Carol shouted, "Leave us alone! I don't want you! Get out of our lives!"

Hamish laughed again then barked, "Clay! Turner! Get that terrorist into the truck. Wilson, stay and assist me in looking after this woman."

The shot that came from the woolshed was followed by the whine of a ricochet as the bullet that hit Wilson's coalscuttle helmet caused him to reel backwards and drop his Schmeisser.

A second shot was followed by Dan's shout.

"Stuart! Carol! Back over here!"

The shots had caused Hamish and his soldiers to turn instinctively and crouch down. Stuart, scooping Wilson's weapon from the ground, seized Carol's arm and headed in a crouching run towards the woolshed shouting, "Cover us! We're coming in!"

A detonation of thunder buried all sound for a few seconds as the pair reached the woolshed steps. A flash of lightning momentarily illuminated the scene as Stuart glanced upwards through the driving rain and saw several figures at the woolshed windows firing their Stens.

As they reached the top of the steps the door was flung open. Both of them dived through the doorway and sprawled on the floor. The sound of splintering, a groan and a thud followed the slam of the door. Bullets from behind the fleeing pair had cut through the door and had hit Dan who had been holding it open. He collapsed and lay motionless on the wooden floor.

Above the percussive din of the rain on the corrugated iron roof Tony's voice shouted, "They're too well armed. Everybody downstairs! We'll cover you!"

The machinery whirred and the wool bale tipped backwards to reveal the familiar gap in the floor.

"Go, all of you!" shouted Tony as he leapt up to the window, fired twice and crouched down again.

Joining him at the window Stuart fired a burst from the captured Schmeisser into the driving rain before ducking down.

"Hard to see anything out there," he said.

"It'll keep them at bay but not for long," Tony replied. Turning to the others he shouted, "All of you. Keep moving! Go down now! We'll follow!"

They all moved to the top of the gap and in response to his command began a rapid descent. Brendan stood at the top of the stairs urging them to hurry. Susan stopped as she drew level with him and seemed about to speak before she followed the others down the ladder. Carol, the last of the group, paused at the top.

"Come on, Carol!" shouted Brendan impatiently, as another bullet whined through the woolshed and splintered against the back wall.

Hesitating, she looked across at Stuart, crouching under the window.

"Stuart, what about…?"

"Do as he says, Carol. I'll join you shortly. Go!"

Springing upright he thrust his weapon through the broken windowpane, fired a further burst and slid back to his crouching position. He glanced back. Carol had gone. Brendan, clasping a pistol, was the last to go. Pausing by the trapdoor, he shouted, "Don't be long, mate!" and dropped out of sight.

On the final rung Brendan missed his footing and sprawled to the floor. As he twisted round he glanced up to hear a burst of firing and to see the trapdoor settling back into place.

"They're closing the entrance," gasped Susan who, with Carol and several other women, was crouched against the wall.

"Stuart," said Carol. "What's he going to do?"

The answer came swiftly. Above them came a loud crash followed by two ferocious discharges.

"Jesus! Grenades!" said Brendan. "Poor bastards. They've got no show!"

Above them the woolshed door opened with a splintering crash. A short was pause followed by the slow tread of boots and the sounds of creaking mingled with the noise of the storm as soldiers moved cautiously over the wooden floorboards.

"They've all copped it," said Brendan.

"No they haven't," came Carol's desperate whisper. There was raw fear in her eyes. Her statement was meant as a question, and she scanned the faces of the others, seeking some form of reassurance. "They can't have."

Susan put an arm across her shoulders. "We'll find out soon. In the meantime we need to keep absolutely quiet."

The others nodded in agreement, even though, with the noise from the outside gale, the chances of their being heard were slight.

"Susan? What about your uncle?"

"He fell asleep about an hour ago. I suppose he's OK."

"Best not disturb him. Wait until the soldiers have gone."

Seeing the searching look in Carol's eyes, Susan tried to smile. "Of course. When the soldiers have gone," she echoed.

By an unspoken consensus they gathered in a group and seated themselves on the earth floor two metres from the bottom of the ladder. The moaning of the wind, the rattling of the windows, the unrelenting rhythm of the rain and the heavy footsteps above created a discord of foreboding – reflected in the drawn features of the group as they huddled together in the semi darkness.

Above them the tread of the boots became heavier and more confident. The sounds of a shouted order, a crash as some object was splintered or thrown to the floor by the searching soldiers penetrated the noise of the storm. On each occasion the group members instinctively looked upwards but all they could see were dark shadows gliding over the narrow gaps in the floorboards. Even the occasional lighting flash did little more than momentarily illuminate the silhouetted figures. After several minutes the sounds settled into a pattern appearing to indicate that although the soldiers were searching, they had found nothing significant. Some members of the huddled group began to exchange hopeful glances.

Suddenly a shouted order brought all movement to a halt. Snatches of conversation drifted down followed by a further order. The footsteps and the shadows appeared to suggest the searchers were all moving in the same direction – towards the woolshed door.

"They're leaving," whispered Susan who still had her arm around Carol. Several of the others nodded in silent agreement. "Just a few more minutes and we'll find out what happened."

There was a momentary lull in the wind and the listening group heard another shouted order.

"Wait!"

Carol started at the sound of Hamish's voice.

The footsteps halted.

"The wool bales! Shoot the wool bales!"

Fearful glances were exchanged as the stuttering of machine pistols echoed and re-echoed above them.

In response to a shouted order the firing ceased.

"Nothing in them, sir," said a soldier's voice.

Hamish voice sounded again.

"There's one more. The small one over there!"

There was a thud of rapid footsteps and from above them came a fresh burst of firing. It stopped abruptly.

"Sir!" shouted a voice. "Look!"

Rapid footsteps were followed by Hamish's excited voice.

"The wool bale. It's fixed to the bloody floor."

The renewed howling of the wind drowned all other sounds. In spite of the dim light the huddled group caught glimpses of silhouetted figures gathering round the trapdoor area.

"If they discover the trapdoor we'll have to make a fight of it," said Brendan in a hoarse whisper. "All move back and crouch on either side of the passage."

They took new positions and crouched down. A rattle of gunfire from above sent a shower of bullets thudding into the floor at the base of the steps. As the trapdoor disintegrated a shaft of light thrust itself into the gloom. Instinctively Carol jumped up and began to move towards the base of the ladder.

"Stop her!" shouted Brendan. Two of the others leapt forward, seized and dragged her down onto the earthen floor.

With a thump an object with a small wooden handle landed on the ground.

"Grenade!" screamed Susan.

CHAPTER 45

"Jesus, what a mess! They've all copped it, sir. The whole bloody lot."

By the flickering light of the kerosene lantern being held aloft by Wilson, Hamish Beavis, with two other soldiers, Clay and Turner, stood on the tunnel floor surveying the carnage. As the swirling smoke drifted upward through the hole in the floor the scene it revealed was gruesome. Patches of blood and flesh were splattered at various sections of the wall and bodies lay in grotesque postures at the tunnel's edges.

The four men gazed silently at the blood soaked scene. The relentless downpour had paused and now the only sound was of water dripping steadily from various parts of the building.

Clay gazed at the nearest corpse.

"Christ, that's Brownie."

"Who?" snapped Hamish.

"Alfred Brown, sir. He was in our regiment. He was a good mate."

"Brown!" answered Hamish. "He was a deserter, Clay. And don't you forget it."

Meeting his officer's angry eyes, Clay nodded brusquely and looked down again.

"Brown was a terrorist." In a sweeping movement he indicated the bodies in the passage. "They were all terrorists!"

"They were all New Zealanders, sir," said Wilson.

Hamish glared at him. "Saboteurs! Subversives! Traitors to their country!"

"Maybe, sir," said Turner. "But, like us, they were all born here."

There was a murmur of agreement from his comrades.

"That's enough. You men still have a great deal to learn. Subversives are subversives, regardless of their nationality. That makes them our enemies." He glared at each man in turn. "Clear?" he demanded.

The soldiers exchanged glances. Their desultory "Yes, sir" peeved their officer who was about to demand a more enthusiastic response when there was a low moan from further down the passage.

"One of them's still alive, sir," said Wilson starting forward eagerly. "Let's have a look."

"Wait!" barked Hamish. "I'll go. Cover me."

The soldiers lifted their weapons as he picked his way carefully forward past two of the bodies.

The groan sounded again. He crouched down. The hair was matted and bloody but the face was Carol Peterson's.

"Bring the lamp!"

The three soldiers hurried forward.

Snatching the lamp from Wilson's hand Hamish shone it directly on to Carol's face. Her bloodied hair seemed to have been caused by a cut across her left temple. The blast had torn away her tunic and part of the blouse underneath, revealing one of her breasts. Crouching motionless Hamish stared fixedly at her.

A cough from Wilson brought him hurriedly back to reality.

"Don't just stand there, you men!" he barked.

The soldiers exchanged glances.

"What do you want us to do, sir?" said Turner.

Standing up Hamish glanced around. Nearby a door sagged on one hinge revealing a small cubicle with a bed frame and a straw mattress.

"Lift her up and put her over there on the bed. Wilson, you take her shoulders, Turner her feet." He turned to the remaining solider. "Clay, come over and support her back."

The three soldiers moved into position and, on a nod from Wilson, began to lift Carol upwards. She groaned aloud.

"Gently, you bloody morons!" barked Hamish. "I want her alive."

Turner glanced at the other two, raised his eyebrows and grunted.

"You say something, Turner?"

"Me sir? No, sir."

"Keep your mouth shut and get on with it, then."

Picking their way gingerly through the debris the soldiers carried Carol into the cubicle and carefully laid her on the mattress.

"Now step back!"

Turner had noticed a blanket lying in a crumpled heap at the foot of the bed. He picked it up and began to spread it across her.

"What the hell are you doing, Turner?" demanded Hamish.

"First rule of first aid, sir. Keep the patient warm."

Hamish glared at him.

"Permission to carry on, sir?" said Turner meeting his gaze.

Hamish grunted and nodded curtly.

Standing near the head of the bed, Wilson bent forward.

"This looks interesting, sir,"

Reaching across Carol he pulled out a drawing pin and removing a small black and white photograph from the wall near the bed, studied it carefully.

"It's her. This girl."

Turner peered over Wilson's shoulder. "That bloke with his arms round her. It's Johnson the terrorist. Maybe she was his girlfriend or something."

"Give it here!" Hamish snatched the photograph from Wilson's hand. "It could be valuable evidence."

He peered intently at the photograph. A street photographer had taken it outside the Chief Post Office in Queen Street. Stuart, in a university blazer and tie, was standing with a smiling Carol who had her arm through his. She was wearing a frock Hamish recognized as one she had often worn to work.

With a snarl he crumpled the photograph in his hand and let it fall to the floor. He stared at it for a moment and then glared at the three soldiers who were gazing at him in astonishment.

"What are you three staring at?" he growled.

Clay looked down at the crushed photograph. "You said it was valuable evidence. And now you've thrown it away!"

"Are you questioning my actions, Clay?"

Glancing at his two companions and then back at Hamish, Clay raised his eyebrows and shrugged.

Hamish stared uncertainly at the trio and then barked, "You men, go back upstairs and undertake a thorough search of the building!"

"Another search of the building?" asked Turner with a quizzical look. "They're all dead up there."

"Do as I say!" He jerked his head towards Carol. "I now need to interrogate this prisoner."

Again the soldiers exchanged glances.

"Interrogate the prisoner?" Turner made no attempt to hide his incredulity.

"Are you a bloody parrot, Turner?" shouted Hamish. "I will not stand for any more disobedience. You men are to get out of here and carry out my orders. Clear?"

"As a bell, sir," answered Clay. "We are to search the area upstairs that we've just searched while you'll be interrogating the prisoner."

"Got it in one, Clay," replied Hamish sarcastically. "Now carry on!"

The men turned and began to walk towards the stairs. Wilson, the last to leave, stopped and turned back.

"Just one thing, sir."

"What is it?" demanded Hamish impatiently.

The soldier's tones were measured. "If you have any trouble, you will let us know. Won't you, sir."

Before Hamish could reply the men had gone but as they mounted the stairs he heard the echoes of their subdued laughter.

Clenching and unclenching his fists, he stood looking uncertainly in the direction the soldiers had taken. Then turning towards the girl on the bed he smiled. He bent down until his face was right in front of hers. His voice was soft and triumphant.

"At last, sweetheart. At last we're together. At last you're all mine."

Her eyes were closed and she showed no reaction. Fearful she might be dead he put his ear close to her mouth and sighed with relief when he heard her soft steady breathing.

"You've had a tough day," he said aloud. "Never mind, your fiancé Hamish is here to look after you now."

Carol still showed no response. Looking round he saw a battered but serviceable wooden chair lying against the wall outside the cubicle. He placed it by the bed, removed his long leather coat and peaked cap and sat down facing her. She appeared to be in a deep sleep. Tiredness came over him and leaning back in the chair he closed his eyes. He had all the time in the world, now. He was on the winning side, Johnson was dead and Carol was completely in his power.

It had been a long pursuit, requiring patience and thoroughness. The Albany bus driver had recalled four young adults among his passengers, two of who fitted the description of Stuart and Carol. When the searches of the farms in the Albany area proved fruitless he had suggested aerial photographic surveillance. A series of sweeps were made over all the farms in the district and any signs of human activity matched against the known number of each farm's inhabitants – in particular the farms in the vicinity where the group of New Order soldiers had been ambushed in the afternoon after the Albany library attack. Several days later by the side of a back road, the bodies of several New Order soldiers had been discovered. The general consensus was that they had been dumped there and a third late afternoon sweep of the local farms had been ordered. A photograph taken at this particular farm had revealed a truck half-hidden by a tree. It had been a wet day and the tracks showed that the truck had veered off the road. A closer inspection showed several figures on the back of the truck, and two standing alongside it. The following afternoon during a repeat surveillance a rhythmic flashing from a clump of bush near the farmhouse had caused the plane to circle overhead for a few minutes until the flashing ceased.

Certain that his quarry was near he ordered the farm to be put under 24-hour surveillance. He had chosen soldiers like Wilson, Clay and Turner who, having had deerstalking experience, were well versed in moving unobtrusively through the bush, leaving little trace of their passing.

In spite of several narrow escapes the soldiers had managed to observe comings and goings that were clearly not part of a normal farm's activity. Final conformation came when a truck with six people on the back was observed travelling away from the farmhouse in the morning and returning later in the afternoon. Two of the occupants had rifles across their knees.

On reading the reports Hamish had suggested to his superiors that the farmhouse be attacked on a day when bad weather would ensure the inhabitants would more likely to be confined inside. The day chosen had been ideal, as the electrical storm had enabled them to approach the buildings without being observed. Luck was certainly on their side when the first people they saw were Johnson and Carol. After their initial escape in the fierce firefight that had followed, he'd lost several men. When they'd finally entered the woolshed the sight of Johnson's lifeless body lying underneath the bodies of several others had given him little satisfaction. He had desperately wanted the man alive. Still, capturing Carol alive was more than adequate compensation. In the end he had got what he really craved – Carol – now his forever.

He smiled grimly, and lifting up the lamp, let the light fall on Carol's face. She moaned slightly and moved her head away from the light.

"You've had a good sleep, haven't you sweetheart," he said loudly over the noise of the rain that had recommenced its incessant roof rhythm.

His voice echoed around the tunnel and he felt a moment's uneasiness. Then, smiling at his own nervousness, he moved the lamp away from her face and continued his one-sided conversation.

"I've been sleeping, too, Carol. You could say we've been sleeping together." He sniggered. "I'm certainly looking forward to that, my girl."

He glanced nervously around again and then turning back towards her laughed hoarsely. "No-one here. Just you and me, sweetheart."

He reached forward, put his hand on the top of her forehead and moved it lingeringly over her face to the top of the blanket. He paused, and taking the top edge in his hand began to peel it back.

Carol's eyes snapped open. She screamed, sat bolt upright and stared wildly at Hamish.

"No!" Her voice was a mixture of fear and horror.

"It's OK, sweetheart. It's me. It's Hamish, your fiancé. I'm looking after you."

Clutching the blanket to her throat she stared wildly round the room.

"Stuart? Where's Stuart?" she cried.

Seizing both her shoulders he thrust his face in front of hers. "Stuart Johnson is dead. Dead. Shot by my soldiers. There's only you and me now."

She stared at him and then began to tremble.

"You're lying! Stuart can't be dead!"

"He is dead. My men killed him."

Continuing to stare at him she moved her head from side to side in denial.

Angrily he started to shake her. "Listen to me, Carol! Stuart Johnson is d-e-a-d, dead!"

Her eyes gazed intently at him. Her mouth moved and she seemed about to speak. Then she pulled her head back and in a swift forward movement spat straight into his face.

Outraged, he brought his right arm back and swept his open palm across her face.

She screamed and attempted to spit at him again.

"You little bitch!" he shouted. "Johnson's dead! Now you're mine!"

Footsteps could be heard moving across the floor and down the ladder.

"Leave me alone, you murdering bastard!" she screamed.

The three soldiers appeared in the doorway and stood staring at Hamish who was still holding the near hysterical girl by the shoulders. His blow to her face had re-opened the cut in her forehead causing the blood to trickle down towards her right eye.

"What's going on?" demanded Turner.

"Get out!" snarled Beavis. "Get out and wait until I call you."

"I don't think so," said Wilson. "The girl's been wounded. You said you only wanted to question her."

"I don't hold with beating up women," added Clay.

"You don't, do you?" Hamish's voice was high pitched. "Nobody asked your opinions. You're not here to think, just to obey orders! And my orders are to get out until I call for you. Understood?"

The men exchanged glances and Clay spoke again.

"It's understood. But we're not leaving unless the young lady comes with us. She needs proper medical treatment."

Taking a step forward, Clay confronted Hamish.

"Back out there in the rain you said something about a fiancée. Was this girl your fiancée?"

Still holding the trembling girl by the shoulders Hamish stared fixedly at him. He opened his mouth to reply but Clay was continuing.

"That's why you crumpled the photograph up isn't it? That's why you wanted to question her all by yourself. She ditched you for Johnson, didn't she?"

"How dare you speak to your superior officer like that!" His voice was shrill. "Insubordination will not be tolerated!"

With a rapid movement he thrust his right hand into the inside of his tunic. The barrel of his Luger glistened in the lamplight.

"Now get out! Each one of –"

There was a loud report as Clay's single shot took him in the leg. Hamish screamed and clutched at the wound as his half-drawn Luger clattered to the floor.

"No more than he deserved," muttered Clay.

"Yeah," responded Turner. "Joining the New Order was one thing, but taking orders from sadistic bastards like him is not to my bloody liking."

He pointed his weapon at Hamish who was lying moaning on the floor.

"Lie still and quiet or we may have to shut you up permanently."

A whimpering Hamish thrust the fingers of his left hand into his mouth.

Stepping forward Clay sat down on the mattress facing Carol. Fearfully the girl drew back.

"It's OK, miss," he murmured. "Me and me mates aren't going to hurt you."

The others nodded in agreement.

"I think it's best we get you out of here as fast as possible," said Turner.

His companions grunted their agreement.

"You can't stay here, miss. Tomorrow this place could be swarming with soldiers." He glanced at the others. "We could drop you off somewhere."

She looked at them and then nodded.

"Yes, yes. There is a place in Milford..."

Clay held up his hand. "No need to tell us. Better we don't know. Tell us roughly where it is and we'll drop you off."

"What do we do about him?" Wilson jerked his head at Hamish who had crawled backwards and was now crouched whimpering against the back wall of the cubicle.

"Leave him here. He can spend the night among the corpses. Tie his hands behind him, Wilson, just to be sure. Not that the bastard'll get far with that gammy leg. The follow-up group will find and rescue him sometime in the next couple of days." He smiled grimly. "If the bastard's still alive."

Taking his hand from out of his mouth, Hamish snarled, "You'll fucking pay for this. All of you! Shooting an officer –"

Whipping a khaki handkerchief from his pocket Clay stepped forward and swiftly pulling it across Hamish's open mouth tied it tightly at the back of his head.

"Breathe through your nose if you want to live." He turned to the others. "We should get going."

Wilson and Clay led the way. Turner indicated Carol was to follow and, as she mounted the stairs, he kept close behind to ensure she didn't fall. At the top Wilson and Clay assisted her up onto the floor. In the fading twilight the four of them stood surveying the grisly scene. The destruction of the wool bales had created the impression of a freak interior snowfall that had settled gently over the splintered wood and the twisted bodies lying motionless over various part of the floor.

Carol stared at the scene and trembling, turned to Wilson. "Stuart? Is he here?"

Touching her gently on the arm Wilson said, "You don't want to try and look for him, Miss. Hand grenades make a very nasty mess of a body."

Carol winced.

"Sorry. Best you remember him the way he was. Here. I picked this photo off the floor. Managed to straighten it out a bit. Take it and remember him as a man that was alive."

She studied the creased images for a moment and then looked up. Her voice was hesitant and barely above a whisper.

"I- I don't want to stay here. Can we go now please?"

"Yes. Come on," answered Turner. "Follow me."

The rain had eased a little as the group sloshed in Turner's wake towards the truck.

"Up here," said Turner, opening the cab door.

Trembling and groggy from her injury and the knowledge of Stuart's death, Carol had to be helped up by Turner and Wilson who then sat either side of her on the wide bench seat. Clambering into the driver's seat, Clay inserted the key, pulled the choke to its fullest extent and then tugged on the starter lever.

The engine turned over but refused to fire.

"Bloody rain," muttered Clay. He made several more attempts and finally as the engine spluttered into life, he pumped the accelerator pedal vigorously until it emitted a steady roar. Switching on the headlights he thrust the heavy clutch pedal to the floor, graunched the lever into first gear and eased the truck down the narrow road towards the Albany village.

The surface, made slippery by the deluge, caused the truck to slip and slither. Aware that Clay needed his total concentration the others sat silently watching the headlights picking out the rain-filled ruts.

Still trembling from her ordeal, Carol found some measure of security in being sandwiched between the two soldiers whose bodies enabled her to remain upright with little effort on her part. Nevertheless her mind was a confused jumble of images, the strongest being Stuart's lifeless body in the carnage of the woolshed floor. As the truck continued its bumpy journey down the rutted road an inexorable ache of emptiness crept over her skin and crawled into every part of her being.

Eventually they reached the end and the truck swung south onto the main road. A liberal layer of gravel meant it was in better condition than the farm road thus enabling Clay to move through the gears and settle into a reasonably consistent speed.

Wilson's voice broke the silence. "No sign of the others, Clay?"

"Nope."

"The others?"

The men remained silent.

"There were more of you, weren't there?" said Carol.

"More of us? How do you mean?" answered Wilson cautiously.

Wrapping her arms tightly across the front of her body Carol took several slow, deliberate breaths before continuing.

"We thought you might attack us," she began.

"How?"

"The planes had been flying over the area round the farm for the past fortnight. When the weather got bad Stuart," her voice broke for a moment, "Stuart said an attack was a distinct possibility. That's why we posted additional guards down by the sheep pens."

The men exchanged glances.

"I'm right, aren't I?" said Carol.

"Yes, you are," replied Clay swerving to avoid a water-filled pothole and shifting down a gear. "The rest of our platoon was assigned to approach on our left flank through the yard and the pens. We expected them to rendezvous with us."

Carol gave an abrupt derisive laugh.

"They won't. Ever. Our guard squad'll have ambushed them. They'll all be dead. Serves them right!" Her voice broke and her trembling recommenced. "Bloody murderers!"

"Steady, miss," said Turner. "They were only doing their job." He sighed. "I suppose we all were, really."

"What do you think your people will do now?" asked Clay.

Carol hugged herself fiercely to control her trembling. "Our people were instructed to fight off the attackers and then leave to join others," she replied tonelessly.

"Others?" frowned Wilson. "Are there more groups like yours?"

"Maybe. Why?"

"Look, Miss, we're in trouble," said Turner. "We've shot an officer." He sighed. "We're all sick of the whole business."

The other two grunted in agreement.

"We originally joined up for adventure and good pay," continued Turner. "The pay's OK but we never imaged we'd have to kill our fellow Kiwis. Look, Miss, I know you must be feeling really lousy but, well you see we've only got a short time and we'd like a bit of advice before we drop you off."

"About what?" Carol's voice was wary.

"Joining your group," replied Wilson and the others grunted their agreement.

"Well," she said carefully, "some of our recruits did come from you Blitzkrieg Boys."

"Like Brownie."

"Brownie?"

"Yes, my mate Alfred Brown. He was killed by the grenades."

"Yes," replied Carol. "I liked him. He was a good friend," she fiercely bit the inside of her lower lip, "to Stuart."

There was a pause and after clearing his throat Turner spoke.

"What are our chances of joining your organisation?"

"There is a way of making contact," she replied. "No promises. You'd have to be vetted. After all, you are Blitzkrieg Boys."

"Fair enough," said Wilson. "So how do we contact your people?"

Carol sat silently staring at the road unfolding in the truck's headlights. Her thoughts were in turmoil. Were they still 'her people'? Was it still her organization? After the horrors of her relationship with Hamish, Stuart had given her a personal happiness she'd never have thought possible. And now he was dead – and for what? Unsuccessfully she tried to stifle a sob.

"Miss?" prompted Turner. "I'm truly sorry and I don't want to worry you, but it's just that time…"

Jammed in between the two men, Carol was unable to reach her handkerchief. She passed her sleeve across the base of her nose and wiped her eyes with the palms of her hands.

"It's all right," she answered. "I'm not sure what's going to happen to me but I will tell you about making contact."

The men waited silently.

Recruitment procedures had been part of the Fightback training programme and each participant had been required to commit them to memory.

"On any Monday", began Carol, "one at a time catch the passenger ferry from Devonport to the city. Sit on the upper deck near the bow. When you arrive on the city side don't get off. Stay there for the return journey. When the ferry reaches Devonport again get off and walk through the terminal to the end. If no one contacts you, repeat the process. Eventually you will be contacted but you will need to be patient."

"On any Monday?" said Clay.

"Yes."

"What if?" began Turner.

"Don't ask me any more questions because I have no answers. All I know is what I've told you. Nothing more. The rest is up to you." She put both her hands to her head and leaning forward, rested on the dashboard. "God, I'm tired."

"We're almost there," said Clay. They had reached the outskirts of Milford. "We'll drop you off and then we'll have to ditch this truck. It's a bit of a liability."

Two minutes later he turned into a side street and stopped. Turner jumped out and handed her down from the cab.

"Sure you'll be OK?"

"Yes, it's not far from here."

"Good luck," he said and then lowered his voice. "And thanks for the advice."

The door slammed and the truck roared away leaving Carol standing alone on the rain-soaked footpath.

***

The sound of the footsteps and the slamming of the outside door echoing through the woolshed indicated they had left. After listening intently Hamish made a renewed attempt to loosen his bound wrists. He twisted his arms, hands and fingers seeking some point of weakness in the cords. His intense efforts lasted for a brief period before, with a curse of frustration, he fell back against the wall. The loss of blood, the pain that throbbed in an aching rhythm from his thigh and the restrictions on his breathing imposed by the gag made his efforts futile.

The pallid light that continued to shine down the shaft illuminated the motionless bodies sprawled in the narrow corridor. The intermittent din of the rain on the corrugated iron roof buried all other sounds but, as it eased, Hamish became aware of a different intonation – the relentless buzzing of blowflies. Seemingly from nowhere they had begun to assemble and swarm in increasing numbers. Although their main attraction was the dead bodies, some of them began to settle on his face. A vigorous shaking of his head accompanied by muffled curses provided temporary relief but within a few moments the light persistent touch of the tiny feet and probing proboscises began anew on the surface of his skin and around his eyes and mouth.

As the sun went down, the light began to recede. Finally it disappeared leaving Hamish Beavis to battle with his tiny tormentors surrounded by sprawling corpses and enmeshed in a blanket of blackness.

CHAPTER 46

The knock on the door, although not the hammering sound she'd heard regularly over the past few months, still caused her to catch her breath. It was dark outside and the hour was late.

Pulling her dressing gown tightly around her she walked apprehensively down the end of the passage to the front door. The head and shoulders of a figure were silhouetted against the leadlight window. As she approached she called out in a voice that trembled slightly.

"Who is it?"

The reply caused her to cry out and reach eagerly for the doorknob.

"It's me, Auntie Catherine. It's Carol."

Unlocking the door she wrenched it open.

The two women stood staring at each other for a moment and then reaching forward buried their heads in each other's shoulders.

"Carol," whispered Catherine. "I had no idea if I'd ever see you again."

"Nor me, Auntie."

"You're shaking. Come on, let's get you inside."

Gently Catherine led her niece into the lounge, seated her on the couch and switched on the light. She gasped in horror.

"Carol! What's happened? Have you been …?"

"Yes, Auntie I have. All of it. Shot at. Hit and, and –."

Overcome by an unbearable wave of desolation she clung to her aunt and sobbed.

Catherine cradled the weeping young woman in her arms for a long time, wisely not wasting meaningless words of comfort. Finally Carol turned her swollen, bruised and tear-stained face upwards.

"It's Stuart, Auntie. He's dead. He died earlier today. I think all the others are dead, too."

Her sobbing subsided and prompted by her aunt, Carol haltingly began to describe the events of the past weeks, starting with the bus trip to Albany. When she reached the point where she had heard the grenade blasts she broke down and clung again to her aunt.

"I think you should stop talking now, Carol, and let me look at your cuts and bruises."

Sniffing and taking deep breaths, Carol shook her head. "In a minute, Auntie. I want you to hear the rest."

"All right, dear, but just the main points. You can fill in the details in the morning."

"After the explosion," began Carol, "Hamish and the soldiers came down the stairs. I woke up with him staring at me and telling me Stuart was dead. He had this horrible leer of triumph on his face. When I screamed he slapped me across the face and shouted that as Stuart was dead I now belonged to him."

Catherine shuddered.

"My screams brought the three soldiers. There was an argument, Hamish tried to draw a gun and one of the soldiers shot him."

"Shot him? Dead?"

"No, in the leg. They tied his hands behind his back and when he started abusing them, shoved a gag in his mouth. Then they said they'd help me get away. We went back up the stairs; they put me in their truck, dropped me off at the top of the road and promptly drove away. I don't suppose they wanted to be caught helping a 'terrorist'."

Her aunt grunted. "I've had a few visits over the past months from various unsavoury characters including Hamish. As you know I knew nothing and I think they realized that no matter what they did to me I really had no information as to your possible whereabouts. It was pretty frightening at the time but I haven't seen much of them recently."

"What do you think I should do now? I don't want to put you in any more danger but I had nowhere else to go."

As she started to tremble her aunt reached out for her.

"Enough of that, my girl. What you should do now is have a long hot bath. Then I'll have a look at you, although there doesn't appear to be anything broken. After that, a good night's sleep. We'll have time tomorrow to decide what's best to do."

Her aunt's prognosis was an accurate one. The cut on her forehead although running up into her hairline was relatively superficial. The left side of her face was swollen from Hamish's blow and her head throbbed, but otherwise she was physically unscathed. Fortunately, in spite of the traumas of the previous day, Carol was totally exhausted by the time she slid into the sheets, and aided by a strong sleeping pill, fell into a deep sleep that lasted nearly nine hours.

At her aunt's insistence, she spent the next day in bed, trying to read, and fitfully dozing. Another sleeping pill enabled her to sleep through the night.

The following morning the two women discussed the situation at length. Carol, although still numbed by the shock of Stuart's death, made a conscious effort to view her complex circumstances as objectively as possible.

"Let's first look at the situation from the authorities' perspective," began Aunt Catherine as they faced each other over the remains of breakfast. "Do you think the soldiers will inform on you?"

"No. They've got nothing to gain by it. They may even desert. They guessed Hamish had been pursuing a private vendetta against Stuart and me." She put her hand to her mouth and took several deep breaths. "Now that – now that Stuart has been killed the authorities may not see me as being of such importance. After all, no one actually knew we were hiding there. The soldiers who tried to ambush us were all killed and if any of the Albany Fightback group survived the attack, I'm sure they're all long gone."

"But how will you explain your disappearance from Auckland?"

"If I'm asked I'll tell them Stuart was worried about being arrested because of his association with the university. We took off up north and spent the time hiding in the bush. Then we quarrelled and decided to split up. After that I made my way back to Auckland. I was worried about being arrested even though I'd done nothing so I travelled alone and kept out of sight. Eventually I wound up here."

"Sounds a bit flimsy. And what about Hamish? He'll still want to hunt you down."

"Yes, but he may not even have survived the night." She looked uncertainly at her aunt, "I hope not, anyway."

Her aunt smiled grimly. "Never thought I'd ever wish death on another human being, but in this case..."

A loud knocking on the door made them both jump. They exchanged fearful glances.

"I'd better answer it." Catherine said. "If I don't it may look suspicious."

Her features a mixture of fear and uncertainty, Carol reached out and touched her arm. "All right, but be careful. I'll stand by the back door in case I have to..."

"Don't panic. Let me check first," said her aunt, and with a reassuring smile she left the room.

As soon as Catherine began walking down the hall she noticed a brown envelope lying beside the front door.

"Carol," she called, "Someone's pushed an envelope through the door slot."

Cautiously she opened the front door and peered out.

"There's nobody here."

"Let's go outside."

"All right, but we need to be careful."

Stepping cautiously out into the porch the two women looked around. The street was deserted, apart from a passing cyclist who gave them a curious glance.

"No sign of anyone," said Catherine.

"Whoever they are, they're fast movers."

"Come on, back inside."

Returning to the house and locking the front door the pair went into the lounge and sat together on the settee. Using an ivory-handled letter opener Catherine slit the top of the envelope and extracted a single page.

"It's for you," she said.

Carol took the page and began to read.

Message for Carol

- *You are to travel into Auckland City immediately.*
- *You may bring only one small case (the size of a Gladstone bag) with a change of clothes and personal items.*
- *You are to go directly to Albert Park and sit on the seat by the band rotunda.*
- *You are to wait there until we make contact.*
  Note:
  Do not show this message to anyone.
  Destroy it as soon as you have read it.

"It could be a trap," she said. "However, the rendezvous point has been used by our And if anyone had people before."

"wanted to capture you surely they would have come straight to my house and arrested you."

"You're right," said Carol suddenly standing. "While I'm here I'm putting you in danger. There is a network of Fightback groups so let's hope the contact is from them. I'll have to rejoin them. Anyone else I contact will be in immediate danger, including you."

"Carol, are you sure?"

"Yes, I am. Things may improve in the future, but in the meantime, I've got no alternative, if I want to go on living." She paused and sighed. "And I suppose I do."

Seeing her aunt was about to protest she reached forward and gave her a quick hug.

"Come on, Auntie, help me put a few things together."

"Only if you're sure. But I'm coming with you as far as the city. Two women will look less conspicuous than one travelling on her own."

About to protest, Carol saw the look in her aunt's eye and knew further argument was futile. As Carol packed they agreed Catherine would leave her niece halfway up Queen Street and then return home on the understanding that Carol would phone her as soon as possible that evening or the following day.

The trip was uneventful and just before one o'clock Carol nervously approached the Albert Park rotunda and seated herself where Stuart had sat several months earlier. At her aunt's suggestion she had brought a book to read as they both agreed it would look more natural. From her small case she took a copy of L.M. Montgomery's book *Anne of Green Gables*. Catherine had bought it for her as a present for her tenth birthday and she had read it several times during her teenage years.

A few people were in the rotunda and others were strolling past chatting and enjoying the pleasant weather. The normality of the environment and the familiarity of the story calmed her somewhat. As she began to read, Carol discovered that the hardest thing was to resist the temptation to keep looking up every few seconds to check her situation. She resolved to only look up on the completion of each page.

Several times her absorption with the book overrode her fears and she read several pages before suddenly recalling her situation. Even so she forced herself to look up when turning to a new page.

"Follow me."

She jerked her head up. The only person in the vicinity was a female figure wearing a long black coat and a red headscarf standing a few steps away with her back to Carol.

"Follow me."

Thrusting her book into her case Carol stood up.

The woman spoke again. "Come on, but keep your distance."

Trying to appear nonchalant Carol began to follow the woman who was now walking up the path towards the fountain at the northern end of Albert Park. Without looking back the woman turned right and crossing Princes Street entered the university grounds down a sloping path near the clock tower building.

Carol followed her. Two male students carrying books under their arms came walking up the path. As she moved to her left to let them pass one of them stumbled and dropped his books in front of her. She stopped in confusion.

"Sorry," said the young man, bending down to collect his books. His companion, making no attempt to help, looked straight at Carol and jerked his head in a sideways movement.

"All clear," he said. "Follow us, Carol."

The woman had disappeared. The young man, having collected his books, stood up. The pair took a few steps backwards and then turned along a different path. Apprehensively Carol did as she was told. As they reached a smaller path she gasped as she recognized the small door. It was the side entrance of the History Department library.

Both men stopped in front of it. The taller man rapped twice on the door. It was opened slightly. Turning to Carol he ordered, "Go straight in."

She hesitated. The shock of seeing the door had triggered off memories of her assignation with Stuart and the subsequent weeks of tension, violence and betrayal. The coincidence was too strong. It was a trap set with all the vindictiveness of Hamish Beavis.

As she turned away the tall man moved swiftly behind her.

"Get in!"

Seizing her by the shoulders he spun her round and thrust her roughly towards the open door.

She stumbled forward, caught her foot on the doorstep, crashed into the door and went sprawling on the library floor.

The door was slammed and locked behind her.

"Hullo, my sweet."

The room was dark but the voice was frighteningly familiar. Twisting onto her back she starred up at the towering male figure silhouetted against the window. Fear surged through her. Desperately she tried to thrust herself backward with her heels but they slipped on the carpet and her legs sprawled out in front of her.

"Carol." The man's voice was soft and as he bent down beside her the light fell on his face. She gasped and stared.

"Stuart! Oh, my God, it can't be!"

Her arms thrust upwards and wrapped themselves fiercely round his neck causing him to lose his balance and sprawl beside her.

"Stuart," she whispered. Her hands explored his face and she began to sob. "I thought, I thought you were dead. I, I left you in the woolshed. The soldiers said you'd been shot. Stuart. Oh, my darling man."

Gently Stuart put his right hand under her chin and tipping it back, looked her fully in the face. His eyes burned into hers but his voice was soft and low.

"It's me, Carol. I'm alive. Everything's going to be OK."

Simultaneously they locked their arms tightly around each other both revelling in the reality. Suddenly Carol jerked back.

"God!"

"What?"

"We're here, at the university which the Germans took over. Aren't we in danger?"

Chuckling, Stuart shifted his position he moved back against the library wall.

"Come here." He patted the carpet in front of him. "Lie back and I'll put you in the picture."

With a long sigh Carol lay back on the carpet and, resting her head on his lap, gazed up at him, her features still reflecting her disbelief.

"From this position I can watch you and make sure you don't disappear on me." She touched the large piece of sticking plaster above his left eye. "Are you hurt?"

"No not really. Just fairly shaken up."

She touched her fingers to his lips. "Take your time. Tell me from the beginning."

"OK," he responded.

Continuing to run his hand lightly through her hair he gazed down at her. Lit by the faint light from a small high window she looked pale and drawn but the lovely contours of her face,framed by her dark hair took his breath away. Gently he ran his hand down the left side of her face and spoke in a soft voice.

"The library doors are locked and a notice has been put outside stating it's closed today for stocktaking so we should be OK, as long as we're quiet."

"All right, but for heaven's sake tell me how you got here, how you ...."

He chuckled. "Rose from the dead?"

"Exactly."

"Yesterday, when you'd all gone down to hide in the Albany Ritz, we managed to keep the soldiers at bay for a few minutes. Then Tony took a shot in the shoulder. I took a quick look over the windowsill and I saw three of the soldiers running forward with stick grenades. I knew I had no time to shoot them all at once and so I dived into the centre of the woolshed. Just as I hit the floor the grenades came splintering through the doorway and exploded near me. I was stunned for a few moments. When I came to I realized I was half under the bodies of two of our chaps."

Carol shuddered.

"It was hideous but it saved my life. I had received a cut on my head, which bled quite heavily over my face. The grenade concussions must have lifted the bodies so they landed half on top of me. So there I was my face covered in blood lying under a couple of bleeding corpses. I passed out again and was woken by the sound of the soldiers' heavy footsteps. I felt really sick so didn't have too much trouble playing dead. It sounds logical now, but at the time I was scared stiff, particularly when the soldiers started checking the bodies. But it worked. When they shone their light on me I was literally frozen with fear and managed to lie there without moving. Beavis cursed foully when he saw me but then told his men to get on with finding any survivors."

"Meanwhile I was downstairs with the others terrified at what had happened to you."

"I must have passed out again. Next thing I remember was hearing a scream."

"It was me."

"Yes." He kissed the top of her head. "The thundering of the rain on the roof drowned out almost everything. I kept drifting in and out of consciousness and awoke again when I heard the soldiers. They sat down near me and began talking. I went hot and cold when they started grumbling about Beavis's treatment of the girl prisoner as it was obviously you. Then, in spite of the rain, they heard you scream and rushed downstairs. I remember lifting my head to try and see what was happening but I had another dizzy spell. Next thing I remember was hearing you talking to the soldiers. It seemed obvious they were going to help you and consequently I was very tempted to reveal myself."

She smiled grimly. "The soldiers were really on edge. They'd have shot instinctively if a blood-soaked apparition had suddenly emerged from under the corpses."

"That's what I thought, so against all my instincts I just had to lie there. But, in my own defence, I was feeling as sick as a dog and wouldn't have been any use to you anyway."

This time she kissed him lightly.

"Then what happened?"

"Once you left I slid out from under the bodies. I was trembling badly, my head was throbbing like hell, and I threw up several times. I then approached the farmhouse very cautiously and, once I was sure it was deserted, went in and started to get myself cleaned up. Five of the chaps from sheep pen guard squad then turned up. They'd successfully ambushed a Blitzkrieg Boys patrol but as it was obvious the farm had been identified we all decided to leave straight away. We used the radio to contact another support group."

"How did you get away?"

"We used the Lucas Creek escape route."

She nodded knowingly and smiled. "Go on."

"There was a small amount of moonlight so we were able to make steady progress in the two boats and by early morning rendezvoused with reps from the university group – one of them was the chap that I first met by the notice board. I was desperately worried about you and in the hope you'd gone to Aunt Catherine's, I arranged for a message to be dropped off ."

"We both know the rest of the story." She reached up towards him with both arms. "Kiss me, just to prove again this isn't a dream."

The kiss was slow and lingering, a heady mixture of longing, relief, reassurance and passion. Feeling herself becoming overwhelmed, Carol pulled her head back and placed her fingers lightly on Stuart's lips.

"Wait a moment."

"Christ, I want you. Carol!" Stuart's voice was urgent.

"Me too, but I still need some answers."

He sighed and smiled. "Very well, but make it short and snappy."

"OK. First question. Our families. They must be worried sick."

"True. I've arranged for them both to be contacted by our people – to inform them we're alive and well and we send our love, and hope to arrange a meeting with them some time soon. We can't write or phone but at least that will reassure them in the interim."

"I do miss them, Stuart."

"So do I. More than I thought I would. Hopefully, as I said, if the situation improves, we'll be able to arrange something more substantial in the future."

She stared at the ceiling for a long moment, sighed deeply and looked back at him.

"The other thing is," she paused.

"Yes?"

"Brendan and Susan. I was so traumatized by what had happened to you that I didn't give them a thought until the next morning when I woke up at Aunt Catherine's." She shuddered. "I can't bear to think they're dead."

"Brendan's not."

"Brendan. Not dead?" Her eyes were wide.

"No. When the five chaps who'd been stationed near the sheep pens turned up they did a final check of the woolshed to see if anyone was alive. Two of them also went downstairs."

He paused and sighed deeply.

"Go on." Her voice was low but impatient.

"They found Brendan and Susan lying crumpled in a corner behind several others who were dead. There was so much blood and muck around at first they thought they were both dead. Susan's body was badly damaged from the explosion."

Carol shuddered.

"Brendan's face was covered in blood. He didn't respond to the light of the torch and they thought he was dead. Just to be sure one of the soldiers felt for his pulse on the side of his neck and he stirred, moaned and tried to get up."

He paused again.

"Go on, Stuart," said Carol impatiently.

"They helped him up and got him to his feet."

"So he could walk?"

"Yes." His voice faltered. "But they had to lead him."

She frowned. "Lead him?"

"Yes. It's awful. The explosion made him blind."

"Brendan. Blind. Oh, God."

Gently caressing the back of her neck he continued. "He's safe and you'll be able to see him later tonight. He's lost a lot of his old spark, having to come to terms with his blindness, not to mention Susan's death and his guilt at hurting her. He's going to need a lot of support."

"Before you tell me any more, when our men were downstairs did they come across the professor."

"Yes they came across him straight away, still in his cubicle." Stuart shook his head. "He was dead. He was unmarked – must have just passed away in his sleep."

"That wonderful old man." Carol stared unseeingly at the ceiling and then back at Stuart. "What about Hamish?"

"No. As soon as our men found Brendan alive and managed to bring him upstairs we all forgot about anything or anyone else."

"The two soldiers who helped me shot him in the leg, gagged him tied him up and left him in our room. Nobody heard anything?"

"No. If he was alive he did the sensible thing and kept very quiet."

"So he's still there?"

Stuart shrugged. "Who knows? Who cares?" He kissed her gently on the forehead. "You're here and that's the most important thing, my sweet."

"And what about the two German girls, Sophie and Gretchen?"

"No idea. They were in the farmhouse so might have avoided the attack on the woolshed. They weren't in the farmhouse when I got there. Let's hope they managed to get away and somehow link up with the university group."

"Yes. I don't fancy their chances if they're caught by the German authorities. They're not known for their benevolence to people who betray them."

Reaching up Carol touched his cheek.

"You said I'd see Brendan tonight."

"Yes. I've arranged for us to be picked up after dark. We're then being taken by car to rendezvous with a Fightback division in the Waitakere Ranges. It's more rugged and remote than Albany and therefore also safer. Resistance is beginning to spread, so from there we're going to re-group and develop a longer-range strategy."

"Picked up after dark? Hmm. It's still daylight." Her voice was soft and her eyes were glinting.

"Yes. As I said –"

Her urgent mouth was on his. Their mutual hunger was intensified by the gamut of emotions they'd both undergone in the previous twenty-four hours. As Stuart thrust sharply into her Carol winced, gasped and clung to him, her moaning coming from the very depths of her being. Digging her nails into his back she joined him in a long delirious rhythm.

They both collapsed breathing hoarsely. Stuart, lifting his head from beside her face glanced down at her and chuckled.

"Heavens, girl, you've still got half your clothes on."

She moved her hand back under his shirt. "So have you. You're not a gentleman. Just an animal."

They lay together for a few minutes in mutual contentment and then kissed again.

This time their lovemaking was languorous and gentle. Afterwards, as they nestled side-by-side Stuart looked up at the window.

"The sun's starting to go down, my sweet," he murmured. "Our pick-up will be here soon." He smiled. "We'd better make ourselves respectable."

"Another step into the unknown," she replied thoughtfully as she stood up and got dressed.

Suddenly she stiffened.

"Stuart," she whispered. "There's somebody out there."

The scratching by the door was barely audible.

"It's the keyhole," whispered Carol.

"Quick," said Stuart pointing across the room. "Over to that side of the door. I'll stand on this side."

The door burst open and a figure stood silhouetted in the doorway.

"Stuart, Carol, are you in here?"

"Gretchen," gasped Carol. "Quickly, come in and shut the door."

The young German woman stepped into room and closed the door.

Her voice was soft. "Good evening. I am very pleased to have found you."

"How did you escape?" said Stuart.

"How did you know we were here?" added Carol.

"I have my sources. And of course, you will remember that I too am an accredited member of Fightback."

Harshness in Gretchen's tone and an improvement in her speech pattern caused Stuart to ask carefully, "Were you sent here with a message?"

"Yes, in a manner of speaking." She laughed harshly and in a rapid movement reached into her shoulder bag and produced a small Walther PPK pistol. "Both of you stand back against the wall. Now!"

"You traitor," hissed Carol. "Susan was right. She never trusted you."

"Easy, Carol." Watching the German woman intently Stuart moved back against the wall. "Do as she says."

"That's the intelligent thing to do, Stuart." Gretchen repeated her short, mirthless laugh. "After all, your choices are somewhat limited."

"Your English has shown a remarkable improvement," replied Stuart. "And I'm sure it's not due to your being a linguistic genius."

"Your perception does you credit," she responded sarcastically.

"And your being a Jew? Was that also a lie?" Carol's voice was ice cold.

"Me? Jewish?" She spat on the floor.

"Was it through you that the soldiers knew we were going to try and rescue the professor?"

"Yes, Stuart," she answered. Her pistol hand was steady. "But when you escaped and took us to your headquarters I decided my inside knowledge would be very useful to my people."

"And Sophie? Was she in on it?"

"Sophie?" She gave a short laugh. "No. She never guessed. She was far too idealistic. Obviously it clouded her judgment."

"And Brendan? Was he part of your grand strategy?"

Gretchen shifted slightly.

"I was fond of him, of course. And I needed an ally in the Fightback group. He was the obvious one." She gave a thin smile. "He was, as you say in English, 'a pushover'".

"And the attack on the farmhouse. Did you help with that too?"

Gretchen nodded.

"You bitch," said Carol. "All those people, our friends, now dead."

"There are always casualties in war," replied Gretchen grimly. Her voice rose. "But the sacrifices were necessary for the greater good of the Third Reich's New Order."

Carol locked eyes with the German woman. Her voice was slow and deliberate.

"Brendan is still alive." In a barely audible whisper she added, "But as the result of his injuries, he's gone permanently blind."

Gretchen's left hand covered her mouth and her pistol hand momentarily wavered.

"Enough!" Gretchen gestured sideways with her pistol. "Both of you are to walk towards the door. You will then walk up the path to Princes Street. I'll be right behind you." The hoarseness in her voice betrayed her tension. "If you try to run I'll shoot you – in the back if necessary." She gestured again. "You first, Stuart."

Giving Carol a smile of reassurance that convinced neither of them, Stuart walked to the door and opened it. The sun was reaching its nadir and the trees and buildings that dotted the grounds were casting long shadows.

"Up the path."

Moved by a brisk breeze, the branches of the trees sent the shadows flickering and dancing in erratic rhythms across the path and grass verges.

Aware Carol was close behind him, Stuart walked slowly his eyes darting from side to side seeking some way of escape.

"Gretchen!"

A woman's voice rang out causing the trio to stop and turn. From behind the gnarled branches of a tall pohutukawa tree a figure emerged and stood in the centre of the path.

"Gretchen. Where are you going with Stuart and Carol?"

"Sophie," gasped Gretchen. "We are, we are just going for a walk."

Gretchen's PPK had moved close to her waist, concealing it from Sophie's view.

"There is no need for you to come. Stuart, tell her she doesn't need to come with us."

Sophie began to walk up the path towards them.

"Gretchen, what's going on?"

Turning right around Gretchen thrust her pistol towards the advancing young woman.

"Halt, Sophie. Nicht weiter!"

Stopping abruptly Sophie stared at the pistol. She then held out both her arms and began to walk forwards.

"Gretchen. Was ist los? Du kannst nicht..."

Just as the pistol shot sounded Carol leapt forward shouldering Gretchen sideways. The German girl stumbled off the path, tripped and landed heavily on her back. Instantly Carol seized her right wrist. Cursing in German Gretchen tried to free her pistol arm, at the same time flailing at Carol with her left fist. Leaping across the path to assist, Stuart found it difficult to distinguish between the two sets of writhing arms in the fading light.

Ignoring Gretchen's flailing fist, Carol began trying to force the pistol into the air.

She was knocked sideways by Sophie who had come stumbling forward and flung herself across Gretchen pinning the pistol between them.

The German girls' bodies muffled the sound of the second shot. Gretchen gave a brief gasping cry, her right leg twitched and she lay still. Stepping forward, Stuart gently took Sophie by the shoulders and began to lift her up as Carol scrambled to her feet. Sophie's body was limp and heavy and her breath was coming in increasingly rapid gasps as Stuart turned her over and cradled her in his arms.

"God, Stuart. Look at her."

A dark stain was spreading across the front of Sophie's white blouse.

"It must have been the first shot," whispered Stuart. "Yet she had enough strength of will to try to assist you by falling onto Gretchen."

As gently as possible they laid Sophie down in the shadow of a nearby tree. A pale shaft of moonlight fell across her face. She coughed and then reaching up, gripped Stuart's arm.

"Is she, is she dead?" she gasped, between ragged breaths.

"Gretchen? Yes. She's dead. The shot hit her in the throat."

"I'm sorry," said Sophie. "I did not know she would betray us."

Carol placed her hand on Sophie's forehead.

"You are not to blame."

"The Nazis. They corrupt everybody and everything."

"Sophie, there's no need to talk. We have to get help for you."

The sweat that had spread through Sophie's dark hair was now forming a film across her face. She gasped, gritted her teeth and shook her head.

"No. You're in too much danger. I am finished. When I joined *Die weiße Rose* I knew it would be dangerous. But I am glad."

As she coughed again a small trickle of blood seeped from the corner of her mouth.

"No, Sophie, you can't die," whispered Carol, the tears beginning to run down her cheeks.

Sophie's grip on Stuart's arm increased and her eyes burning with a final intensity stared deeply into his.

"We have started to make a difference, *nicht wahr,* Stuart?"

"Yes, Sophie," he replied gently. "We have started to make a difference."

The faintest of smiles appeared momentarily then, with a deep sigh her eyes widened and her head collapsed backwards.

"She's gone," said Stuart, lifting Carol to her feet. "She was a very brave young woman."

Carol buried her head in his shoulder. He squeezed her tightly for a moment.

"We'll have to go, Carol. Every moment we put ourselves in greater danger. Come on."

Taking her firmly by the hand he led her away from the bodies of the two young German women, down the path towards the old barracks wall.

"We've still got time to make the rendezvous."

Carol stumbled, stopped, and leaned against the wall beneath an overgrown musket hole. The pale moonlight highlighted her reddened eyes and drawn features.

"There's no-one around. Yet, somebody must have heard the two shots."

"Maybe. But unless they're part of the New Order, and are armed, the sounds would have sent them hurrying away."

Reaching up she touched his face. "Stuart?"

He glanced nervously around. "Carol, we should be making tracks. The Waitakere Ranges Fightback people will be at the rendezvous any time now."

"I know." She looked at him intently. "I believe we'll win in the end, but I'm scared for both of us."

As he opened his mouth to speak she gently she placed the tips of her fingers on his lips.

Her voice was soft. "Just tell me again that we've promised to look after each other."

He reached up and took her face between his hands.

"Yes, Carol, whatever happens I promise I'll always look after you."

The warmth of her smile was spontaneous.

"Me too."

As the chiming of a distant clock sounded a light rain began to fall. Hand in hand, they moved through the university grounds and emerged onto the dark glistening street.

Author's Notes

Many of the characters in *Uncommon Enemy* are fictional. However a number of historical figures have been woven into the plot. The following is a brief summary of each of them – in the order in which they appear in the story.

Peter Fraser

New Zealand Prime Minister 1940-1949. Fraser was a self-made man from a poor Scottish family who immigrated to New Zealand in 1911. Opposed to New Zealand's participation in World War I, he was arrested and imprisoned for a year due to his opposition to conscription. However, on becoming New Zealand Prime Minister in 1940 he introduced a number of wartime measures including conscription and press censorship.

Walter Nash

After serving as Minister of Finance in the governments of Michael Joseph Savage and Peter Fraser, Nash served as New Zealand Prime Minister from 1957 to 1960.

Joachim von Ribbentrop

A vain man and a favourite of Hitler, he was instrumental in bringing about the Nazi Germany-Soviet Union Pact in 1940 – broken by Hitler with the invasion of Russia on June 22 1941. At the end of World War II he was among the members of the Nazi hierarchy that were tried by the Allies at Nuremberg. His arrogance gone, he cut a sorry figure and was the first of the Nazi defendants to be hanged on 15 October 1946.

Sir Ernest Davis

Mayor of Auckland 1935–1941. A wealthy Jewish businessman who made his fortune from brewing, he was a key figure in the horse racing industry. He received his knighthood for his extensive charitable donations.

Klaus von Stauffenberg

Born into an aristocratic Prussian family, he was an outstanding scholar and successful soldier. Disillusioned with the Nazis – he was never a supporter of their anti-Semitism – he was a key figure in the unsuccessful bomb plot to kill Hitler on 20 July 1944. The German Führer survived, Von Stauffenberg was arrested the following day and executed by firing squad. (His wife Nina Schenk von Stauffenberg died on 5 July 2006 aged 92.)

Sophie Scholl

A student of philosophy and biology at Munich University, she and her brother Hans were members of the student resistance organisation Der weiße Rose (The White Rose). Arrested for distributing anti-Nazi pamphlets, she and Hans were tried and beheaded on 18 February 1943. Prison officials and others who witnessed her execution, commented on her courage. Nowadays, in Germany, she is a highly respected historical figure.

Other notes of historical interest:

German Anti-Nazi Resistance Groups

Although The White Rose is probably the most well-known, other German groups who opposed the Hitler's regime included Edelweiss, a Catholic student group founded in Bavaria prior to the outbreak of war, the Werner Steinbrink Movement, the Alfred Schmidt-Sas group, Die Meute (The Pack – as in hounds) in Leipzig, the Kittlebrach Piraten in the Ruhr, and the Verbrand in the foothills of the Alps. Resistance was difficult and reprisals were swift and savage for the courageous members of these and other groups and individuals.

Non-Germans in the German Army

During World War II hundreds of thousands of foreign volunteers swelled the ranks of the German army, serving as front line soldiers or in supporting roles such as drivers, sentries or storekeepers. Soldiers from Denmark and Norway fought in the SS Standarte Nordland division, Dutch and Belgians in the Westland division and thousands of Russians and Ukrainians served the German army under Russian general Andrey Vlasov. Of particular note were the Cossacks (forcibly repatriated to the Soviet Union at the end of the war) and the French Charlemagne Division (part of the Legion des Volontaires Francais) who fought with distinction in the 1945 Battle for Berlin.

Nazi Germany Atomic Research

Fission, the basic process that makes nuclear weapons possible, was first discovered in Berlin in December 1938 by a team led by German physicist Otto Hahn. Members of the scientific community outside of Germany thought that the Nazis would be the first to build nuclear weapons and in August 1939 émigré Albert Einstein warned President Roosevelt of the threat. The threat increased when Germany overran Western Europe, capturing ample supplies of uranium in Belgium, and the Norsk Hydro

Plant in Norway that produced heavy water. In response, Roosevelt launched the Manhattan Project that developed the bombs dropped on Hiroshima and Nagasaki. Although, during the war, Germany was the first nation to develop and use jet fighters (Me-262s) cruise missiles (V1s) and ballistic missiles (V2s) it was overtaken in atomic bomb research by Britain and the USA. The reasons for this are still disputed by scientists and historians – highlighted by the publication in 2005 of a new book *Hitler's Bomb* by Berlin historian Rainer Karlsch who claims that the Nazis actually conducted three nuclear weapons tests during the war.

Die Fahne Hoch (Raise High the Flag)

The origins of this Nazi anthem are described in Chapter 16. An interesting historical footnote is that Horst Wessel's melody was based on an old folk tune common in Northern Europe. The same folk tune was used years later as the basis for the Christian anthem *How Great Thou Art.*

Acknowledgements

Some writers work in isolation, keeping their work concealed until it is presented to a publisher. In my case I found the assistance of family, friends and colleagues invaluable. Even though I didn't always accept their advice, their honest comments were always stimulating and thought provoking, and greatly assisted me in the crucial process of maintaining an objective perspective.

For their frank and useful comments on the content, and the perils of publishing, special thanks to Brad Bradley,

Clive Brown, Diane Brown, Lyn Brown, Alan Dormer, Cathy Dunsford, Graeme Lay, John McKenzie, John Morton, Christine and Paul Parker, John Paton, Gary and Anne Jenkin, Philip Temple and Frank Wallace. For their assistance with German history and language, thanks to Henrike Hepprich, Alan Kirkness, Jennifer Moeckel, Stefan Resch and Karsten Schwardt. For their perspectives and experiences of the wartime generation, thanks to Mervin Brown and Margaret Dawson. For his creative ideas on the cover design, thanks to James Menzies. For the perspective of the newer generation, thanks to my boys Karney, Christian, Shane and Justin. For advice and guidance on matters military, thanks to Brian Hirst and John Phipps. Thanks also to other family members including Patrick Jackson, Cherry Reynolds and Dean Reynolds for their help and encouragement, and finally to Bess, my wife and best friend, for her on-going support, and for always helping me to keep my feet on the ground.

And to all my friends, neighbours and colleagues that have been part of my life on the North Shore, thanks for the memories.

Sources

Researching background material involved drawing on my own knowledge of New Zealand, and in particular the North Shore where I grew up. Visits to East and West Germany, Poland, Czechoslovakia, and Russia in 1966 had sparked my initial interest in the issue of German occupation. During my research, a European trip that my wife Bess and I took in 2004-5 to cities such as Berlin,

Dresden, Prague and Warsaw added considerably to my insight.

As well as numerous documentaries and feature films a number of books proved particularly valuable in the course of researching for *Uncommon Enemy.*

Laurie Barber, *War Memorial: A Chronology of New Zealand and World War II,* Auckland, Heinemann Reed, 1989

Michael Basset, *Tomorrow Comes the Song: A Life of Peter Fraser,* Auckland, Penguin, 2000

Anthony Beevor, *Paris After the Liberation 1944 – 1949,* London, Penguin, 2004

Alan Bullock, *Hitler: A Study in Tyranny,* London, Penguin, 1952

Robert Cowley, (ed) *What If? Military Historians Imagine What Might Have Been,* New York, Pan Books, 1998

Dan Davin, *For the Rest of Our Lives,* Auckland, Blackwood & Paul Ltd, 1965

Michael Dobbs, *Winston's War,* London, Harper Collins, 2003

Richard J. Evans, *The Coming of the Third Reich,* London, Penguin, 2003

Alison Harris, and Robert Stevenson, *Once There Were Green Fields: The Story of Albany, New Zealand,* Auckland, Publishing Press, 2002

Robert Harris, *Fatherland,* London, Random House, 1993

Peter Hoffman, *Stauffenberg*, McGill-Queen's University Press, Montreal, 2003

Mary S Lovell, *The Mitford Girls,* London, Abacus, 2001

John Mulgan, *Man Alone,* Hamilton, Pauls, 1949

Vincent O'Sullivan, *Long Journey to the Border: A Life of John Mulgan,* Auckland, Penguin, 2003

David Pryce-Jones, *Paris in the Third Reich,* London, Collins, 1981

Christopher Reich, *The Runner,* London, Headline Book Publishing, 2000

Anita Shreve, *Resistance,* London, Abacus, 1993

Keith Sinclair, *A History of the University of Auckland 1883 – 1993,* Auckland, Auckland University Press, 1993

C.K. Stead, *Smith's Dream,* Auckland, New House Publishers, 1993

Auckland University College yearbooks, 1939, 1940

The Third Reich, New Jersey, Time-Life series, 1989

Also by John Reynolds

Books

Writing Your First Novel

Robyn Hood Outlaw Princess (based on the musical)

Musicals

Robyn Hood Outlaw Princess – Music Gary Daverne

Starblaze: Music: Shade Smith

Windust: Music: Shade Smith

Valley of the Voodons: Music Shade Smith

Sink the Warrior: Music: Shade Smith

The Littlest Elf: Music: John Reynolds

Pirates and Petticoats: Music: Mal Smith

For further information visit the author's website

https://drjohnreynolds.wixsite.com/dr-john-reynolds *or contact him by email: jbess@xtra.co.nz*

Youtube channel: youtube.com john reynolds writer

Author Bio

John Reynolds is a New Zealand freelance writer, teacher and broadcaster. He has travelled and worked in a variety of countries including London, Canada, Zimbabwe, Malaysia, Australia and the USA. He has also travelled through Western and Eastern Europe, Scandinavia, and Russia. All of these experiences have informed his writing.

He has written the plot and lyrics for five full-length musicals: *Robyn Hood Outlaw Princess* (music by Gary Daverne), *Starblaze*, *Valley of the Voodons*, *Windust* and *Sink the Warrior* (music by Shade Smith), two novels *Uncommon Enemy*, *Robyn Hood Outlaw Princess* (based on the musical), and *Writing Your First Novel* - a book for aspiring fiction writers.

A qualified teacher, he has a BA (History) University of Auckland,
MA (Educational Technology) San Jose State University California,
and a PhD (Film, TV and Media Studies) University of Auckland.

He is an experienced radio and television broadcaster and public speaker and enjoys doing presentations to groups about his writing experiences, either in person or through social media.

Contacts:

Website: https://drjohnreynolds.wixsite.com/dr-john-reynolds

Email jbess@xtra.co.nz

Reviewers and readers' comments

"A fast-paced, action-filled novel"

"A well -researched, deeply provocative book"

"A story of love, betrayal, and patriotism"

"This book is definitely a must-read for readers of all ages and nationalities"

"I found that I couldn't put it down"

"A fast-paced, action-filled, suspense-ridden novel which will have the reader not wanting to stop except for a cappuccino to keep the energy going to reach the end."

"I really enjoyed Uncommon Enemy *and at 79 years of age I can safely say it's been a long time since a man kept me awake until 3.30 in the morning."*

Add your review to the book on Amazon.com to help other readers find the author's work.